HENNY

on the

COUCH

HENNY

on the

COUCH

A NOVEL

REBECCA LAND SOODAK

five
spot

NEW YORK   BOSTON

5 Spot
Hachette Book Group
237 Park Avenue
New York, NY 10017

www.5-spot.com

5 Spot is an imprint of Grand Central Publishing.
The 5 Spot name and logo are trademarks of Hachette Book Group, Inc.

The publisher is not responsible for websites (or their content) that are not owned by the publisher.

Printed in the United States of America

Binder's Code: RRD-C

First Edition: April 2012
10 9 8 7 6 5 4 3 2 1

Library of Congress Cataloging-in-Publication Data

Soodak, Rebecca Land.
Henny on the couch / Rebecca Land Soodak.—1st ed.
    p. cm.
  ISBN 978-0-446-57426-6
  1. Self-realization in women—Fiction.   2. Upper East Side (New York, N.Y.)—Fiction.   I. Title.
  PS3619.O66H46 2012
  813'.6—dc22
                                    2011011097

For Mitchell, of course,
and
Rubin, Ellis, Cassie, and Shay

HENNY

on the

COUCH

1

2007

I knew the paintings immediately, even though I hadn't seen him in years. If I'd been downtown, say Chelsea or Nolita, I would have been prepared. Even SoHo would have made sense. In those neighborhoods, I always braced myself for the possibility of seeing his work around any corner. And yet, in all these years, I never had.

My neighborhood, however, was a whole different story. The Upper East Side is not a hotbed for superstars of the contemporary art world. The dead masters, absolutely. But Oliver Bellows, I did not expect.

I felt it like an assault.

This doesn't have to be a big deal, I reasoned, composing myself. It'll be interesting to see his work. I tugged on Trudy's leash and we crossed the avenue, but as I got closer to the street-level window I became cautious, as if the bold canvases could poison me. That had been my strategy all those years ago. I'd loved his work, but after everything happened, I pretended that he, and by extension his art, was like bleach, something to be handled very carefully, or not at all. Benign in the right circumstances, but too close, possibly lethal.

I stood in front of his abstractions while New York City navigated around us. It was as if Trudes could read my sense of anticipation, because her tail slapped my side and she gave me her *where are you hiding that tennis ball?* look, which I ignored. Ever accommodating, she switched gears and settled on the pavement while I stared straight ahead.

His work still moved me. My eye kept going to one painting in particular. It was saturated in burgundy and shades of blue and I marveled at its balance of form and color. For a split second, I considered buying it. Michael will like this, I thought. It belongs with us. Then I remembered. My desire for the burgundy canvas was completely absurd, but for that instant it had been pleasant to consider.

I glanced down the avenue toward my shop; the red-and-white-striped awning might as well have been a flag, reminding me of where I belonged. I felt a pang of guilt at having left Willa to deal with the Burke birthday party alone. Updos and face paint for a bunch of four-year-olds was more manageable with an ally...but it was my day to pick up the kids. Willa understood.

Suddenly it occurred to me that he could be in the gallery that very moment, observing me. This was to be avoided at all costs. I couldn't give him the satisfaction. Being moved after all these years was one thing, but for Oliver to witness it seemed like a betrayal to Michael.

I looked in, afraid to see him, and was disappointed when I didn't.

Instead, there was a stunning woman with very short hair focused on the computer. He's probably slept with her, I decided. She glanced up. I must've tensed, because just as she smiled, my codependent cocoa Labrador leapt in excitement. Her paws pressed against the window, making loud clicking sounds on the Madison Avenue glass.

"Trudy!" I scolded, pulling her down. "You crazy girl." With a flick of her leash, we darted away. It took a block and a half for me to calm down, but once I did, I realized now that the canvases were out of my vision, I missed them. This scared me. It's just his work, I rationalized while stroking Trudy's ears. Nothing more, nothing less.

Of course, every couple of years I'd searched for the latest news on Oliver. I knew of his success. He lived in London, was married. Last I checked, they didn't have kids, but I'm sure there was still time. And I followed his work. From behind the barrier of my computer screen, I watched his evolution. He was predictable without being stagnant. I remember feeling pleased that he'd maintained that signature brushwork.

Seeing his paintings in person didn't have to be as disturbing as that first search had been. *That* had been difficult. Adam was just two and a half and Henny a newborn. On top of already losing me to Little Scissors, my busy boy now had to share me with my brand-new baby girl. I was terrified that neither was getting what they needed. And worse, that it would haunt them for years.

That's when I found out about the Browning Arts Fellowship. I couldn't hide from Oliver's newsprint face and familiar name. Oliver had the fellowship while I had engorged breasts the size of tissue boxes. I was devastated. All I wanted to do was sleep, and I would have, if the salon and my babies hadn't needed me.

"Why are you crying, Mommy?" Adam had asked while we were snuggled in front of the TV.

"Because sometimes *Clifford* makes Mommy sad." Though only two, he'd rubbed my hand empathically, as if he too occasionally found the big red dog disheartening. This only made me more miserable. He deserved better.

I couldn't confide in Michael. My grief was too extreme. He'd have needed reassurance, which would've required dishonesty, or disloyalty. Since I was up for neither, I let him think I had some sort of postpartum depression, which in a way I guess I did.

But that was years ago. Max hadn't even been born yet, and now he's three! Yet another reminder of how fast time flies—not that I needed reminders.

Trudy and I walked up the avenue as I tried to convince myself that seeing Oliver's work in person didn't need to be jarring. I didn't want to spend time healing from it. Our lives were full. Happy. There wasn't room for an emotional setback. Then I remembered the shampoo purchase order—if the delivery didn't come by tomorrow, I'd have to give them a call.

I shrugged. Oliver's paintings. "No big deal," I told Trudy, who wagged in agreement. As we passed each exquisite boutique, I reminded myself: He's an artist, and back there was his art. A fact. Nothing more, nothing less.

Then I picked up my pace and we headed toward school.

2

1986

I feel the drunken crowd walk into the diner before I see or hear them. Like a blast of air-conditioning, they alter the room. I taste my grilled cheese on rye. It's Saturday night and all I've done so far is wash my clothes and order this sandwich, which although delicious, I'm ashamed of. They seem around my age, barely legal to drink. I wish I hadn't gone to eat so close to campus. What was I thinking? I might as well wear a sign around my neck: *loser*.

One boy is captivating. This, I notice immediately. But the group is loud; it makes me uneasy. Still, I try to watch the beautiful boy, but each time I peek, he catches my eye and I look away. I'm certain if he hasn't already dismissed me, he will. They are too happy for my taste anyway, doing ridiculous things with the salt and pepper.

I decide they are idiots.

"*Garçon!*" The beautiful one stands and claps his hands. One, two, a gesture for the waiter.

Entitled asshole. With a conspiratorial eye roll, I convey my disgust to the server, but he thinks I'm unhappy with the grilled cheese. "It's fine," I try to reassure him, but his English is not good. He doesn't understand the source of my displeasure and points to my full glass of water.

"No, no, it's fine." I look at the group, worried they are watching me. "Forget it," I mumble, unable to explain. The waiter shrugs and moves toward the boisterous table. I was mistaken—he is not my ally.

I rummage in my bag. Please, please, let me have remembered

a book. I cannot bear to stare into nothingness in such close vicinity to people who do not hide behind literature on Saturday nights. Nikki Giovanni saves me. This way I can position myself as an intellectual, deep in concentration.

Their laughter is distracting. I read at them and everyone else who's ever made me feel inadequate.

I'm new to the city. Though I'm taking classes at Columbia, I'm part of the continuing education program, not a *real* student, which to me makes all the difference. Thankfully, a friend of my mother's helped me get into the dorm; otherwise, I think there's a very good chance I'd become one of those New York casualties you hear about who's found by a disheveled landlord there to investigate the stench of cat piss and rotting flesh.

My loneliness, when it strikes, is brutal—though my fascination with New York is a helpful remedy. I study city women the way med students memorize anatomy. I take it all in. The bag (Chanel with a gold chain), the shoes, the hair. I am determined to understand the uniform of the different neighborhoods. Determined to belong.

I walk hour after hour, learning the streets. When I'm downtown, I take pride in deciphering the illogical West Village. West 10th turns into West 4th, Greenwich is both an avenue and a street. I discover that knee socks and a miniskirt are welcome in Alphabet City but suspect on the Upper East Side. Like a mantra, I recite, Central Park West, Columbus, Amsterdam, Broadway, Central Park West, Columbus, Amsterdam, Broadway, because real New Yorkers know the order of the Upper West Side avenues.

Yesterday, I followed a mother and teenager on Ludlow Street. I overheard the woman tell her daughter, "Because no one fits bras better..." The girl seemed so accustomed to her mother imparting practical information that she paid her no mind. She wasn't disrespectful exactly, just dismissive, as if her mother's wisdom was no more notable than waking up each morning with the ability to walk or talk. Or breathe.

I pierced my belly button and stalked knowing women in Balducci's, so one day I'd be able to mimic the way they picked out melons, cheese, and coffee. I have waited a long time (as long as any twenty-one-year-old can wait for anything) to live in Manhattan, and now that I'm here, I'm anxious to start the rest of my life.

But as I witness the beautiful boy and his friends so clearly connected and happy, I'm filled with loss. Here I am, in this magnificent, bustling city, but around public joy I'm reminded of what is finally gone.

I push my sandwich aside, no longer hungry. At least I've gotten thin. Some nights I lie on my lumpy mattress, touching my jutting ribs and hip bones, and remember my first. He didn't mean much to me, though in fairness, given the circumstances, no one could've punctured my icy shield. I'd lie under him and watch his face twisted and unfamiliar. It was pleasurable enough, but that wasn't really the point; I needed something sex provided. Not love. Something even harder for girls to come by on their own; he'd made me feel worthy. But just when he was push, push, pushing me to some faraway place, I knew it was also a warning that he'd be pulling out soon, and I'd once again be left feeling nothing at all.

He'd been kind and dependable, a good choice for my first. But if it hadn't been him, I would've settled on someone else, many someones if necessary. I didn't tell him much, but neither of us noticed. Had the boy required more from me, I would've had to acknowledge what was happening around me. Thankfully, he left me for a narrow-hipped girl named Cindy, which was lucky, really. Because even though I didn't love him, leaving would've been hard.

I glance at the group. The loud boy is sketching a girl wearing black. She has a dancer's body, small breasts free beneath a Clash T-shirt. Of course he would sketch the striking girl. I feel clumsy; his attention on the graceful one makes me angry. What a poser he is, drawing her in a diner. A diner, how pretentious! Then I remember that I'm the one reading poetry. I wonder if they're sleeping together. I've only had sex once since the funeral several months ago. It had been my way of saying goodbye. Seeing them reminds me of that loss as well.

What would it be like to be with the beautiful, loud boy, I wonder. His confidence is arresting. The ballerina tries to see his sketch but he crumples it. I wrongly perceive the gesture as one of perfectionism.

"Fuck you, Oliver," she says.

Oliver. Behind my book, I practice saying it. Oliver. I like how many movements my mouth needs to make just to say his name. Like a waltz, quite possibly making it the most enticing name known.

After my plate has been cleared and my coffee refill refilled, I know it's time to go. I dread walking near them, ashamed of my loneliness. But I gather my things and saunter toward the cashier, deceptively oblivious of Oliver and his friends. I dig in my bag for money and berate myself when I can't find any. As I search my jeans, my mind pulses with: I'm such an asshole; I'm such an asshole. Finally, I find some singles in one of my back pockets.

And then, when I turn to leave, he is standing right next to me. I hadn't heard him approach and am startled. I want to flee but maneuvering my body around his isn't an option; my brain will not let me choreograph such a task.

He stands close. If I were to put my hands out ever so slightly (which I don't, but if I did) I wouldn't have to straighten my elbows to touch him.

"For the serious girl…" he says, offering me a folded placemat just like the ballerina's.

I pause. Because I've been watching his every move, I know he is handing me a drawing. I should pretend I have no idea what it is, but I can't figure out how to do this. So without meeting his eyes, I take it and leave quickly.

If I said thank you, neither of us heard.

3

2007

Michael and I hustled among the throngs of Saturday night moviegoers. Like most married people, we had a system. I got the seats while he got the popcorn.

"Get a small," I told him, worried about his cholesterol (and belly). He returned with a medium, which I pretended not to notice, and handed me M&M's I hadn't requested but appreciated nonetheless. I reminded him to turn off his phone and he read trivia questions aloud, even though I'd seen the answers while I was waiting.

During the first three minutes, one of us inevitably whispered, "Are you in?" which really wasn't necessary. We always knew whether the other was hooked or not. Besides, for me, liking the movie mattered little. There was no place I'd rather be on a Saturday night than next to my husband in a darkened theater.

In the taxi home we sat close. Michael stroked my leg, knee to thigh.

"I'm thinking of painting again," I said. Though the desire had been brewing for a while, seeing Oliver's paintings the other day accelerated it. I still hadn't told Michael about the gallery. Oliver was always a loaded topic, and now didn't seem like the time.

"You should," he said, moving his hand higher.

"You think?" I shouldn't have mentioned it. I didn't want him to notice if I didn't follow through.

"I do." He nudged my knees apart. I looked at the cab driver through the rearview mirror and wondered if he could see us.

"Then again, Little Scissors..."

"That's why you have a partner," said Michael.

"Yeah, but it's not fair to Willa if I just check out."

"Shhhhh," he whispered, placing his hand on my crotch. I closed my eyes and ever so slightly rocked into him.

We bought the *Times* on the way home, and as we walked into our building I wondered if we had enough milk for the morning. Suddenly I was torn between reading the paper and being with my husband. Michael didn't seem conflicted.

"How was everything?" I asked our sitter, Beth.

"Great. I made them turn off the computer and we actually baked cookies," she told me.

"Fun," I lied. Even with my best of intentions, baking with my kids was usually an ordeal. I looked at Beth and vowed to be more patient. Who cares about eggshells in the brownie mix?

"They wanted you guys to taste them." Beth presented cookies slathered in thick frosting and carefully applied rainbow sprinkles. They looked like love.

"Of course." I chose one with raisin eyes and a chocolate chip smile. I could just imagine Henny's concentrated expression as she created this masterpiece.

"Oh. I almost forgot, Max had a nightmare," said Beth. I braced myself.

"He was crying for you. Don't worry, I handled it," she added proudly, mistaking my expression of guilt for one of alarm.

Perhaps going out every Saturday night was unnecessary. I glanced at Michael as he scanned the front page.

"He couldn't find Chocobunny," Beth continued. "It was under his bed."

I nodded, familiar with the routine, and opened the fridge to calculate our coffee-cereal-milk quantities. It would be close.

"He loves when you rub his back," she said. "Works like magic. He fell right back to sleep."

I looked at her. Was she implying I didn't know how to soothe him? A flash of anger came over me. Thankfully, the cookies brought me down. Anyone who could supervise that endeavor deserved my admiration.

"I'm glad you were there," I said, which was also true. I *was* glad Beth was there. That, and the exact opposite of glad, something Michael didn't understand at all.

"Alrighty then," Michael said. He wanted the girl out. Michael was adept at sensing when my scale was tipping more toward mother than woman, a situation that did not usually bode well for him.

I grabbed the *Times* from the kitchen counter and headed for our bedroom.

"Come on, girl," Michael said to Trudy, who was already following him to the door.

"Get milk," I urged, adding "please" a few seconds too late.

When Michael returned, he called from the den, "You up?"

"Barely." I paused in the middle of an article from the magazine section.

"Guess a blow job's out of the question..." he teased, which I pretended not to hear. Silence filled both rooms until Michael turned on the TV. Relieved, I listened to my husband listening to the laugh track of comedic situations that were not our own.

Mondays weren't usually hectic at Little Scissors, but early September was the ceremonial trimming time for hair brittle from chlorine and Long Island rays. Customers who hadn't seen each other all summer were busy exchanging updates on sleep-away camp and trips abroad. The shop echoed with whirling blow dryers and children's pleas for their mothers to buy rainbow-colored back-to-school pencil cases and sparkly hair accessories. Willa had been right; upgrading the gift shop had been a great move.

One tyke sat in a race car, center stage, none too pleased by the experience of his first haircut. Tears left tracks on his splotchy cheeks while his mother and nanny stood off to the side cajoling him with silly faces and an impromptu jig.

"Check for lice," Willa whispered to Ava, one of our newer stylists. Camps are a breeding ground for them. Each autumn we inevitably got the thankless job of informing an unsuspecting parent that their precious one's scalp was teeming with parasites.

"Gross," Ava whined at the thought. Willa shrugged. After a dozen years in business, very little fazed her. I never would've gone ahead with this place if Willa hadn't agreed to join me. I got the idea a few months before Michael and I were married. I'd gone to a swanky salon far too expensive for my prior, single self. But there I was, soon to be a Mrs.; I looked around in amazement. For several hundred dollars a pop, confident women were being tended to. One stood out, though. She was pregnant—swollen and seemingly miserable. I remember wondering whether she'd bring little Susie or Billy to this place. Somewhere between my blowout and handing over Michael's hard-earned cash (by then I'd quit my job at a high-end wallpaper showroom), I began envisioning a salon that catered only to kids.

Michael had loved the idea from the beginning. He found investors practically overnight, which made me feel fortunate, yet frightened. I knew I was lucky to be set up in business, but at the same time, I was completely dependent on him to make it happen. That's when I approached Willa. I'd actually been closer to her girlfriend, but I'd always liked Willa, and more importantly, I'd trusted her. She'd been aching for something more dependable, having spent most of her twenties auditioning for plays and landing only the occasional commercial.

When I asked her, a slow smile started to form on her face. Unbeknownst to me, she had a small inheritance to invest and was a few hours shy of an abandoned cosmetology license. It was the perfect match; she coached me while I got my hairstylist's license, and I enabled her to make a change. But what she really provided I wouldn't have been able to articulate at the time. I needed someone from my pre-Michael life around while I was busy becoming a whole new me.

Willa moved across the shop to answer the phone, pausing briefly to blow bubbles toward the hysterical boy—stopping him mid-sob. It was a rare child who didn't respond to her, even with her tattoos.

Brightly colored peonies, lilies, and lotus flowers covered her right arm like ivy; a nonconformist's celebration of life. Her left side however, was far less festive. Spanning from fingertips to shoulder was a weeping willow. Dark and light green leaves dripped down her arm. Beneath the hearty trunk was a maze of roots that despite being intricate capillaries connecting tree to earth always reminded me of the impermanence intrinsic to all living things...until I looked away.

Despite the ink, Willa had gentleness about her. She wasn't meek or submissive; it was more that she carried herself with quiet purpose, which, depending on the day she was having, or the observer, came across as either serenity or sorrow. Occasionally I'd try to imitate her demeanor, but you can't fake authenticity.

The bustling shop was making my head spin. Bills needed filing and I kept forgetting to ask someone to empty the overflowing trash can in the bathroom. Plus, a part-time worker who was supposed to be on tomorrow's schedule had quit this morning and I still hadn't found anyone to cover for her. I contemplated putting myself on, but didn't want to reopen that can of worms. After I had Henny, I'd stopped cutting hair. I'd felt pulled in too many directions, so I'd surrendered the scissors to Willa and found my niche in payroll and purchase orders. These I could do at my own pace and in silence.

I scanned the schedule book. Even if I wanted to step in, tomorrow was parents' day at Max's preschool. Not to mention, my day to pick up the kids. Everything will get done, I reminded myself. It always does.

I checked my watch. Beth would've just gotten Max and they'd be en route to pick up Adam and Henny. I looked out the display window—at least it wasn't raining. I returned my attention to a sale I was ringing up. The customer kept adding items that caught her eye: kiwi conditioner, pellets that turned the tub water purple, packets of smiley-face tissues. I was thrilled to be racking up her balance, but a line was starting to form, creeping into our already cramped shop. I was sweating and craved calm.

"Excuse me," a woman said to Willa. "Any chance my daughter can get in today?"

"We're completely booked," Willa answered without looking up.

"What about Ava?" I asked.

"Ava"—Willa scanned the schedule—"might be able to squeeze you in."

"Which one's Ava?" the woman asked. Willa pointed to her.

The customer shook her head no. "I don't think so," she said. "She looks like a scared little mouse. I prefer...confident women." The nerve.

"Do you now?" Willa asked. Usually she responded to difficult customers with a penetrating stare, but she was smiling.

I studied the customer. Tall and svelte, she looked like she'd stepped off a movie set. She wore gabardine trousers and a silk shirt, all in the mauve/beige family. And she had perfect cheekbones. Perfect cheekbones and the ability to wear mauve—probably the quintessential characteristics of elegance.

I grabbed the appointment book. "Ava's an excellent stylist," I said encouragingly,

"I don't even want a haircut," said the svelte one's surly daughter.

"A trim, Leah. Just a trim." The woman scanned email on her phone. "Come to think about it, tomorrow might be better. I've got to get back to the office."

"Well, *I'm* available tomorrow," said Willa. "And no one's ever accused me of lacking confidence," she added, smiling.

The woman extended her hand over charm bracelets and troll pencils. "Victoria Layton," she said, shaking Willa's hand.

"You're off tomorrow," I reminded her. "The commemoration." I shouldn't have said anything. It had been six years since 9/11. If Willa wanted to skip the ceremony, it was none of my business. It's just that I'd adored her girlfriend. But if hitting on Mama Mauve was preferable to listening to thousands of names being called at Ground Zero, who was I to judge?

"It's supposed to rain," said Willa, writing Leah's name in the book. Right, I thought to myself. This is about rain.

On the bright side, my scheduling problem was now solved.

"Ahh, Kara," a customer called. "Toilet's backed up."

4

1972

I am only seven years old, but this much I know: I should not be looking up. Real New Yorkers don't care about majestic buildings that scrape the sky, but they make my tummy giggle, so every few seconds I peek. How do people *not* look up, I wonder, as I watch grown-ups busily move about their lives. Someday I hope I get to be up real high, able to look down on the street. My mother grabs my hand and pulls me along.

I can't believe I'm actually here. If I could swallow New York City whole and bring it back to Cleveland, I would. I love everything about it, even the diner by the bus station where I ate scrambled eggs while my mother clanked her coffee and kept checking her watch. If I lived here, I'd eat at that diner every morning.

It feels like we walk the streets for hours. I want to ride in a yellow taxi like I've seen in the movies, but I can tell my mother is in the mood to say no. She's been grumpy since the bus. I know better than to bother her with childish requests. Besides, I like to watch the ladies in beautiful clothes, so I barely notice my aching feet. These New York City Mary Janes seemed more comfortable at the May Company. I look down and wonder when they stopped being shiny, before or after breakfast, because on the bus I sat carefully, wiping any accidental fingerprints.

The neighborhoods change as we make our way from 42nd Street through midtown and into the park. My heart quickens when I see the horse-drawn carriages.

"Maybe later," my mother says, adding the *maybe* again lest I misunderstand.

Her pace slows when we approach a white building. "No matter what she says," my mother warns gravely, "she doesn't define you. Pay her no mind, do you understand?"

"Who?" I ask, suddenly afraid. But she's already disappeared into herself, so we enter the building.

My mother tells a man in uniform that Mrs. Adler is expecting her. I want to ask who Mrs. Adler is, but my mother is being still and serious so I practice being still and serious too.

Once inside the elevator, I study our reflection on the shiny doors. I stick out my tongue and tilt my head from one side to the other. When she doesn't scold me, I settle down as we chug our way to Mrs. Adler on the twenty-eighth floor.

The first thing I notice is the woman's bug pin. It's an ant maybe, but I'm not sure because all bugs look the same to me. This one has green jewels for eyes and tiny little pearls at the ends of its antennae. I can't decide if it's ugly or beautiful, so I settle on both. It is both.

"You shouldn't have brought the child, Juliet, you know that," the fancy lady says. My mother grips my hand. It is the first time I've ever seen her this way. I think maybe she's scared. I want to tell her not to worry because I definitely won't break anything, but it doesn't matter...the lady isn't inviting us in.

From the doorway, I see a rug made out of fur in a sunken living room. The couches are whiter than snowstorm snow. I am tired and want to rest on the rug. It looks soft and I think it would feel good to bury my hands in the fur. There's a wall of windows, and I know this is my chance to see the people on the street from way up high. Maybe there's a girl just like me looking up at this very moment. But I stay where I am.

"I thought it was time you two met. This is Kara Caine," my mother says, undeterred.

"Pleased to meet you," the woman says, not looking at me.

"Thank you," I answer, glancing at my mother to see if I did it right, but she stares straight at Mrs. Adler, so I look to the floor. The lady doesn't even notice my shoes.

"I'm sorry for your loss, Sophia," my mother says, but I don't think she sounds sorry at all.

"Yes, well..." Mrs. Adler starts, not bothering to finish her thought.

"It seems there's been a mistake, though, and I think you are just the person to fix it." My mother's polite words don't fool me. She is not being nice to the lady.

"A mistake?"

"Oh, well, the obituary, which was lovely by the way, said that Arthur is survived by a wife, but there is no mention of any children. I think we both know that that's not the whole picture, now is it?"

I am mesmerized by gold curtains blowing in the pristine room. There is a painting of a girl with long brown hair wearing a blue leotard. I took ballet once. My mother watched the class through a hall window. Afterwards, she was silent. If I'd been any good, she would have told me.

I see a stone figure on a shelf, and will forever associate Greek artifacts with this moment, when my future is being decided by my mother's quiet words to Mrs. Adler.

For a moment, neither speaks. "I can't believe you're doing this to me," the lady finally says.

My mother meets her stare. "This isn't about you."

"It was made clear that the initial sum relinquished all of the child's rights to any future negotiations."

"Kara!" my mother yells. "My daughter's name is Kara." Hearing my name makes my heart pound; I don't know what I've done wrong. Then I realize she's yelling at Mrs. Adler, but knowing this doesn't quiet the thumping.

"With a K," my mother adds through gritted teeth. "It's a lovely name, don't you think?"

Mrs. Adler bristles.

"I'm sure the *New York Times* fact checker would note the K," my mother continues. "I suspect they're careful about that sort of thing."

We are told to wait in the foyer. I hear Mrs. Adler on the phone somewhere in the apartment.

"Mama, the windows," I whisper, wanting her to see the breezy dance in the faraway room.

"Not now, Kara, please!" Her eyes are fierce. I go silent.

Mrs. Adler returns with a manila envelope, looking weary. "My husband was buried last week, and you're descending on me like a vulture," she says quietly.

"Yes, I imagine losing Arthur is painful." My mother removes the envelope from Mrs. Adler's chalky blue hands. I check my own little-girl hands, relieved they are not wrinkly like the lady's.

"This is it, Juliet," the tired woman says. "No more."

"It's not my fault your husband was so"—my mother pauses and looks at me—"friendly with sopranos a third of his age." She laughs nervously.

"Yes," Mrs. Adler says, "he was always after the understudies. The real talent was far too threatening."

We get a white horse, and I like white horses best. The trees are black against a violet sky and I pretend it is the olden days before cars were invented, but I quickly grow bored of the game. This ride is longer than I expected and I'm getting cold. My mother sits quietly with her eyes closed. I know she isn't asleep, but she looks like she's dreaming nonetheless.

It is coming-home time for the city kids. From the carriage, I watch Jamaican nannies speak with thick accents to girls dressed in plaid skirts. I wish I hadn't gotten the patent leather. They're not even shiny anymore. I hate my mother for not knowing red or navy nubuck would have been better. The horse man gives us a wool blanket but it's scratchy and I don't like the smell.

It all seemed so much better in the movies.

Maybe because I know we are leaving anyway, I want to go home.

"One more stop," my mother tells me.

By the time we get to Lincoln Center, there are crowds of people. Chatter canopies the night air. My mother walks with purpose, clearing a path through the perfumed masses who wear stylish coats and sparkly jewels. I wonder if she's taking me to a party. Then I see we're at a theater. I anticipate going into the already open doors, but she leads me past them, and we turn a corner. I have to run to keep up.

"Come on, there isn't time to dawdle," she says, but she's not angry. I like it when my mother isn't angry. We enter through the musicians' entrance. She picks up something from the floor that looks like a small magazine. Many years from now I will read this playbill and find out that my deceased father, Arthur Adler, composed this opera. But for now all I care about is keeping up with my mother. I don't want to lose her down this long corridor.

Instruments are playing all at once, like a mumbled greeting just for us. When we turn another corner, the resonance grows. It isn't music exactly, but I like it all the same. If excitement had a sound, this would be its song.

"We'll sit here," she says, sliding her body to the floor. I'm worried what'll happen if someone finds us, but my mother doesn't seem concerned, so I sit next to her and rest my head in her lap. I must've dozed, because when I come out of a haze, there is silence, and then applause. I don't move. Like thunder, the orchestra begins.

In time, I hear singing. And though I've never been taught, and certainly never heard it before, I know this is opera. I want to see the lady who is singing. My mother's body tenses, like a statue or the dead. And then out of nowhere, like in a dream, but I'm awake, she sings.

Just like the lady, my mother sings.

Shocked and baffled, I listen. It is like finding out she can fly, or talk to tigers, or speak Chinese. I listen and listen and listen some more. My mother sounds like loud magic as her tears settle on the cold floor.

5

2007

Parents' day at Max's preschool was almost over. I calculated if I got out of there in the next twelve minutes, fifteen tops, it would still be possible to do a quick grocery run and be on time to pick up Adam and Henny. I could have the groceries delivered. Then if homework went smoothly, I'd take the kids on their scooters while Max and I walked Trudy. This way I'd be able to pass by the gallery.

Since first seeing Oliver's paintings, I'd managed to pass by his show regularly. It would only be up a few more weeks. I knew I was a tad obsessed, but I wasn't hurting anyone. It's not like I was sneaking out to meet *him*. Plus, soon it would be too cold for the kids to scooter.

Max's smiling teacher read *A Dinosaur Comes Over for Dinner* while my little ventriloquist sat among his classmates and mouthed each word. I was getting a kick out of him when a woman whispered to me, "I think he's heard this one before." If I'd ever met her, I didn't remember her name.

"It's his favorite," I said.

"He's obviously a literary genius," she whispered. The woman next to her glared at us.

Once the story was over, I resisted the urge to grab my bag and macaroni necklace, but there was still the curriculum presentation, which the teacher assured us would be brief. I guess after attending so many preschool orientations, I'd become a bit jaded, because I was thinking the preschool curriculum could pretty much be summarized by, *share and don't bite your neighbor.*

"What's your philosophy on enriching kids who are numerically gifted?" the glaring one asked. I settled in as if watching a nature show that had nothing to do with me. I, too, had once been similarly conscientious, but now as the perky teacher addressed the question, I looked around to see if I was the only one who found enrichment for wealthy three-year-olds irritating.

"An animal unit is coming up and we'll incorporate numbers in a fun way." While the teacher spoke, I studied the children's beaming self-portraits, enjoying the display of big, smiling lips and wide eyes in greens, blues, and browns; their art was optimism personified. Perfection. My eye went to Max's. I imagined him pounding a crayon to create those freckles. I guess I wasn't so jaded after all.

"Your kids are naturally curious; they thrive when investigating their worlds."

It was true. Just today Max seemed to be thriving when he investigated his testicles. "Them my grapes, Mama?" he'd asked.

"Encourage them," the helpful teacher...encouraged.

I do that, I thought, remembering how after explaining his anatomy, I'd *encouraged* him to wash his hands.

"Each child will research his or her favorite animal. Use magazines, newspapers, and of course the Internet," said the teacher.

I looked earnest and engaged, but really I was remembering how the last time Max used the computer, he kept licking the little ball on the mouse.

"See how fast you can jump in the stroller," I said.

"I wanna walk. I'm not a baby."

"I know you're not a baby, silly. Do babies know every word from *A Dinosaur Comes Over for Dinner*?" The grocery store was twenty blocks away. This was the only way we could possibly make it on time.

"I know every word."

"I know you do, and babies definitely don't know how to jump in their strollers, so come on, kiddo, jump in. We've got places to go."

"No! Big boys walk and run and jump and hop. I can hop, Mommy, wanna see?"

If I skipped the latte, he could walk for a few blocks. "Two blocks," I offered. "You can walk or hop or jump for two blocks and then in you go, deal?"

I maneuvered the stroller around his classmates and the grown-ups responsible for them, while Max counted his hops. I considered rethinking the whole gifted with numbers thing, but then he skipped seven and eight, and hesitated after eleven.

"Are you heading east?" asked the woman who'd noticed Max reciting the story. "We'll walk with you. Zoe loves Max," she said.

"Same." I had no idea which one Zoe was.

"I'm Morgan."

"Kara Caine Lawson," I replied. I'd long ago learned that cultured Manhattan women provided their full name clearly, with a slight hint of pride. After all these years it still felt awkward. Nonetheless, I'd honed the skill.

"Nice to meet you, Kara Caine Lawson." Her smiling hazel eyes had soft wrinkles around them that made her look as if she was always on the verge of laughing, a physical reminder that life shouldn't be taken so seriously. She wore little makeup and had rock-star hair—straight, streaky, and cut in long, choppy layers.

"So, how about that animal unit? Good times ahead," Morgan said, rolling her eyes. "As if we have nothing better to do."

"Seriously," I agreed, wondering if she worked.

The kids ran ahead. That Zoe was adorable. I liked her red cowboy boots.

"Freeze," Morgan yelled, stopping her daughter well before the curb. "You guys want to get some pizza or something?" she asked.

"Can't. I have to go to the grocery store before getting my other kids."

"How many kids do you have?"

"Three. And a dog." I readied myself for the impressed look that usually came. Manhattan families rarely had more than two children, and while Max's arrival had created chaos, I enjoyed the awe that frequently came my way, but this Morgan had no response. In fact, part of me wondered if she'd even heard.

"*I* should go grocery shopping," she said. "But I'm not in the mood."

"Not in the mood. What a novel idea," I said.

"Yeah, well, we still have milk, so how bad can it be?"

"My husband gets grumpy if we run out of Diet Coke," I said, pretending to complain. I assumed we were having one of those moments when women put down their men in order to bond.

"My husband can get his own damn Coke." Before I could contemplate whether I was being judged for keeping house and home stocked with sugar-free soft drinks, she yelled, "Zoe, watch the poop!"

I prayed Max wouldn't step in dog crap—then we'd be late for sure. "I hate when people don't clean up after their dogs," I said. "I mean, no one's making them have a pet."

"Oh please, Zoe's a shit-stepping moron. If there's shit around, she's stepping in it."

And just like that, I made a new friend.

6

1986

I've seen Oliver plenty of times on campus, but I always busy myself with something very urgent to do straight ahead. I'm not sure, but I think his eyes followed me. Or maybe I just imagined it. This time he's sitting on the floor in the student lounge. I consider saying nothing yet again. I'm afraid if I speak to him I'll find out that he frequently sketches lonely girls in diners, and in fact, it meant nothing. None of his friends are around, but still, approaching him feels difficult. I haven't showered and my hair is crazier than usual. To make matters worse, earlier a pierogi escaped my mouth midway between applesauce dunking and chewing, and now my clumsiness is displayed prominently on my chest.

But mostly, I am just plain afraid.

"Thank you for the drawing," I say, finally mustering the courage. When I first looked at it a few weeks ago, I was astounded. My face had been shielded by curls and a book, but somehow he captured my melancholy mood. I looked insecure and vulnerable, yet somehow striking and strong. Even though it embarrassed me, I loved the drawing.

"Do you like it, serious girl?" He looks up from the crossword, as if expecting my interruption. It's Thursday, one of the harder puzzles, and he has very few squares left. This makes me nervous. I'm not good at puzzles.

"I did. I mean, I do. I mean, yes, thank you." I resist the urge to touch the grease stain.

"You are very welcome..." He waits for me to tell him my name.

"Kara," I say. "With a K," which makes me sound like an idiot, but at least he remembers me. He tells me his name is Oliver while I fidget with my shirt. I nod awkwardly, which seems to amuse him.

"Do you always sketch girls in diners?" I ask.

"Only the inspirational ones," he volleys. I am flattered that he's just called me inspirational; that I'm not alone in the grouping remains undetected.

"Are you always so...slick?" I am pretending to be irritated by his confidence. I have seen enough movies to know that serious girls do this around cads. My mother always appreciated a cad.

"Are you always so...intense?" he teases.

"Says the guy doing Thursday's puzzle." I stand, not knowing what more to say. I want him. We are in agreement, he is worth wanting.

"You're flirting with me," he says, looking me over from head to toe. He has a way of zeroing in on me, as if no one else existed.

"I'm not a virgin," I answer, startling us both.

"Hello." He pretends to cough. I'm nervous, but I don't look away; there is no doubt about it. I momentarily have the upper hand and I enjoy the power my invitation has provoked.

His loft is an industrial space near Columbia. On the ground floor is Disker Vacuum, a retail and repair shop that seems to have been around since before electricity. After Disker, the next two stories are filled with art students and squatters, including, as I later find out, the ballerina—exotically named Eden. Conveniently, he has no roommates.

Oliver unlocks a massive door and I follow him down a narrow hallway. The old floors reverberate with his swift step. Now that we're here, he seems remote. I feel like an intruder. He throws his keys on the counter and disappears behind a large canvas to open a window.

"Shit," he says, mostly to himself. Apparently he left some brushes soaking in a canister, which is bad, but he doesn't explain why.

I size up the large room. Every surface seems to explode with his art, which makes it hard to know where to focus. Canvases are propped against the walls. Most are paintings of women; faceless figures in dreamy, graceful poses. I carefully step over thoroughly used brushes and dented tubes of paint to get closer to his work. I am mesmerized by the background in one of his larger pieces.

"That's from last year," he says. I nod and study it while he wipes a brush with a filthy rag. I sense he's watching me, and even though my desire to explore his work is sincere, I can't help but wonder if I am succeeding at the endeavor. I notice that the back of his couch is splattered with paint—surprised by his carelessness, even if it is in the name of art. I look at each canvas. Even the dry palettes in shades of blues, reds, and browns seem worthy of my attention.

"I love them. They're...amazing," I say, which sounds stupid and flat even though it's how I feel.

"Thanks." He stares at me. I wonder what he sees. Surrounded by his world, I feel bland.

"Fuck it, these can wait." He throws the brush aside. "Do you like Dylan?" He signals for me to follow him to the back of the apartment.

I stop in front of one easel. "Is this that girl from the diner?" It's hazy and imprecise, but something about the figure reminds me of the ballerina.

"Eden," he tells me.

"Is she your—"

"Model?" he interrupts.

"Okay..." I giggle. "Is she your *model?*"

"She is." He flashes a smile.

"Is she your...anything else?"

"Yes."

"Oh." I look down.

He laughs. "Relax, serious girl. She's my friend. But tell me you're not one of those crazy possessive types?"

"I am not one of those crazy possessive types."

"Good. Because even though you're cute as hell, I'm not ready to go steady."

I agree with him wholeheartedly. Meaning, I lie.

"Although if you want, I can get your name tattooed on my ass..."

"Shut up!" I slap his arm.

"Suit yourself." He gently pushes me in the direction of his room "Just in case though, it's Kara with a K, right?"

His futon smells like pepper and turpentine and even that I love. At first, I'm giddy. I find everything exciting—his rough face on mine, how he grips my hair when we kiss. But I tense up when he goes for my jeans. I want him, but I suddenly feel modest. He turns on his side and starts to touch me. I am wondering what we look like from above. I'm glad I wore my burgundy knee socks; I like the way they contrast against my pale thighs.

"Here?" he asks. I hesitate, consider lying. He moves his fingers and asks again. "Here?"

I can't answer. I want to but I can't.

"Show me," he persists.

I reluctantly move his hand so he can touch me just so. I watch him watching me and hope I don't smell. It feels good, but I'm too nervous. I want him to stop. I'm aware of music coming from another apartment as his fingers circle me. I sort of squirm so he'll climb on top of me.

"What do you want?" he whispers in my ear, which I think sounds cheesy, except it sends chills through me. Even so, I don't answer.

Finally, he pushes into me. It's like nothing I've ever experienced. Immediate and thorough—how filled up I am. Until now, as compelling as this whole Oliver experience has been—the sketch in the diner, the flirtatious banter, being among his phenomenal art in this Hollywood-hip apartment—none of it has prepared me for this. And even though he's the reason, the root, the cause—my altered state seems deeply personal. Mine alone to experience, this sudden awareness of what my body is capable of feeling.

"Where are you?" he asks, stopping.

"Here." I force myself to keep looking in his eyes.

After, I want two things at once: to curl into a ball, and to flee. But I do neither. He pulls his comforter over me and hops out of bed, cuing "Tangled Up in Blue." It's so loud I fear for his speakers. When he goes into the other room, I exhale. I want to check how I feel to foreign fingers, but it's no use. I cannot isolate the awareness of touching from being touched. At least I smell like him.

I can't believe I'm here. I relive how it felt to have him watch me, but it's too embarrassing so I push the image away and take in the details of his room. There are large industrial windows, but I'm unwilling to leave his bed, so I don't check the view. A mug of cold coffee rests on an overturned milk crate and tucked in the mirror over his dresser is a postcard of Einstein sticking out his tongue.

As I gawk, there's a part of me focused on only this: I am transformed, no longer homely. I want to look in the mirror to check. I don't know if this will ever happen again, a terrifying thought that has me strain through Dylan's tempo for the sound of him in the next room. Is this a beginning? I really hope it is. Maybe Eden truly is just his model. He did sketch me when she was there. That has to count for something.

He's everything I'm not. Brilliant, creative, witty. Being around him alters me. It doesn't matter if this monumental change is microscopic, invisible to the human eye. I know it's real. It's like he's granted me a VIP pass to his planet, and although I am still me, I'm no longer the same. I always wanted to be . . . no longer the same.

I lie in his bed. I haven't been here an hour, but something important has happened, and I am well aware, this is no small thing.

7

2007

It was two o'clock, also known as the calm before the storm. The Mommy-and-me mob had come and gone, and we still had a half hour or so before the elementary school–aged throngs arrived. I switched off various DVDs and returned trains and stuffed animals to their bins. Willa had just come back with lattes for our much-needed afternoon jolt. With Trudy at my feet I took a sip. Perfect. I kicked off a clog and petted her with my bare foot. I swear that dog purrs.

"Victoria is some sort of marketing genius," said Willa. It seemed lately she'd been bringing up the woman-in-mauve every chance she got.

"According to Victoria," I grumbled. Willa stared at me as if trying to decide what to say.

"I'm sorry." I looked down at Trudy. "I shouldn't have said that."

"Agreed."

I stroked Trudes and tried to come up with a remedy for the silence. "I mean, if you like her," I started, not finishing the sentence. Even if I did find Victoria pushy, she was the first woman Willa had even given a second look to in six years.

My mind flashed to the morning the planes hit. I'd been trying to get Adam to a sing-along class, but an inconsolable Henny was slowing us down. She hated the stroller.

"Put her in your pocket," Adam suggested, his term for the baby carrier. He was right, though; she settled into me. I was sleep-deprived and behind schedule, but the crisp September morning was invigorating. We were letting go of summer; that cool breeze a promise of autumn approaching.

"A car, Mama. A car."

"Yes, Adam. A car."

"Clouds, Mama. Clouds."

"Yes, Adam. Clouds."

We walked across 86th Street while I tried to block Adam from noticing the bagel shop. *Maybe later* was a concept we were still working on. Then I saw the crowd gathered in front of an electronics store. At first glance I assumed there'd been a robbery, but as we got closer, I saw their somber faces. Something big was happening.

"People, Mama. People."

"Yes, Adam. People," I whispered, placing a hand on my now-sleeping Henny. From behind the display glass, people were watching TV. For a split second, I recalled clips I'd seen of crowds watching Kennedy's motorcade, images that had always seemed quaint to me. I nudged my way in, feeling more curious than frightened. Never again would I be so cavalier.

A plane had crashed into the World Trade Center. Fire. This was impossible. People kept looking across the street, toward downtown, but it was no use, we couldn't see anything. Not yet. Hours later, smoke and the stench of burnt plastic would waft uptown and linger for days. But those first hours, the picture-perfect fall day remained unscathed; the cruel blessing of survival.

The crowd grew around me; strangers all watching. We stood in silence as the mammoth building only four miles away spit flames and smoke. (And later, dear God, people.)

"A fire, Mama. A fire," said Adam.

"Yes. Yes," I whispered. My heart was pounding. The World Trade Center was on fire. Nothing made sense.

My eyes were glued to the television when the second plane hit.

"What the..." someone said. I clutched the stroller. For a moment I didn't know what to do.

"Damn!" said a teenager, breaking my trance. I turned the stroller so Adam couldn't see.

Michael. I needed Michael. I'd just left him brushing his teeth. He was going in late today. His office was midtown, nowhere near this ... but none of that mattered. I needed him.

Just as I grabbed my phone, it rang.

"Kara," said Michael.

"I know. I know. We're in front of P.C. Richards." Later he'd tell me he had no idea what that had meant, but at the time, he didn't ask.

"Honey." He paused. "Go to Willa."

Dear God! Oh no. "Oh my God," I said.

"Go," he said softly.

My city seemed silent. All I could hear was my breath and pounding heart. People were out, but there was no bustle. No honking cars. No random conversations. Street cleaners were still, Rollerbladers stone-faced. I glanced at strangers but quickly averted my eyes. In those first hours, you didn't know if the person coming toward you had a husband, or daughter, or friend down there.

"Where we going, Mama?" asked Adam.

"Let's go see Willa." I hoped he didn't sense the panic in my voice.

Once outside their apartment, I hesitated. This was the beginning of nothing I wanted.

"Willa, it's me ..." I called. The buzzer was still blaring when we reached the first landing, and for a moment I was annoyed it might wake Henny; a thought I was quickly ashamed of. I held Adam's soft hand and climbed the stairwell.

"Sixteen, seventeen, eighteen," Adam counted while I bargained with God. Maybe she was upstairs and not in that blazing tower. She could have called out sick, or taken the morning off. But Willa's girlfriend was a sous-chef at Windows on the World. Loved her job and worked hard. It was Tuesday. She was there. She was there and I loved her and I loved Willa ...

"Thirty-one, thirty-two, thirty-three ..."

Adam's voice got softer when we reached their floor. The door was open. We were still holding hands when we entered. Hanging on the refrigerator was a photo of them, taken in Provincetown a few summers back—they were looking at each other, laughing.

"Willa," I whispered.

She was sitting on the couch with the phone in her hand. The TV was on. Peter Jennings was reporting that a few minutes before nine o'clock, the South Tower of the World Trade Center had been hit by a commercial airliner.

"We were on the phone," said Willa.

"A second commercial plane appears to have hit the North Tower minutes ago," continued a calm Jennings.

"We were on the phone," Willa repeated.

I didn't know what to say. I stood like a fool.

"It sounded like a sonic boom," a caller was telling the anchorman. "Or an earthquake," she continued.

"There are unconfirmed reports that there has been a possible hijacking of a commercial airliner," continued Jennings.

Willa punched numbers into her phone, listened briefly, hung up, and tried again.

"Willa," I started. Adam looked at me with big eyes and giggled.

"We were on the phone and then nothing..."

"Anyway, Victoria is a marketing genius." Willa's voice brought me back to the present. "And she thinks we can be getting *much* more publicity."

I stared at my friend and smiled.

Just then, Trudy's ears perked up. Susan, a longtime customer, was tapping on the window, trying to get our attention. With her was six-year-old Carly, sitting in a wheelchair that resembled a stroller.

"Perfect timing," I said at the door. "No one's here."

While they waited on the street, Willa and I scurried around gathering the balloons from the cutting stations and sticking them (and Trudy) in the back office.

"Get *Nemo*," I said to Willa.

"And lower the ringer," she reminded, handing me the phone. Last time we'd had to stop Carly's haircut because she became so agitated by the incessant ringing. With the little girl's known triggers tucked away, I motioned for Susan. She pushed her daughter up the ramp and parked her near the back wall. The girl stroked her hands over and over again.

"Hi, Carly," I said. She was one of the few clients I still handled myself. Her mother pressed play and slid into the chair next to her daughter.

I unclenched Carly's fingers and sprayed water into her palm. She kept her eyes glued to the show, but for a moment it seemed she relaxed her hand into mine. It was smaller than Henny's. And bluish, as if she had poor circulation. I didn't know what was wrong with Carly and I'd never asked. I just followed what Susan suggested a few years back and used steady movements when trimming her hair. Tender enough to be sensitive, but casual so as not to condescend.

Every few minutes Carly released quick, guttural yelps that startled me despite their regularity. I glanced at Susan; her eyes were closed.

I sectioned and combed carefully. Occasionally I stroked her long straight hair the way I did Henny's.

When I was done, I asked Susan if she wanted a blowout.

"Do I look that bad?"

Willa and I looked at each other. "No ... I just thought you might want a pick-me-up ..." The unspoken reason, *because my babies can talk and walk and play*, hung in the air between us.

Carly had her first seizure at Little Scissors. She'd been just under a year old. The beginning of her slow decline. I used to wonder how Susan had the strength to return to what must have felt like the scene of the crime, but after the first few times, it occurred to me—coming here was the least of Susan's worries. She had bigger fish to fry.

The bell on the door jangled, announcing Willa's three o'clock. The younger of the Lamb boys heaved his backpack onto the bench and began to rummage through it.

"I don't have a pencil," he said to his mother.

"Thanks, but some other time," Susan said. For a moment, I'd forgotten my offer.

"Where's your pencil case?" the mother asked. Carly yelped, this one louder than the others. The mother and older boy glanced at Carly, and then Susan.

"Bet he lost it," said the older brother.

"Ha!" The younger boy produced his pencil case while Carly made her noise again, even louder than the last. All eyes were on her.

"She's trying to talk to them, isn't she?" I asked.

"She is," said Susan.

"That's incredible," I whispered.

"I know."

"Yes, aren't they nice boys?" I said to Carly. "They're exciting, aren't they?" I could feel their nervousness, but I didn't care.

Susan chimed in. "Yes, they do seem like nice boys, don't they?" She touched her daughter's cheek. Carly didn't respond or even look in our direction. She continued to rub her hands in the robotic motion, but there was no doubt about it—in her own way, she was reaching out to them.

I held the door as Susan maneuvered the chair onto the sidewalk. Sunlight and squeals of the recently dismissed children seemed out of place, even though they weren't. It was three o'clock on the Upper East Side.

"What's wrong with her?" the younger of the two boys asked his mother.

I walked quickly to the back office so I wouldn't have to hear the answer.

I sat at the kitchen table and tried to block out the noise around me. Michael was down the hall on the phone. Every few minutes his authoritative voice released an encouraging laugh. It was one of the reasons he was so successful; he conveyed the perfect combination of confidence and good humor.

Miley Cyrus was crooning in the living room, something about the tragedy of love gone wrong. Henny kept restarting the song and Miley's lament would again build to a crescendo. The boys were in the playroom, their cartoons competing for the airwaves. I took a deep breath and returned to the toy catalog. I was trying to predict the next fad so I could order wholesale in plenty of time for the holidays.

"Mom!" Adam yelled. "Make her turn it off." Henny wailed in opposition.

"We can't hear our show," Adam urged.

"We can't!" Max agreed.

"Less noise, please," Michael said good-naturedly. But their arguing escalated. "Honey…" My cue to intervene. As I passed his office he mouthed *thank you* and shut the door. I heard his muffled voice, "Yes, three kids. They're amazing. As I was saying…"

I grabbed headphones from the shelf above the speakers and plugged them in, instantaneously eliminating Miley's pain. Henny protested, but I silently placed them on her ears and she too went silent. Adam and Max retreated to Japanese animation and relative peace was restored, thus enabling me to return to my orders.

A few minutes later, Michael's door opened. "Unbelievable!" he said, sounding excited. "Un. Fucking. Believable."

I looked up. "What's going on?"

"I just hung up with a firm in Seoul! There might be a project…"

"A project? In Seoul?"

"This guy was interested. I could hear it."

"Interested… in what?" I asked.

"In partnering on international projects," Michael explained, sounding dejected. "It's the way of the future, Kara. Asian markets are spearheading global development."

I nodded. My husband wanted to be a spearheader while I was overwhelmed by quantity decisions for the Laugh-and-Learn Puppy.

"Garrett and I were just talking about tapping into Asia," he said mostly to himself.

"Of course you were." This was a familiar scenario. Michael and his partner's grand dreams frightened me. It didn't matter that their firm had already wildly surpassed our expectations.

"It's a first conversation," he said calmly. "I'm sure they're talking to West Coast firms as well." I could sense Michael was handling me. I hated being handled.

"I've got to call Garrett," he announced, turning away.

For a moment, I considered calling out to him. *Tell me more*, I might have said. Or, *Sounds phenomenal*. But I sat unmoving and listened to him down the hall.

"Guess who I just got off with..." he said, again shutting the door.

I returned to the order form while snippets of Michael's conversation seeped into my consciousness. I attempted to reassure myself. International markets don't happen overnight. Besides, everything will work out, it always does. With each new mantra, I tried to cultivate my own version of Michael's certainty. Then I decreased the quantities, pushed send, and got an early start on dinner.

8

1975

A few hours before the girl is to arrive, my mother says, "If we're going to have a slumber party, we'll need supplies." I don't usually have friends over, so we stand in the A&P and try to figure out what normal girls need. It's like an important test, one neither of us wants to fail.

When we get back, my mother sighs in swift surrender. She releases her purse, keys, and the brown bag of treats onto the Formica and heads upstairs. She always needs to rest after an outing.

Looking around, I imagine the groceries waltzing out of the bag and into the cupboard, but nothing moves. Except time. Even though the kitchen is clean, I smell something stale. Something I'd never notice unless the girl was coming over.

The frozen pizza is easy, I know where that goes. Caked snow swathes the freezer shelf. I pinch a piece off and make it disappear on my tongue. I want to open the Freihofer's chocolate chip cookies, but it might be better if I wait for the girl. I hope the new snacks don't give her the impression that I think this night is special. I already know the importance of appearing more casual than I feel.

With rigid wrists, I hoist myself above the sink and look out the window. Our backyard meets another and I like to check if anything is going on. Our neighbor is sitting outside her sliding glass door. I watch her smoke a slow cigarette. Maybe she hears the phone, or her baby, because she jumps, as if startled, and then takes two quick puffs before flicking the butt across her yard. As she exhales, she sees me and waves. I quickly look away. She must've gone inside, because when I peek again, she's gone.

I watch the gray-green grass. My swings sway toward me, and back again. Since our storm windows are down and have been for two years, the scratching metal sound doesn't penetrate the kitchen. Only the hum of our Frigidaire and my mother's TV. When I tire of the yard I return feet to floor and put the rest of the food away.

I don't like waiting. I look out both front windows, the one in our den where I can see down the street (no cars), and the dining room window, which has a lesser view, but more space to do handstands. (Two cars, neither is hers.)

It is unanimous, Miss Minnesota is the prettiest.

"How does she get her lips so shiny?" I ask.

"Lip gloss," my mother answers, not looking up from *Cosmo*.

"I wonder what it tastes like," my friend says dreamily. I lick my lips, hoping they'll shine like Miss Minnesota's.

"Men like shiny lips, girls. God's honest," my mother says.

My friend is in heaven. She's not allowed to watch Miss America pageants and *Cosmo* is off-limits, too. I hope I remember to take the magazine so we can flip through it before we go to bed. I think she'll like the quiz. For a moment, I am proud of my mother. Or something similar to proud.

"Don't be fooled into believing talent wins you a man. Talent is nothing compared to big shiny lips," my mother says, laughing. I turn to her, and for the first time notice her full lips. They are every bit as beautiful as Miss Minnesota's, and the rest.

My friend is captivated; I can always tell when my mother has that effect on someone.

"I ask you, does talent make you a better kisser? No, it does not," she says, not giving us a chance to answer.

She rests in her chair, and for a moment looks weary. But not her

vibrant red curls; they are so alive they seem ready to bounce her
out of the den. Her kohl-smudged eyes dance between the magazine
and the pageant. When Miss Rhode Island sings "Summertime" my
mother's eyes glisten. Something is wrong. I know it, and I don't
know it, all at the same time. She bites her cuticles. Then the contes-
tant misses a few notes and I check my mother. "Oh sweetheart," she
mutters to the girl on the screen. She shakes her head dismissively,
stands, and asks if we want more chips.

I jump up. "I'll get them!" But I'm too late. She's already halfway
to the kitchen. I watch her red kimono sleeve gather as she reaches
for the snacks. Moving about, her hair grazes silk; she looks like fire
before it spreads. I try to imagine what I would think if I didn't
know her. I check my friend, but she is focused on applying fuchsia
polish to her gnawed nails.

My mother soundlessly snatches her bottle from under the sink.
Her loose gown reveals a flicker of the beige nightgown she remem-
bered to put on. This is a great relief because I forgot to remind her.
Hopefully, it's a sign I can relax.

An abandoned Salem smolders in the ashtray. I turn chalk-sized
ash into dust while Miss Massachusetts plays "American Pie" on the
xylophone. Or is it Miss South Dakota? I'm not really sure, but I like
the song all the same.

She serves Ruffles in a green plastic bowl, as if we eat crisp chips
in clean bowls every night. Then she returns to the kitchen for three
glasses; each clinks with ice, hers louder than the others. I don't usually get to drink red punch in the den, but it's like she's making a
deal with me, one that requires careful hands and silence. I look
away and try to sip the juice so it will stain my lips cherry red.

While I paint streaks of blue on my toenails, my mother returns
to the kitchen to make her phone calls. I wonder if my friend is listening too.

"And then what happened?" my mother asks.

My friend probably isn't paying attention, but just in case, I walk
carefully to the television and turn it up. When I get back to my
spot, rug fur is stuck in two of my toenails. I knew it was a risky

move, but I'd hoped for the best. It's my fault, I reason, wishing I'd been more careful. I pick the fibers from their tacky resting place.

"No way! You're a riot, baby," my mother says, her not-funny laughter growing louder.

"Your mom's cracking up." My friend looks at me, but I am busy inspecting my nails. I squint to see if the smudges are noticeable. We have a half an hour, I think to myself. An hour, tops. The pageant won't be over, and I'm beginning to worry.

"I bet Miss Minnesota wins, it's so obvious," I say, trying to sound bored.

"Yeah, but you never know," says the girl.

"I'm getting tired," I add.

"Come on, Daddy, come show me some love," my mother says with perfect annunciation.

"Is your mom talking to your dad?" the girl asks.

"My dad's dead," I say, liking that now she looks uncomfortable. Maybe I won't show her *Cosmo* after all.

"You son of a bitch," my mother yells. "It's one goddamned night. You make it sound like forever." I stare at swimsuits and heels.

"Don't you hang up on me," she yells. A moment passes. "Asshole!" Even though I can't see her, I suspect she has to concentrate in order to mount the receiver to the wall. I have seen this dance before.

My friend looks at me and giggles.

"This is boring," I say again, this time shutting off the TV. "Let's go upstairs," I declare, not asking. I grab the chips and my punch. The girl follows nervously.

"Talent gets you nowhere, girls," she yells from the kitchen. "You heard it here first."

She is shuffling things around in the refrigerator. Whenever she's angry, she throws old food away. It's like she has no tolerance for soggy, limp evidence of time passing.

I lock the door behind us, which buffers the sound of breaking glass.

"She just gets grumpy is all," I explain.

"My mom too," says the girl, but I know she is lying. I can tell.

We listen to records. Sister Sledge coaxes us into a sleepover mood again. But later, when the girl asks cautiously to use the bathroom, I decide that she and I will never be friends.

I carefully open my bedroom door; the hum of Johnny Carson and calm comes from below. Leading her to the bathroom, I act as if it is all a big, boring burden.

I'm glad when the girl finally falls asleep. I'm used to being alone at night, and only able to unwind in solitude. I tiptoe downstairs and turn off the TV. I could cover my mother, but that would require looking at her.

My body warms the cold sheets. I remember my toes and am not surprised when I feel jagged bumps and pieces of scratchy shag. It doesn't matter, though. I have just decided the blue is ugly.

As I drift to sleep, Miss Minnesota and the others dance in dresses made of jewels, their lips shimmering through the night. And in the morning, when I look in the mirror, I see a stubborn mustache, crimson proof that my plans don't always work out.

9

2007

Morgan and I sat in the playground while Max and Zoe played in a vile sandbox that seemed to give them enormous pleasure.

"I think some kid found a syringe in there once," I said.

"Urban legend," yawned Morgan. She lay on the blacktop and closed her eyes.

"You're probably right. Still, I always scope it out," I said. "Just to be safe."

"Just to be safe," Morgan echoed.

"Arthur, that shovel isn't ours," a young father said as I scanned the park. Henny was watching some girls on the monkey bars. Join in, I silently pleaded. Why did she always hold herself back? Adam was riding his scooter around the perimeter with his friends. I marveled as he swerved past the younger kids, unstoppable.

"Where's Michael?" asked Morgan.

"Home. Working."

"I should be working," she said.

"And Eric?" I asked.

"I don't know. The gym, maybe. He's taking Zoe later so I can have some alone time."

"Nice." I hoped I didn't sound resentful.

"I need it," she said. "If I don't get time to just *be*, I can't write. I know it sounds like New Age bullshit, but..."

"I wish Michael stepped up once in a while."

Morgan was a successful novelist. She had work that mattered to her and a husband who spent time with their daughter so she *had time to just be.* It seemed Michael was hardly ever alone with the kids anymore. Besides school, Beth had become my only reprieve, and that was always tinged with guilt, especially if—like tonight—it wasn't for work. No wonder I wasn't painting.

"Trouble in paradise?" Morgan asked, sitting up.

The morning had been difficult. Michael had secluded himself in his office while I ran around like a madwoman trying to get the kids fed and the apartment in order. Just when I'd finally gotten Henny to practice violin, the alarm company called about Little Scissors. Apparently Willa had arranged for Ava to open and she'd punched in the wrong code. By the time I got it resolved, Henny had refused to continue. I'd acquiesced, which pretty much ensured a similar argument was in my future.

Then I took it out on Michael.

"Do you think you could help out here?" I'd barked from the hall.

"When's Beth coming in?" he'd asked without looking up. In that moment, I'd wanted to slap him. I knew that by tonight, we'd be a man and a woman, instead of coparent negotiators—but until then, he seemed like the enemy. Still, I didn't want to sit in the playground complaining to Morgan about him.

"Just a lot of homework and violin bullshit."

"Mmmm."

"At least Adam finished everything." That this was my son's accomplishment, not mine, was a detail I chose to ignore. I wanted to enjoy the sun baking my back.

"No, no, Arthur! Put it down," the father said. Morgan and I watched him chase his son. "Arthur, give it to Daddy."

"Poor bastard," she mumbled.

I used to get so embarrassed when my kids took others' toys. But now I thought little Arthur looked sweet. I wanted to reassure this father. Tell him that the stage passes. But when I smiled, he shook his head in irritation. I remembered how Michael used to hoist Adam onto his shoulders and haul him from one slide area to another while I followed close behind, swelling with pride.

"Arthur, give it to Daddy. Arthur! Come back here, Arthur!"

I searched for Adam. He and his friends were on the benches, a sculptural mass of discarded scooters nearby. Sweaty and laughing, he was still more boy than big, thank God. Our eyes met. For a moment he looked puzzled by what was certainly my serious expression. I smiled reassuringly. He nodded and looked away.

Morgan and I relaxed into the afternoon. We facilitated the occasional bathroom break or popsicle run, but mostly we talked about her latest novel and Little Scissors. By the time Beth arrived, Morgan and Zoe were heading out. Maybe I'd skip going to the shop and get a manicure instead, I thought while I watched them go. Or I could pass the gallery...

"So I've been thinking about Max's Sippy cup situation," Beth said tentatively.

"Oh?"

"I think it's important for his development to drink from a big boy cup," she said.

"Well, that's an interesting idea." I was stalling. She was right. Max was three and certainly able to drink from a cup. But he loved those Sippy inventions, and frankly, so did I. He was making progress drinking like a big boy, but doing so without spilling still took concentrated effort. Perhaps I'd be willing soon, like when he was tall enough to reach the paper towels.

"I mean, it's important for him to feel a sense of competence, you know, because of his birth order."

I was beginning to rethink the Introduction to Child Development class we'd just paid for. (A gift. The class coincided with Max's preschool hours and she wanted to go back to school.)

"I mean, Henny still spills a lot, so I was thinking if Max practiced more now..." She looked at me.

"Look, Beth, while I care about Max's developmental milestones," I ventured, "I also care about my carpet." I was going for humor. She obliged me with a giggle.

We both remained silent for a moment. Maybe she was right. It was true that Henny spilled so often that we'd all come to expect it.

Besides, I knew when I hired Beth that her dream was to one day open a daycare, which meant she took her job seriously. I adored her. I did. But I kept feeling a competitive jolt whenever she tried to educate me on my kids.

With Adam, I'd strived to be the perfect mother, often meeting his needs before he even had them. I'd arranged my hours so I could go on every field trip, and I didn't just know the names of all the kids in his class, I'd befriended the mothers and nannies as well. I'd taken pride in being able to recite his beloved books, and made it my business to attend every birthday party with the guest of honor's preferred Power Ranger or Disney Princess perfectly wrapped in colorful paper and crisp bows.

When Henny came along, though it had been difficult, I tried to keep up with all that. It had still seemed like a worthy ambition. Any attention Adam had had, Henny deserved as well. And then Max arrived. What a humbling experience that had been. Suddenly I had more kids than hands. Something had to give. Motherhood with a capital M stopped being my aspiration. It wasn't failure if I changed the rules. With Adam and Henny, there'd been nightly baths in warm, sudsy water. I sang *no cold babies* in silly voices and wrapped them in lush towels, drying and hugging in one delicious burrito-baby move. After Max, they'd holler, shivering and with blue lips, "Mom, there are no towels, can we just dry off with toilet paper?"

Excellent idea, kids.

I looked at earnest Beth. For close to two years she'd been trying to come up with sensible ways to improve me or my kids. Her suggestions were usually right in theory, but in practice they lacked one crucial ingredient—me. That I was their mother and already doing the best I could never really figured into Beth's equation.

Maybe I didn't want to change. Or couldn't. But despite the fact that I frequently felt inadequate or guilty, I think I intuited the solution wouldn't be found in doing more, or *being* more, for my kids. In fact, I sensed striving for maternal perfection might be part of the problem.

Beth stared across the playground. "Um, listen, I was going to tell you this later, but maybe now's as good a time as any," she started.

"I'm listening."

"I've found another job."

I felt as if I'd been slapped. "Wow," I said, thinking about the tuition check we'd just written last week.

"Yeah, you guys have been great. You have. But I think it's time to move on," she chirped.

"I had no idea," I mumbled. "How long have you been thinking about this?" My voice was off. I had to look away.

Beth was quitting!? Now what? My mind was racing. Autumn was always such a crazy time. Now we'd have to put getting used to a new sitter into the mix. Guess this pretty much meant I'd be putting painting on the back burner. Again.

"I think it's been coming for a while," she said. "I mean, you don't need me the way I want to be needed."

"What are you *talking* about?" I asked, thinking about Morgan's *time to just be.*

"I mean, you need someone, but you don't need *me*. You don't need my expertise. I wanted to contribute to you, and..." She paused, as if asking for my permission to speak candidly.

"Go on."

"And I think I really could've helped you, if you'd been open to it." Helped me! Jesus. My mind flashed to all the times she'd suggested better ways to discipline the kids. Maybe I should've been more amenable to star stickers on the Good Boy chart.

"Wow. You really hate those Sippy cups, don't you?"

"I just think Max should have the opportunity to..."

I couldn't bear to hear her thoughts on Max's maturation. She was a beautiful young woman and I liked her, but she was a kid, for God's sake. So what if my three-year-old slurped from a Sippy every now and then? I was responsible for their whole lives, not to mention Little Scissors and Michael's firm. We both had employees counting on us. And let's not forget, the country house in Kent. Yes,

I was aware it was a privilege—and I was extremely grateful—but that didn't change the fact that I sometimes found the responsibilities daunting. I'm sure none of this occurred to Beth. There were nights I was so anxious about our ventures that I skipped reading to the kids and opted to watch *Seinfeld* instead to calm myself.

"So where are you going?" I asked, thinking about how I'd break it to the kids. Max would take it the hardest. He spent the most time with her. I looked at him happily maneuvering a train around his unwieldy sand roads. But he would be fine. Sitters moved on. I'd learned that when Bonnie left. She was a nursing student, and after she got her degree she'd gone to work in a clinic. I'd been terrified that Adam and Henny would be devastated, but actually they'd handled it fine. In fact, so much so that I remember wondering if maybe I too could easily be replaced. Michael had reassured me, and I think he was right. "What matters is that *we* remain constant," he'd said.

"I always wanted to move downtown," Beth said. "I mean, it's so much more laid-back." As if I'd never been below 57th Street. "And the timing is perfect because a friend's friend needs a roommate. The apartment is so chill."

"It sounds great," I said, hurt. I decided I'd tell the kids that it was time for Beth to have a downtown adventure. We'd throw her a little going-away party. I'd get cupcakes from Eleni's. Henny loved cupcakes.

"And it all fell into place because I found a family who lives only a few blocks away," Beth said. "Both parents are doctors," she added with pride, as if this now made her an honorary doctor as well.

"And the kids are adorable! A baby and a two-year-old."

No kids were more adorable than mine, I thought, as I caught two girls rolling their eyes while they waited for Henny to take her turn at hopscotch.

"So now you're giving two weeks' notice?" I asked. One of the hopscotch divas seemed to exhale in exasperation when Henny went back to the beginning. She probably lost count, I thought with a sigh.

"About that..." said Beth.

"How long?" Of course she wouldn't give us two weeks: she already had a job and didn't need a recommendation.

"I was hoping for next Friday. But if you need me..."

"Friday's perfect," I said. And it was. Because anything longer would've required admitting that I couldn't do it on my own, and it would take a lot more than Beth leaving to get me to do that.

Just as the elevator doors closed, I remembered it was Henny's library day. I tried to press door open, but it was too late. My kids looked at me.

"Library book?" I asked. Henny shook her head no.

"Uh-oh," said Max while Adam stood in the corner with Trudy, pretending he didn't know us. We rode down, let our neighbors shuffle past, and went back up. With her sad puppy eyes, Trudy looked at me as if I'd lost my mind. *Hello? You forgot to get off. See? We're still on the elevator.* But after a couple of floors, she slumped to the ground. At least Michael had already walked her, I rationalized.

Henny ran in to retrieve the book. "I can't find it!" she yelled moments later. A low-grade headache was becoming high-grade, so I swallowed two Advil with the last sip of sweet coffee and went to help.

"Are we going to be late?" Henny asked.

"Yes, we are." With no hint of reassurance, I headed to the corner of her room and lifted an empty basket. The words *Library Books* were elaborately written in different-colored markers. An example of my wasted time.

"Unbelievable," I mumbled.

"Don't yell at me," Henny whined.

"That was not yelling, Henrietta," I said. "When did you last see it?"

"I don't know."

My head was starting to spin. I pictured Henny's teacher, Miss Nathanson. I hated being late. Where was it? I scanned the room while Henny shuffled papers on her desk. The boys looked at her and then me.

"Where's the book, Henny?" My voice startled her. Great, I'm the bad one. Michael never scolded the kids, which only irritated me more.

"What am I going to do?" Henny complained. "Miss Nathanson told us not to forget our library books on library day."

"Yes, I know she did." I banished the vision of an unprepared Henny, deprived of picking a book while the others merrily made their choices. This wasn't the time for her to learn the consequences of disorganization. The punishment far exceeded the crime. Especially since no matter what anyone said, if a second grader didn't have her books on library day, it was the mother's fault, not the child's. And no one knew better than I that a daughter shouldn't be sentenced for her mother's misdeeds.

But was it too much to ask that the library books ended up in the book basket?

"Perhaps next time you could put your library books in this basket here, the one marked, *Library Books*. An excellent place for them, don't you think?"

Henny was applying stickers to an old spiral notebook. I watched as she dug in her desk to retrieve a pair of scissors. My phone vibrated. It was Ava; she was supposed to open this morning.

"I'm racing," I explained, watching Henny.

"I'm sick as a dog," said Ava. She added a cough for good measure.

"Uh-huh." I tried to remember the day's schedule. With a raspy voice, Ava explained her symptoms. If she was really sick, I didn't want to be a bitch; if she wasn't, I didn't want to be a sucker. We hung up and I called Willa, but it went to voicemail.

I contemplated whether it was possible to drop everyone at their respective schools and make it in time to open the salon. I was fairly certain Ava had a tight morning schedule. I called Willa's cell again. Voicemail.

While I was trying to figure out if I should leave a message, Henny was carefully cutting slivers of paper. She seemed completely unaware of what was going on around her.

I hung up. "What are you doing?" I snapped at Henny, but she paid me no mind. "Do you hear me?" She continued cutting.

There was something about the way she continued cutting—oblivious to what was going on around her—that filled me with rage. Without thinking, I hurled the library basket toward the bookcase near her desk. It clanked and tumbled to the ground, my unpredictability firmly established. I needed to control myself, but there was a more powerful part that quashed any meager protests, including my own.

"Your books are not my responsibility," I ranted. "I try to keep this place organized, but if you can't do your part, *you're* the one who won't get to take out books, not me!"

I stood fuming and again thought of Michael. Maybe if he spent more time with his children, I could get to be the reasonable one, for once.

My babies stared back at me with wide eyes. Evidence of my enormous power. I aggressively flipped through stacks of books, rearranging ones that had been thrown in haphazardly. When I saw that stupid basket, my rage came tumbling back. My ability to anticipate this very problem had done nothing.

It occurred to me that my children had no choice but to listen to my hysterics. What could they do? Tell me, *Mom, you're overreacting, take a few minutes alone, try to calm down*? Not a chance. In fact, the ability to do that might be the very definition of freedom.

"You *must* be more responsible around here," I heard myself say. "You're old enough to keep your rooms neat. Look at this. Jesus." I held up an expensive sweater I'd bought Henny a week earlier. Obviously she'd taken it off and just tossed it on the bookshelf.

"Clothes go in the hamper. Do you want to wear dirty clothes to school?" The threat floated in the air. I threw Henny's pajamas and yesterday's dirty outfit in the bin.

"It's not my job to wait on you guys hand and foot!" I paused and thought of Beth. "And it's not a babysitter's job either! You've gotten so used to having a nanny around that you don't know how to pick up after yourselves." I blamed them, though of course I'd been the one responsible.

An image from my childhood came to mind. Alone in the kitchen, packing my lunch, while my mother lay on the couch, hungover.

"You guys have no idea how lucky you are," I continued. But when I glanced at them, they didn't look lucky at all; they looked frightened.

I exhaled. Even that resembled her.

"Which book are we looking for anyway? The one on weather?" I asked.

"That was mine. I returned it yesterday," Adam said, sounding relieved. He looked at Henny guiltily.

"Well?" I demanded. "It's not my library book." I had no memory of it, which meant Beth had read to her. Shame whacked me. Finally, an antidote to my anger: failure.

"*Ivy and Bean*," Henny answered.

"Did Beth read it to you?" I asked, knowing the answer.

Henny nodded hesitantly. I imagined the two of them nuzzled together as Henny listened dreamily. Great. Beth read and I raged. I tried to visualize where she might have left the book and even considered calling her, but I didn't want to admit defeat.

"Did she read the book after school, or before bed?" I asked with the seriousness of a sleuth.

"I don't know," Henny answered in a daze.

I released a long, slow breath. "Think, baby," I coaxed her. My warmth sounded foreign. Why did I forget this was always the better approach?

As if a lightbulb went off, Henny shouted, "At bedtime."

"Did you want to *sleep* with the book?" I asked. She always wanted to sleep with the day's most adored treasures. I looked under her bed and grabbed two stuffed animals and my lost slipper; I threw them on her comforter.

"How about that?" I said to myself when I found a flashlight

Michael had been searching everywhere for. I didn't bother scolding Henny. The loot was damning enough.

"Aha!" I held up the book.

Max sat agreeably in his stroller and we walked the few blocks to school. Adam and Henny squabbled at the curb. "Walk," I commanded.

Anyone looking at us would know right away that I was undone. A fuming mother implied one thing: failure. My responsibility was to get three well-fed, happy children to school on time (with library books). Effortlessly. While there is zero prestige in this feat, *not* accomplishing it is a failure of one's own.

I looked at my brood. I'd always sworn I wouldn't be like my mother. I wished I had remembered that being late (and unprepared) was better than being late, unprepared, and abused. Even Trudy looked dejected. I was desperate to turn the morning around. Perhaps they could still go to school happy. I knew I'd feel guilty the rest of the day, but the magnitude of guilt was still in my control.

"Let's start the morning over," I suggested.

They didn't answer.

When we arrived, I tied Trudy to the gate and took comfort in the fact that other kids were still trickling in. At least we weren't the only ones. In the entrance hall, I moved to kiss Henny. She surprised me by leaning into my embrace. Even though second grade was waiting, for that moment, she didn't seem to want to let go. I don't deserve this love, I thought miserably. Adam nodded an obligatory goodbye, while Max gazed at his siblings. I still had to get him to preschool, and at this rate, there was no way to be on time to the salon. But I hesitated; I needed to watch them make their way down the long corridor.

People and that elementary echo disappeared. I marveled at how normal my babies seemed. Certainly to me they were exceptional, but there was no question about it, they were also utterly ordinary.

Just like all the others. I watched until the end, when they turned the corner and went on their way.

Ready now, I retrieved Trudy and patted Max's hair. I was finally calm. My children blended in.

That evening I unpacked Henny's backpack. Tucked among math sheets and memos was *Ivy and Bean*. I held the book in front of her, blocking the TV. "You checked it out again?" I asked in disbelief.

"We didn't have library today," she said sleepily, shifting to see the TV.

"Why not?!"

"I don't know. I think they switched it to Thursday." And she returned to her show.

10

1986

It takes a week of sitting in the student union to run into Oliver. When this fortuitous event happens, I'm thankful that the planets have so kindly aligned themselves. We speak briefly, but I can tell he's about to leave. He kisses me. Even though I've been thinking about him nonstop since our afternoon together, his lips are unfamiliar. They are warm and the coffee I taste on his breath feels like an invisible secret, only for me. When he turns to leave for class I am determined to appear casual, nonchalant. This is as effortful as it is dishonest, but I figure some of the best strategies are.

He doesn't call. I gave him my number when I was at his apartment, but still, he doesn't call. I dial information and end up staring at my scribbled writing, unable to figure out a way not to sound pathetic. Unsure which is worse, sounding pitiful or another night without him, I sit quietly.

Then I dial his number.

"Hello, hang on," Oliver yells into the receiver. It sounds like he throws the phone down. I assume he's painting. My heart pounds as I listen to the Grateful Dead blaring in the background. He doesn't yet know it's me. I hear him lower the music, but I quickly hang up before he comes back. I worry he'll guess it's me, but I'm still glad I hung up. He's painting. I would hate to bother him. And most of all, I don't want to be like my mother.

*   *   *

A few days later, he walks into the student lounge looking disheveled and preoccupied. I am in the exact location where we first spoke, but he doesn't glance in my direction. I tell myself it means nothing, even though I always pay homage to this spot whenever I walk in; then again, I'm sensitive that way. I watch as he stands on the commissary line and debate if I should go to him. It's obvious he needs coffee. I'm afraid if I approach, he'll reject me. I try to contain my brewing panic. Hunched, he heads for the door. Just as I think he's going to leave without acknowledging me, he stops before the exit and looks across the lounge directly into my eyes. I can't breathe. I'm suddenly like an asthmatic on a frigid day, not really in danger, but in need of a moment to acclimate. Hand to temple, he salutes me. By the time I smile, he's gone.

I sigh. The recognition, though slight, is restorative. Like the first dose of an antibiotic. Much better than not at all.

Finally, he calls from Ralph's. "Come have a drink," he says, with what seems like nothing to lose. Before I've even hung up, I want to sprint to him. I have a paper due and shouldn't go, but I know better than to grapple with the inevitable.

"I can't stay long," I say as I slip next to him at the mostly empty bar.

"A Molson for the killjoy," he tells the bartender.

"Make it a Diet Coke," I say, taking a sip of Oliver's beer. "Seriously, I've got to write a paper."

"So what you're saying is you'd very much like to come over." He leans in to kiss my neck. I am cold from the walk over, but that's not why I shiver. I can feel my eyes sparkling, so I steady myself.

"What I'm saying is I have to get a good grade on this fucking Virginia Woolf paper."

"You sound like an angry feminist; I'm sure you'll do fine."

"You think? It's pretty dense." My Women in Lit class is one of the few things I still care about that doesn't involve him. I like the professor. When the class discussions get going, she scoots onto her desk, kicks off her shoes, and smiles. It's like she thinks what we have to say is worth waiting for. I don't want to ruin it.

"You don't know how hard Woolf can be," I tell him.

"No, my love, *you* don't know how hard *I* can be."

He says he'll only be a few minutes in the next room, so I wait on his bed. I look at my watch. If I don't start my paper, I won't be able to get it in on time. I hear the shuffling of canvases and consider offering to help, but I sense he needs a minute alone.

I don't want to open *A Room of One's Own*. These past few weeks, I've become accustomed to the persistent background din of waiting for Oliver. Classes are half absorbed, sleep only partially restful. My focus is perpetually divided between the task at hand and hope. Now that he's in the next room, I have trouble letting go of longing. I feel pathetic, but knowing this provides no solution.

I reluctantly begin reading. As I attempt the famous text, I imagine imminent prestige, as if reading Woolf will grant me access to a secret society for the educated elite. I don't desire knowledge as much as a yearning to be perceived as scholarly.

But there's a slight problem. What started as procrastination and distraction has bloomed. I sit in Oliver's room, on Oliver's delicious bed, and this raisin-sized problem grows. It becomes my plum-sized problem, and it is this: I do not know what the fuck Woolf is trying to say. I think I understand her basic assertion, that in order for women to create fiction they need a room in which to do so. Evidently, she maintains, they also need money. This makes sense to me because I figure it's probably fairly difficult to be inspired while hungry. But then I reread every twisting sentence and try to comprehend why her essay goes on for a hundred and ten more pages. One minute a woman is wandering around campus, the next she's talking about crocuses. With every unwieldy paragraph, my mind fails. I'm able to read the words on the page, but her message eludes me.

So I come to a familiar conclusion. My bewilderment implies something. It means: I am dumb. I can't. I don't matter. And perhaps the most dangerous of implications, the one to be hidden at all costs, is that my stupidity must be kept a secret; neither spoken nor explored.

I try again. I follow a woman into a library and past a party and all the while what I am really doing is...waiting for Oliver. With each twisting paragraph, I grow bored.

It never occurs to me that the problem is anywhere but within me.

"Did you start without me?" Oliver asks when he finally comes to me.

"I was about to," I say, tossing *A Room of One's Own* to the floor.

"Seriously, I was giving you some time to get work done. Any luck?"

"Yeah, thanks. She's brilliant." And I'm not.

At first I worry I'm not doing it right, but he guides me up and down until I know his pace. I fall asleep tasting him, which is almost as good as an orgasm of my own.

Much later, I wake. Laughter and the scent of pot seep into his bedroom. I consider joining them, but can't bring myself to move. Lying in his vast bed, I strain to hear the voices but fall into an uneasy sleep.

In the morning, his canvas greets me, the ballerina's unmistakable form displayed in blues and browns. I study it while they lie on his scarlet couch nearby. Eden at one end, Oliver at the other. They are fully clothed, except for bare, dirty feet.

Neglect permeates the loft, a full ashtray on the coffee table, brushes bathed in paint resting on a wannabe Pollock floor.

I return to Oliver's room and dress quickly. She is his muse. It's a beautiful painting. When I walk past them again, I pause at the canvas. He has captured her grace and beauty, but that's not what makes the painting magnificent. I squint so that I see only the swirling colors, blurring the figure, ignoring the form. I don't know how long I'm there, enveloped by Oliver's art.

"You're Kara," Eden whispers.

At least he talks about me. "Hi," I say softly.

"I'm Eden."

"Hi," I say again. She makes an event out of stretching. Unhurried and entitled. I look around the room for something crucial that might require my attention.

"Do you want pancakes?" she asks.

She cooks here? "No. Thanks, though."

Oliver stirs, which is alarming. I don't want to talk to him. Fortunately, he settles back to sleep. Eden rises and glides to the bathroom.

I see one of his paintbrushes off to the side, away from the others. It appears discarded, practically an invitation. I have no plan for it, but pick it up.

"I'm not sure if he has eggs," she yells from the bathroom. I hide the paintbrush in my satchel, convinced he won't miss it anyway. I hear her moving around and decide to make my exit. Taking a deep breath at the door, I slide open the echoing bolt.

"So you're sure?" She seems to appear out of nowhere. "Because I found eggs." She leans against the wall as if she's seeing me off.

"I'm sure. Thanks, though." I sound so boring... so blah.

She smiles. It is a perfectly warm expression. Who are you to him? I want to ask. Or perhaps give her the play-by-play of last night.

"Next time, then." She touches my arm.

I manage to smile. Then I push open the massive metal door and step into the day.

11

2007

I stood on the corner of 90th and Fifth and looked around. I never tired of Central Park in the fall. Its magnificence sparked my gratitude, the kind one feels when she knows things could've just as easily gone another way. The chilly air made all things feel possible.

I was waiting for Morgan. The plan was to walk a few loops around the Reservoir before we needed to pick up the kids. "I've got to address this ass situation," she'd said when she invited me.

"Ahh yes. I have a similar situation."

Now I was waiting. She was almost fifteen minutes late. I checked my phone. No message. There were, however, about a million emails regarding soccer snack. One mother wanted to enforce an *organic only* mandate, while another debated the pros and cons of prepackaged cookies. They were hitting *reply to all* and clogging my inbox. As quickly as possible, I was emailing the snack mother (and only the snack mother) and volunteering to bring an unspecified nibble, when I heard Morgan calling from across the street.

"Sorry, sorry, sorry." She waved her hands in the air as if surrendering. I tucked my phone in my sweatshirt pocket and watched her approach.

I waited for her tell me what had kept her, but she didn't. Everything about her radiated self-assurance; her toothy smile framed by glossy lips, the way she sashayed toward me, her solid hug hello. I'd been annoyed, but now that she was here, I just wanted to catch up.

"Emailing your lover?" She motioned to where I'd deposited my phone.

"I wish."

"Oh?" She raised an eyebrow.

"Kidding," I answered a bit defensively. "I was just reading these endless emails."

"Something up at the salon?" she asked.

"Soccer snack."

"Ah." She nodded.

"It's unbelievable actually. *Harry loves cauliflower, Molly needs grapes*," I mocked. "They might call a meeting. A possible vote!"

"Hilarious," said Morgan. "I should put that in my book. Endless emails about the minutiae of motherhood."

"But who'd read it? The reality is brutal enough."

"Oh, I'm not worried," she said. "I've a very loyal following." It was true. Morgan's debut novel had been a breakout success. The second one received mixed reviews, but her fans had come to her defense. Now she was working on number three. Or trying to.

"How's the writing?"

"I'm a tad distracted, actually."

"Anything serious?" I asked.

"Just...distracted." It seemed like she was holding something back, but I didn't want to come off as prying. "Seriously, emails from soccer moms is just the sort of social satire my editor loves," said Morgan.

"I guess..."

"Could be dangerous, though," she said. "One wrong move and you're perilously close to woman-bashing."

"That's a bit extreme," I said.

"Not really. Wealthy white women are the last group it's acceptable to deride," she said.

"I don't know..." I said. Was this true?

"You're right. Let me amend that," Morgan said. "Wealthy white *mothers*. They're hated even more."

"These women aren't victims. I mean, read some of this." I offered her my phone, which she shooed away. "They sound like housewives from the fifties. Did we learn nothing from Betty Friedan?" I asked.

"Or do we boost our own sense of self by putting these women down? The old *I'm nothing like her* defense."

"Seriously? Soccer. Snack," I said.

"Look, they bug me too," said Morgan. "They do. But there's a part of me that can't shake the feeling that what's important to women is always devalued. As dull as sliced oranges may be—they matter to our kids."

I thought of Adam. Last night he'd cornered me as soon as I'd gotten home. Hadn't even taken my jacket off *and* had to pee; but he was electric. I couldn't make him wait.

"We did this experiment with water," he'd said, "...and you'll never believe it. We actually *measured* the water cycle. You know about the water cycle, right, Mom?"

I nodded and hoped he wasn't about to quiz me.

"When the sun warms the surface water," he continued, "water evaporates into the atmosphere. And guess what carries water vapor?" He waited for me to answer.

"Uh..."

"Wind!"

"Wind." I repeated.

"Wind!" he said again. It was like our old game. My job was to echo. To nod. Smile. In that moment, Adam hadn't needed a dialogue; he'd needed an audience. An echo. And not just any echo; me.

"So if something matters to our children"—Morgan put her hand on her heart—"dare I say, to our country's children...how could it possibly be trivial?"

"Now you're fucking with me," I said.

"A little, but not entirely."

"Maybe they just have too much time on their hands," I said. "I mean, get a job. A life. Volunteer. Something!"

"Got it." She smiled. "Their crime is being wealthy."

"No, their crime is these boring friggin' emails."

"Fair enough." Morgan laughed. "Fair enough."

Adam's game was almost over and I wanted to be ready. I checked the doughnuts. Safe in the knowledge they were exactly as I left them ten minutes earlier, I carefully took a sprinkle from the bottom of the box without touching any frosting. I glanced in the cooler one last time. The oranges and juice boxes would be here when the thirsty boys arrived.

I noticed two couples in the distance. They were in their mid-twenties and I marveled at how young that now seemed. The *Times Book Review* was tucked under one's arm, which reminded me that I hadn't read it, much less a book, in a long time.

I wondered if the women wanted to marry these men, have their children. In my twenties, I used to gawk at married Manhattanites, but I'm not sure young women do that anymore. I wanted to study the men; try to discern whether they might be in it for the long haul. I imagined these couples a few years from now…transformed into coaches and cheerleaders for teams named Red Dragons or Green Giants rather than sexually charged twenty-somethings en route to Isabella's for mimosas and egg white omelets.

As they approached, I felt the urge to burrow in the cooler for cover. Maybe Morgan was right. Maybe I had internalized some sort of self-hatred. Or maybe I just didn't want my existence assessed, perhaps diminished or defined, by my children's recreational pursuits. It didn't comfort me that my children adored those pursuits and I adored those children.

Before the freedom-flaunting ones had wandered onto my turf, I'd been happy on the sidelines. Henny and Max had found some kids to run around with while the adults watched the game. I loved being in the park, and was impressed by Adam's strength. When he scored a goal, he'd subtly look in my direction to check if I'd seen. I'd nod and convey from half a field away that I was here and that he mattered.

Also, the regular coach was out with shingles and Michael had stepped in, foreplay as far as I was concerned. I watched as he encouraged the boys in a noncompetitive, politically correct way. I hoped that later, despite all the homework I'd be required to facilitate, I'd recall this moment and rally the energy to fuck him. The coach of the Red Dragons looked very good indeed.

Now I felt self-conscious.

I had a fantasy that I gave the young couples a piece of my mind.

You will not always be supple and carefree. In a blink of an eye, you too will age, and in all likelihood, procreate. So I ask you this one pertinent question: What do you think will happen if your lovely legacies fancy kicking a white ball around on an autumn day? What then, immortal ones, what then?

I will tell you. Not only will you watch your offspring kick that ball across the field, but you will make sure there are oranges available by halftime. And by available, I don't just mean cut. I mean, you'll see to it that there are no visible hanging white strings. You think you won't, but you will. And do you know why you'll do this? Do you? Because suddenly and without warning, what's important to your kids will become important to you.

The Red Dragons descended. I stood back so they could reach my perfect oranges. Glad to have remembered a garbage bag, I held it steady as they tossed in their peels while reliving the exciting parts of the game.

I looked up just in time. When the couples finally passed, they didn't glance in my direction.

The weekend sun settled behind the distant West Side high-rises, washing our apartment in an evening blue hue. Max was already asleep, collapsed just after his bath. His hair was still wet when his syncopated breath filled their room. I quietly shut the door and passed Michael's office. He was returning emails while Adam sat next to him reading a book. They were wearing the same expression—serene absorption. I savored the image.

I wondered what qualities I'd inherited from *my* father. As far as my mother was concerned, he'd been responsible for two things: impregnating her and destroying her budding career with the Metropolitan Opera. Suffice to say, she hadn't been particularly enthusiastic about any genetic reminders. Now that I was a mother of children whose father I adored, I realized what a loss this had been.

Michael glanced up. As if reading my mind, he offered a comforting smile and I was immediately transported back to the present day. I found my way to Henny's room. She was on the floor playing with her dollhouse. As usual, her clothes were strewn about. This time I just threw them in the hamper and straightened some of her art projects. She glanced at me and then continued to play. I poured a half-full bottle of water into our surviving lima bean plant, one of my most treasured possessions from her preschool years.

I scanned the bookshelf. I couldn't remember the last time she'd read to me, a fact I was ashamed of. I'd delegated that task to Beth last year, after my attempts kept deteriorating into slammed doors and tears. But she was older now. I wanted to see her progress.

We nestled together on the purple couch. As soon as I opened the book, her body went rigid. She sat without making a sound.

"What's the first letter?" I asked.

"D?"

"Not D..." I said slowly. I was surprised. She was stymied on the word *Bob*.

"B?"

"Yes. B. B for bear. Buh, bear," I said. She pursed her lips to make a B sound, then silently studied the word.

"What's the next letter?" I asked.

"O?"

I nodded. "And what sound does O make?"

"Ohhh."

"Good. In this word, though, it's Ah." I waited for her to put the Buh and Ah sounds together, but she didn't.

"Buh, Ah..." I prompted.

"Buh, Ah," she repeated.

"Good," I said. "Now add the last letter." But she sat silently.

"What's the last letter, Henny?" I was growing impatient.

"D?" she asked, as if we hadn't just gone over this.

"Not D. See? Just like before, right there." I pointed. How could she not have remembered?

"B," she said quietly.

"So what's the word?"

"Buh, Ah. Buh," she said.

"Uh-huh." I could see she was trying. I felt a surge of compassion, quickly followed by frustration, punctuated by fear.

"Buh, Ah. Buh," she repeated.

"Can you put it together?" I wanted to scream—*Bob. It's Bob!*

"Buh, Ah. Buh," she said again.

"Bob," I said warmly. "See? Bob."

I knew she was trying her best, but her best wasn't getting her anywhere. Henny was not learning to read. Her first-grade teacher had told us she'd catch on. That any delay would right itself after a developmental spurt. But I was beginning to think maybe not. Maybe something was off with my baby girl.

"It's okay, sweetheart. You're just tired," I said. "My turn." I moved the book to my lap and pointed to each word as I read, careful the whole time not to let her see the thick tears that had formed in my eyes.

12

1975

I ride my bike with all my might. House after house whizzes by. A garden here, a porch there. I pretend I'm in a movie and the camera is following me through these streets. I glance in a window as a family sits for dinner. Several doors down a wagon has been left on a perfectly manicured yard. I pedal, knees jutting rhythmically, unaware of my breathing or the creaking old bike. Grass grows in between cracks in the cement, but I expertly steer away from the jigsawed sidewalk, navigating a curb with ease. This, I think, will make me seem cool in my movie. Down a ways, a garage door has been left up, treating me to a splash of two cars neatly tucked away. I move on.

I can practically see myself onscreen, crazy red hair blowing behind me. I imagine the opening music as I pedal faster. Fleetwood Mac maybe. My speed feels necessary, as if life depends on it, but of course in reality, no one is chasing me and no one is waiting. Except for my mother, but she doesn't count.

I used to make believe I was someone else—a girl from a big exciting family, with lots of noise. Fancy clothes, too. But now when I try to picture what my movie might be about, I only see myself pedaling. Destination and story elude me.

I wonder if my mother will have company tonight. If so, I hope it's Uncle Andy because Uncle Phil calls me Kara Mascara, whereas Uncle Andy doesn't say much at all. As I get closer to the hill near my house, I count. That's my trick. I don't look ahead to see how much farther I have to go; instead, I count to one hundred keeping my eyes peeled to the ground. If I do it right, the downhill will take me by surprise, but today I keep peeking, desperate for the descent. When it finally comes, I pedal with all my might. My feet can't keep up with the spinning so I lift my legs straight and fly down the hill, feeling powerful and free, even though I'm neither.

And then I see my mother. She's in our driveway flipping through the mail. I can tell she doesn't expect to see me; we both wear the same *oh-there-you-are* expression. She's my mirror. Our connection isn't exactly tender, but it's predictable and solid . . . what I know as home.

And then her expression changes. Something isn't right.

A blue station wagon is backing out of the neighbor's driveway headed right for me. Two seconds more and it would have hit me. But my mother's silent warning, the one just before her shriek, has saved me. I veer sharply to the right while the car backs out and then continues on. I am safe, but without thinking, I clench the front wheel with both my feet.

It is impressive, really—the arc of flight. Fast and slow, all at once, I soar over my handlebars. I sound like sneakers in the dryer, pummeling, pummeling, pummeling—I land.

She comes to me, furious.

"You were going too fast. Are you okay? Jesus, Kara. Jesus. You took it too fast." She is touching me. Inspecting.

"I'm okay!" I snap, hiding my burning knees and elbows.

"Did you hit your head? I couldn't tell. Did you? Did you hit your head?" I pull away from her and spit into my stinging palms. "Honestly, Kara. You nearly gave me a heart attack!"

Our eyes lock. For a moment it's like we're both waiting for the other to do something. She reaches for me again, tries to stroke my hair. It's not that I don't want her. I do. But stronger is my need *not* to want her. I am frightened and hurting; but also, I'm enraged that she's frightened and hurting too.

"I said I'm fine," I bark. She flinches. I know I should be nicer, but something stops me. She pats the front pocket of her denim jacket and with trembling hands lights her Salem on the second try. The deep inhale rights her.

I push my mangled bike to the garage while she gathers her mail and purse from the driveway. Seeing her hunched on the pavement fills me with shame. I dawdle so she'll go in the house before me, then I take one last look at the now dark day.

Without even trying, I realize something about my movie. It doesn't matter if I'm moving toward something or trying to get away. I may only be ten years old, but I'm suddenly aware that there's very little difference between the two.

13

2007

Maybe I was being paranoid, but when I stopped in front of the gallery window, I could've sworn Trudy looked at me with her big doggie eyes as if to ask, *Really, again?*

"Yes, again," I answered defensively as two men passed. It was official. I'd become one of those women who talked to her dog on the street.

But the burgundy painting was still in there and I couldn't resist a quick peek. It soothed me. And I didn't feel guilty, either. Since Beth had quit I'd yet to hire anyone, and I only had one more interview scheduled. Michael just assumed I'd figure it out. *I'll like anyone you like*, he'd said. So my thinking was—if he's not going to help, I have every right to this indulgence. Some people destressed with yoga; I had this.

Who was I kidding? I was completely full of it. Michael never pointed out that after all these years I'd not once changed a light-bulb or any of the other million things that fell under his domain. We were a team. So why was I standing outside of Oliver's show, yet again?

Go to work, I told myself.

But I stayed put. I wanted to know if he painted any people. I tried to see into the back of the still closed gallery...but I couldn't tell. Every search I'd done proved he no longer did figures, but I wanted to make sure.

Okay, then. I was ready.

"Come on girl." Loyal Trudy stood. "See? That wasn't so bad." She looked at me with total devotion, her wagging tail my signal she was ready for our next adventure. Unlike me, she didn't hold a grudge.

Morgan sat at the big-kid cutting station sucking on a lollipop while I told her about Henny. "I've never seen anything like it," I said. "I'd help her sound out a word, and then a few seconds later, it was if she'd never seen it."

"Yeah, but are you comparing her to Adam?" she asked.

Was I? Adam did start to read about ten minutes after learning the alphabet. Perhaps I was holding Henny to his high standard.

"I mean, *children learn at different rates*," Morgan said, mocking our kids' preschool teacher.

"Right," I agreed. But seconds later, I was doubtful. I mean, Morgan hadn't been there.

"Look, my sister-in-law went through this," she said. "If you're worried, get her evaluated."

Evaluated. God, I hated how that sounded. Evaluated. Yuck.

"But don't do it through the school," she said. "In case they try to use it to kick her out or something."

"They can't do that," I said. "Can they?"

Morgan shrugged. "They were horrible to my niece."

"Yeah, but she was in private school," I said. "They can't kick Henny out of public—"

Just then, Willa and Victoria came in from the back room. I had no right to resent Victoria's presence; and yet I did. I made the cursory introductions. Victoria told Morgan that she had devoured her first two books, but before Morgan could even respond, Victoria handed her a business card. "We have an excellent book publicity division," she said. "We work with all the major publishers. You should let your editor know."

I wasn't in the mood for networking; my mind was on Henny. Did she really need an evaluation? How would I explain it to her? Now I wanted Michael.

"And... actually," said Willa, "Victoria also works with several Madison Avenue shops in the neighborhood."

"With impressive results, if I do say so myself."

I suddenly understood where this was going. "That's great," I said.

"I'm certain I could get Little Scissors covered in all the regional publications," Victoria added.

I glanced at Willa, hoping to convey my desire to change the subject, but she was beaming at Victoria. I was startled. Willa had always been radiant, but now she seemed different. Even if I wasn't crazy about Victoria, there was no denying that since they'd been seeing each other, Willa seemed happier. Given our long history, this mattered to me.

And then the phone rang. "Which publications?" I asked while answering.

"This is Mrs. Murphy, the school nurse."

"This is Kara." The tenor of my voice silenced them. "Are the kids okay?"

"Henrietta's fine," she reassured me, even though I could hear my girl crying in the background. "But there's been an accident. You should come."

"Oh my God," I said when I saw her, which made Henny start to cry again. The front of her sweatshirt was covered in blood. Even though the nurse had told me over the phone that Henny had run straight into the jungle gym, knocking out her two front teeth (baby ones, thank goodness), in that instant I thought she'd been shot.

"You're fine," I said, hugging her. "You're okay." I released her for a moment and held her at arm's length. "Let me see you," I said, stifling my horror.

Henny opened her swollen lips and revealed a bloody space where her teeth used to be.

"Well, would you look at that?" I pretended to marvel. "You look older somehow." I squinted. "I guess knocking out a few baby teeth ages a girl."

A slow, blood-crusted smile started to form on her face, melting my heart.

"We're looking for her teeth," Mrs. Murphy informed me. "But she probably swallowed them." Lovely.

"What about the tooth fairy...?!" cried Henny.

"Not a problem," I said. Henny looked to the nurse, who nodded with authority. "I'm sure this happens all the time," I continued. "Tooth fairies understand."

The pediatric dentist was exceptional. She gave Henny purple sunglasses to wear during the X-rays. "And I can keep them, Mama," Henny kept telling me, even though I'd been standing next to her when the doctor said so. Luckily, there'd been no bone fracture or damage to her permanent teeth.

Exhausted, we walked toward the avenue to hail a cab. I glanced at my email. A shampoo supplier wanted to schedule a sales meeting. Henny was chatting about something, but I wasn't really paying attention.

"Look!" she yelled, pointing across the street. An elaborate graffiti mural was painted on the far end of a handball court. I was reminded of the artist Basquiat. He started as a graffiti artist. And then I thought of Eden.

Out of nowhere, Henny bolted into the street.

"Henny! Stop!" I tried to grab her sweatshirt but she was too fast. "Henny!"

A taxi came at her. All other sound evaporated; there was just this: the taxi's blaring horn merged with my tragic cry for Henny.

The car screeched to a stop. Henny froze, her outstretched hands touching the hood of the cab. The driver must have been terrified, because for several seconds he continued to pound on his horn. Henny remained unmoving.

I ran to her and pulled her out of the street, breaking her trance. "Sorry. Sorry," she cried.

"You must be careful!" I touched her all over. Arms, face, chest.

"I didn't see him. I didn't," cried Henny. Time folded into itself. I became ten years old. "I'm sorry, Mama. I'm sorry."

She's okay, I kept telling myself as I clutched her shoulders. "Please, Henny! I can't take it. You must be careful!" *You nearly gave me a heart attack!*

She nodded. I couldn't let go of her. No child of mine had ever been so close to death. "You must!" I said again—as much a prayer as a command.

It was more than I could take. Not only was she a mess, crying for the millionth time today, but I was flooded with memories. First of Eden, then my own childhood near miss; a near miss witnessed by my mother. How little I'd understood at the time.

There's a certain kind of powerlessness when confronted with the knowledge that one's own callousness, even the kind committed in ignorance, can't be undone. I'm sorry, Mama. I'm sorry, I silently echoed my daughter.

I glanced at the magnificent wall in the distance. Henny'd been excited. She hadn't meant to be careless. Still, I was shaking. I needed to calm down.

"Can we go see?" she asked, pointing to the mural. She was ready to move from this moment to the next.

I sighed, completely drained. Henny wiped her nose on her sleeve and looked up at me.

"Okay. Yeah. Sure." I grabbed her hand, so small and soft in mine, and we crossed the street.

That night I went through the motions of our regular routine— homework, dinner, bath; but really I was counting the minutes until the kids were in bed and I could talk with Michael

"What do you mean, you're worried?" he asked, muting the TV.

"Just that. I'm worried," I whispered. The kids had just gone down. I didn't want them to hear us.

"I thought you said there was no permanent damage."

"Not her teeth. Her." Michael glanced at the TV. "Something's wrong," I added.

"What do you mean, *something's* wrong?"

"Something's wrong." I shook my head. Perhaps it's universal— the impatience of wanting to be known without needing to say.

"She's...flaky," I started.

"She's always been flaky," said Michael. Which was true.

"But this feels different." He looked at me. "It does."

We sat quietly for a moment. I felt like I was arguing a case when what I wanted was to curl up into him. The divide felt unbearable. I was drained. I wanted to crumble. But this was not the time; I had Michael's attention.

"Okay, for one thing, I don't think she's learning to read," I attempted.

"Okay..."

"Seriously. She's not getting it."

"Is her teacher concerned?" he asked.

"I don't know." I didn't like the question.

"So she didn't call..."

"Why do you always do that?" I interrupted. "I'm telling you that *I'm* worried and the only way you'll take me seriously is if someone else agrees."

"That's not what I said." Michael was getting annoyed.

"Okay." I tried to mellow out. He never responded when he felt under attack. "What *are* you saying?" I asked.

"I'm just trying to figure out if other people in her life are also concerned, because..."

"Because then you'll believe me," I spurted. I couldn't stand not being taken seriously. I'd finally recognized something was off, and I needed Michael to be interested in what I had to say.

"No. It's not that," he said sternly.

I was quiet for a moment. "You should have seen her. She ran right into the street." Tears came to my eyes.

His face softened.

"Without even looking!" I wanted him to come to me. "It was terrifying...and..." I looked to make sure he was listening. "A little bizarre."

"Bizarre?"

"She just *ran* into the street!" Even thinking about it made my heart pound. "Right after running face first into the jungle gym two hours earlier. Jesus." I tried to push the image of a bloody Henny out of my mind.

"She's clumsy." Michael smiled.

"But what about the reading?" I looked at him. "I don't think she's improving."

"What do you mean, you don't *think*?"

I started to feel defensive. "Forget it."

"Look, I'm exhausted," he said, as if I too hadn't been going all day. "It's getting late," he added.

"I had a really busy day too, Michael." What did that have to do with Henny? Even though he swore he respected what Little Scissors had become, whenever I wanted more from him, it seemed there was an unspoken suggestion that the salon wasn't worth the trouble since his firm earned five times what the shop brought in. Not to mention, Michael had negotiated the fantastic lease, and even though he'd deny it, I always felt the consequence of that help was that I should never intrude upon him with demands. If I couldn't handle my domain, perhaps it meant something should go.

"I've been really swamped lately..." His voice drifted off as his eyes moved from the TV to me. "All I'm saying is if Henny's teacher isn't complaining—how far behind could she be?"

"Well, I'm not so sure we should *wait* for the teacher," I said.

"Okay, what do you think we should do, then?" he asked, trying to conceal his irritation. Michael had twenty-three employees, many of them top architects in their own right. He was accustomed to being the boss and didn't like me dictating his evening schedule.

"What do I think *we* should do?" I repeated. "You haven't even asked what I'm worried about."

"You told me what you're worried about. Henny's flakiness. And her reading," he said as if I was testing him.

I wanted to talk about it, recount the details of my concerns. I was worried. I wanted him to be worried too. Maybe then we'd figure out how to handle this together. Michael only had energy for the bottom line.

"Forget it. I'll handle it," I said.

"Great, you do that. I'll be over here, handling everything else, how about that?" he said.

"I'm sorry?" I asked sarcastically. I silently started to list the doctor appointments he never scheduled, much less attended, the school forms he never filled out, the homework struggles he never witnessed...

"You haven't exactly shown any interest in *why* I'm so swamped at work," he said. "I'm busting my ass on the Wartels design while competing with a West Coast firm for projects in Seoul..."

"Seoul? What projects?"

"I told you about this," said Michael. "We're trying to break into the Asian markets. Big opportunities."

"That's happening?" I exclaimed. "I thought that was just a conversation."

"I'm not the only one deciding, Kara. I have a partner whose opinion matters."

"Well, this partner thinks you're already spread too thin. This partner, the one you enjoy sleeping with every now and then, can't even get your attention to discuss a crisis, and you don't even *have* the Asian market."

"So now it's a crisis," he said. "Will you relax? Henny is healthy and beautiful and you need to slow down."

"Just long enough for the Yankees to win the World Series?" I was seething.

He was quiet for a moment. My heart was pounding.

"I work hard, Kara, and yes, if I want to watch a game, I will. I don't need your guilt, and I definitely don't need your permission."

He didn't yell. He didn't need to. I heard him loud and clear.

14

1987

S ince I took the paintbrush a few weeks ago, Oliver and I have only had sex once. It makes me crazy to be around him and not be *with* him. I'm included when they all go to an opening or the pub, but he treats me like the others. I feel like a dog who once received a treat for heeling. I keep waiting in anticipation, but nothing comes my way.

And then Andy Warhol dies. We meet at Ralph's, where Oliver and other aspiring eccentrics parrot tributes lacking in punch. Our parents' generation had Kennedy and King, Vietnam and the first walk on the moon. I suspect for most of us, divesting in South Africa is too theoretical and Iran-Contra too remote. Even though there's inescapable poverty a block in either direction of us, it's like we're shielded by Columbia and our comparative good fortune. Still, we yearn for a cause worth yearning for, and tonight Warhol seems to fit the bill.

Oliver's fingers are wrapped around his glass like little smooth sculptures in an elegant embrace. Apparently art as commerce is inevitable. I track his whiskers from chin to jaw to cheekbones. I'm startled when he releases a laugh.

Someone toasts to the life and death of the artist. Oliver smiles as he raises his glass, but I detect a slight hesitation before he takes a sip. There's a Knicks game on to the right of the bar. I don't care about basketball, but the moving image keeps drawing me in. A Springsteen song is playing, but it's so loud here I can't figure out which one. My chair is bumped, which brings me back to the group. And then I realize Eden is staring at me.

Oliver refills my glass. She sees that too. Usually she's a participant in these conversations, but tonight she's quiet.

The discussion moves to Warhol's most recent collaborator, Jean-Michel Basquiat.

"We met him," Oliver informs the table. He looks at Eden, waiting for her to corroborate. "Remember?"

She nods. "It's the first thing I thought of when I heard."

"He's a fucking genius," says Oliver.

"He idolized Andy," Eden says. "Must be devastated."

"You guys *know* him?" I ask. I wonder what other exciting experiences they've shared.

"Not only didn't he go to art school—he didn't even finish high school!" Oliver says, ignoring me. "You don't see him in Intro to fucking Oil."

"We met him at Canal Paint," Eden tells me. "He was cool."

"Basquiat at Canal Paint! I'll toast to that," says a guy sitting across from her.

"Was he shopping?" another asks.

"For canvases," Eden answers.

"Unstretched," Oliver clarifies.

"It's not like we *know* him." Eden looks at Oliver but he ignores her.

"Those guys don't waste time dissecting the masters," Oliver says.

"He was intense, though," Eden tells me. "In a good way." I nod, thankful that at least *she's* paying attention to me.

"I mean, they're innovators…" continues Oliver.

"*Were* innovators," Eden mutters. I smile.

"…They don't concern themselves with theory, and in the meantime, they end up altering the whole fucking discourse."

I'm not sure what he's saying exactly, but I like that he's passionate, even if he does feel far away.

"I mean, Warhol takes the most lowbrow bullshit of our culture and turns it into art. He doesn't embrace or reject—"

"You do know he's dead, right?" Eden interrupts.

Oliver looks irritated. I find myself wanting to come to her defense.

"Fine. When Warhol was a living, breathing artist, he didn't embrace or reject consumerism, he transformed it."

"Transformed it how?" I ask.

Oliver smiles as if he's grateful for the opportunity to elaborate. I've become his audience, a role I'm comfortable in.

"Well, for starters, he took images that were so predictable they were practically invisible—and turned them into a whole new entity: art."

"He knew those images once reflected a real person or a real thing, but they'd become oversaturated. Take *Mona Lisa*," continues Oliver. "That image is no longer a reproduction *of* the painting. It's become a symbol *for* the painting. An emblematic shortcut, if you will. A logo."

Oliver looks to see if I'm following him. I am, but even more important to me is my desire to convey the *appearance* of understanding. I suspect this relates to his point, but I keep it to myself.

"Warhol understood symbols. He played with them. Manipulated them and got famous doing it. And then, in a postmodern twist of fate, his work became so known, such a part of the public's consciousness that it too became a symbol of a symbol of a symbol." Oliver's face is flushed.

"That's innovation," he says. "And I'm not sure if it can be taught. Maybe it has to be unearthed. Discovered. A task for the artist. He either can or cannot."

"And you? Have you discovered where your art fits in?" I ask quietly.

"No," he says. "I haven't. But I haven't stopped trying either." He flashes a smile.

"So you're in it for the long haul!?" declares Eden. "Come hell or high water, you're unearthing the shit." She's so cool. They both are.

"Hell yeah! Abso-fucking-lutely," Oliver yells. "I want it all. Beyond my wildest fucking dreams!"

"You tell 'em, motherfucker," says the guy next to him.

Oliver finishes his beer and slams the mug on the table. Then he jumps up and pounds his chest like Tarzan—howling and all. Everyone laughs. I'm fascinated. He doesn't just divulge his dream of grandeur, he declares it. His aspirations don't leave him paralyzed by self-doubt, nor is he resentful or bitter. Basically, he's the opposite of my mother.

And then in front of everyone, he kisses me hard and on the mouth. "Thanks," he says.

"For what?" I am elated by his public display.

"For reminding me what's important. What I need to do." I have no idea what he's referring to.

"It's simple," he says. "Real artists believe in themselves."

Oh.

Soon after, he leaves. But the kiss has appeased me. I don't feel desperate. The others move to another topic—the latest *Star Trek* movie. Eden scoots her chair closer to me. "I'm bored," she says. "What should we do?"

I have no idea, but instead of trying to come up with something, I'm busy digesting that she wants to hang out with me. The group argues about the commercialization of Hollywood. I like big-budget movies, but don't say so.

"Put me out of my misery," she whines while chipping away at her black nail polish. "I know!" She leans forward. "Wait. Do you know how to roller-skate?"

There are many things I cannot do—knit, apply mascara without looking, pitch a ball, bake cookies, sew a button, climb a tree, open my eyes underwater (or dive without holding my nose), diagram a sentence, figure out my part of the bill, arm wrestle, tell a joke without stammering, play chess, parallel park, order without first scrutinizing the menu, jaywalk, open a bottle of wine, remember how many days there are in May (or is it June?), juggle, whistle, sing in tune, read a map, roll a joint, make origami, fold a fitted sheet, bowl, build a fire, walk in heels, surf, remember models' names (or designers'), stomach the taste of gin, yoga, leave a lecture early...but *roller-skate?* That I can do.

We take a subway to the Staten Island Ferry. She stops at a flower stand and holds up two bouquets—royal blue carnations with near-dead baby's breath and lime green daisies. "Aren't they magnificent? Oh, Kara, how will I ever decide?"

I roll my eyes. "The ferry's leaving."

"You're right! We'll take both." She gives the vendor some wrinkled bills and offers him a daisy. "In memory of Andy Warhol," she says. "The innovator."

"Come on," I urge.

"May he rest in peace," she yells as we run for the ferry.

She weaves daisies and baby's breath in my hair so I can be a Ferry Fairy. I pretend I'm above this sort of thing, but the truth is, being around her makes me feel little-girl giddy—or at least the way I imagine happy little girls might be.

When we get to Roller Drama, sweaty skaters are milling around the entrance. My heart pounds as we move through the crowd, but as soon as the door opens a song from the seventies puts me at ease. I try to tell Eden that I know every word, but she can't hear me. She laces quickly and is off.

I remind myself that I know how to do this as I make my way to the floor. Another old song comes on. I can't find Eden in the crowd, but I'm not worried. Flashing strobe lights transform everyone into a slow-motion robot. I feel like I'm in a dream.

I step out. My body has remembered. I laugh; and when I realize no one can hear me, I laugh again. Eden comes from behind and screams something exuberant. I clumsily convey my approval by punching the air with my fists, which inspires several animated strangers to do the same.

The night moves on. Guys approach us, and even though I enjoy their attention, none compare to Oliver. Eden, however, enchants them all. She has this way of being flirtatious without encouraging anything serious. It's impressive, actually.

On the ferry back, we sit on the outer deck. The cold air quiets us. I take in the view—Lady Liberty in all her glory, the glittering lights of the World Trade Center, the sound of the wind.

"I wish I could fly," she says, staring into the night. "Just soar above the city. Away from it all. Do you know what I mean?" she asks.

I am surprised by how she looks in need of reassurance. Maybe she's not invulnerable. It's strange to see her this way.

"I used to feel that way," I tell her. "But I kind of did it. Escaped." I motion to the magnificent skyline.

"That's right. You're a small-town girl. Ohio, right?"

Small-town girl? I think of my mother and cringe. "So what do *you* want to escape from?" I ask, hoping it has nothing to do with Oliver. Could she be in love with him?

Eden stares at me. "I don't know. I just…well, I guess you could say, I lack clarity."

"About?"

"Everything." She smiles at me. "But so what? Like most things, I'm pretty sure feeling bad won't last forever."

And then I make myself a promise. I don't hoot and holler like Tarzan, but it's important all the same. This whole night has been the opposite of lonely. And from here on out, it's where I want to live.

15

2007

I darted around the apartment tossing magazines into the recycling, feeling guilty I'd never gotten around to reading them.
Tucked between bills and a picture Henny drew were two birthday
invitations for Adam; thankfully, there was still time to respond. I
threw breakfast dishes in the dishwasher, poured soapy glop, and
proficiently flipped switches. The mechanical whirl was comforting;
life could be managed.

The final nanny applicant would be here soon. I really hoped
I liked her. The kids were watching TV in the playroom; I'd only
introduce them if this girl, Liza, seemed like the one.

The first thing I noticed was her hair, long and hastily pulled on
top of her head. I wondered if she was the type who got ready without a mirror, or if rather, like me, her disheveled style required careful attention. Regardless, I liked her hair. She wore a corduroy bag
across her chest. It was from Old Navy. I'd considered buying one
as a knock-around, but in the end rejected it as too youthful. Even
though the girl wore it well, I saw I'd made the right decision. My
day for shabby bags had come and gone.

Her porcelain features seemed rebelliously punctuated by a tiny
diamond in her nose. She looked like a teenager, which I suppose
until recently she was. I had the disturbing realization that this girl-
woman was closer to Adam's age than mine, which didn't seem possible. Henny would fall in love with her, I thought. She's a wonderful
combination of princess-pretty and hipster.

Interviewing people was hard for me. For one thing, I was cursed with a superb memory. Before I got married, I was always the one trying to prove myself. In fact, it was one of the first things I noticed about Michael; he answered to no one. So after I sold his firm three hundred thousand dollars' worth of hand-painted silk wall coverings, I accepted his invitation to dinner.

Now, whenever I interviewed anyone, here or at the shop, I felt I owed it to my younger self to put applicants at ease.

I greeted Liza and gently touched her arm, a gesture that felt both rehearsed and sincere. I offered water or juice; she chose water. We sat. I smiled while she took an awkward sip. I tried to ignore the inherent power difference and behaved as if this was a nice chat with a would-be friend. Of course, this strategy had backfired in the past. Having convinced candidates of my fundamental goodness, I ended up feeling awful when hiring one meant not hiring another. I dreaded those calls, sweating and stumbling when I finally made them.

"We're not looking for someone to wait on us," I said, trying to decide what I thought of the nose ring. "And I set my own hours, so I'm around a lot." I remembered how happy Beth had seemed when she told me about Dr. Mom's schedule.

I asked Liza if she considered herself hardworking, but what I really wanted to know was: Are you invested in improving me? I may never be voted best mother, but then again, I'm not nursing a Dewar's all day either, so I figured I was ahead of the game. Or at least I was better than *my* mother, which was probably what most parents strived for, anyway.

"I can be difficult," I warned. "I'm obsessed with keeping this place organized." I pushed the library book fiasco out of my mind.

Liza sat with perfect posture and reassured me. "Oh, I'm anal when it comes to organization."

"Organization is good," I told her. However, the word *anal*, not so much.

"I really need someone who can focus on the details, like if a toy is left in a restaurant, that kind of thing." I opted not to tell her about the time one sitter sent Henny to preschool without underwear. In a dress. In winter.

I tried to think of appropriate questions, but none came to me. Would she kidnap my children? Fall in love with my husband? Would Michael view her twenty-three-year-old body and be reminded of what mine no longer was? I looked at her clear skin and touched my face, hoping the lovely perimenopausal acne had cleared up. Thankfully, my forehead felt smooth.

Please don't steal from us, I silently requested. Perhaps my dresser drawer, second from the bottom, left side, wasn't the best spot for my jewelry.

"The job comes with a separate-entrance studio apartment, right next door. It's small, but we think it's a nice perk." I paused for what was typically an enthusiastic expression, and she obliged. "It's great because the sitter gets her own Upper East Side apartment," I continued, "and we're guaranteed a punctual nanny." Translation: Please don't ever be late.

I decided she didn't look like a thief; however, I wondered if she would rummage through my belongings. That's what I used to do when I babysat, but I was a teenager then.

She was telling me something about being a camp counselor a few summers back, but I wasn't listening. I was trying to discern if this smiling girl who appeared so wholesome she could have modeled for soap was really a crystal meth addict who would take Max on drug runs.

I looked at her clothes. She had a nice style for a girl on a budget, which made me wonder if she'd resent the abundance in our home or around the neighborhood. I didn't want to be judged for an occasional Bergdorf bag. And how would she view our countless Legos, Thomas Trains, and Barbies, especially when my kids had zero sense of how privileged we were? What would she think when they whined that they *needed* that stuffed animal/computer game/ sweatshirt with the rhinestone puppy? Did the fact that I almost never gave in once I said no counteract the other fact that our budget was rarely the reason?

I uttered none of these concerns; instead I stared deep into her eyes for signs of malevolence and asked if she had experience watching three kids. I suspected I'd hire her regardless, but it was a reasonable question. I hoped she wouldn't give me cause to be doubtful, because I wanted this girl, Liza, to be the one. She didn't have to perfect. I was done with perfect. Plus, I decided I liked the nose ring.

"Do you have any questions for us?" I asked.

"Well, sure. Let's see..." She asked about a typical day—the children's schools and activities. She was impressed that Henny played violin and seemed to know a bit about tae kwon do. Before I could introduce her to the kids, Adam came into the kitchen, glanced at her, and retrieved an individually wrapped string cheese from the fridge.

"Adam, this is Liza; Liza, Adam."

"You must be the three-year-old," she said, leaning across the counter island.

"Uh, actually, I'm ten..." Adam stammered, looking at me. She smiled.

"Ha. Ha," he said, getting her sarcasm.

"I forgot to mention that I love to cook," she said to me. "Will that be a problem? I mean, this being your kitchen and all."

"You love to cook, do you?" I could feel Adam looking at me.

"Gee, Mom, will that be a problem for you?"

"No. I don't think that'll be a problem." Adam and I high-fived each other as Henny and Max wandered in.

"Who are you?" asked Max.

"And why are you high-fiving?" added Henny.

"I'm Liza," she told them. "And I think it's because I can cook."

"Cool," said Henny. "I like your nose earring."

Max walked over to Liza, pulled her to his level, and inspected her nose. "I don't," he concluded. Liza smiled.

A few minutes before we were winding down, the kids retreated to the back of the apartment and I asked about her family.

"It's just my mother and me..." she said.

I could certainly relate; but I sensed there was more. Our eyes

met. It seemed like she was trying to decide if she should tell me
something.

"...and she's in jail," she said. I nodded. Later I'd worry that this
had made me seem patronizing. But in that moment, I held my gaze
and wondered if one day I'd tell her about my mother. I waited before
daring to speak. I wanted to know the story, but resisted asking.

"Fraudulently obtaining prescription drugs," she whispered, even
though there was no way the kids could hear. "Also known as doctor
shopping."

"Got it," I said, as if I was the most relaxed person on the planet.

She hesitated. "Maybe I'm saying too much."

"Not at all." Although I wasn't really sure. But then I decided
these details weren't important. It wasn't her fault her mother was
an addict. I questioned whether I'd been similarly determined, yet
fragile, at the same age. Probably, I suspected.

I'm sure she needed a job and place to live, but, I realized, I too
needed something. I needed someone who wouldn't judge me.
Someone who just might believe I was a good enough mother. So
while others might have assumed that her mother's incarceration
predicted future problems, not me. I considered it a sign.

Max and I were already at the café when Morgan and Zoe arrived.
Getting seats by the window had been part of my plan; I had a direct
view of Oliver's gallery. The kids sat on the filthy, coffee-stained rug
and used wooden stirrers and pink packets of artificial sweetener to
create a city.

The place was nearly empty, just an older man reading the sports
section and a woman who appeared to be in her thirties typing away
on a laptop. I tried to discern if she had kids. She wore a wedding
band and Dansko clogs, a good sign, but one never knew. I hoped
so; otherwise, I anticipated bitter stares if our three-year-olds acted
like three-year-olds.

"My agent thinks this book has an excellent chance of going to
auction," Morgan announced.

"Auction?" I asked.

"Publishers competing for the privilege of my acquaintance." She let out a hearty laugh. The woman at the computer glanced in our direction. Morgan didn't seem to care about dirty rugs or irritated patrons, something I found fascinating. Her brash voice made me nervous so I kept moving closer, but she just chattered away. Whether she was completely oblivious or unapologetically self-accepting, I wasn't sure. Either way, I could've used some of that bravado.

"We need babies for our city," Zoe said, placing sugar packets in pretend houses.

"And trains, we need trains too." No game was complete unless it included a train.

I considered pointing out Oliver's paintings across the street, figuring if nothing else, it made for a good story. But I resisted. Words had a way of making things more powerful than they otherwise were; and I didn't need to give Oliver any additional power. Instead, I half listened and hoped my glances across the street went unnoticed.

"Yeah, last year's article in the *Times* didn't kill my career after all," she said. "Never trust reporters," she said. "Like he was ever interested in my *process*. He even used his wife—said she loved my work." Morgan shook her head. "Opportunistic motherfucker."

The gallery wasn't open but the paintings were illuminated. I kept trying to gauge if the people passing by looked in. Just how successful was Oliver Bellows? I shifted in my seat in an attempt to better concentrate on Morgan.

"So, what does Eric think about your book?" I asked.

"He doesn't," she said.

I looked at her.

"He thinks about how much money it'll make, but if you mean, does he like the book—he hasn't mentioned."

"Is that a problem?" I asked.

"Baby, that's just the tip of the iceberg."

This surprised me. She'd made jabs at her husband before, but this seemed different. "Well, what's the rest of the iceberg?" I asked.

She sat back in her chair and watched Zoe, who was deep in conversation with Max. I peeked across the avenue. The striking woman
was unlocking the door. I tried not to study her every move.

"For starters, he wants another kid," she whispered.

"And you?" I asked.

She sighed. "I'm forty-one. It took me three years to get pregnant.
I was so pumped on hormones I could barely produce a coherent
thought. I don't know how I even finished that book." She stirred
her coffee. "And after I sell this one, I'll have revisions, there'll be a
book tour. It's hard enough to leave Zoe..." Her usual self-assurance
was gone. I wondered if she was about to cry.

"Not to mention the fucking." And she's back, I thought.

"Go on." I smiled.

"There is nothing sexy about *having* to fuck," she said, followed
by, "Zoe, do not eat the sugar."

"You too, Max, cut it out."

I tried to picture how Michael and I would've resolved this issue.
We'd both always wanted two kids, so that had been a no-brainer.
Then there was the night he landed the Nobu account. I'd had
too much sake, but not too much to stop a fine, fine moment in
an attempt to maneuver the extremely difficult task of getting my
diaphragm from the nightstand drawer, but then he said...don't,
and I stopped what I was doing and looked at him, and then he said
don't again and I laughed, and then he laughed, and then one of
us stopped laughing, probably me, and then the other did too, and
thirty-eight weeks later, Max arrived. We called him Baby Sake for
a while; until Henny did. I smiled to myself. Then I remembered I
was mad at Michael.

Morgan watched the kids; I watched the gallery.

"Do you guys talk about it?" I asked. Michael and I still hadn't
revisited the subject of Henny's reading.

"Sort of. Well, we used to, anyway."

"Does he get where you're coming from?" Though really I was
wondering, Do you get where he's coming from?

"He wants Zoe to have a brother or sister. For us to be a family of four." She said it with disdain. "But the facts are the facts. I'm forty-one."

I nodded. Not because I agreed with her. Rather, I was familiar with how difficult it is to be compassionate when someone you love wants something you don't.

"Besides, empathy isn't going to solve this one." She leaned in close. "In fact, empathy just might get my ass pregnant." Then, without letting go of my gaze, she placed her palm in front of Zoe's mouth. The little girl hesitated slightly before spitting three soggy pink packets into her mother's waiting hand.

On the way home, I listened to my messages. Willa wanted to discuss some marketing ideas. She sounded more professional than usual, which I found annoying. I'm sure Victoria had put her up to it. I sighed. The last thing I wanted right now was to put extra energy into Little Scissors. I suddenly felt ready to talk to Michael.

"Hey," I said when he picked up. "You busy?"

"What's up?" He sounded overwhelmed, but like he was trying to be present because he knew I needed him.

"I'm still worried about that thing." Max probably wasn't paying attention, but just to be safe, I spoke in code.

"Henny?" he clarified.

"Uh-huh."

"Her flakiness?" he asked.

"Yeah," I said. "And the other."

"Reading."

"I think I should call her teacher," I whispered. "But also... maybe she should see someone. Like... a private educator." I was being squeamish. I could tolerate the word *educator* better than *neuropsychologist*. "For an evaluation."

"That sounds reasonable," he said. "Get a few opinions..."

"I think so." I sighed with relief.

"All right then." We were silent.

"Okay," I said.

"Okay," he repeated. It was tolerable to hang up because neither of us wanted to. I thought of Morgan. I might not have her confidence or success, but I did have this. My marriage. I was proud that I hadn't wasted another moment staying angry at Michael. And while it wasn't exactly a victory, it was restorative. And at that moment, on that afternoon, restorative felt very close to enough.

When we got home, Max retrieved his beloved Chocobunny and joined Adam watching TV. "He's doing it again," Adam yelled. Whenever Max was exhausted, he liked to suck on Chocobunny's ear.

"Stop slurping," Adam warned.

"I like slurping."

"Honey, it grosses out your brother," I said.

"It doesn't gross me out. It *is* gross," Adam said. I stand corrected, I thought, rolling my eyes.

Henny and Liza were at the kitchen table, an early reader in front of them. I kissed Henny's head.

"How's it going?" I whispered, not wanting to interrupt, but unable to resist. Liza looked up and silently conveyed that it was taking Henny forever to finish her work.

"Let me just ask," I started gingerly. "How long has Adam been watching TV? Because he should get going on his homework."

"He already did it," Liza answered.

"Oh. Wow." I was impressed. "A few days in and you've already got things under control."

On my way to make the calls, I checked on the boys. All evidence of a dispute was gone; they were lounging like satisfied zombies. In the privacy of my room, I left messages for Henny's teacher and the *educational evaluator*. Then I called Willa.

"The landlord said he's sending us a plumbing bill," she said. "He's blaming us for backups in the rest of the building."

"That doesn't sound right."

"I know. Can you talk to Michael?"

I told her I would.

"There's something else." Willa sounded nervous. "I asked Victoria to put together a marketing proposal."

"Okay..."

"She has some excellent ideas. I think you'll be pleased," said Willa.

"Sure. Fine. When it's ready, I'll take a look."

"It's ready."

"Oh. Okay." I paused. "But I've recently reviewed our numbers. I'm not sure..." This was a complete lie. I hadn't reviewed anything.

"That's the point; publicity can take us to the next level."

The next level—she sounded like Michael. Why was everyone interested in the next level? I could hear kiddie music playing in the shop. My tranquil bedroom accentuated my guilt. "I'll be in tomorrow, I'll get it then."

"Fair enough," she said, before taking another call.

I sat on our bed and stared out the window. Someone was home in the apartment directly across from us; every few moments a shadow moved behind the blinds. A few floors above them, a housekeeper was on the terrace. Sweeping, maybe; I couldn't tell. And then she was gone. I'd never noticed that you could see our building reflected in some of the windows across the street. I thought about getting my camera, but instead kicked off my shoes. In the distance a siren droned. Even that lacked conviction.

I looked around my room. Everything was in order. It was a beautiful room. I lay and stared into space, not the least bit certain of what to do next.

16

1977

It is All You Can Eat Shrimp Night at Ponderosa, but I want the junior steak instead.

"No fries for me," my mother announces, leading her almost empty tray around the metal track. I slide mine behind hers and consider my options. Hesitating, I look at my mother.

"Sweetheart, the Beverly Hills Diet is not for children," she tells me, so I take a bowl of fries. The crispiest ones I see.

"It's working, though," she says. "Look how loose my pants are." My mother lifts her sweater so I can see. There are people behind us. I'm afraid we're taking too long. I have one last difficult choice, pudding or Jell-O? I weigh my options. Pudding. Definitely. Now all I have to do is decide which flavor and resolve the whipped cream situation. Dinner is a lot of work. For me, choices usually are.

My mother cuts her steak with authority. I wonder if the shrimp would've been better. Suddenly, my belly hurts and the meat looks gross.

"This is really going to work, kiddo. I can just feel it." For a second, I think she's still talking about her diet. "I mean, people don't care where they buy laundry detergent, so why wouldn't all your little friends' parents get it from us?"

I lick the whipped cream off of a dry, cracking cherry and swallow it whole, like a pill.

"And teachers! Teachers are a great resource. And Libby! I forgot about Libby." She seems excited by her brilliance. "I need a haircut anyway, it'll help me to look more professional. So while she's snipping away, I'll explain the whole Amway business model. It's perfect."

"Meeting Larry is going to turn out to be the best thing that's ever happened to us. You mark my words." While she continues talking, she takes out a cigarette and pulls my tray closer. She alternates between a drag from her Salem and my fries, all while digging in her bag for a piece of paper. "Who else? Who haven't we thought of? Who do we know that wants to be rich, rich, rich?"

"Are we going to be rich?" I ask.

"Of course we are, sweetheart."

"So, what are we now?" I know better than to mention Mrs. Adler or the trip to New York City, but I still remember.

"We have enough, don't you worry about that." She frowns a little. "But it's different when it's money you've earned. You do know that, don't you?" I nod. "It's important to earn your own money, Kara."

I nod again even though I don't really see what the big deal is. Money is money. But I'm not in the mood for a lecture, I want to go home. It's Wednesday. *One Day at a Time* will be on soon. I like the pretty sister. Plus, I need to go to the bathroom.

"In fact, that's what I'm going to tell your little friend's mother. Even though she's not hurting for money, what with that lawyer husband of hers. But that's what I'm going to tell her. There's a difference when it's your own money."

I figure now is not the time to point out that my mother knows very little about having a husband or an income. I want to watch my show. "I have to go to the bathroom," I announce.

"Hurry up," she says, checking her watch. "I have to get back. Larry might call."

On my way to the bathroom, I wonder if he's coming over again. I like my mother's TV better than the one in the den. The last time Larry came over, they'd talked about the benefits of concentrated detergent versus the diluted stuff they sell in the A&P. I had liked the glossy Amway pamphlets that were scattered on the white Formica, so I'd arranged them in a pattern. When I'd squinted, they looked like a tapestry tablecloth.

"So, you're telling me you can do forty loads of wash for what would normally take twice as much detergent?" she'd asked Larry.

"That's what I'm saying," he'd said. Instead of pointing out that he didn't *invent* the laundry detergent, I'd concentrated on the pamphlets.

"These aren't for play, sweetheart, this is business," Larry had informed me as he scooped them up and stacked them in front of his notebook. I'd looked at my mother to see if she'd yell at him, but she just kept talking.

"I think that's brilliant. It's probably even *better* for clothes if you don't use so much..."

"Soap," Larry had said, finishing her sentence.

"Soap," she'd agreed. I'd wanted those pamphlets and she didn't even care.

"Who washes your clothes?" I'd asked. "You or your wife?"

My mother broke the silence. "Who does the wash really isn't the point, Kara." Even though I was just a kid, I'd known that who did the laundry was very much the point.

I walk into the Ponderosa ladies' room and my nostrils are immediately assaulted by air freshener. I can even taste it. I try not to breathe as I pull down my Levi's with the orange label and scratched-off measurements. I sit on the toilet and tear a piece of toilet paper.

Then, on my underwear, I see it. I nearly jump. For a second, I think the brown is a bug. I don't like to kill bugs, not because I like them, just because I'm afraid of them. But it's not a bug, I see that now. I know what that is.

I sit for a moment. I am sort of scared, but giggly. In awe, but also proud. I touch myself. If I had any doubt, I have now confirmed it. I am wet, but it is a different kind of wet. This wet is also dry.

I smell my fingers and am reminded of something that I can't quite place. I wipe and look at the evidence. Then I wipe again, and look some more. It is the most fascinating thing I have ever seen. I crumple clean toilet paper and put it in my underwear, hoping this will do.

I wash my hands slowly, watching myself from above.

"I got it," I say when I return to the table.

At first my mother doesn't understand. Then a smile spreads across her face and she gets teary. "Oh, honey." She jumps up and hugs me. I roll my eyes and hope no Ponderosa patrons can tell what's going on.

The car is dark and the suburban streets empty. An occasional headlight makes shadows dance along the dashboard, briefly landing on my mother. Each house we pass, I glance in. Seeing a person or a TV on is rare, so when I do, I feel lucky, like I've won a prize.

"It's very good timing, actually," my mother tells me. "I was wondering how the detergent handled blood."

And then I figure it out. My swing set. That's exactly what it is. I smell my fingers again. It is fainter now, but I know I'm right. My blood smells like rusty old swings. I'm certain, but surprised I remembered. A long time it's been since I was on a swing.

17

2007

Morgan's apartment was smaller than I expected, with clutter everywhere. Dishes decorated with dried marinara were piled on the coffee table and Zoe's dolls and books were sprawled across the counter. Typed pages marked up with purple ink blanketed the desk and oriental rug. Though I'm sure she had a system, it didn't look that way. Still, despite her chaos, she seemed completely present while I complained about Willa's plans for Little Scissors.

"Victoria's thorough. I'll give her that."

"So what's the problem?" asked Morgan.

"Money, for one thing."

Morgan cocked her head. "Really?"

"Yes. Victoria's expensive," I said more forcefully than I'd intended. "She asks for three months up front and doesn't even guarantee that we'll get publicity."

"So what *does* she guarantee?"

"That she'll pitch stories. Write press releases. She says she has contacts everywhere: *New York* magazine, the *Times*, *Big Apple Parent...*"

"And if she's successful, what happens?" Morgan asked.

"If she's successful, then Little Scissors is rebranded. It'll be like that candy store...you know, the one near Bloomingdales."

"Dylan's?"

"Yeah, Dylan's. Little Scissors will be like the next Dylan's Candy Bar." I slumped into the couch and sighed.

"Yeah, that'd be terrible," Morgan said. "Success beyond your wildest dreams."

"Those aren't my wildest dreams," I said. My mind flashed to Oliver. Many years ago he'd compared himself to Warhol and Basquiat. He hadn't just admitted his dreams; he'd owned them.

"So what are?" asked Morgan. I had a brief vision of spreading paint on canvas instead of peanut butter on whole wheat, but I stayed silent. I'd sound pathetic. She waited.

"I want to paint." My voice was soft; I sounded like Henny.

"Really?" she asked. "You paint?"

"I used to. About a million years ago." I glanced at her. She was a real writer. She probably thought if I had any talent, I'd have pursued it long ago. I should've kept my mouth shut.

"Well then, I guess you're long overdue."

Wait. What?

"I didn't even start writing until my thirties," she explained. "I mean, I kept a journal, but I never took myself seriously."

"What changed?" I asked.

"A lot of things. I finished therapy, for one. Or quit. I don't know." She took a long slow sip of coffee. "And you know what else?" She looked at me; I was completely engrossed. "Amy Bloom." she said.

"The author?"

She nodded. "I read an interview where she said her writing aspirations took off in her thirties. Said if she didn't take her career seriously, no one would. This completely inspired me. I started my novel that night."

"Really?" It almost sounded too easy.

"You'd be amazed what can happen when you have a role model."

"Forget a role model," I said. "I need time. Time would be nice." The kids, the shop, Michael . . . they all flashed in my mind.

Morgan shook her head. "Are you sure? Or do you need permission?"

"Permission?" I didn't like how that sounded.

"Are you waiting for someone to tell you it's okay to pick up the brush?"

"I have a lot on my plate," I said. Thankfully, I restrained myself from reminding her that having three children is very different than having one.

"You do. Absolutely. I guess what I'm saying is, you'll never know if this is worth pursuing, if you don't... pursue it." She looked at me. I felt like a petulant teenager.

"I mean, most artists don't have the luxury of quitting their day job," she said.

"What's your point?"

"I'm saying, maybe this isn't only about time."

There was no denying that there were a few times I'd had the opportunity but still hadn't picked up the brush. It had been a while since I'd told Michael I was going to paint.

"From my experience—it took more than just a room of my own," Morgan said.

"And money. Woolf said a room and money." I was surprised that I'd remembered that essay from college. Maybe I should give it another try.

"Right, a room and money."

"And a nanny... did Woolf say anything about a nanny? Let's not forget the nanny." I was teasing, but there was no question that if Liza hadn't been working out, this conversation would've been moot.

"Right. A room, money, and a nanny." She looked like she wanted to add something but wasn't quite sure what. "And courage," she finally said. "Wait, not only courage—willingness."

"Willingness? What's willingness got to do with courage?"

"Oh, believe me... they're absolutely related," she said. "The willingness to suck."

"The willingness to suck." This was a fascinating idea.

When it was time to leave, Morgan handed Max a sandwich bag of animal crackers for the road. "So are you?" she asked while the kids were silly with goodbyes.

"Am I what?"

"Are you willing?"

"Willing to paint?" I asked.

"Willing to fail," Morgan clarified. Somehow, miraculously, making it not sound so bad.

The next morning I woke to the clanging of clean dishes being put away. It was Liza's early day. "Good morning," I said, heading straight for the coffee. The room was filled with a warm, bitter aroma that reminded me of asparagus. A large pot was on the stove, boiling slow and steady. "How long have you been up?" It was seven-fifteen.

"Since five," she said. "I wanted to try that new sunrise Jivamukti class. It was great—I might make a habit of it."

"What's this?" I removed the lid as Michael came into the kitchen.

"Soft millet miso porridge," she answered proudly.

"Oh dear." I returned the lid.

Michael cocked his head while pouring a cup of coffee. "Good luck," he said to Liza.

"Just be open-minded," she said to us. "It's delicious. Really. Tastes like regular oatmeal, practically."

"But does it taste like Lucky Charms?" I asked. "Because they're magically delicious."

"But are they magically macrobiotic?" Liza replied. Michael raised his coffee, as if toasting her, and left the room.

She was so good-natured that her attempt to improve our eating habits didn't even annoy me. I mean, if she could get them to eat that sludge, more power to her.

Liza placed three bowls in front of my waiting children.

Max spoke first. "No." He pushed his bowl to the center of the table, walked to the fridge, and took out a box of chocolate milk. As he chewed on the straw he seemed to be watching us, curious as to what would happen next.

"Mom?" Adam asked.

"Look, guys...Liza worked hard on this soft millet miso porridge," I said, trying to keep a straight face. I grabbed Max's discarded bowl and enthusiastically tasted a spoonful. Bitter vegetable mush, with a surprisingly sweet aftertaste. Not bad, though decidedly not good either.

"Delicious, in an interesting way," I said.

"Really?" Adam said, not buying it. "Porridge?"

"Go make a bowl of cereal," I mumbled. "It's sort of sweet," I told Liza.

She shook her head knowingly. "Carrots."

"This is sweet, too," Adam said, pouring his cereal. "Marshmallows."

"Laugh now," Liza chided, "but that there is some serious brain food."

"Good thing I'm already smart," Adam said with a full mouth.

Henny held her nose and shoveled in three spoonfuls.

"You are a kind and daring person," I told her. She smiled.

"Hey, no problem," Liza said to Adam and Max. "More for us, right, kiddo?" she asked Henny, who nodded reluctantly.

That afternoon, I plowed through my purchase orders. Liza said it was the millet. Who knows? Maybe she was right.

We entered the Upper East Side institution that is Lester's Clothing. The boys pushed past Henny and made a beeline for the mechanical horse ride in the shoe department.

"Do they have clogs?" Henny asked for the millionth time. Liza and I exchanged looks of exasperation. When Henny wanted something, she was relentless.

"I told you, clogs are very hard to walk in."

"But I can try, right? I can try."

Max waited on line for the ride. There were two boys ahead of him, and a little girl had just started her turn, so Adam opted to peruse the nearby Yankee shirts instead.

"Mommy," called the girl on the ride, "I need more quarters."

Her mother lazily opened her wallet and handed the older daughter some change while I signed my name to the waiting list. A salesman in wrinkled trousers walked out of the back room and called the next name on the list.

"Welcome to hell," I said to Liza.

Henny wandered the shoe display, touching shiny loafers and sparkly sneakers, while I found a cluster of chairs and set up camp for what would be our home base for the next hour. I kept expecting Henny to ask my opinion on a pair, but she seemed deep in thought, very far away.

"You can't go again," Max informed the girl on the ride. "She can't go again, right, Adam?" he yelled.

Adam looked up. "You can't go again," he said halfheartedly.

"My mom said I could," the girl whined. The two boys who were also waiting stepped off the line and stood on what could only be described as the sidelines while the girl's sister tried to deposit the quarters despite Max blocking the slot with his sticky hand.

Liza and I looked at each other and then at the child's mother, who was energetically texting someone.

"Do you want me to step in?" Liza asked, like a ventriloquist.

"Not really," I whispered. "My money's on Max."

"Definitely," she agreed, as Adam went to investigate.

Twin girls from Henny's grade came in. "Great minds think alike," their mother said to me as she signed the list. The girls sat across from us. Without a word, one opened a book; the other took her mother's phone and began to play a game. Neither said hello to Henny. I looked to see if her feelings were hurt, but she didn't seem to notice.

"It's his turn. Then his turn. Then my turn," Max said, pointing to the boys who'd stepped aside. The girl stayed put.

"Your brother should move his hand," said the sister to Adam.

"Your sister should share the horse," he replied.

"Mom!" the older girl yelled. "This boy won't let Abigail have a turn." The woman looked up from her handheld and surveyed her precious ones in distress.

"Oh, for God's sake," she said with a sigh. "Just let the little boy have his way."

"It's not fair!" whined the girl, not moving.

"She had a turn," Max yelled to the mother, who ignored him.

"His turn, his turn, my turn!" Max insisted.

The mother of the twins looked at me with a raised eyebrow.

"Lawson," a salesman called from the list.

"We're up," I told my boys, with pleading eyes.

Adam shrugged. "Whatever." So perfect was his demonstration of the intrinsic meaninglessness of all mechanical rides that without a word Max relented and followed his big brother to the sneaker section. The girls looked dejected, even after the coins were inserted and the monotonous galloping resumed.

"Do you have clogs?" Henny asked the salesman after her brothers had been helped. Adam was playing on his phone and Max was testing out his new sneakers by jumping over a stool.

"Max, enough," I said sternly.

"Over there." The salesman pointed. Henny had spent the last twenty minutes mere steps from the display.

"Where?" she asked. The clogs were right in front of her.

"Right there, honey," I said, pointing. Adam looked up briefly.

Henny gazed in a different direction. I'm pretty sure the twins were watching us.

"No, sweetheart, right there," I said.

"To your left," the man added. Henny remained baffled. I jumped up to show her just as my phone rang. The number was unfamiliar and I was about to let it go to voicemail, but by the third ring, I was curious.

"Mrs. Lawson? This is Miss Nathanson, Henny's teacher, returning your call." I stepped away from Henny while motioning that she could try on blue clogs; Liza looked annoyed.

"Yes, hi," I said quietly. "Thanks for getting back to me."

"I think we should speak in person," Miss Nathanson said unemotionally. "How's next week?"

I nervously wiped my hands on my jeans and looked for a pen.

With eerie calm and Miss Nathanson's voice running through my mind, I bought Henny the blue clogs. It was the least I could do.

18

1987

My Woolf paper is late, but instead of dealing with it, I fold creased laundry I washed days ago. I've been daydreaming about painting. I want to, but it feels stupid. Like how I used to play with my mother's makeup or try to walk in her shoes. I grab Oliver's paintbrush and fall on my bed. The bristles are soft on my cheek and lips. I touch myself through my jeans but reject the idea. Only Oliver will do. I smell the stolen brush; the turpentine, a venomous scent. I rationalize that I'm not a true thief—just a young woman in love. Guilty all the same.

On my way downtown I consider turning back. Each time the subway doors open I look at strangers for an answer: Continue my errand or head uptown to safety? I have no appetite for Woolf, sufficient enough reason to stay on the train. I'd thought about asking Eden to come with me, but I'd been afraid she would've told Oliver. Another girl might have asked him for help, or at the very least taken a painting class; but I refuse to have a witness. Compelled to go it alone.

I surrender at West Fourth Street. The creative pulse of downtown is like a gas seeping into the stilted mass-transit air. The urban anonymity makes me feel hopeful. Or powerful. Sometimes I confuse the two.

I have a fantasy that I'm a famous artist. All I have to do is get off at Canal Street, head to the paint shop where they saw Basquiat, and commence the rest of my life.

When I return, my urgency is less urgent. Sitting at my desk, I stare at the hastily bought tulips. They don't really inspire me, but no other subject emerges. I briefly understand Oliver's necessity for Eden. The bodega flowers taunt me: Real artists believe in themselves. I busily stall by arranging earrings on top of my dresser. I fold scarves, draping one over the desk lamp, filling the room with an amber hue, which pleases me.

I lean in to my reflection and pick whiteheads, washing away evidence with a dripping blue cotton ball. I glance at the tulips. Real artists believe in themselves.

My familiar reflection occupies me. I concentrate on specks of gold in the greens of my eyes and practice. First, a carefree smile, then a seductive gaze, and finally, my typical expression, serious. I think my freckles may be less visible than when I was younger, so I squint to check. I am about to call my mother to ask her if it's just my imagination, but then I remember, and because I am looking in the mirror, I catch myself in the act of remembering. It is a bizarre moment. Most people never get the chance to see how they appear when they grasp that their whole life will never be the same. I try to repeat the expression, but I'm unable to go from startled, to sad, to very much alone.

My mother would have liked Oliver. Considered him the real thing. That was her ultimate compliment, rendered rarely, and never in reference to me.

"Some people just have it," she said one night when her Streisand album ended with that scratchy needle noise, quite possibly the saddest sound ever. Her glass was empty—she'd soon be asleep. On my way upstairs, I paused. I'd never told anyone, but I always suspected *I* had a hidden talent. And even if I wasn't yet sure what it was, I sensed its presence. But that night on the stairs, I figured I must have been wrong. If my mother thought I was the sort of person who had *it*, I'm sure she would've have said so by now.

I don't want to think about my mother. I want to paint the tulips. I study my image, searching for signs of her legacy in my curved nose and the shape of my eyes. Our resemblance is obvious, which makes me worry for my future. But I can't shake the seed of "what if…"

Even with the tulips taunting and the uninvited memory of Streisand and Dewar's, I see for a moment (longer than brief, but shorter than forever) that quite possibly, I just might be something very close to beautiful.

And then I am ready, the tulips quietly waiting.

19

2007

I was supposed to meet Morgan at the reservoir, but to get there on time I needed to leave right then. Instead, I moved about Little Scissors rewinding hair dryer cords while Willa's eyes followed me. Though I hadn't told her, she seemed to sense I was about to leave. She's like Trudy, I thought. Only Trudes anticipates a long delicious walk, and I suspected Willa's afternoon would be far less satisfying. I tried not to feel guilty.

"So that's that?" asked Willa.

"I just think getting publicity before we're ready isn't sound business sense."

"If we increase our customer count, it is." Ava was cutting a toddler's hair. The mother glanced at us.

"The financial obligation is substantial," I whispered. "Even more than I'd expected."

Willa motioned for us to move to the back. I considered grabbing my coat and leaving; but of course, I followed her. "I don't get it, Kara. Most people would kill for this opportunity."

I leaned against the wall. "We'll lose customers if we can't handle the increase," I said quietly.

"The best businesses have tons of reviews posted in the window. Why do you think that is?"

"I don't know...so they can rationalize that laminator expense."

Willa never laughed to humor me. "I'm guessing because it's good for business. All I'm saying is, Victoria can make it happen."

"For a cost," I mumbled.

"Yes, for a cost. A discounted cost. Lots of businesses pay for PR," she said.

"We never have."

"I'm sure Michael's firm did," said Willa.

"Okay...I don't see how *that's* relevant."

"I think we should do this," she said quietly. "I do. I want more for this place. It's like I've been asleep, and now I'm awake." Great, she's playing the dead girlfriend card, I thought.

"I want Little Scissors to be a destination—not just a neighborhood shop." She sounded like Victoria's puppet, but still, her sincerity was obvious. I wasn't ready to admit it, but deep down I knew we had a serious problem.

"I can't do this right now. I've got an appointment." I left out that I was off to meet Morgan.

She looked as if I'd slapped her.

"I'm sorry, but I do." I struggled to get my jacket on. Nothing felt easy. "I'll see you later," I said, wondering exactly when it was that I'd started lying to Willa.

Morgan was waiting at the corner. "Do you mind if we skip the Reservoir? If I don't get coffee, I'm not going to make it to pickup."

"What about the ass situation?" And Trudy, I thought.

"My ass situation needs coffee." But she didn't look exhausted. She looked elegant. More coiffed than usual. Hair sleek and straight, eyes lined in smoky charcoal. "My treat," she persuaded.

"I guess I can tie Trudy outside; she does love the occasional stroke by a random stranger."

"Who doesn't?" asked Morgan.

We went to E.A.T., a bustling lunch spot near the Metropolitan Museum. I scanned the room and was glad that I didn't know anyone. I felt terrible about Willa and wasn't in the mood to see and be seen. But as soon as Morgan started to speak, the world faded away.

"I'm not saying I'm proud of it, I'm just saying it happened."

"Weren't you scared?" I asked, not believing my ears. She'd answered some man's personal ad on Craigslist. At her country house, no less. When she was supposed to be writing.

"Of course I was scared. That was part of the thrill."

"But he could've murdered you, been one of those maniacs who cut you into tiny pieces. Turned your spleen into an appetizer."

"I see you've given this some thought."

"Apparently."

"There was something about him I couldn't resist." She told me she'd intended for it to just be an email flirtation. She'd been tentative at first, but he'd convinced her to meet.

"Where?" I asked.

"The movies."

"The movies!?" I made it sound like an affair that started at the movies was particularly vulgar.

"A little movie house," she clarified.

"What movie?" I sounded like Henny—the way she focuses on irrelevant details.

"A French film. About a waitress," Morgan said.

"Figures," I mumbled. "So how'd it go from watching a movie..."

"A film," she teased.

"From watching a film to...you know."

"Let's just say, he was...persuasive," she said.

I looked at my salad, suddenly fascinated by mesclun greens. (For one, they aren't only green, there are shades of purple and red; none of which I shared with Morgan.)

"Actually, more like instructive. Commanding, even."

Yes, yes, I nodded. I wanted more water.

"Things pretty much progressed from there." She motioned for the waiter; apparently she wanted more water as well.

I didn't want to be judgmental. Especially since there was a part of me that thought she was brave. The same part that kept thinking about Oliver.

Michael would've been devastated if he knew how often my mind drifted to Oliver. Maybe this obsession was more dangerous than I'd considered. I mean, Morgan actually did it. She cheated. I needed to stop thinking about him. No more making up scenarios about what it would be like to suddenly run into him. No more passing by his show or googling his work.

But as soon as I vowed to put an end to the musings, I realized I didn't want to. The daydreams had become my respite. And even more distressing—I doubted I had the ability to stop.

I was irritated. Feeling conflicted wasn't part of my plan. I'd never gotten a bittersweet *The Way We Were* moment of closure, and I yearned for it. Michael took what he wanted when he wanted it, I thought to myself, knowing full well a Yankee game was different than my longing for Oliver.

Morgan clearly needed to talk, but I didn't want my silence to imply approval. Even if I didn't want to be judgmental, complicity didn't seem right either. I worried I was not only condoning her affair, but all infidelity. Even a potential one of mine.

I loved my husband. When I garnered the energy, I even loved fucking him; that wasn't the problem. But the truth was that I missed the thrill of the conquest, the sense of adventure inherent in the unexpected. Sometimes marriage was hard. Listening to my friend talk about multiple orgasms was one of those times.

"Do you think Eric suspects anything?" I immediately regretted speaking her husband's name.

"Not at all." She frowned.

I hadn't even met the guy and I already felt sorry for him.

"The crazy thing is, I don't even feel like I cheated on him," she said.

I tried to hide my astonishment.

"Promise you won't judge what I'm about to say . . ."

"I promise," I said while judging her.

"No, I can't . . ." She hesitated.

"I won't," I lied. What more could she possibly tell me?

"Okay, well . . . I like it a little rougher than Eric does," she whispered. I nodded as if I heard about this dilemma from all of my friends.

"Eric knows, but he's not into it. Not since Zoe, anyway. I guess the thought of pounding his daughter's mother isn't exactly a turn-on."

"Madonna-whore syndrome. Happens to the best of them." Though not to Michael, thank God.

"Somehow I thought being with a stranger wasn't much worse than getting myself off while fantasizing about one."

I set my fork down and leaned in. "Yeah, sure...one and the same," I whispered.

She smiled. "Thanks for not judging."

"Morgan, I want to be a good friend. I do. This just sounds... risky." And then I thought about my daily jaunts past the gallery. I pictured myself each morning, choosing an outfit while thinking in the back of my mind, Today might be the day I see him. It might not be the same as fucking a stranger, but it was a secret.

She took a bite of greens; I mirrored her move. In that moment, I wanted to be like she appeared—self-satisfied. Sexy. Strong. But the tangy vinaigrette scorched my throat; I sipped water and resisted the urge to flee.

"So, how did you leave it?" I asked.

"You don't want to know." But I did.

"You're going to see him again?" My voice sounded tense.

"I can't not see him," she said, which sounded like a cop-out to me. "Seriously, I'm fixated."

I knew what that felt like. As much as I missed the chase, I didn't miss the desperation. Michael never devastated me in that way, like I kept expecting him to in the beginning. My dependable husband never kept me waiting. I felt grateful. I forgot that what Michael and I had, we'd both created. Meaning, of course, it was something either of us could destroy.

"Not only am I totally addicted to this man," she said, "but after he left, I wrote three chapters! That's more productive than I've been in years!"

"So he's your antidote to writer's block?"

"I never said I was blocked. I'm just saying, he fucked me, several times actually, and suddenly my creative juices were flowing."

"So to speak."

She smiled. "But enough about me. What's up with you?"

"I can't follow that! Jesus."

"You know what? That's just it," said Morgan. "I needed drama! Excitement. To shake things up. I mean, this always knowing what's going to happen next, I think it's killing me. I do." She looked angry. "Can you can understand that, even a little?"

I hesitated. "Yes. I can."

She took a sip of chardonnay. "There I go again. Seriously, let's change the subject. Tell me something. What's going on? How's Henny?" Morgan tore a piece of bread.

"Fine. She's fine. We're meeting with her teacher next week."

"Good. Good." She nodded. "And you? Are you painting?"

"Not really." She studied me. "Okay, I'm not painting, but I'm not ready to talk about it, either." Though I did like that she was grilling me. It was as if my not painting was finally important to someone other than me. But I couldn't tell her my truth. That I was terrified I'd be even worse than I'd been years ago.

"I told you I fucked a stranger and you can't talk about painting?"

"Yeah, well, mine's humiliating."

Her laugh silenced the room.

A few mornings after Liza's unsuccessful porridge, the kids sat with Michael, eating.

"Pass the millet miso," said Adam. Making fun of Liza's glop had become a family joke; luckily, she was good-natured about it. Still, talking about it when she wasn't here felt wrong.

"Easy now," Michael said, as I handed Adam a plate of warm raisin toast.

"Did you know Liza's mother's in jail?" Adam asked Michael.

Henny put down her spoon. "Is she a robber?"

"No. She's not a robber," Michael answered and glanced at me.

"It's kind of complicated," I started.

"Are there train robbers?" Max asked. We all looked at him.

"Train robbers?" said Adam. "You mean, people who steal when they're on the train?"

"No! Train *robbers*. Robbers who *take* trains."

"Don't be stupid," Adam said. I gave him a look.

"I like trains," Max told his cereal.

Henny still seemed worried. "Basically, Liza's mother was going through a hard time," I explained, "...and to try and make herself feel better, she took drugs."

"Wait. Drugs?!" Adam exclaimed.

"What are drugs?" Henny asked, looking between Michael and me.

"Drugs are like a dangerous medicine some grown-ups use, but they're very bad," I said.

"Then why do they do it?" asked Henny.

"I'm never going to do drugs," Adam announced. "They're disgusting."

"Disgusting," said Max, looking at Adam.

"I don't know why..." I started to say.

"Because they're stupid," Michael answered. I shot him a look. Michael knew I didn't like to condemn addicts.

"I'm not really sure," I said. "Maybe because some people think that when they're sad, it's going to last forever."

"Did Liza tell you about her mother?" Michael asked Adam, who shrugged.

"Well," I said. "I think as long as *Liza* doesn't do bad things, it doesn't matter what her mother did."

"That's true," Michael agreed, trying to make nice

I took a sip of coffee and stared at him. My handsome husband was dressed in a stunning gray suit. His purple-and-red-striped tie popped against the white starched shirt, which reminded me, I still had to drop off the dry cleaning. I thought about Morgan's need for excitement and figured the dry cleaner probably wasn't what she had in mind. Michael looked like a man who had places to go. For that moment, envy surpassed love.

20

1980

We've waited months to find out who shot J.R., and the show is about to start. "I think the lady did it," I tell my mother. We're in position on her queen bed. I consider mentioning my social studies test, but decide there's really no point. It's not like she can magically change my grade, so I push the vision of red ink out of my mind. Luckily, she doesn't keep track of these things. In fact, when it comes to school, she asks little. I think we both prefer it that way.

"Don't get any on my bed." She hands me the popcorn. The bowl turns her blanket warm. I welcome the salty taste, letting the fluffy white parts dissolve in my mouth. We're not exactly cuddled next to each other, but I can feel her leg, and our pillows overlap. "Which one, his wife, or the other?" she asks.

"The pretty one."

"They're both pretty."

"The quiet pretty one," I tell her.

"The brother's wife? You think *she* shot J.R.?"

I don't elaborate. The opening song is on and I want to savor every moment.

"That's what I need. I need a J.R.," she says, stirring the ice with her pinkie.

"But everyone hates him."

"Not women, Kara. He's got power. Nothing's sexier than power." I like when my mother speaks this way. Confiding in me is proof that I'm sophisticated.

"I like him too. He's cool," I tell her. Until then, I liked J.R.'s brother. He's cuter, with curly dark hair. But now that she's explained it to me, I agree. J.R. is better.

"That's exactly what we need," she tells me. "Our very own J.R. Ewing." She opens a new pack of cigarettes and with a flick of her lighter she makes fire appear. Sweet smoke and her lemon perfume glide in my direction.

"It figures," she says when it's revealed who shot the powerful oil-man. "It's always the other woman, Kara. She's the world's enemy. I wouldn't be surprised if they blame this whole hostage situation on adulterous women."

I can't hear my show, but asking my mother to be quiet isn't an option. I stare at the TV and hope for a happy ending. Out of the corner of my eye I watch my mother finish her drink well before the ice has melted. She seems deep in thought, blowing slow angry smoke toward the ceiling.

"Those poor married men. Sweet souls, tricked into sin by conniving whores." She reaches under her bed.

I don't want to be her confidante anymore.

"Better watch out, Kara. If you're not careful, you could become one of those evil women." She empties the stashed bottle into her thirsty glass and tries to tickle me, as if her rant is a big joke, rather than a solemn warning.

I sit quietly. I'm not stupid. When I grow up, I'll *never* be like her. I have plans. I'll marry a man and have his babies. I don't know what else I'll do, but that much I know.

That I can get right.

21

2007

Henny and I stopped for a snack near Oliver's gallery. She needed to get her homework done before violin and I figured it was as good a place as any. I stole glances at the burgundy painting while Henny took bird bites of grilled cheese. At this rate, she'd never get done in time.

In a few days Michael and I were meeting with her teacher. I wondered what Miss Nathanson would say if I told her that the workload was too much. I rummaged in Henny's backpack for her book. "Just the first few pages," I cajoled. My phone vibrated. It was Morgan. We hadn't spoken since her confession at E.A.T.

"Can't talk now," I answered. "I'm with Henny and she's just about to start her homework." I purposely spoke loud enough for my girl to hear.

"Sorry. Real quick... tonight, I'm with you," said Morgan.

"Huh?" I handed Henny her book, which she set next to her plate.

"If Eric calls, we're going to a nursery school meeting."

"Morgan..." I signaled for Henny to pick up the book.

"You're right. A show. Broadway. You got free tickets."

"I don't know... We haven't even met. Do you think he'll call?" I watched Henny spread a thin line of ketchup on a fry.

"No. But just in case."

"I really hope he doesn't..." I didn't want to be in cahoots with her, but I didn't want to say no, either.

"Thanks, babe. Really," she said.

"Wait. What are we seeing?" Henny painted another fry.

"I don't know. What do you think?"

"What's new?" I asked.

"*Spring Awakening*?"

"Saw it." I pointed to Henny's book. She put it in her lap.

"Fine. *Spamalot*?" asked Morgan.

"Supposed to be excellent, but we want to take Adam."

"Take Adam where?" Henny asked.

"A play," I said.

"What play?"

"It's called *Spamalot*, you wouldn't like it."

"I want to go," Henny told a French fry.

"Any other suggestions?" I asked Morgan.

"You do know this is pretend..."

"We loved *Jersey Boys*," offered an older woman sitting at the next table. Her friend nodded in full agreement. I smiled.

"Are you kidding me?" Morgan laughed, overhearing. "I'd rather the nursery meeting." I glanced at the women, glad they couldn't hear.

"*Mamma Mia!* was excellent," said the other lady.

"*Mamma Mia!*?" I asked.

"That Abba thing? Please."

"What's *Mamma Mia!*?" asked Henny.

"A play," I whispered. "What about *Hairspray*?" I asked Morgan.

"Fabulous," agreed both ladies.

"Fine, *Hairspray*," said Morgan.

"No, wait." I was worried it would get back to Michael, and then he'd think I'd already seen it, and since I really did want to see *Hairspray*... This was making me crazy.

"You see? This is why I never get tickets," I said.

"Yeah, it's so hard to make pretend plans."

"Fine. *Spring Awakening*." The ladies did not approve. "*Spring Awakening*," I said again, shifting my direction ever so slightly away from them. "This way, if Eric asks about the show, I'll be able to answer his questions."

"Excellent. Thinking on your toes. Well done," said Morgan.

"He better not call," I said.

"Thanks Kara. You're the best." And then she was gone.

I took a sip of water, a failed attempt to cleanse my soul. "Sorry," I said to my girl. "You ready to read the first page?" I asked in the most loving tone I could muster.

"I'm not done with my fries." She looked as if she wanted me to argue with her. I waited as she chewed.

"All right, *I'll* read the first page." I articulated each word while Henny studied the diner.

"Your turn," I chirped.

"What's ketchup made of?"

"I don't know, tomatoes, I guess."

"But what else?"

"Come on, sweetie, what's this word?" I asked, pointing.

"How come Max loves ketchup but hates tomatoes?"

I looked out the window. Across the avenue a handsome couple peered in the gallery window.

"Should we?" asked Henny.

"Should we what?"

"Tell Max about the tomatoes."

"I don't know." They entered Oliver's exhibit and I returned my attention to Henny.

"That's a sight word," I said. "You're supposed to know those just by looking." When Adam was her age, he'd memorized all the sight words; perhaps I'd mention this as well.

Henny looked at the page. "Fox," she said.

"Don't just use the pictures," I said.

"Miss Nathanson said I could."

Henny started to read, but it seemed like she'd memorized the gist of the story and was parroting it back to me. I motioned for the check. "Come on, we'll finish after violin." I scanned the bill and tried to push my guilt away. My patience was shot and I sensed Henny was getting cranky as well. I tried to make a game out of packing her backpack, but she passively plodded away.

Finally, we made it outside. I held her hand and looked down the avenue for a cab. I vowed to be more patient. Loving. A better mother.

"I'm not going." Henny let go of my hand.

I balanced my bulky bag, Henny's backpack, and the dreaded violin. It was the cabs' change of shift time, and if we didn't get one soon we'd be late. Henny continued to whine. I looked around, hoping no one was watching.

"You're going to violin, Henny," I said.

"It's not fun, Mama. I don't want to."

"We honor our commitments." At least some of us do.

"No. I'm not going!"

"Look, Henny, there's nothing you can say to change my mind." The gallery owner was holding the door so the couple could exit. They all appeared sated and self-assured.

"I'm not. You can't make me." She began to cry.

A cab slowed, but when the driver saw us, he seemed to think better of it and accelerated, his off-duty light suddenly illuminated.

"Bastard," I hissed.

"I hate it, Mama. I'm not going."

"Look at my face, Henny." I lifted my sunglasses so she could see into my eyes. "Do I look like I'm going to change my mind?"

Undeterred, Henny carried on as I searched for a cab. I would have liked nothing more than to skip violin, something that never occurred to my daughter. But today was Music Theory. Period. If I gave in so easily, what else would I allow her to miss? (Why wasn't she learning to read?) And what about her future? (Why wasn't she learning to read?) Today it was violin, ten years from now, who knew what. (Why wasn't she learning to read?)

"I'm not going, I'm not!" Her face was turning red. She wiped her nose with the back of her hand, and then her hand on her jeans.

I started to question my stance. She looked exhausted. I felt her head, though not in a nurturing way. Usually she was agreeable; what if she was coming down with something? But I couldn't change my mind. I'd already made her look into my eyes. My word had to be more important than her comfort. It was too late to turn back.

"You don't care about me!" Henny cried. Across the street, the couple lingered by the display window as two young women entered the gallery.

"All you care about is Little Scissors! You don't care about me! You don't!"

I knew she was tired, but it didn't matter. Like blood, my anger circulated on its own. I should've surrendered. Called it a day. Taken my little girl home. But I couldn't see past Henny's tantrum. How could she be so ungrateful? Didn't she know that she and the boys were all I cared about?! And Michael, I added, more out of loyalty than genuine feeling.

A cab stopped. The driver lowered the passenger window. "I'm about to go off duty," he warned. If my destination was too far away, he'd move on.

"Ninety-fifth and Madison," I said. Henny was still screaming.

"Get in, lady, but the kid has to shut up."

I too wanted Henny to stop, but how could he speak that way? I looked downtown. There were no other cabs.

"You heard him, Henny. Hush!" She wailed louder.

"Teach her some manners, lady." He drove off, abandoning us on 72nd Street.

I was filled with fury. I bent to eye level again. The violin case bumped the pavement and Henny's backpack knocked my bag off my shoulder.

"You ungrateful little brat. If I *ever* behaved like that with my mother...You stop it right now!" I secretly squeezed her arm for emphasis. She tried to wiggle away.

"You're hurting me," she whimpered.

"What makes you think you have a choice about how you will or will not spend your time?" I admonished her. "If I ever, *ever*, spoke to my mother..." I said, my voice trailing off.

We finally got a cab and made it to the music school a few minutes after class had started. I took her to the bathroom and angrily washed her face, then led her to the room. She went right in, joining the others on the rug. I couldn't face the mothers or nannies yet, so I returned to the bathroom and splashed cold water on my own face.

Methodically, I put soap on my hands, lathered, and watched as the
suds slid off, leaving a path of skin as they made their way down
the drain. I applied lipstick and tried not to cry, but it was no use.
I sat on the toilet and rocked back and forth, covering my eyes. My
mouth was open, ready to release a sob, but for a few moments, no
sound came. Just tears of shame.

In time, someone knocked. I worried a line might be starting to
form, so I blew my nose into a rough paper towel and splashed my
face again. I smoothed my appropriate cashmere sweater over my
gray skirt and tried to regain my composure, but my blotchy red face
gave me away. Someone knocked again. I had to leave the bathroom;
it was no longer my turn.

I joined the mothers and sitters in the lobby. Some used the time
to make grocery lists or check emails. Others read. But I simply sat,
and tried to determine exactly when it was that life landed me on
95th and Madison, instead of all the other places that existed in the
world, where I would never go.

I looked at Michael sitting in a chair meant for a seven-year-old.
His knees were perched above his sloping thighs and his feet seemed
too big to settle comfortably in front of him. Over his head was a
bulletin-board collage of orange construction paper pumpkins that
framed smiling second graders. I could easily picture Michael as a
freckle-faced little boy, and for an instant he was replaced by a little
Max or Adam. But my husband was not a little boy, he was a father.
A frightened one.

"I was glad to get your message," Miss Nathanson started,
"because it's better not to wait for parent-teacher conferences." She
paused, as if uncertain whether she had our attention. She did. "I
assume you're concerned about Henny's progress."

I nodded, as if my heart was not in my throat.

"Let me start by showing you some of her classmates' work, so you
can get an idea of how other second graders are doing." She placed
papers in front of us, but I made no move for them. I didn't need to

look at other children's work in order to know Henny was nowhere near her peers. Michael reviewed the papers, but I was pretty sure he didn't know Henny's work well enough to make an informed comparison.

"So her reading isn't improving?" I asked.

"It's not."

"Her first-grade teacher had some of the same concerns," Michael started, "but she thought Henny would go through some sort of spurt and things would click in." I nodded. That is what she'd said.

"Well, that's the thing; it isn't," said Miss Nathanson. She sat quietly, letting us absorb her words.

There was a sour smell coming from the closet. Perhaps an uneaten sandwich lurked in the cubbies. I briefly considered mentioning it, but it occurred to me that I wasn't here to make suggestions.

"Is this news to you? Did you know she can't read?" asked Miss Nathanson. She probably didn't intend to sound accusatory; nonetheless, I looked at my hands.

"Well, I knew she was having trouble..." My voice trailed off. What could I say? I knew exactly what she was describing. I had an intense urge to kick Michael in the shin, but I resisted. This was no time for violence; Henny was in trouble.

"What about math, how's she doing in math?" Michael asked.

"Well, she's making one-to-one correspondence, but I'm afraid she's not up to grade level in math either." Miss Nathanson sat with an empty legal pad and a few clean folders in front of her. She was a young, new teacher; I suspected these made her feel important, but to me, she looked like a child playing dress-up. When she wasn't speaking, her lips settled into a pursed grimace.

"What are you saying—that she should go back to first grade?" asked Michael. I decided Miss Nathanson's eyebrows needed waxing.

"We don't send children back a grade." She emphasized the word *back*.

"Are you saying she shouldn't have gone to second grade?" I asked.

She averted her eyes, uncrossed her legs, and shifted in her seat. "I really can't speak to that."

"Okay..." said Michael. I knew he was getting annoyed. My eyes told him to relax. I pushed my chair a little closer to him.

"Look, I know this is hard to hear," she said.

"That is true," I agreed. My voice sounded cold even though I knew this wasn't Miss Nathanson's fault. Come to think of it, her ridiculous lips weren't her fault either. The waxing, well, she was on her own there.

"What do you think? That she's not trying hard enough?" said Michael, which embarrassed me. I knew that wasn't what she was suggesting. "Because she can be flighty sometimes, even at home," he added.

"Actually, I think she's trying *very* hard. To the best of her ability," said Miss Nathanson. "Which is what I find deeply concerning. Especially since I suspect Henny is aware that her best efforts aren't enough."

"Enough?" Michael repeated, as if he could catch the teacher in a lie.

"Enough for her to keep up with the other kids," she said softly.

"So she knows she's lost," I said.

"Yes. She does. And I imagine that is a very lonely place to be."

My nose burned as I thought of Henny, baffled and alone in this colorful classroom. Michael and I looked at each other, and then at Miss Nathanson. My eyes filled with tears, which her eyes mimicked.

"She's gotten into the habit of pretending she understands. I see her on the rug and I can tell she has no idea what's going on, but when I ask if she has any questions, she just shakes her head no and peeks at her neighbor's work."

"Cheating?" Michael asked.

"Not cheating. She's just...lost," said the teacher.

"So what do you think we should do?" I asked.

"Well, it's your legal right to request an evaluation," she paused. "That would be the first step to getting Henny special services."

"Special services?" Michael barked. He was often brusque when he felt threatened. Usually whispering *epidural* helped—our short-hand for when I was in labor with Adam and Michael had interrogated the anesthesiologist—but this time I said nothing and waited for Miss Nathanson to answer.

"I really can't speculate," she said.

"But you're a teacher; you must have some sense—" Michael challenged.

"*Legally*, I'm not at liberty to speculate," she interrupted. It was the second mention of our legal rights. I wasn't sure why she was being so official, but at the time, I didn't care. I wanted to see my daughter. I wanted this meeting to end and to go home and see Henny. All I'd been doing lately was yelling at her. How could I have been so stupid?

"We need to think about what you're recommending," Michael said. "I'm not sure we want her labeled."

But I didn't need to think. I'd already spoken to the evaluator, Dr. Stockland. The first of five appointments was in a few weeks. I wasn't sure why Michael was hesitating; nevertheless, all I really cared about in that moment was getting home to my girl.

"I need to document this meeting," the teacher said as we stood to leave. She opened one of the blank folders, which turned out to be legitimate after all, and handed Michael a pen. He scribbled his signature and threw the form on the desk. Moving robotically, I retrieved it and sat back down. It was titled *Parental Notification of Academic Deficiency.* I skimmed the form, not really digesting it. About to sign my name, I attempted it again. Perhaps if I really tried to concentrate. But the second time was the same as the first. Like an unknown language or a difficult poem, the words danced across the page. I signed it anyway.

The next day I bought paint. Like hungry sparrows the cans beckoned while I multitasked. Dishes were swiftly loaded into the dishwasher and counters wiped clean. I gathered strewn toys and scattered magazines and returned them to where they belonged. After I made the boys' beds, I headed for Henny's room with her sneakers and colored pencils in tow. For some time, I studied the large wall facing her bed.

Without consciously thinking about it, I could see what wasn't yet there. I'd forgotten that. I'd forgotten how when you're lucky, inspiration chooses you, not the other way around. Besides, I thought, if Oliver Bellows could become an international art star, I could paint a goddamned wall.

I started the mural that day. Except for the mandatory breaks for nourishment and the bathroom, I focused on the wall. My worries floated in my mind as I mixed Benjamin Moore baby blue and vanilla cream. Morgan's affair, Willa's lofty plans, Miss Nathanson, Henny's evaluation—they all diminished as I glided bristles across the wall.

At first I listened to music, but when the playlist ended, I couldn't be bothered, so silence and the city din became my melody. I was painting.

Much later, there was the click of our front door. I braced myself. I didn't want to stop, but the kids were home. "I'm in here," I yelled.

"Liza's teaching me the monkey bars..." Henny called from down the hall. Adam and Max were behind her; when they got to the door, Adam's jaw dropped.

It was Max who spoke first. "Mommy! You painting."

After a barrage of questions (when did I learn—in college; what's it going to be—it's a surprise; can *I* paint on the wall—no) they went about their evening. Sounds washed over me—dishes clanking, bathtime squeals, Michael's baseball game—but I kept to the task. (Even when they argued with Liza about putting toys away.)

During one break, I called Willa. I didn't go into specifics, but I told her I needed a few days away. She sounded hurt, but even that didn't stop me. My life would have to wait. I could not, would not be roused.

Michael and the kids were great. The boys were even gracious about letting Henny bunk with them for a few nights, which was very sweet and fortunately novel enough to distract them from my neglect. I missed my old oils, but the process of mixing colors and immersing brush into paint was every bit as intoxicating as it had ever been. Perhaps even more so.

In other words, my time was well spent.

"My very own flower fairy!" Henny squealed when she saw it.

"My turn!" said Max.

"It kind of looks like Henny," Adam said. This hadn't been my intention, but I realized he was right. The resemblance was obvious.

"Trains. Dinosaurs. Baseball..." Max listed his favorite things. "Okay, Mommy?"

"Unbelievable, Kara," said Michael. "Absolutely unbelievable."

"Really?" I asked. "You don't think it's trite?" I whispered. I didn't want to ruin it for Henny. "I mean, a *fairy*?" But my momentary mocking was quickly replaced by a sense of loyalty. Many years ago, Eden had braided flowers in my hair and called me a Ferry Fairy. This nymph was mine. I felt protective.

"That's just it," started Michael. "There's nothing formulaic here. She's...arresting, actually," he said, not taking his eyes off the wall.

"I think it's the use of line here." I pointed to sections I'd outlined bold and thick. It's true, the figure looked strong. And beautiful. Adam was right—it looked like Henny.

"I love it," declared Michael. And I believed him, because every time we had guests over, he found a way to maneuver them to that end of the apartment. Until he invited the pizza guy in. After that we agreed to let any display of my decorative skill happen organically. Except for Morgan. Morgan, I invited a few days later. She and Zoe came for a playdate, and while the kids snacked, I led her down the back hall.

"Don't feel like you have to like it or anything, I mean, it may not be your taste, and believe me, I get that. Nothing's worse than having to fake enthusiasm," I rambled.

"Do me a favor..." said Morgan.

"What? Anything. What?" We stood in front of Henny's closed door.

"Relax. I mean, who gives a shit what I think?"

"Uh, me," I mumbled, opening the door. Morgan swooshed past.

"Wow," she said.

I sat on Henny's bed and deconstructed the word *wow*. Morgan nodded as she studied the wall. At one point, she moved closer as if examining the brushwork. Every hair follicle stood at attention while I waited for her to elaborate. What are you thinking? I wanted to scream.

"It's really...fun," she said.

"Thanks." I looked down.

"You should be proud."

This I did not like. In fact, I think I blanched. I tried not to be overly sensitive, but *You should be proud* felt patronizing. And fun? Roller coasters are fun. (Except not to me, I get nauseous. And I hate waiting on line.) My mural was not fun. You may be wondering how a fairy could be anything but fun, and that is a valid point. But this fairy, though whimsical, was also pensive. There was depth to her frolicking. And nuance. Fun? I don't think so.

"You're going to keep going, right?" she asked.

"Keep going? You mean add more?"

She shook her head. "No, I just meant you're going to keep at it. Painting."

My face felt hot. Did she think the mural was lacking? Or had been a waste of time? Should I cut my losses? Move on? Dear God, did she think I was a bored woman with a hobby? I tried to stop this flood of insecurity. It's Morgan, I told myself. You adore her. She adores you. She'd become my mentor, my cheerleader, but now I felt deflated.

"Yeah, well . . . we'll see," I said.

Morgan nodded. "It's wonderful." She smiled. "Thanks for sharing it with me."

Thanks for sharing it with me. This sounded hollow. Like when someone apologizes by saying, *I'm sorry you feel that way.* My head was spinning. I contained myself. She'd complimented me; I knew this, but I'd wanted something more from her. So I did what I always do. I pretended it was enough.

"Well, thank you for looking," I said with a smile. "Much appreciated." For a moment our eyes met. Then I put a gentle hand on her shoulder and guided her out. Without looking back, I flipped off the light and shut the door.

Liza was a different story. I didn't know it at the time, but her reaction was the one I'd return to again and again—like a gift I gave myself when I carried heavy groceries or had trouble falling asleep.

Early one afternoon, I passed by Henny's room and saw Liza lying on the floor. When she noticed me, she hopped up.

"Sorry, I was just—" she started.

"It's okay. Really," I interrupted. "Flattering, in fact. You liked it enough to...linger." I hated how full of doubt I sounded.

"Linger? This is where I come when I want to...disappear." Then, as if rethinking the confession, she stepped back. "It sounds stupid."

"No."

"You're so lucky." She looked sad.

"Liza." In an effort to comfort her, I was about to diminish my life. But I *was* lucky. I didn't know what to say, so her name hung in the air.

"Do you know how lucky you are?" she asked. There was longing and maybe the smallest sliver of malice, but mostly she seemed curious, as if she'd never been acquainted with a certain kind of happy.

"If I had talent, I'd never worry..." She paused.

Worried was my baseline emotion, but saying so was out of the question.

"...Worry about whether...I matter," she said. I used to feel that way around an artist I knew.

"But I guess when you're a mom, you *already* know you have a purpose," Liza said. "Some moms, anyway."

"Yes, well, my mother walked away from her purpose," I said, remembering her magical voice. I never talked about her, but something about Liza made me want to.

"My mother's purpose is Oxycontin. Pathetic, but true."

I wanted to tell Liza that no one was perfect. People make mistakes. To warn her that her mother, however flawed, wouldn't be around forever.

Liza motioned toward the mural. "But this...this is a calling. "Kids *and* talent!" And with that, she left the room.

Was this a calling? Or was I just a bored woman with a hobby? "Maybe," I said, unconvincingly, to no one at all.

22

1987

I wake to someone banging on Oliver's door. I'd been dreaming about my mother, but as I tumble into consciousness, the memory dissipates and only grogginess remains.

I elbow him. "Someone's here."

He grunts.

"Oliver." I nudge him again.

"Sleeping." He rolls to his side, pulling the comforter with him. The pounding stops and is replaced by the grating buzzer.

"It's probably Eden," I say. I usually see her when I stay over, but last night she didn't stop by. Oliver thinks she met someone; maybe he's right.

I throw on one of his T-shirts. "I'm coming, I'm coming," I yell. As I clump down the hall the buzzer stops and the banging returns. It's not even seven o'clock.

"Okay. Jesus." I slide the deadbolt and fling open the door. It's a stunning woman with long gray hair and Oliver's deep blue eyes.

"You're not Eden," I say.

She looks me up and down. "You're not Oliver." She reminds me of some movie star—but I'm not sure who.

"May I?" She motions inside. "I don't mean to be rude, but I'm in dire need of the facilities." She moves past me, depositing her bag on the couch. "In the meantime, dear, how about waking my son?"

"It's your mother!" I pull the covers off of him. "Seriously, come on. Your mother's here."

"Shit."

"Did you know she was coming?"

He stretches. "Isn't she in Rome?"

"How should I know? I thought she lived in London." He throws on jeans, forgoing underwear, and asks if I've made coffee.

"Uh, no." I say it like I'm dumbfounded and annoyed, but really I'm in awe of his nonchalance. That, and the sight of him in those jeans.

"I need coffee."

I take my time getting ready—shaking out yesterday's clothes in an attempt to make the obvious appear less so.

They mirror each other. Coffee cup cradled in one hand, elbow on the counter, the aforementioned eyes. He's telling her about his classes. She compliments his Eden series. I find his mother intimidating as hell, but Oliver's adoration is obvious, which I love.

"How's Fredrich?" he asks her.

"I'm sure he's fine." She shrugs.

"I'm sure he's not."

"And your father?"

"They're good. The baby's cute."

"Better him than me," she mumbles. "I've had a terrific season, by the way. Busy." She sips her coffee.

"Mother tinkers with photos," Oliver informs me.

And then it hits me! "You're Renee Rand!?" I knew she looked familiar. "I can't believe you never told me," I scold Oliver.

"Didn't I?"

Politicians, movie stars, models—she's photographed them all. I can't take my eyes off her. They continue their conversation as if they're accustomed to giving outsiders time to absorb her prominence.

"And where are you from, dear?" Even though Oliver's introduced us, she's yet to use my name.

"Kara's new to the city by way of Ohio," he says. His mother nods.

"But my father was a New Yorker," I hear myself say. It's the first time I've ever told anyone. I can practically see my mother standing here in Oliver's kitchen, silently warning me. *Don't do it, Kara. It won't give you what you want.* I push her out of my mind.

Oliver looks at me bemused. "I'm sure I told you," I tease. "He was a composer. Arthur Adler," I say as if I've said it a thousand times.

"Arthur Adler! No kidding. He was quite accomplished," says Renee Rand.

I smile politely.

"He died too young," she says.

Looking grief-stricken, I agree with her. Though in actuality, I'm thrilled to finally reap some benefit, besides a financial one, from my lineage.

"Did you inherit his musical talent?" It's like she's seeing me for the first time.

"Sadly, no." I consider telling them both that I *have* been dabbling in oil painting, but I don't.

"He was wonderful. Very charismatic," Renee declares. "How old were you when he died?"

Again my mother's image comes to me, and she looks mightily peeved. "Seven," I say courageously, as if I'm stifling a lifetime of sorrow. To my imagined mother, I telepathically communicate that this conversation is none of her business.

"I remember everyone was shocked. It was so sudden," Renee says. "Heart attack," she informs Oliver.

I tell her she is correct. My father, Arthur Adler, died of a sudden heart attack.

"I photographed them," she says. "With Sophia, his first wife. I never knew they split up."

I swallow. "Uh, they didn't." My mother gives me her *I told you so* expression and then she's gone.

"Oh." Renee stares at me. "Did you...did Sophia know about you?"

"We met."

"Your mother had to know that he was never going to leave her. They were one of *those* couples..."

"Mother." Oliver shakes his head. He isn't angry at her, but he knows she's out of line.

"He had quite the reputation as a ladies' man," she says.

No shit.

"So how long are you in town?" Oliver changes the subject.

"Leave the day after tomorrow. Los Angeles. I'm at the Waldorf. A car's waiting outside. I just wanted to surprise you."

"Yeah. Thanks for that." He smiles at her.

"You know, you should let your friend here be a reminder." She motions in my direction. "Birth control. It's not just a woman's responsibility."

"Mother!"

"Well it's true!" She winks at me. "Aren't I right, Karen?"

I tell her she is. And though I don't look at Oliver, I sense he agrees—we should be better about this. Rubbers every time. Or maybe I'll go on the pill. And the part about being called Karen—that, I just ignore.

23

2007

From down the block I saw red and purple balloons tethered to the bench outside the shop. For the rest of the day the bouncing bouquet would be a wonderful lure; but at that moment, it signaled two things—I was late and Willa wasn't.

"Howdy," she said, handing me a latte.

She never brought me coffee in the morning. "Thanks." I dropped my bag behind the counter.

"Did you already have a second cup? I was guessing not..." I rummaged in the desk for Sweet'N Low.

"Already put it in," she said.

"Oh, thanks."

Willa turned on a jazz station, trading the silence for bopping rhythm. Even though this was more appealing than the usual barrage of kiddie nonsense, it made me edgy. I took a sip of the too-sweet coffee.

"Missed you around here," she said. It was the first time we'd spoken since I painted the mural. Now I felt guilty, an emotion the coffee only exacerbated.

I surveyed the shop. She'd repositioned one of the display shelves, placing the tall one next to the red cutting station. It looked great, opening up the whole back wall. Still, we'd never made changes without consulting each other. "This is great," I said, vaguely motioning toward the wall.

She leaned against the desk and smiled. "I was hoping you'd approve."

"So, anything I should know?" I asked.

"No. Not really. I refused the conditioner shipment. They screwed it up."

"Supposed to be shampoo," we both said at the same time.

I checked the appointment book. "Busy. That's good."

"Yeah, the numbers are up."

"Look, Willa, I know I haven't been pulling my weight lately." I was all set to tell her about the mural. I wanted to explain what a luxury it had been to have the freedom to paint. And how time had seemed to disappear. And what it was like to temporarily feel as though I hadn't needed anyone or anything. Probably the way booze was for my mother, I imagined. But Willa's ten o'clock arrived— twin four-year-old girls.

"No problem," she said. "We'll figure it out."

This is the easygoing Willa I know, I thought, while watching her help the sisters with the delicate task of determining who got to sit in the pink car. And as the day progressed, I settled into the familiar routine of the salon. The peace I'd felt while painting began to fade. The real world was encroaching.

That afternoon Liza and the kids stopped in to use the bathroom before heading to the Ancient Playground in Central Park. Max made a beeline for the lollipops.

"Max," warned Liza. Then, as if remembering that for now she was second in command, Liza asked me if Max could have one. "I have sliced apples," she whispered.

"One," I informed them both.

Adam and Henny were near Willa's station. "Tell her," he said. Henny acted like she had no idea what he was referring to. "About lunch," he prompted.

"Huh?"

"What happened at lunch, Henny?" I could tell she was playing dumb and I didn't appreciate the charade.

"I dunno." She started to arrange Willa's combs and brushes.

"Henny." Her passivity was infuriating.

Adam spoke first. "Mrs. Clancy freaked out because Tyler Booth and Ronnie Stonewell were hitting each other with their lunch-boxes..."

"Who's Mrs. Clancy?" I asked.

"The lunch monitor," answered Adam. Henny's back was toward us, her shoulders stood at attention.

"She turned out the lights and told everyone to be quiet..."

"I didn't hear her!" yelled Henny.

"Yes you did," Adam said. Then to me he explained that Mrs. Clancy has a loud voice *and* she turned off the lights. He glared at his sister.

"I didn't. I didn't."

"So what happened?" I asked, touching Henny's arm.

She pulled away. "Nothing."

"Mrs. Clancy told her that it was disrespectful to ignore adults. Made her throw out all the garbage that was left on the tables," said Adam.

"Adam, just because *you* heard Miss Clancy..."

"Mrs.," they said in unison.

"Just because *you* heard Mrs. Clancy...doesn't mean Henny did." Henny glanced at me and looked away.

"You weren't there. It was embarrassing!" Adam turned to his sister. "Why'd you cry?" He didn't wait for an answer. "You shouldn't have cried! Crying makes everything worse."

I hated to hear him speak this way. He was my first baby; where was this coldness coming from? Perhaps I'd been so worried about Henny that I'd been neglecting Adam. I pictured myself painting and shuddered.

"Mrs. Clancy sounds like an asshole," I blurted out.

"Shall we?" Liza asked the kids. They hopped to. When I spoke, they were never so compliant. Perhaps they just wanted to get to the park, I reasoned. I kissed Max's head, and gave Adam's shoulder a pat, but when I turned to look for Henny she was already out the door.

*   *   *

Morgan and I sat on the floor in an empty part of the children's section while a Barnes and Noble employee read to squirming preschoolers. Every few minutes I could hear them reciting in unison, "Or I'll huff and I'll puff, and I'll blow your house down." I was grateful that Max was finally entertained without my needing to build train tracks or perfect the tenor of my choo-choo.

But my relief was fleeting, and not because of the rain either. New York had been pummeled for days (buckets of it setting records in Central Park). Everyone was talking about it; rain was the great social equalizer. My mother talked about the weather. And even if my socks were mysteriously moist, given my waterproof boots, and my raincoat and umbrella responsibilities (one Batman, the other Magritte's clouds) were putting me over the edge, I didn't want to discuss it. Though to be fair, I didn't want to talk about Henny's first appointment with the neuropsychologist later that day, either.

"You're a good person to ask," Morgan said. "What should I make for dinner?"

"Here we go."

"What?"

"That feels like an insult. How come that feels like an insult?" I asked.

"I don't know. Because you're a grumpy bastard..."

"I *am* a grumpy bastard." Though as usual, being around her was making me feel less so. Even if she did think my mural was fun. (Fun!) We sat for a moment. Morgan checked her phone.

"So no suggestions?" she said. "Tuna casserole? Chicken stir-fry? Nothing?"

"If tuna casserole isn't an insult, I don't know what is."

"I think cooking is chic," said Morgan.

"Tuna casserole is not chic," I said. "Being a *foodie*, maybe. But tuna casserole? I don't think so."

"If you say so."

"I'll give you chicken stir-fry, though, that can go either way. It depends if you use a wok." I waited for her to argue, but she seemed preoccupied. Come on, I thought. Make fun of organic ginger; begin a diatribe on the subjugation of chicken. Something, anything, so I could enjoy these last few minutes before Liza arrived and I'd have to get to Little Scissors. Liza would stay with Max while I ran to make the deposit. Then Adam and Henny pickup. I'd have a half hour to drop Adam at a playdate and get Henny to Dr. Stockland's. "Aren't you politically opposed to making dinner?" I prodded.

"Yeah, well, it's amazing... the power of guilt." She tossed her phone in her bag.

"Oh," I said. "That."

"Yeah, that."

"So... how's *that* going?" I asked.

She looked at me with sly eyes. "It's... intense, actually."

"The sex... or the relationship?"

"Oh honey, the sex *is* the relationship." It looked like she was about to go for her phone again but thought better of it.

"There's no reception in here," I told her.

"I know." She slumped against the wall. "Compulsive phone checking. It's a lovely side effect."

"Are there other lovely side effects?"

"Well, let's see. An unrelenting yeast infection, but for me, that pretty much goes with the territory of phenomenal sex."

"Okay, I am going to say this one time and never again." I paused. "*Phenomenal*? Really?"

"Yeah." She nodded. "Phenomenal." I felt her eyes on me. "Trouble in paradise?" she asked after a moment.

"No. No. It's not that. We're fine." She raised an eyebrow. "We are!" I repeated.

"The sex?" she prodded.

"The sex is fine," I said.

"Ouch." She rolled her eyes.

"Stop. Don't do that. It *is* fine. Good, even. Very good. In fact, if there was a problem, and I'm not saying there is, but if I were to put words to any minor flaw...it would be quantity. Not quality. Definitely not quality."

"Okay. Okay. I get it. That's great," she said. "So, up the quantity."

"Yeah, well, I think that falls under the category of easier said than done."

Two nannies parked strollers near us, which was good, because I needed a moment to get over being annoyed. Michael was my husband. My lover. My man. She'd crossed a line. I waited until they were out of earshot.

"Just because it's not phenomenal—" I started.

"I want phenomenal," she interrupted. "And as often as possible, thank you very much."

"—doesn't mean that it's not something equally essential."

"Equally essential to phenomenal?" she asked.

"Okay, I'm not sure sex with the same person, year after year, can keep being phenomenal every single time. There. I said it. But that doesn't mean it can't be something else. Something other than phenomenal but just as necessary."

"Oooh, I like that," she said. "Like how Led Zeppelin and Brahms are different, but...essential."

"You like Zeppelin?" I asked. "I like Zeppelin!" This felt like an amazing development.

"I do not *like* Zeppelin," she said.

"Me too, me too." I had the urge to list obscure songs to prove I wasn't a "Stairway to Heaven" kind of girl—"Moby Dick," "The Rain Song," "Going to California"—but then I remembered I wasn't fourteen.

She checked her phone. I pretended not to notice.

"We're supposed to meet later," she explained. "But he hasn't told me where."

"He will, though, right?" I asked.

She shrugged.

"That would make me crazy."

"That's kind of his point," she said. "Keeps things unpredictable and...intense."

"Does it work?"

She looked across the room at her daughter and then leaned in close. "Like a fucking charm."

I ever so slightly pulled away. "How often do you see him?" I asked.

"It changes. A couple times a week. Sometimes less."

"And...is that enough? I mean, how does it work?"

"How does it work?" she teased.

"Unless you don't want to talk about it."

"He texts a time and a place, and I go," she said.

"Just like that?"

"Just like that."

"So he'll text five o'clock, the Pierre, and you...go," I said.

"Pretty much. Except it's the Bowery, downtown. And sometimes there are...instructions."

"Instructions?" I knew this would open me up for more information than I wanted. And yet I couldn't resist.

"Instructions. Get naked, wait facedown, legs spread." She said it like she was reading her grocery list. Skim milk, bread, soda. Jesus.

"And that time...he was an hour late!" she said.

"Oh my God, I would shoot myself."

"Shoot myself? No." She shook her head. "I'm forty-one years old. He's a genius. By the time he got there I was sooooo—"

"...Don't say it, please, dear God, do not say it." I put my hands over my mouth.

"I was so—ready," she said, laughing. "A genius, I tell you. I thought those days were long gone."

"And what if you can't get away?" I asked.

"I can."

"Okay then." My mind was spinning. "Are you ever afraid you'll run into someone?" I asked.

"Already happened. Rochelle Shurl," she said.

"No." Rochelle Shurl was the nursery school director. The very proper nursery school director.

"He wasn't with me," she said. "I told her it's one of my writing spots."

"Unbelievable."

"Okay, you want to hear the fucked-up part?" she asked.

"Didn't I just hear the fucked-up part? Because I'm not sure I can handle more."

"Not the fucked-up *sex* part. The part about Eric. Me and Eric."

"Okay..."

"I like him more," she said. "I mean, who would've thought being with someone else would lead to that?" She looked at me. "Sometimes we're at home, just hanging out, and there they are, Eric and Zoe...making macaroni, listening to *The Sound of* fucking *Music*, and I look at them and I can't believe it, how happy I am just to be looking at them. Like, I like the sight of them. The whole thing. My husband. My kid. The way they use spoons for microphones and dance around singing *raindrops on roses*. It's...sweet," she said.

I imagined the scene. It made me sad. She was going to lose them. I could feel it.

"And I think to myself, this is family. My family. My sweet little family." Her eyes welled up. "How can both be true?" she asked. "The overarching, profound need to be pounded by a man I hardly know, versus..." She stopped, as if searching for the words.

"Versus loving your husband," I ventured.

"Versus loving my family," she corrected.

"Am I late?" Liza asked, startling us.

"Not at all," I answered. Morgan burrowed in her bag and pulled out some lip gloss. She's putting on a mask, I thought.

"Still pouring?" Morgan asked while examining her reflection in a compact.

"It's intense," said Liza. She slinked out of her dripping jacket and draped it over Max's stroller.

"Today's Henny's first appointment with Dr. Stockland," I told them, trying to shift any lingering focus away from Morgan.

"Why didn't you say so?" Morgan asked.

"I don't know. Probably because we got to talking about..."

"Recipes," said Morgan. "I love a good recipe."

"No. You love a phenomenal recipe."

"Who's Dr. Stockland?" Liza asked.

"I've heard he's great," said Morgan.

"Let's just hope he can live up to his reputation," I said.

"Who?" asked Liza again. I could've sworn I'd told her about the evaluation when we discussed the Miss Nathanson meeting, but now that I was sitting there, I realized I hadn't.

"Henny's going to a doctor who specializes in evaluating kids," I explained.

"Evaluating kids?"

I nodded. "Basically it's a neurologist who gives a bunch of intelligence tests to see—"

"Neurologist. Yikes," said Liza.

I ignored her and continued. "It's a whole process. It'll take five or six sessions. But the idea is we'll know more about how Henny thinks. What she's good at. The specific areas she has trouble in."

"What's the goal?" Liza asked. It was an excellent question.

"Well, I guess they're looking to see if she has some sort of... learning...issue," I said.

"Does she know about this?" asked Liza, sounding horrified.

"We told her last night."

"You told her she might have a learning issue!?"

"No...I told her she was going to a doctor who knows a lot about how kids learn, so we could figure out how to help her better."

"What'd she say?" asked Morgan.

"She wanted to know if she was going to get a shot." I smiled at the memory.

"She must be terrified," said Liza.

"Actually, once she found out she wasn't, she seemed fine."

"The whole thing sounds horrible," said Liza.

"Horrible?" Morgan challenged. I started to feel nervous.

"I'm sorry, but it does. To me." I didn't know how to respond.

"*How* many times does she have to see this guy?" asked Liza.

"Five, I guess. Maybe less." Though the doctor never suggested it might be less.

"What if I read with her more?" Liza suggested. "I'll go slowly. Sound out each word." She sounded panicked. I glanced at Morgan and wondered what she was thinking. Zoe was already reading and Henny had three years on her. I found Max and Zoe in the crowd; she always talked circles around him. I wondered if Morgan thought my kids were slow. I shouldn't have told anyone about this.

"I'll practice those words...what do you call them?" Liza asked.

"Word wall words."

"Word wall words. Maybe if we did them in the morning."

"Maybe," I said, though I didn't really think so.

"They have these flashcards," Liza continued. "They probably sell them here." I glanced at Morgan. She rolled her eyes.

"I just need to find out what's going on with her," I said kindly. "You know, so we can figure out what to do."

"Does this guy know she's only seven?" asked Liza.

"That's totally reasonable," declared Morgan.

"I was always so lost in school," I explained, hoping I could make Liza understand we were doing this out of concern. "I guess it's good we're noticing early."

"What was your problem?" Morgan asked, which startled me.

"I don't know. I was just...uninterested," I said. Was that it? I wondered. Maybe *I'd* had a problem? I'd never considered it before.

"Well, Henny's very interested," said Liza. Then, looking at Morgan, she added, "I should know. I'm the one who does her homework with her."

I felt like I'd been punched. I looked away from them and had a brief fantasy of slapping Liza across the face. But what Liza said was true. She was the one who sat patiently with Henny most afternoons. Morgan stared stone-faced at Liza, then, as if dismissing her very existence, looked at me and said, "Anyway, you're doing the right thing; getting a *doctor's* opinion." I could've kissed her.

I checked my watch. I still had a few minutes, but I had to get out of there.

"But won't taking her to some doctor just make her feel bad about herself?" Liza asked.

"I hope not." I'd feared the same thing.

"I'm sure he's terrific," Morgan reassured me.

"I'll keep you posted," I said to Morgan, then, realizing how that sounded, added, "Both of you, I'll keep you both posted."

I gathered my gear and stepped over other people's children to reach Max. I kissed him on the head and zigzagged out of the congested store. Standing under the canopy, I listened to the downpour cacophony, deep and hollow. Shoppers scooted past me with their exasperated New York City *excuse me*'s, but I just stood and watched raindrops ricochet off the pavement. My city was in a downpour blur.

I took a deep breath. Then another. And made my way in the rain.

24

1981

I can't decide which Lip Smacker I like better, watermelon or Tootsie Roll. I don't want Mr. Mancini to see me smell them, so under my desk, I pull off one cover and, using my fingernail, scrape some off the waxy stick. I casually smell the glop under my nail. The chocolate aroma makes me hungry. Looking around my math class, I determine no one is watching and eat it while my peers dutifully learn about triangles. I'm no fool. I know I'm not supposed to eat Lip Smackers, but I love the sweet taste and figure since they're for kids, they can't be poisonous. I scoop another clump, watermelon this time, glance around the room, and lazily bring my finger to my tongue.

I am bored; this helps pass the time. I don't care about triangles, and even if I did, my mind will not grasp what Mr. Mancini is trying to teach. He doesn't notice I'm lost. My face looks engaged while my brain contemplates Tootsie Rolls and watermelons.

Like all of my classes, it lasts forty-two minutes, which is something I like about middle school. In elementary, except for lunch and my frequent escapes to the bathroom, I was trapped in the same room all day. In twenty-one minutes, the bell will ring, and I'll get the rush that comes with a challenge. Will I be able to get to my locker, find *Our Town*, and be on time to English? If I remember my combination, I can make it. My face turns red at the idea of walking in late again and having everyone watch me make my way to an open seat.

I think my combination is 44-17-27, but as soon as I say it to myself, I'm doubtful. Maybe it's 44-27-17. I look in my spiral, but can't find where I thought I wrote it down. The whole thing is making me nervous. Now I'm not even sure if it starts with 44.

I return to happier ponderings, this time making a game of chance out of the taste test. Without looking to see which one it is, I scrape it. Then, without smelling, I rub some on my lips and, like a piece of soft candy, I take a bite of the mystery balm. It's Tootsie Roll, which disappoints me. This feeling of loss is how I figure out that I like the watermelon best.

I don't yet know that leaving decisions to chance isn't the best way to choose.

The sound of pencil on paper brings me back to Mr. Mancini. Even if I'm baffled by his instruction, I like his pleasant voice. He's not an attractive man, yet something about him is appealing. I don't understand why this is, so while I listen, I try to figure out what it is that makes me feel this way.

I wonder if he thinks I'm pretty. He's not a pervert or anything, but still, it seems like he sees something in me. Something that makes me look away. Maybe he does think I'm pretty. Or maybe he can tell that at night I think about what it will feel like to be older, or beautiful, or touched by someone else's fingers.

He is telling us we'll need to study. I only know the one with the right angle. There will be a quiz soon, but I don't hear when. I am busy wondering why Mr. Mancini wears a tie. None of the other teachers do, which makes me wonder if he likes ties, which makes me wonder what it would be like to someday take a tie off a man.

I ask Ryan, a popular boy who sits next to me, when the quiz is. We've been in the same school forever, but we never really talk. I'm not hated by boys and girls like Ryan, I'm just invisible, like the caste system was decided long ago. Ryan tells me Thursday, which means I have a few days before I have to think about math. This puts my mind at ease. I hope I'll remember to study. I jot down *Math quiz, Thursday* in my notebook, a note I'll find long after the quiz has come and gone.

25

2007

Henny fell asleep in the cab, her body heavy with exhaustion. I looked out the window and watched the neighborhoods change as we drove down West End Avenue and turned onto 86th Street. At the light, a group of teenage boys crossed Broadway. Besides being fettered by backpacks they'd never admit were too heavy, they seemed carefree. Adam was only a few years younger than these boys. I tried to imagine him similarly self-possessed. By his age, I'd been navigating my neighborhood for years. I remembered the wind in my hair and how powerful I'd felt soaring down those hills. I wondered when Adam would start to wander the city alone.

I glanced in the buildings as we passed Amsterdam and Columbus, but Henny's rhythmic breath pulled me back. I watched her sleep. My guilt was vast and illogical, as if I should somehow be able to protect her from grueling assessments and any resulting weariness. At least she liked Dr. Stockland. She'd said so after the first visit. It was strange waiting for her during their sessions. Every so often, I'd hear her faint voice through the walls. Even though I couldn't make out what she was saying, I could tell if she was finding something difficult. It's like her uncertainty seeped under the door and summoned me, leaving me poised and ready, until a moment passed and I realized there was nothing for me to actually do.

I closed my eyes when we got to Central Park. I liked to see if I could sense when we were on the East Side. At Fifth Avenue, I had a clear view into the Metropolitan Museum's Temple of Dendur. In the midst of this vibrating city was a spacious and tranquil exhibit from an altogether different time and place. It seemed otherworldly, and yet there it was. The city still did this to me—infused me with awe.

When we passed Madison Avenue, I leaned forward. "Instead of Park, can you take Lex?" I asked. Whenever possible I liked to avoid Park Avenue. It was my private homage to my mother. Mrs. Adler had lived on Park.

When we pulled up to our building, Adam, Max, and Liza were in the lobby with a muddy, happy Trudy. They had that fresh-from-the-dog-run look of fulfillment. Henny greeted Trudy by kissing her ears. I exhaled.

I knew a storm of homework, baths, and dinner was brewing, but when we got into the apartment, I allowed them a few minutes to relax while Liza and I unpacked backpacks and got started on dinner. Neither of us mentioned Henny's appointment. It seemed as long as we avoided the topic, we were fine. In fact, I enjoyed our calm, seamless choreography as she sliced a red pepper (Max's sole vegetable) and I washed the lettuce. By the time the conversation turned to her boyfriend, Nate, the salad was done, and she was already unpacking Max's stroller.

"He says he hates Woodmere, so there's no sense in me going all the way out there for a stupid anniversary dinner." She held up Max's latest treasures, sticks and dry, crumbling leaves.

"Toss them." Liza hesitated, so I added, "I'll take the blame." I hoped she didn't think I was callous for no longer saving every jewel my kids brought home. Even though I felt varying degrees of remorse when they landed in the garbage, I didn't change my mind.

"So you haven't met his parents?" I asked, while she rinsed out a Sippy cup.

"No, but he's not that close to them, so I don't really care." I watched to see if she would separate the straw device so she could thoroughly clean the spout.

"I thought you said his mother helped him get an internship at her cousin's law firm?" She wasn't removing the insert. I tried to figure out which would feel worse—correcting her or tolerating the knowledge of the lurking rancid cup.

"Well, yeah, but she drives him crazy. Besides, they sound like snobs, so I'm not that into it."

I'd deal with the cup later. She was probably distracted by the thought of Nate's family. I passed her the plates, remembering how terrified I'd been when Michael introduced me to his parents—and we'd been engaged by then. He was their adored only child; I'd worried they wouldn't think I was good enough for him, but they'd been lovely.

I handed her the silverware and made a mental note to call Simone. I'd always appreciated that she and Dennis weren't the stereotypically intrusive type of in-laws. Until recently, they were political science professors at Syracuse. We used to spend holidays together, and Simone particularly seemed to enjoy the kids, but then they shocked everyone by retiring to one of those golfing communities in Palm Beach. For a second, I wondered what kind of grandmother my mother would've been—but I quickly pushed the thought away.

I watched Liza wiping the counters. While I didn't have a crystal ball, I was fairly certain Nate wasn't going to the dinner alone because he hated his family or milestone festivities. But instead of Liza suspecting anything was amiss, she acted like she didn't care. I guess skin elasticity wasn't the only difference between us. When I was her age, I was so needy. In fact, it took meeting Michael, who wanted me as much as I wanted him, to change that. I suspected that if Liza had a chance with her Five Towns law student boyfriend, it was better that she wasn't pushy.

"You can always come to Kent with us," I offered, knowing she'd decline. Who could blame her?

Just then, a sleepy Max came into the room. "Where's Chocobunny?"

Liza walked to the stroller, which I found odd, because there was a long-standing rule that Chocobunny did not leave the house. Occasionally Max would ask, but my answer was always the same. Some items were just too precious.

"Oh my God," Liza said, looking through the kids' sweatshirts in the otherwise empty stroller bag. "He took it to the playground," she said, stating the obvious. My heart ricocheted off my ribs as I looked from Max to Liza in disbelief. Chocobunny was gone.

Max became hysterical. I wondered which was causing more pain, the reality of his loss or the universal feeling that results when the terrible thing your mother warned you about has happened.

Liza stayed with the kids while I took to the streets. I searched the soon-to-be-dark neighborhood between our apartment and the playground. Doorman after doorman shook his head when I asked if they'd seen the frayed bunny. Some offered words of encouragement, but many returned blank stares. I wondered if they thought me an overly indulgent, hysterical mother. I cursed myself for the times I'd been similarly judgmental of my peers and vowed future loyalty.

I scanned gutters and curbsides. With crystal clarity I could conjure the bunny in my mind, but memory has no bearing on the world of lost possessions. An impossible sort of powerlessness: not being able to replace what's loved and easily imagined, but gone.

I sensed that the people returning to the neighborhood noticed my darting eyes. Maybe it was time to give up. I tried to think of the situation from a spiritual perspective. Perhaps this was meant to be.

Fuck that, I thought. This wasn't fate; it was Liza. My Chocobunny rule was clear, and yet here we were, and Max was suffering. My mind drifted to the countless movies and TV shows I'd seen where affluent women were portrayed as terrible mothers. I was sick of the ever-attentive and nurturing young nanny archetype and the corresponding self-absorbed vessel that birthed accessories she didn't care about.

Where were these vessels? I thought angrily. I'd been living on the Upper East Side for over a dozen years, and I still hadn't met any. Even the wealthiest women I knew, a.k.a. the ladies who lunch set, the fanciest of fancy, hell, even that math enrichment idiot, were all attentive and loving to their kids. Imperfect, most definitely. But attentive and loving, without question.

I'm sure Liza felt terrible (though she hadn't uttered anything resembling an apology), but she was *not* devastated. *I*, however, anticipated sleepless nights ahead where I'd obsess whether Max would ever feel truly safe again. Then I had a horrific thought. What if she'd done it on purpose? What if Liza was so disgusted by my children's privileged little lives that she used Chocobunny to settle the score? How could I have been so stupid! I'd hired a girl with a family history of criminal activity. How idiotic of me to think that she could have gotten away unscathed? My own insecurities had brought Liza into our lives and now she was inflicting intricate, passive-aggressive punishment on my children.

I hesitated at the iron gate. Shadows danced in the mostly empty playground; I felt like an intruder. But I thought of Max and entered. Swing silhouettes and slides stood bare and waiting. The usually bustling playground was a faraway memory. I was spooked and missed the street and all things familiar. Though not quite running, I got out of there. It was time to head back.

I scribbled my number for some of the doormen I'd already spoken to. They said they'd keep an eye out, but I'm sure they were just humoring me. My phone rang. "Any luck?" Liza asked tentatively.

"I'm afraid not." I heard Max howling in the background. Anger and guilt returned. Where was that fucking bunny? "Tell Max I'm still looking," I said as Michael beeped in.

"Where'd we get Chocobunny?" Michael asked. He'd obviously spoken to them. I gave him the name of the store in the West Village and we hung up.

There was a young man in a blue uniform, picking up litter. For years I'd seen these men around the neighborhood. They were in a program that offered petty offenders the option of community service instead of jail time. I was dubious whether prettying the already pristine Upper East Side qualified as community service, but until that evening I'd never spoken to any of them directly. "Excuse me, sir," I said. No response. "Excuse me," I repeated.

His skin was a rich blue-black. We both seemed startled, only one of us by his beauty. When I had his attention, I became self-conscious, barely able to speak. "Have you seen a brown stuffed bunny? Looks like a rag?" I worried he too would think of me as a silly mother of indulged ingrates. My eyes filled with tears. He looked at me for what felt like a long time.

"Yeah, I saw that thing," he said. "Check the garbage. The one across from the park." I ran the two blocks back to the playground, my long tweed coat and crazy hair soaring behind me. I felt more like my mother than ever before. We were one and the same: full of sheer desperation juxtaposed with hope. Hope instilled by a stranger who probably didn't have extra to give.

Except for some discarded coffee cups and leftovers from the Viand Coffee Shop, the first can was empty. I peeked in the next, greeted by an awful stench. There, under a half-eaten sandwich and what could only be dog shit wrapped in the *New York Times* metro section, was Chocobunny. I cautiously retrieved him, shaking off any debris. I wanted to hug him, but didn't.

Michael rang again. "They went out of business."

"I found him," I cried.

I looked for the man in uniform, wanting to thank him, but he was nowhere in sight. I suspected he was probably the one who'd tossed Chocobunny in the first place, but I didn't care. My city was restored. People seemed to have a bounce in their step. I held up Chocobunny for one doorman, who gave me a thumbs-up. If this had been a musical, I'd have tap-danced all the way home.

When my phone rang again, I assumed it was Michael. "Guess what?" Willa asked.

"No idea." My heart fell. I loved her, but in that moment, I wanted to enjoy the victory.

"I have the perfect solution," she said.

"Okay..."

"We should expand."

I stopped walking. "Expand," I said. There were clues to how I felt in the way I said this word. I didn't raise my voice on the second syllable, the universal way to turn a statement into a question. As in, ex-pand? Nor did I mimic the way she'd said it; a socially acceptable stalling tactic while one contemplates or digests an idea. Expand, as in, huh, how about that? What an interesting idea. No. I said it like someone who realizes that a meeting of the minds isn't going to be possible. I said it like an acceptance. A recognition that this just might be the beginning of the end.

Expand. As in, the most apathetic way one could utter the word.

"It solves a lot," Willa said. "We could move to a larger space. I mean, the water pressure's for shit. The landlord's obnoxious and you know he's going to raise the rent. But we can relocate. This way, we're able to accommodate more customers. We'd probably have to hire some new people, but that could be fun, actually. And Victoria will get us the press..."

The whole time she spoke, I hovered above our conversation— half listening and half fascinated by the fact that she had no idea how there were few things I wanted less than *more* Little Scissors. But here is the thing about being sanctimonious. While I was busy recognizing Willa's lack of attunement, I completely missed *her* clues. The subtleties of where she was coming from.

"Because it's time, Kara. Time for a change." I held Chocobunny in my cold hands and tried to usher her off of the phone. There was a woman walking toward me. She was wearing a flapping rain jacket. When she got closer, it sounded like sails whipping in the wind.

"Kara, if we found the right space..." continued Willa; but I was already gone. The woman in the jacket reminded me of a Bonnard painting I'd always admired, the one of a woman walking in the rain. And then it hit me, this was not some random woman; it was the elegant gamine from Oliver's gallery. I wanted to see who she was with, which is how my eyes finally, after twenty years, landed on Oliver.

"Oh my God."

"Are you okay?" asked Willa.

"I've got to go."

"Promise me you'll think about it," she said before I closed my phone. I shook my head, as if he were an Etch-A-Sketch image I could easily erase. There was no doubt about it; Oliver was walking past, deep in conversation with the woman. They entered a brilliantly lit prewar building. He'd aged, of course. Was gray around the temples, lines more chiseled than drawn, but there was no question, it was Oliver.

I'd imagined running into him so many times, but none of my fantasies played out like this. It happened so quickly. He hadn't even seen me. I looked in the lobby. They were gone. I couldn't deny it any longer. Having just come so close to him, I owned what I'd been hiding since I first saw his show. It was time to talk to Oliver. I could force myself to resist, but I didn't want to. I sensed he had something I needed. Something only he could give. I didn't want to be disloyal or dishonest, but I doubted I could convince Michael of something I didn't fully understand. He'd only feel betrayed.

It would be lovely to push pause on my life, but with bittersweet wisdom, I knew that sort of thing only happened in the movies.

I looked at Chocobunny, lucky to have found him. His frayed fur and soft self reminded me I had somewhere to be. With gratitude mounting and guilt not far behind, I made my way home.

"About Chocobunny," Liza said, as she was leaving. I looked up and was startled by her pallid face. If she'd been withholding an apology, it seemed only because remorse was stuck in her throat, like a levee on the brink of disaster.

"It's okay," I said. "No worries." And I meant it. I felt terrible for ever doubting her.

"I shouldn't have let him..."

"Really, Liza, it's okay. We found him," I said. "I mean, we're so lucky." But when she turned to leave, her long shift finally over, it occurred to me that my luck and hers were not one and the same.

26

1987

Eden and I make our way down the sweater aisle of Cheap Jack's, a vintage shop in the East Village. I'm looking for retro granny dresses or men's wingtips in my size, but a black cardigan with mismatched buttons catches my eye.

"Mothballs," Eden says. "You'll never get the smell out." I know she's right, but I'm not in the mood for advice. "Renee Rand's a classic narcissist. You shouldn't let her get to you," Eden insists.

"Is that your professional opinion?" Eden's parents are psychiatrists; she gets like this sometimes.

"The world revolves around her. Luckily, Oliver's in her orbit. Otherwise, he'd be impossible."

"She kept calling me Karen..."

"Because you had nothing to offer her, so basically—you didn't exist."

"Huh?"

"She's a nasty bitch." Eden takes off her sweatshirt and pulls a flapper dress over her tank top. "The real question is—what did Oliver do about it?"

"Oh, he totally noticed, but what could he do?"

Eden raises an eyebrow.

"What?" I ask defensively.

"Nothing." She goes to the mirror. I follow her like a hungry stray.

"I mean, it was clear she wasn't going to listen anyway," I explain.

Eden shrugs. "If you say so."

"And the good news is, it doesn't matter. She left yesterday."
Eden steps out of the dress. "Well, that's a relief," she says.
"Right? I mean, out of sight, out of mind," I say.
She looks at me as if I'm crazy. "Yeah, right." Eden laughs. "Absolutely. Especially when it comes to mothers."

Oliver and I spend the next weekend together—or more precisely, with his art student friends. Friday night there's a poetry reading, and Saturday everyone meets at the Met. He's not all that demonstrative, but he makes up for it both nights at his place. We're at the point where we know each other's bodies—what to do, how to do it—but are not so familiar that anything's become routine.

On Sunday afternoon, he's ready to paint. I can tell; he gets that look where it's obvious his mind is somewhere else. I consider going home. I don't even have a toothbrush here, and I've been wearing the same jeans all weekend. (Though I do get to wear his T-shirts, which I love, of course.) Still, maybe I should go back to my room and start my own painting. But I don't.

He's working on Eden's odalisque pose. Using shades of gray, he paints a scarf draping over her. It comes to me like lightning; the scarf should be yellow. I long for a contrasting color (yellow, it has to be yellow), but I'm silent. We both concentrate on the canvas. He exudes confidence in his process, not once looking in my direction. I think of my tulips. They now seem precious compared to Oliver's Eden. I am no longer convinced yellow is the way to go.

"Do you want me to leave?" I ask. I don't want to disturb him, but something feels off. He seems different. Moody. Distant even.

"Hmmmmm?"

"Is it okay if I hang around awhile?"

"Well, I'm working. You know I'm working, right?" What does he mean by *You know I'm working, right*? Does he want me to go? I don't want to.

"Obviously, you're working. I like watching you."

Oliver's silence hangs in the air. I want him to give me a sign that it's okay if I stay, but he isn't. I wish I hadn't asked. Then it would be up to him to claim his space. I close my eyes, hoping this makes me appear serene, reflective. His silence is humiliating.

"Look, Oliver. I don't want to bug you. Just…"

"Just what, Kara?" His irritation is undisguised.

"Just… are you mad at me?"

"I wasn't, but I'm starting to be…"

"I'm sorry. I don't want to bug you."

"Good."

"What does that mean?"

"What does *what* mean?"

"Good. When you said good, does that mean, good, you want me to leave? Or, good, like, as long as I'm quiet, I can stay?" I despise the sound of my voice.

"I don't get it Kara…" Oliver puts his brush down and wipes his hands on a rag. He is graceful, composed. He squeezes pigment on the palette. My thought of yellow returns.

His movements seem calculated: He arranges the brushes on the cart, replaces the cap to a tube of paint, wipes the outside of the turpentine container. With each slow gesture, I want to rip every piece of hair out of his scalp. "…If you know I'm working, and we've been hanging out all weekend, why do you want to stay?" Before I can answer, he adds, "I'm just doing my thing, I'm not good company."

I am distracted by all the things I shouldn't say. Begging would be honest, but of course, I know better. I am desperate for him. I don't care if we speak. He doesn't even have to acknowledge me; I just want to be near him. I have schoolwork I could do, or other responsibilities, but nothing compels me. No interest, errand, or pursuit. My only desire is not to be rejected by Oliver.

Panic brews. "Look, why don't we stop talking about this. You work." I wonder if he detects the slight tremble in my voice. "I'll go in the other room. Maybe take a shower or something. How's that sound?"

Again, he says nothing. He stands back from the canvas and squints. I look at his back, shoulders, and ears. His ears look angry.

I just need one word, one gesture. A shrug maybe, any tiny sliver of an invitation.

Then it occurs to me that he probably isn't answering because he's deeply engrossed in his art. That's it, I figure. His absorption is his way of conveying that of course I can stay...as long as I understand that he is not to be disturbed. Oliver is driven. It's what I love about him. I understand that. I want to support his artistic pursuit, not interfere with it. He is brilliant.

I will just relax, take a shower maybe, watch him paint for a while. Yes, I tell myself, his absorption is his invitation. I am relieved, because for me, only two places exist, with Oliver and not with Oliver. I am thankful that again tonight we'll be together.

I turn toward my plan, my mission almost in action, when I hear him. Quiet, but unmistakable. "I think you should leave."

27

2007

It was Liza's birthday and law school Nate was taking her to Momofuku. Gone were her usual jeans and T-shirt featuring a band I'd never heard of. Tonight Liza wore a flowing black tunic over charcoal skinny cords. Gray suede boots landing just below her knee replaced her usual Converse high-tops. But it was her hair that was most transforming. I'd given her a gift certificate to one of the hipster salons downtown, and they'd done a great job. Whenever Liza turned, her glossy hair swished, as if somehow a breezy draft was aimed only at her. Michael did an imperceptible double take, which I interpreted more as shock than attraction. Regardless, he busied himself with the weekend section of the paper, while I grated Parmesan for my guys.

"Liza! You look like a lady," said Max.

"Thank you, Max." She curtsied.

"Now you look like a princess." Henny giggled. Adam glanced up, only to quickly return to his pasta, dismissing her beauty as ten-year-old-boys are apt to do. Liza and I exchanged amused glances.

"Are we ever going to meet Nate?" I asked. Sometimes I'd hear their voices through the thin walls, but I could never make out what they were saying. Maybe it was misguided, but I thought if I saw him, I'd be able to discern whether he was trustworthy.

"Not tonight. He's coming from work, so we're meeting at the restaurant."

I nodded, feigning approval. She'd stopped in for her weekly check; she didn't need to be interrogated. I wondered if she'd also wanted some company. I remembered long ago feeling lonely whenever I got ready to go out. Perhaps the anxiety of a night on the town was lessened when friendly eyes witnessed the exit.

"Well, I'm off," she said, grabbing her navy windbreaker from the hall rack. I didn't want to hurt her feelings, but her jacket spoiled the outfit.

"Liza," I started. "Do you want to borrow a sweater?" I took my black cashmere wrap from the closet. "It's going to be cold later," I added, as if the loan was related to weather.

"No good?" She looked down self-consciously.

"No, I just thought…" Michael shot me his *tread lightly* warning and moved to the obituaries.

It fit her beautifully. I told her she could keep it. "Are you sure?" she asked.

"Absolutely. It never looked right on me," I said, as if she was doing me a favor by taking it off my hands. I knew full well that it's hard to enjoy what you have to give back.

"Thank you," she said, checking herself in the full-length mirror.

For a moment I wondered if I should've saved it for Henny, but Liza reminded me of my younger self. Obviously, ridding her of her navy windbreaker wouldn't substitute for a healthy, dependable mother; but I figured I was doing something.

She studied her reflection. I caught a glimpse of myself standing behind her and turned away. In part, I wanted to leave her to the private act of scrutiny. But also, I suddenly had a need to avoid watching her embark on a night out in which all things were still possible.

Just as Michael and I were settling in to watch a formulaic detective show that involved clever sleuths and pretty prey, Liza's phone rang in her abandoned jacket. I considered not answering, but I worried it might be her boyfriend calling to say he'd been delayed.

"Hello. Liza's phone." I held her cell like a thief who didn't want to leave fingerprints.

"Lizzy, it's me, can you hear me?" the woman screamed. It sounded like she was calling from a bustling bar or the subway.

"Hello," I shouted. "This isn't Liza, this is…"

"Lizzy, I can't hear anything. I hope you can hear me," she yelled.
"Hello," I screamed. "Call back and leave a message." But the
woman kept talking. Her desperation was obvious.

"Happy birthday, sweetheart." It sounded like she was covering
the receiver with her hand, because I heard a muffled *shut the fuck
up*. Across the living room Michael sat watching our flat-screen,
ignoring the work papers on his lap. It scared me how far away he
seemed.

"Lizzy, can you hear me? Can you, Lizzy?" she yelled.

"Yes." The only answer I had.

"The happiest of happy, sweetheart," she continued. I tried to
make out the background voices, but everything blended into an
echo. So that's what prison sounds like, I thought.

"...not fair of you. So think about it, Lizzy. Think about it." I
listened to the mother's strained tenor. "I hope you'll change your
mind, just...just come visit. Maybe then I can explain. Lizzy, come.
I'll explain. If you'll let me..." A moment later, she screamed goodbye and the connection went dead.

I held the phone, Liza's phone, to my ear, relieved by the sudden
silence. With a pounding heart, I concentrated on my surroundings
the way a frightened child up from a nightmare might take in her
bookcase, curtains, a special stuffed animal.

I replayed the mother's words. What did she want to explain and
why wasn't Liza letting her do it? I wished I hadn't answered the phone,
but I couldn't pretend I hadn't now—the call was in her phone log.

That night, I woke at 3 a.m., in a puddle of sweat. I kept my eyes
closed and tried to trick myself back to sleep, but my nightgown
stuck to my skin. Egyptian cotton did nothing to lessen my sweaty
chill. I wondered if I had a fever, even though I didn't feel sick. So
this is a night sweat, I decided, feeling old. I'd heard these could
start years before menopause. So here I am, I thought.

I'm sure there are people who find the middle of the night peaceful; but for me, being the only one awake inevitably leads me to

imagine some unspeakable adversity where I lose everyone I love. I lay drenched next to Michael and took comfort in his each faint snore, in-out, in-out. *I am safe*, I silently said as I tried to match his breath, hoping it would lull me back to sleep. But my drenched gown couldn't be ignored; I was both frozen and sweltering. No matter how I shifted I couldn't get away from the sweaty sheets.

Finally, I gave up and got out of bed. Shivering, I took off my nightgown and let it fall to the floor. For a moment I considered turning on the light to see if it had left a wet print, yearning for proof of this experience, but I didn't want to wake Michael.

I shut our bedroom door with a soft click and went to check the kids. Henny's room was filled with a rosy glow. I leaned in to her face, wanting to get as close as I could without touching her, so I could feel the warmth of her sleep, be enveloped by her sweet smell. I took in the beauty of her room: the fairy mural, her pink Guatemalan quilt, her tattered Molly doll wrapped in Max's old baby blanket. The room was everything I didn't even know I'd wanted when I was her age.

Earlier that night, she'd answered my *I love you* with *I love you more. Not possible*, I'd told her. Now as I watched her sleeping, it occurred to me that my love for my mother never approached the strength of my love for my kids. I wasn't sure if this was because of the mother I'd had, or the mother I'd become.

I went to the boys' room. Max had kicked off his train quilt and Chocobunny was lodged between the wall and his bed. I put everything back in its place. So easy to fix some things. And there was Adam; his night sound—serious and strong, just like Michael's. I flipped off the nightlight and headed for the living room.

Pulling a cashmere blanket around me, I settled into the couch and had almost drifted into sleep when it came to me. I hopped up and scurried for my keys. Trudy lifted her head, which made me feel like I needed to explain myself, but luckily, she dismissed me without question. In the elevator down to the basement, I wondered if our doorman would see me in the monitor; what would he make of this middle-of-the-night descent.

I could hear hissing in the mechanical room all the way down the hall to our storage unit. Every scary movie I'd ever seen flashed in my mind, but after a few minutes I convinced myself that there was nothing to fear among these clanging pipes and buzzing overhead lights. Still, I kept looking over my shoulder as I turned the key. Once inside, I felt safe surrounded by artifacts Michael and I cherished enough to keep despite years of disuse.

I found the canvases right away; they were exactly where I'd left them over a dozen years ago, the week Michael and I moved in. My old paintings greeted me, but the lighting was poor, and I wasn't ready to inspect them anyway, so I dispassionately flipped through them like inventory. They weren't the reason I'd come; it was the still wrapped, bare canvases I sought, the ones stored in the back.

My oils, on the other hand, were harder to locate. It wasn't until I'd searched two boxes that I remembered I'd stored them in the wicker picnic basket that was on top of Michael's hockey gear. Maybe we should get rid of some of this stuff, I thought, but devoting a weekend to that chore seemed like torture.

I was struck by how dusty and dented the basket was. Even that had aged. It was hard to believe so much time had passed since the day I bought it. We weren't even married, though we must have been engaged, because I remember how I'd walked around the store in a fog while Michael stayed in the furniture section. I'd thought, I am now a woman who shops in places like Conran's on Astor Place. I'd wanted a souvenir—some evidence to reinforce this new reality. It didn't feel celebratory, exactly. More like, practice. And that picnic basket wasn't simply beautiful—it seemed full of the promise that there would be romantic jaunts and happily-ever-after endings.

I balanced the basket of oils and canvases as I relocked the door. I'd still need turpentine, but there was no point in looking for any down here.

Once I got back, it occurred to me that the what-to-do-next part of my plan hadn't quite crystallized, which for about thirty seconds seemed particularly funny; then I pulled everything out of the front hall closet and made piles for Goodwill and the garbage. My late-night art supplies had a new home.

As quietly as possible, I hauled two bags to the garbage room on the other end of our hall. On my way back, I heard a door unlock. I didn't want any of my neighbors to see me, so I hesitated before turning down our corridor.

"Do you have a busy week?" an invisible Liza asked. I couldn't hear his reply. I peeked around the corner. Nate was broad-shouldered and wore a dark peacoat and even darker hair. Although they were hugging, it was obvious he was already gone even though he hadn't yet left. I quickly ducked back.

"Happy birthday, kiddo," he said. Kiddo? Oh dear.

I wasn't sure, but I think they kissed. Then he must've headed for the elevator, because Liza called his name, as if she'd remembered something important.

"Thanks for dinner," she said. I could see her shadow on the wall—so close, I was filled with panic and shame. But I didn't move away; instead, I held my breath.

"I almost forgot," said Nate. "Your birthday. I didn't have time to shop—but didn't you tell me you liked this scarf?"

"I love it," she said. "It smells like you."

Steps away from them, I closed my eyes in pity while she assured him that she cherished the *gift*. And then the elevator arrived, piercing the late hour with amplified elevator sounds—and he was gone, leaving her to the illusion of an almost empty hall.

I waited longer than necessary until it seemed the whole building went still before slinking back. But once inside, even with the fresh scent of a potentially close call, I was filled with a quiet kind of knowing, a hard-won wisdom, a sad triumph. The eavesdropping and smuggled art supplies aside, I was no longer that girl.

Before my eyes were even open, I could tell I'd slept later than I'd wanted. Sunlight filled our room and Michael's side of the bed had that empty-for-hours feeling. Adam and Henny were arguing in the other end of the apartment, something about the Xbox. Michael's voice was nowhere to be found, but the white noise of cartoons informed me of Max's whereabouts.

It was almost ten o'clock. My body felt lifeless. I thought about turning over or, worse, sitting up, but rejected the idea as too taxing. I felt hungover, and tried to think if I'd had any wine the night before. Then I remembered waking covered in sweat and spying on Liza after my late-night errand. With a heavy hand I searched blindly, finding the cold, damp, sheets. So I hadn't imagined it.

I had to get up. The kids must be starving, I thought, knowing Michael's culinary ability was nil. Adam and Henny's angry voices were approaching. I didn't want them to see me in bed so late. Images of my mother passed out came to mind.

I hopped up and scooted past them, shutting the bathroom door between us.

"He cheated," Henny cried.

"He's being a sore loser," Adam yelled. I looked at my reflection, stunned to see my swollen eyes. My hair was matted on one side, and sticking up on the other.

"Guys, give me a minute." I pulled sticky strands off my neck and confined my hair in purple elastic. I studied my forty-two-year-old face. I'll bet I was once beautiful, I thought, squinting to see if I could conjure up my old self. I supposed one day I'd look back on my *forties* with nostalgia. Lifting the sagging skin on my face at my temples, I imagined my younger self. I always assumed my mother had grown haggard by accident or poor planning, like if she'd only used night cream and lightened up on the booze, her skin would've stayed smooth and supple. I let go of my cheeks and then lifted them again to compare. Perhaps a facelift was in my future, though I knew they didn't really make women look any younger. Just wealthier. Which might not be such a bad consolation prize, actually. This would be a good thing to get Morgan's take on.

What would my mother have looked like, had she aged? And then it occurred to me. I was the age she'd been when she died. It was astonishing I hadn't thought of this sooner.

"Mom!" Henny screamed.

"Are you listening?" followed Adam.

I looked in my tired eyes and tried to remember hers.

"I just want to play alone," Adam yelled. "Can't I practice the next level without her?"

"We share in this family," Henny shouted.

"Where's your father?" I hoped Michael could hear me. Even though I had to get them breakfast, I quickly moisturized and applied lip gloss and mascara. I couldn't bear to start the day looking like her.

Michael sat at the kitchen table, warm coffee and the Sunday paper in front of him. He was chiseled and unshaven, and I knew from across the room just how he'd smell. The waxy Apple Jacks bag had been removed from the box and orange cereal speckled our granite island. I shoved the plastic bag back, but it bulged, just as I knew it would. I tried not to glare at my husband.

"Hillary is getting some bad press," he said. "I think Obama is going to benefit from this Blackwater debacle." I poured coffee and took out the eggs. By the sounds in the next room, Adam and Henny had called a truce and were back to their game.

"Can I help?" Max asked as I heard Liza open our door.

"I'm getting my jacket," she called. Her hair was still straight and she wore Nate's scarf like it was a badge of honor. I was surprised to see her return my sweater, neatly folded, to the hall closet, but I felt a certain satisfaction knowing that my canvases were secretly stashed so near.

"I can get it dry cleaned," she offered.

"Oh. No, it's fine." I guess she decided not to keep it after all. "Listen, Liza, I didn't mean to intrude, but you left your phone here, and I answered it without thinking."

She looked at me. I tossed eggshells into the disposal and handed Max the whisk.

"Anyway, your mother called. It was really loud in the background, and I think she thought I was you." I waited to see if she'd ask me to explain. "I'm sorry, I shouldn't have intruded," I went on nervously. Liza said nothing to save me. I started to feel resentful, but soldiered on.

"Anyway, she sounded nice," I lied. I offered Max a slice of bread to dip into the eggs and dragged a chair over to the stove for him to stand on. Then I showed him the hot parts of the skillet and dropped a soggy piece of bread into the crackling pan. Liza found her phone in the parka and scrolled through her calls.

"I think she wants you to visit," I said after a moment.

"Yes, she's mentioned that," said Liza.

"I thought things were good between you two." I tried to remember what made me assume that.

"Well, as good as they can be, considering she's a lying drug addict who gets indignant when anyone points it out."

"Oh, is that all?" I joked, hoping she'd appreciate the banter.

"Seems so."

"Liza," I began, knowing I should stay out of it. "Your mother sounded like she wanted to explain something."

Liza looked at me with a raised eyebrow.

"Sorry. I'll shut up," I said.

"It's fine," she said. "But really...there's nothing to explain. Nothing new, anyway. She always says the same thing. *I didn't plan on getting addicted. Things got out of hand.* Blah, blah, blah. I've heard it all before. Usually when she's wasted, but still, *I* remember, *I* wasn't the one in a blackout."

I nodded, understanding more than I cared to. "Sounds hard," I offered, with a hollow thud. She rolled her eyes, and soon after, left for the day. I hoped she knew I meant well. Sometimes she seemed so connected, and then other times cold and moody. I wished I'd kept quiet. Or better still, not answered her phone.

I could feel Michael's stare. If I looked up, he'd tell me I should back off. He'd remind me that Liza was an employee and it was one thing to let her into our lives, but quite another to become so involved.

But I didn't want to have that conversation.

Out of the corner of my eye, I saw him fold the city section and move to real estate. He probably didn't want to have that futile chat either. So I put another piece of soaked bread into the pan and poured orange juice and chocolate milk punctuated by straws. I lifted Max off the chair and placed French toast on plastic plates. I called Henny and Adam, and then I called them again. I did all of those things, and probably a few more. But I did not look at Michael. That, I did not do.

28

1980

I lie on my mother's bed and watch her getting ready. She told me she's going out with the woman from down the street, but she's lying. Larry's wife took their kids to Pittsburgh. I've become skilled at listening in on my mother's calls. It's easy, really. I just lift the receiver while holding down the disconnect button. Then very slowly, I let it go. Most of the time, she doesn't even notice. That's how I found out they're going to the Ground Round. Larry is friendly with the bartender, which probably makes him feel important. Somehow I know better, because I rolled my eyes when I heard that part, but my mother giggled. I couldn't tell if she really found the news funny, or if she was just grateful to be going somewhere with him besides her bedroom.

She looks at her image while spraying White Shoulders on her neck and wrists. Then she slowly massages lotion into her legs. I look away for a moment because my mother has turned into a woman. A woman about to meet a man.

"I won't be late." She thinks this is a comfort, but it's not. I know she'll stay until it closes. Once she's out of here, coming home is the last thing on her mind.

She dabs powder on her already pale face. I want to be the beautiful woman getting ready, or, barring that, I want her to be as lovely as she looks on this night when she is about to swallow discount drinks with another woman's husband.

I tell her to wear her Frye boots, but she doesn't. Instead, she chooses black pointy heels bought on sale, at Sears.

"Not bad," she says to herself. Then she applies frosted peach lip gloss and offers me some. I slouch toward her and carefully paint my lips. They feel smooth and slick and special, but after I look in the mirror, I wipe it off. I'm too young for silky lips and too old for pretend.

Before she leaves, I act as if she's already gone. Out of the corner of my eye, I see her hesitate at the door to the garage, but I don't look her way. I could reassure her that I'll be fine, but I can't help my last-minute pout that I try to disguise as engrossment in *The Love Boat*. I come back with a monotone *good night* in response to her tentative one.

I watch the show until I hear the garage door go down, then I scan the den as if somehow she might have magically left a part of herself behind. Only her sugary scent lingers while headlights reverse themselves away from me, offering one last flash of shadow, and then nothing at all.

29

2007

Michael drove the city streets as if he were in his Audi and not my tank of a minivan. We'd left later than planned, and he was trying to make up time. I looked at the kids in the backseat. Despite Adam's surly expression, they were a beautiful bunch. My babies weren't babies anymore. Life was moving so quickly.

"It'll be fun, you'll see," I said as much to myself as to Adam.

Even though I'd been attending the Thatchers' party for as long as Michael and I'd been together, I too was nervous. I usually just stayed in Michael's sphere, but this year I'd know more people. Both Morgan and Victoria were Thatcher regulars, Morgan by way of her literary agent, Alana Musk, who was a close family friend of theirs, and Victoria had just been hired by Lisette Thatcher to do PR for her foundation. I suspected Victoria would spend the afternoon working the room—I wondered how Willa would fare. Despite seeing her almost daily, life seemed to be taking us in different directions. I missed her. Or more precisely, I missed missing her.

I think for Michael this party was an annual reminder of his achievement. Paul Thatcher had given Michael his first corporate project—reconfiguring offices on two floors in an East Side building. The timing couldn't have been better. An increased demand for office space was brewing, in part fueled by the city's recent tax incentives for new construction. Paul Thatcher went from operating a small investment firm's properties to becoming one of Manhattan's top-tier real estate developers, expediting Michael's ascent.

*   *   *

Henny and I held hands as we walked across the Thatchers' field. In the distance were the New Yorkers I most envied: clever men and women who had figured out a way to make a (substantial) living combining art and commerce. I took in our surroundings. Reds and browns blanketed the Litchfield Hills. As a landscape painting, this foliage would look too quaint, but for an afternoon out of the city it was magnificent. Even the aloof guests seemed to sparkle. I allowed myself to appreciate the pristine blue of the storybook sky and released my fears into the crisp air.

"I swear, it's like a movie," I said to Henny.

"What movie?"

When Adam saw the hayride, he forgot his miserable mood and convinced Henny and Max to check it out. Like the other prepubescent city slickers, my kids seemed transformed by the treat of being able to run free outside.

Michael was intercepted at the cocktail tent by Garrett, who murmured something about several investors he *had* to meet. This affair was more than just a party—it was a networking opportunity where big business went down.

"You made it," Morgan called from across the crowd. She grabbed two glasses of chardonnay from a passing tray and made her way to me. "Come, I'll introduce you." What she didn't know was how much I hated mingling, but I said nothing and followed like a naughty puppy. Any newly acquired confidence diminished with each tentative step.

Morgan introduced Alana, a fifty-something blonde woman in orange cashmere. She was mid-conversation and barely glanced in my direction. "It's just that I don't know anything about this Obama guy," she was saying to a tan man with sandy hair who looked vaguely familiar.

"Oh please, this is Hillary's time," Morgan joined in.

"You're just saying that because you're a woman," said the tan man, who might or might not have been on *General Hospital*.

"You're just saying that because you're a misogynist," Morgan retorted. They clinked glasses, declaring a truce.

I could hear parts of conversations going on around me. I took a sip of wine and tried to concentrate on the topic at hand.

"I recently spent some time in Dubai," Alana announced to our growing circle. And blah, blah, blah, blah, blah, Chinese art market, blah, blah, blah, blah, blah, Russian businessmen.

I gave up trying to follow and started nodding each time she paused. I wondered if I was losing my hearing and took a gulp of wine. I hated getting older. I secretly touched my thighs, feeling my fleshy flesh. I don't typically rely on beverages in stemware to boost my confidence, but after a few minutes I traded my empty glass for a glistening full one. Cheers, I said silently while studying Morgan. She was everything my mother always wanted to be—captivating, clever, and successful. I felt proud to be around her.

"Oh, Dubai is absolutely phenomenal," said an older woman. "My favorite trip, not including the safari I took, of course."

"Yes, but nothing beats Kenya," Alana concluded. In my mind, I kept repeating her words. Nothing beats Kenya. Nothing beats Kenya. That settled it; I hated her.

"Well, you can't compare the two. Kenya's God's country," Morgan said, "and Dubai's essentially man-made."

I shook my head in emphatic agreement. Oh yes, Dubai is man-made. Perhaps I should switch to water during the meal.

"Have you been, dear?" the older woman asked, perhaps noticing my fervor.

"Oh no, but it sounds..." I searched for the right adjective, settling on far too many. "Magnificent. Impressive, astounding."

I probably couldn't find Dubai on a map, and frankly, the whole place irritated me. Not in any informed political sort of way, but rather because I had no idea how a whole (magnificent, impressive, astounding) country had materialized while I still knew nothing about it. In fact, the first time Michael mentioned it, I thought he was messing with me.

Just then, Victoria and Willa approached us. I nearly did a double

take. Even among this theatrical crowd, they were a dramatic couple. So entwined, they wore each other like accessories; a balancing
act that involved wineglasses, an alligator clutch, and intermittent
caresses. Still, both their poise and connection seemed genuine.

"Fabulous," Morgan said, motioning to Willa's hair. She'd worn
it piled on her head and braided in a splash of silk leaves and dried
berries.

"Thank you." She smiled. I noticed that despite being wrapped in
a fringed leather shawl, she still managed to reveal pellet-hard nip-
ples under a flimsy silk tee.

Victoria offered a collective hello and then asked Morgan if her
editor was in attendance.

Alana leaned in. "Alana Musk…" She extended her hand. "I'm
Morgan's agent." I suddenly perked up.

"Victoria Layton. Public relations. My firm has an excellent—"

"I know who you are," Alana said. "I represent Felicity Boehme's
new book."

"I've known Felicity for years."

"I'll say. She owes her career to you." Victoria simultaneously
smiled and shrugged. They discussed Felicity's upcoming fiftieth
birthday party while I pretended not to listen. I found them fascinating. Even though I was envious of their success, I was still able
to respect their accomplishments, even the manipulative way they
communicated their authority. But around them, I felt insignificant,
which immediately led me to categorize them as Mrs. Adlers. Said
another way, I promptly (and privately) despised them.

"So, Morgan, what are you working on these days?" Victoria asked.

"Excellent question," answered Alana. "The great American
novel, of course."

"That was last year. This year, I'm going for the greatest American novel," Morgan said.

"Do tell," said a woman who joined the actor.

"Oh, it's just a little tale about work and love," she said.

"In that order?" asked Victoria.

"Another fine question," said Morgan.

"She's always dodgy when she talks about a work in progress," Alana explained.

"Am I?" Morgan batted her eyes.

"Why?" I asked, as all eyes shot in my direction.

"Why am I dodgy?" asked Morgan.

I rolled my eyes. "Why is *in that order* a good question?"

"Why do you think?"

"See, every question with a question," Alana said.

"Do I?" Morgan's eyes twinkled. Again, the blond actor and she clanked glasses, which seemed to upset his lady friend.

"Is my wife entertaining everyone?" a man asked with pride. So this is Eric, I thought, starting to feel anxious. Then I reminded myself that I wasn't the one cheating on him and I quietly absorbed his presence. He was taller than I'd expected. And he looked like a runner, or maybe someone who snorkeled. Basically, he was earthier than the finance frat boy I'd imagined. And based on the first thirty seconds of my assessment, he didn't seem like a chump or a bastard either.

"She's charming as usual," a perky woman in a tight sweater answered.

"That's my girl," said Eric, sliding his arm around Morgan's waist.

"Oh good, you're here. I want to introduce you to Kara," she said as I stood a little taller. Avoiding eye contact, I shook his hand. Morgan looked adoringly at her husband, which made me feel sorry for them both. I found Michael across the swarm; his eyes anchored me. And then they were gone.

"So, you're the artist who's not making art," Eric said.

"Yes. I mean, no." I glanced at Willa and was relieved to see Victoria expertly steering her toward a gregarious group in the other direction. "I mean, not really."

"So, how do you know Morgan?" Alana asked, seeming slightly interested.

"Zoe goes to school with my son." The artist who's not making art sounded better.

"Zoe?"

"Morgan's daughter," I prompted.

"Yes, of course. Do pardon me, but I think that's Ahmet over there. He just got back from Dubai."

I scored a lukewarm dumpling from a lukewarm waitress.

"Don't mind her," Morgan started. "She's...what's the word?"

"A bitch?" whispered Eric. I smiled.

"Who cares? She's great at what she does." Morgan listed Alana's authors as Michael approached with Garrett and Garrett's wife, Paige. I introduced everyone and kissed Paige hello, once on both cheeks. She was from Belgium, and while I haven't yet made it to Kenya (or Dubai), I knew how to greet people like Paige, no matter how long they'd been stateside.

"Sasha, join us," Paige said to a woman behind me. Michael whispered something to me about Garrett that I couldn't quite hear, and I was vaguely aware of Morgan extending her hand to Paige's friend. A waiter offered me another dumpling, which I greedily gulped, eager to counter the chardonnay. How my mother tolerated this feeling was baffling. With a full mouth, I glanced at the newcomer.

"And you are?" Morgan asked Sasha's companion while I swallowed the dumpling whole.

"Oliver Bellows," answered my first love.

Michael looked at me. I could tell the others recognized his name. They offered spirited introductions that bordered on aggressive. Even Michael seemed excited, although in a moment of solidarity he withheld his usual handshake. Oliver and Sasha (the stunning woman from the gallery) nodded with each announced name. As the salutations neared completion, I stood mute and waited for Oliver's eyes to land on me. I watched as familiarity replaced his courteous expression.

"Kara Caine," he said, with a gradual smile.

"Hello, Oliver." I sounded like a woman in control.

The group looked back and forth between us. All movement turned into slow motion. Like when I'd been in late labor with Adam, I was keenly perceptive to every pulsation. I sensed the group would've given anything to know our story. This public recognition was a vindication of sorts, no less sweet for being long overdue.

Sasha spoke first. "Oliver's been indulging our American sensibility with an exhibition at my gallery." I remembered Oliver indulging my American sensibility, but I didn't say so.

"Yes, well, you're a difficult woman to turn down."

"There's a story there, I suspect," Morgan said flirtatiously.

"How long since you've shown in the States?" Paige asked.

"Not since I left Gagosian." As if that answered the question.

"Not including the MFA, of course," Sasha added. I'd read about that three seasons ago; I'd avoided Boston like the plague.

"And of course, the MoMA show in the spring." Sasha beamed at Oliver, who took a sip of wine.

"I heard about that," Morgan said.

"What an accomplishment," added Paige.

I felt like I was going to be sick. How had I missed the MoMA announcement? Not only hadn't I heard about his extraordinary achievement, but there was a time when I knew *all* the museum schedules a year out. I felt as if I'd been living under a rock.

"Where's your gallery?" Morgan asked.

"Seventy-first and Madison," Sasha answered. I held my breath while Morgan seemed to calculate the block.

"That's near Little Scissors," said Michael.

"Little Scissors?" asked Sasha.

"I own a children's hair salon," I explained. Everyone nodded. I looked around for Willa, but she was nowhere in sight.

"We're there all the time!" said Morgan, gently punching my arm. "The coffee shop where we always get..." Midsentence she glanced at Michael and seemed to realize there were some things she still didn't know. "...coffee. Occasionally, I mean. Sometimes." She took a slow sip of wine.

"Do you, now?" Michael asked, raising an eyebrow. I wiped my mouth with a cocktail napkin.

"So, Kara." Oliver paused. The sound of his voice saying my name belonged nowhere near my husband. It reeked of experience. "A hair salon, you say..."

I nodded.

"And have you seen my show?" he asked.

"Uh, no. Well, just from the street."

"Ladies and gentlemen," said a party planner with cinematic timing, "please make your way to the dining tent. Lunch is served." There was clanking and scurrying as our group dispersed, taking their cocktail-party attention spans with them.

"I will catch you later," said Morgan. She and Eric sauntered away, his arm at the curve of her back. Only Michael lingered next to me, standing tall.

"Michael, this is Oliver Bellows. Oliver, my husband, Michael Lawson." There. I made it. Did either of them know how difficult this was? The two loves of my life shook hands.

"I hope you'll both check out the show," Oliver said. Always about the art.

"Love to," Michael answered for us. I wanted to look at Oliver, but when I did, I felt guilty and looked away. It was like being in a trap. Michael noticed when I looked, and Oliver when I didn't.

Michael leaned in to me. "Good luck," he whispered, followed by a kiss on my neck. "I'm going to catch up with Garrett and Paige. Remind me to tell you what's going on." I watched Michael inform Oliver that it was nice to meet him. Likewise, Oliver responded.

I was told I looked well. And I replied, a bit defensively, that in fact I was well, lest there be any misunderstanding.

Henny and Adam came running toward me with Max following behind, his face covered in blood. I knew he was fine and that in fact none of my children were particularly worried, but this was a public nosebleed, so we wore masks of concern. At home, Max would've gone to get the *nose towel*, an old red terry rag, saved for injuries or the convergence of dry, cold temperatures and a certain nose-picking fixation.

"Excuse me." I ran to help Max, impersonating Carol Brady.

Several waiters offered cloth napkins while my children basked in the limelight. I made eye contact with Oliver's serious stare before following a woman in a maid's uniform (a maid's uniform!) to the guest cottage (the guest cottage!), where we freshened up.

Oliver startled me outside of the bungalow. "These must be your children."

"Who's that?" Henny asked.

"Guys, this is an old friend of mine. Oliver Bellows. Oliver, this is Adam, Henny, and Max."

"How's the nose, big guy?"

"It stopped," Max said, inserting his pointer finger. Henny pushed it away.

"It happens all the time, you know," Adam informed my old friend.

"Well, it was nice to see you," I said.

"And you."

I headed toward lunch, pretending I was ready for the exchange to be over.

"Kara," he called. I turned as the kids kept walking.

"I'm off to Paris and then back to London," he said. I nodded. I'm off to Paris, too. Or the pediatrician. Same difference.

"But I'll be back in the spring. Before MoMA opens," he said. "Should I call?"

I paused. I didn't want my hesitation to imply that I thought the invitation was meaningful. He just wanted me to see his work.

"So, you'll come?" he asked as he entered my information into his phone.

"Sure. Sounds wonderful." My voice was calm and confident, and not at all filled with excitement, or dread.

I found Michael and the others dining on butternut squash ravioli. They were engaged in a heated debate about Frank Lloyd Wright's original color choice for the Guggenheim exterior. I offered an informed opinion and leaned into Michael, listening and laughing at just the right times. I even chatted with a woman I'd never met. I helped the kids make intricate ice-cream sundaes, and spoke cleverly about a recent op-ed. And as the day wore on, I kept my secret. The flutter of excitement, all mine to enjoy.

30

1987

Exactly eight days have passed since Oliver asked me to leave, if you include that day, which of course I do, because starting my count on the first full day without him would only make it day seven, and even if it hasn't been an eternity, it's definitely been more than a week.

He isn't in the student union—no surprise, since he hasn't been there the other million times I checked—so I head to the library. Sitting outside halfway up on the cold steps, I'm almost content. Of course I am desperate to run into him, but I enjoy watching students come and go. The ones in groups are foreign to me, so I seize snippets of their conversations, hoping for a clue. I like this detachment. These *peers* are only a curiosity; not so long ago, they were my goal.

Next, I walk the three minutes to Ralph's. My plan is to enter purposefully and head for the bathroom, even though I don't need to go. This will allow me two things: the possibility of bumping into Oliver and a chance to apply lip gloss in front of a mirror. After I've achieved one of these goals, I walk to the subway. I tell myself maybe he's coming home from some downtown adventure, but I know I am grasping at straws. It doesn't really matter. I want to run into him and the subway seems like a possibility.

First one train, then another, but none of the passengers are Oliver. I buy a token, which makes me feel like I'm not a brokenhearted stalker, but rather a girl with a reason to be underground. I hold my head high, not out of pride but because it's the only way I can investigate each incoming commuter for Oliver's wavy hair, Oliver's eyes, Oliver's rescue from another night without him.

I give up and move to the scene of the crime. Grilled cheese is out of the question, because the mint tea I order barely stays down. I practice what I would say if he walked in right now. This has become one of my favorite ways to pass time. I'll casually ask what he's been up to. Make a joke, some coy version of *fancy meeting you here*. Or maybe a *do you come here often?* jab. After all, not so long ago, he sketched me here. It was the first time he made me feel more beautiful than I am.

I leave two messages for Eden. Seeing her would be fun; it usually is, but since Oliver sent me away, contacting her has become strategic. I hope my motive isn't obvious, I think as I dial her again. I hang up on her machine, remembering this might be the weekend she's visiting a friend at Oberlin.

I finally find relief in painting. This time, I am my own subject. I study my eyes in a hand mirror and reproduce the image on a tiny canvas. I learn that the top and bottom of my iris is hidden by my upper and lower lids—intercepting the circle of color. And my eyelashes stop being my eyelashes. Instead they are transformed into these wonderfully unpredictable arrangements of hair in varying depth and direction. Each pupil has a tiny white square of reflected light—placed in slightly different parts of my eye. It's a tedious sort of concentration, where time and longing disappear. After two days, I declare the painting complete and prop it against my window, pleased. But before I've cleaned the last brush, I call him.

"Hey, serious girl, where've you been?" This I don't expect. I have no pithy comeback for casual. A poignant moment of rejection is more what I'd had in mind. Possibly tears. But a friendly chat catches me off guard.

"I've been, um, well, I've been really busy."

"You coming over? Eden's back. She's making lasagna." I can hear her yelling, *Kara-Kara*, in the background.

"Um, I guess I could for a little while..." As if everything is normal.

"Bring beer," he says before hanging up. I sit on my bed, needing to review each word of the conversation. Eden's back. I guess she did go away. Still, I'm annoyed that she didn't call me first, but I figure holding a grudge isn't going to do any good. Next, I consider the beer. Not just the beer, but the direction: Bring beer. I'm not one for diagramming sentences, but I'm fairly certain *bring beer* qualifies as a command, which is really very nervy, I think. At least he wants me there. I'm still not clear how Eden's lasagna fits in. I consider searching my Jung textbook for the universal meaning of lasagna, but I don't want to overthink things. After all, I'm in a hurry.

I look in the mirror with excitement. I know his attitude is insulting, he didn't even bother to say goodbye before hanging up, but the sick thing is, I don't care. I want him even more now. I glance at my miniature self-portrait and feel a pang of guilt. *What are you looking at?* I silently scold.

I try to take my time. I don't want to appear desperate, so I purposely make each movement intentional. When the phone rings, I assume he's calling to remind me not to get light beer. I remember how he once complained about Eden drinking light beer. I allow the phone to ring a second time when it occurs to me that perhaps he's calling to apologize for hanging up so quickly. I don't want them to think I'm so annoyed that I'm not coming; they might make another plan.

"Hello," I say, worried I'm too late.

"Hi, Kara, it's Professor Benton, Mary Benton. I was hoping we could discuss a few things."

"Professor Benton, oh, I, I thought you were someone else. I'm, I'm just on my way out," I am in no condition to chat with Professor Benton.

"Oh, no, not now. Not over the phone. Let's set up a time to meet."

"Uh, yeah, sure," I say, dreading the idea.

"Does Thursday work for you?" she says, as if asking. "And Kara, bring *A Room of One's Own*." At the end of this conversation, I'm the one who doesn't say goodbye.

31

2007

I couldn't stop thinking about seeing Oliver at the Thatchers'. I'd replay our brief exchange and my face would burn when I remembered his eyes meeting mine. Interestingly, Michael couldn't keep his hands off me. We didn't speak about the encounter, but it was as if seeing Oliver ignited something in Michael as well. He explored my body with renewed fervor, fucking me with enthusiasm. His zeal was infectious. It was as if a balance had shifted and Michael's way of regaining equilibrium left my body raw in the morning. At the time, I assumed Oliver was the catalyst, and my guilt the accelerant. It didn't occur to me that Michael had a secret of his own to absolve.

So, my clandestine rendezvous took a backseat. I still wondered what meeting him would be like, but it was months from now. And he could change his mind. It had happened before. So the obsessive immediacy paled. Oliver was a fantasy, whereas Michael was available—in the next room, a phone call away, inside of me.

Morgan and I had plans to meet for a manicure, but I was going to cancel. I still had bills to pay and next week's schedule needed revamping. It was just as well, I figured. I wouldn't be good company anyway. Later, Michael, Henny, and I were meeting with Dr. Stockland to go over her evaluation. I'd gotten so used to Henny going to those appointments that I'd forgotten that at some point we'd actually learn the results.

Also, Willa was late. Her customer had been waiting for at least ten minutes and seemed to be getting tired of trying to keep her toddler entertained. "Can you call her again?" she asked.

I dialed Willa. "I'm not sure what's keeping her," I said, hanging up when it went right to voicemail.

"Maybe she's on the subway," the woman offered just as Willa came in.

"I'm so sorry." As usual, her movements were graceful as she placed her bag behind the counter and adjusted her smock, but I could tell she was excited about something. "How is everyone?" Willa asked.

I looked at the customer. "Fine..."

"Good, good."

"What's up?" I asked.

She paused and looked at me. "I just met a broker!" It took me a moment to understand what she was saying.

"Are you looking for a new apartment?" asked the customer. "Because my cousin's a broker."

"*That's* why you're late?" I said.

"Not me. We're moving the shop," Willa told the customer. "Expanding, actually." She glanced at me. "*Thinking* about it, I mean." Willa tousled the girl's hair. "Now, what are we doing today? Just a trim?"

The woman nodded. "How exciting. You're staying in the neighborhood, I assume."

"Nothing's been decided," I interrupted, feeling my face burn.

"True. Nothing's been decided. But yes, to answer your question, we'd never leave the neighborhood," said Willa. "It's our home."

"Did you actually *sign* with her?" I asked. Commercial Realtors were notorious for their underhanded deals. Michael had tons of contacts. If nothing else, it was foolish not to ask his opinion.

"Not yet. She seemed great, but I want to talk to Victoria. She knows everyone."

"Oh, well that's good," I said, hoping the customer wouldn't detect my snide tone.

"We'll talk," Willa said calmly. "Get some names from Michael too, if you want." I was about to tell her that of course we should speak to Michael, until I remembered I didn't even *want* to move. I shuffled my papers. I'd already been uneasy about Dr. Stockland, and now this. I had to get out of here. I called to Trudy, who hopped up. Suddenly, meeting Morgan seemed like an excellent plan.

We sat next to each other in hot pink pedicure chairs with vibrating capability (if we were so inclined, which we weren't). A piped-in version of *Pachelbel's Canon* might have succeeded in creating a luxurious mood if there hadn't been a gaggle of eleven-year-olds getting twenty-dollar manicures a few feet away. I searched the faces of the Korean women while they buffed the girls' nails. Which was worse, I wondered—polishing girls who fail to make eye contact, much less use words like *please* or *thank you*, or waiting in an empty shop for customers (and tips) to trickle in.

I considered telling Morgan about what just went down with Willa, but I didn't want to think about it. Actually, I didn't want to think about anything.

"Razor?" asked Morgan's pedicurist, shorthand for *Do you want me to shave your calluses so your heels feel as smooth as a baby's bottom?*

"Hell, yeah," answered Morgan. My pedicurist looked at me. I nodded a polite hell, yeah, as well.

"I just can't believe you never mentioned Oliver Bellows," Morgan said. I fought the urge to shift in my seat at the mention of his name, but instead I concentrated on the woman with the razor.

"It was a long time ago," I said.

"The Mesozoic Cretaceous period was a long time ago. You fucking Oliver Bellows was practically the day before yesterday."

"I don't think so," I whispered.

"You know what I mean."

"I just don't like thinking about that time, okay?"

"Oh sure, I understand," she said. "I don't like remembering my affair with George Clooney either." The two pedicurists looked at each other, and then at our toes.

"Well, for one thing, he wasn't *Oliver Bellows* back then. He was just... Oliver."

"Just...?" Morgan challenged.

"Well, he did always seem... bigger than everyone else." Except for Eden, I thought.

"Now you're talking." Morgan poked my arm.

I closed my eyes and inhaled through my nose. I wanted quiet. The giggling girls, chamber music that was so overplayed it was no longer beautiful, Willa, silent scorn from the woman massaging my legs... all of it. I wanted it to disappear. "Seriously, I just can't *chat* about this."

"Okay, fine. Your call. But might I just point out one thing?" Morgan asked, no longer smiling.

Go on, I nodded.

"I don't *chat*. Ever."

"Right," I said, getting annoyed.

"I'm serious. I figure, if you're worth talking to, I might as well be real," she said.

"Except when it comes to your husband." I regretted it the moment I said it. I braced myself for her anger, but I was wrong. She looked wounded.

"I deserve that," she said, looking down.

"Morgan, look, I shouldn't have..." I knew coming here was a bad idea.

"No, you're right. I'm lying to my husband." She leaned toward me. "Eric loves me and I can't get this asshole out of my system."

"It sounds awful," I said.

"It is. But then..." She hesitated. "... it isn't."

I wasn't sure I wanted to hear it.

"You know, as fucked up as this whole situation is, at least I feel— vibrant. I'm out there, living." She sat a bit taller in her seat. "I mean, I may be destroying my marriage, making a huge mistake, but I'm in the game. As imperfect as I am, I'd rather this than..." Again, she hesitated, as if she had almost said something she hadn't intended.

"What?" I asked.

"I'd rather be making a mistake than playing it safe all the time." She looked at her toes.

"Jesus, am I being paranoid, or is there something you'd like to say to me?" I asked.

"No, you're not being paranoid, and no, there's nothing I'd like to say."

I was stunned. "I guess the best defense is an offense." I took out my wallet. Now I had to get out of here, too.

She sighed. "Maybe so. Maybe I'm just rationalizing my sordid affair. But still, sometimes you're so private it seems—shut off, bordering on judgmental. I mean, you won't even tell me about your past fling with Oliver Bellows, much less anything more current or real."

"You think I'm *shut off*? That I *play it safe*?" I said, as if I had no idea what she meant.

"Look, I don't mean any of this. I'm fucking impulsive, right? Forget it. Who cares what I think?" But that was the problem. I cared. What she thought and what everyone else did too.

"Okay, you want me to speak up? Not hold back?" I spewed.

"Uh, yeah."

"I think you should end your affair." I paused. "Like, yesterday."

Morgan watched as the woman applied the trendy plum polish (aptly named Wicked) to her toes. "But how do you really feel?" she asked.

"I'm worried."

"Are you sure that's your main motivation?" Morgan raised an eyebrow.

"What? You think I'm jealous?" I asked.

She shrugged. "I don't know. You keep a lot in, Kara."

"See? You told me to be real, but the moment I tell you something you don't want to hear, you turn it into a criticism of me."

"You're right. You are," she said. "But it's still a valid question," she muttered.

"What's the question?" I asked.

"Is it that you want me to work things out with Eric, or is even the *idea* of someone leaving her husband too threatening?"

"Threatening to what?" I asked.

"You name it. To always doing what you're supposed to. To being a good girl. To all things predictable and the fucking status quo. I mean, there could be a ripple effect."

"A ripple effect?"

"Yeah."

"The ripple effect of divorce?" I sneered.

"Like cooties. Only worse."

"But I don't *want* to leave," I said, but it wasn't the whole truth. Over the years, even when Michael and I'd been at our best, it wasn't far away—curiosity about the other life. The one I might have had if I hadn't chosen him. And with those thoughts an unwelcome sensation—something like regret.

"Okay. Great. Good for you," she said. "I'm an asshole. It's my guilt talking." She inspected her toes. "Is there an opening for a bikini wax?" she asked her pedicurist.

"Wait. There is something I've been wondering," I said. Morgan settled back into her chair. "What did you really think of my mural?" I asked.

"Your mural?" She seemed genuinely surprised.

"I mean you complimented me, but it sounded like you were being polite."

She sighed. "I wasn't sure what to say." I braced myself. "I think you have real talent. I do. Absolute potential to be..." She hesitated. "Phenomenal." I smiled. "But you're just beginning. Finding your way."

"So you think I have a long way to go?" I asked.

"Don't do this. Don't give me so much power. I think your mural is beautiful. I do. I also think you're finding your way. Your style. Hell, maybe even your subject matter." Her eyes were serious and tender. I had to look away.

I'd ask for this. I knew she was right. I was a beginner. I concentrated on the woman painting my toes. Suddenly I detested the pale pink shade.

"You really have to keep that in check," said Morgan. "Making art is lonely. Believe me, I know. But you can't look to your audience for reassurance. It'll be your death. Or the death of your art, anyway."

"Yeah, yeah, yeah." I sounded like Adam.

"Look, take it or leave it. All I know is there are plenty of writers and painters and fucking tuba players out there who have made it only because they didn't give a shit what anyone thought." She looked almost angry. "They took themselves seriously. In fact, for the most part, I think that's what always makes the difference between the successful and everyone else. It's the ultimate deal-breaker."

"Believing in yourself?" I asked. She nodded. "What about talent? Talent's necessary, no?"

"Yes, talent. Of course talent. But there are plenty of talented tuba players who quit because they didn't believe in themselves."

"Now that's a damned shame." I said.

"Right?"

"But you're my friend; can't I look to my friends for validation? I mean, there's a difference between a friend . . . and my *audience*."

"Yeah, well, as soon as I looked at that fairy, I turned into your audience. Sorry. I don't make the rules. Now, if you'll excuse me, my bikini needs some Brazilian tending to." She carefully stepped down from the pedicure station and followed a technician into the wax room.

I sat there, spinning. In theory, I knew she was right. Artists need to take themselves seriously, not rely on others for validation. It was the same thing Oliver had said all those years ago—real artists believe in themselves. Which left me with the gnawing suspicion that I might not have what it takes.

Michael and I sat on Dr. Stockland's cocoa corduroy couch and listened as he explained dyslexia to Henny. He'd just given Michael and me the detailed results of the evaluation, and now he was helping us talk to Henny. I stared at his patch of flyaway curls that went from ear to ear on his otherwise bald head. On the table next to him sat a jade plant, its plump leaves coated in dust; nourished, but

imperfect. Even though I was intent on his every word, I kept peeking at his surroundings. Despite the lax housekeeping, his office was
peaceful. A teak desk stood off to the side; on it were two pencil jars,
both covered in faded collage. Probably treasured Father's Day gifts
from long ago, but I couldn't be certain.

"That's why I can't read?" Henny asked, breaking the silence.

"Well, here's how I think of it," Dr. Stockland started. "The
reason you're having trouble learning to read is because your brain
understands the letters differently than the way most other people
do. And those terms—dys-lex-ia and attention deficit disorder—are
just a fancy way of explaining that." Henny sat still and let his words
sink in. I suppose that's what Michael and I were doing as well.

"So dyslexia is more than just switching letters around, like..."
Michael paused as if trying to come up with an example.

"Dog and God," the doctor interrupted. "I love that one." Michael
and I smiled awkwardly. So far, we didn't love anything about this
new world.

"But what does it mean for her future?" I asked, glancing at Henny.
I didn't want her to see how concerned I was, but I needed answers.

"If you mean, will she learn to read, the answer is, yes, she will."

There was a collective sigh of relief.

"I will?" I looked at Henny on the couch. Tears filled her beautiful blue eyes. I was flooded with memories. Her lost library book,
arguments over homework, my rage when she wanted to skip violin...I felt deeply ashamed. I was supposed to be better than my
mother. Selfless. Attuned. Patient. Henny's pain took my breath
away. And with it, a familiar jolt of humiliating failure.

"Yes. You will," Dr. Stockland answered.

Henny looked down, shielding her face with her hair. Sunlight
found its way through a gritty window and landed on her. I wanted
to comfort her, but I stayed where I was.

"But I haven't," she said.

"You will," Dr. Stockland countered. "There are all sorts of strategies for teaching kids with dyslexia and ADD."

"It's because..." Henny started.

"We'll get you the best tutor out there," Michael said.

"We will," I added.

"It's because..." Henny tried again.

"You can give us referrals, yes?" Michael asked. Dr. Stockland raised his hand, stopping us from interrupting. He was right; we needed to listen to Henny.

"It's because...I'm dumb," she said, turning red.

"No, Henny," I said.

"Sweetheart," Michael whispered. Henny started to cry.

"Actually, these results show the exact opposite. In fact, you're quite smart."

"No! You're just trying to make me feel good. I can't read and I'm in second grade, and, and..." She wiped her eyes with the back of her hand. "I'm dumb. I know it." Henny lowered her head. Her shoulders shook as she sobbed.

This time I moved to her. I wanted to stroke her face, wipe away her tears, but when I tried to push her hair to the side she pulled away.

"Even Max can read some, and he's a baby."

"Oh, honey," I said.

"Henny Lawson, you are not dumb," Dr. Stockland said sternly. This got her attention. She looked at him. "In fact, in some areas, you tested way above your age."

"I did?"

"You did. Your vocabulary is that of a sixth grader and you're way above average in your ability to make sense of the information you hear. And your imagination...your ability to describe the things you think and feel...you're off the charts."

"That doesn't surprise me," Michael said. "She's a dynamo." I knew it was breaking his heart to watch Henny so sad. I loved him for trying to add some levity.

"In fact, it's because there's *such* a discrepancy in Henny's cognitive strengths and deficits that a learning disability is presumed."

I knew it was irrational, but the term *learning disability* bothered me the most. Somehow, dyslexia and attention deficit disorder sounded manageable, distinctive even. But learning disabled was

different. To me, it made her sound seriously impaired. Handi-
capped. I thought of the little girl from Little Scissors—Carly, the
one in the wheelchair. I looked at Michael as if he could magically
read my mind.

"Still, even if reading and concentrating are tricky," Dr. Stockland said to Henny, "it doesn't mean you're dumb or you can't do it.
It just means those things may take you longer."

Again, we sat in silence.

"Did either of you have trouble in school?" asked the doctor.
Michael shook his head no. "Because there's often a genetic link."

"Some," I answered. They looked at me. "I don't remember if I
had trouble learning to read, but I do know I didn't always understand what I was reading."

A memory came to me. I must've been ten or eleven. "One time..."
I started. "I had to take one of those standardized tests, and I remember needing to reread every sentence. No matter how hard I tried to
understand those boring passages, I was lost. Other kids were handing in their booklets, and I wasn't even close to being done. Each
story was just a bunch of jumbled words on the page." My ears were
burning as I spoke, but Henny was riveted.

"When it came time to answer the questions, I had no idea which
one was right. It was a terrible feeling." I looked at Henny and the
men. "So, do you know what I did?"

Dr. Stockland and Michael shook their heads no. "You guessed,"
answered Henny.

"I guessed." We smiled at each other. "Each and every question. I
just looked at the choices and guessed. Because you know what was
more important to me than not knowing the answers?" Both men
glanced at Henny, but this time she didn't know.

"What was most important was...that no one find out." All these
years later, I could still picture the kids in my class and how I pretended I was proud to hand in that booklet. I'd told everyone the
test was easy.

I didn't like thinking about that time, much less speaking about
it. But, for Henny...for Henny, it was worth it.

"What about your mommy?" Henny asked. "Did she yell at you a lot?" Guilt knocked the wind out of me.

"Mommy's not going to get mad at you anymore," said Michael.

I tried not to get defensive. I did. "And Daddy's going to help with homework once in a while, because he's so much more patient than Mommy." Yeah, right.

"How did your mother handle your struggles?" Dr. Stockland asked, redirecting the focus.

"Mommy's mommy drank too much," Henny informed him. I guess the evaluation was accurate; my daughter comprehended things beyond her years.

"She wasn't so involved," I said. I didn't like to talk about this, either.

"Do you think it's possible she had her own learning issues?" he asked.

Did she? "I'm not sure."

"You know, until fairly recently, learning disabilities were misunderstood. And girls especially fell through the cracks."

"Why's that?" asked Michael. I looked at my watch.

"For one thing, they're not typically hyperactive, which makes them less impulsive. Adults notice misbehavior. It's the kids who make waves that get identified—and are more likely to get treated."

"It's true," I said softly. "No one noticed how lost I was." So please, Henny, don't hate me.

With just a few minutes left of the session, Dr. Stockland asked Henny to wait in the waiting room so the grown-ups could speak alone. He gave us a referral for a tutor who specialized in dyslexia. "But there's something else I should mention." The doctor paused. "Medication. There are medicines out there that can improve focus and one's ability to process information."

"Medication?" Michael exclaimed. "She's seven years old!" Looking back, I don't know why we were so surprised by this. Many New Yorkers, including kids, were on one thing or another. Still, I never thought of it in regards to our family.

Dr. Stockland wrote the name of a child psychiatrist on the

back of his business card. "You're sure this isn't a bit extreme?" said Michael.

"Treating perceptual and focusing deficits with medicine can be very helpful," said the doctor. Michael shook his hand, but I knew he was dubious.

Henny was looking at a magazine. "What's this?" she asked, pointing to a model.

"A tattoo," I answered. Michael grabbed his raincoat from the closet; the hangers clanged.

"All over her feet?"

"It's a special kind. A henna tattoo."

"A Henny tattoo?!" my girl asked excitedly.

"Not Henny." I rubbed her head. "Henna. It's a dye used on top of the skin, it's not injected."

"Injected?"

"Like a shot," I explained. "Henna tattoos don't last forever like real ones do."

"Cool." She stayed seated. I wondered if this new world of henna tattoos lessened the intensity of her diagnosis. "Can I get one?" she asked.

Michael wanted to go. I felt impatient as well, but maybe she needed a minute. Perhaps it took her longer to move from one thing to the next. I signaled for him to relax.

"I don't know. Kids don't usually get tattoos."

"But you just said they don't last forever."

"It's true. I did." I sighed. "I wouldn't even know where to go." Maybe there was a place in the East Village, but would they do kids? In that moment, I'd have gotten her anything.

"You should do them at Little Scissors," said Henny.

Michael looked up from his BlackBerry. "You should."

"Hmm. We could call them Henny tattoos," I said. My daughter beamed.

As we waited for the elevator I asked Henny what she thought of the session. She shrugged.

"We knew you were smart," said Michael. "This proves it. Just because you're having trouble doesn't mean you won't learn."

"You get that, right?" I asked her. She nodded. "Because we know you're a capable, delicious, smart girl. And—and we only want you to feel good about yourself."

"Do you have any questions?" Michael asked. "Because that was a lot to take in."

"Yes!"

I readied myself. Go on, we both nodded.

"Can I get a Henny tattoo?"

32

1981

I stand in my neighbor's upstairs bathroom and look out the window. There's a blue hue coming from my mother's room. Other than that, our house is dark. "Whatcha lookin' at?" Laura asks. She's four, aware of my every move.

"The sky," I tell her.

"Sky," repeats Harry. "Sky, sky, sky." Holding on to the tub, he pulls himself up. Laura offers her brother a boat, which he promptly throws at her.

"Make nice, Harry," I tell him.

"Nice, Harry." He has the biggest brown eyes I've ever seen, and though I try not to, I laugh.

"Don't laugh at him," Laura scolds. She hands him another boat, which he throws at her again.

"Make nice," she bosses.

"Nice!" he yells. He takes the boat from Laura and flings it in her direction. Finally he tires of this game, plops down by the tub, and sucks on a soapy washcloth.

"Does your mom let him do that?" I ask. Laura ignores the question and dunks her head under the water.

"How many minutes was that?" she asks when she comes up.

"At least ten," I tell her.

"Did you see the bubbles?"

"Couldn't miss them."

Harry falls asleep in his crib and Laura and I settle in and read

Put Me in the Zoo and *Are You My Mother?* As usual, we skip the page where the mother bird unknowingly wanders past her baby. "That could never happen," Laura tells me.

"Not in a million years."

When she, too, is asleep, I sneak into their parents' room. I know this is wrong, but I want to see what a real couple's bedroom looks like. Though their bed is made, it still looks sloppy. Makeup is neatly organized on the bathroom counter. I steal a squirt of lotion that promises to diminish my cuticles. Until then, I hadn't realized this was something I should be keeping track of. The red sandals are the coolest in her closet. I count the man's wingtips: two pairs of brown and three black. Sneakers, too—old ones and a new pair.

Downstairs, I stand at the open refrigerator and swallow two large spoonfuls of rice with raisins and soggy nuts that remind me of bettles. Next, the leftover chicken. I try to get the tinfoil just right so they won't notice. They always tell me I can have whatever I find, but I'm sure they don't expect me to eat this much. For dessert, I eat clumps of butter with brown sugar mixed in and other equally disgusting concoctions.

Every few minutes, I look out their kitchen window. Her room is still flickering, blue. Thankfully, mine is in the front of the house where they could never watch me. From my mother's room, I once saw the father's naked chest when he stepped out of the shower. He didn't know I was watching. He kept moving about the bathroom, talking to his wife who must've been in the other room. I was glad I couldn't see more than his chest, but I kept looking anyway, just in case.

Their phone rings. "When are they coming home?" my mother asks.

"I told you, around eleven." I can hear her smoking. "I probably shouldn't tie up the line."

"How are the kids?" she asks quickly.

"Fine." I don't want to talk. I'm working on a new collage. Random shapes cut from old magazines. This one's in shades of red. I like it better than the yellow and green ones at home.

"You okay?" I know I sound impatient.

"Of course I am, Kara Mascara." And she hangs up. Eleven o'clock comes and goes; I start to pace. I've already folded the afghan and packed up my things. All evidence has been wiped away from the kitchen. I go upstairs again. The kids are sound asleep. I intentionally leave Laura's books on her nightstand as proof I'm a good babysitter.

I hope my mother doesn't know I'm late; she hates when plans change. I keep checking her window; it looks the same. After Carson's monologue, I dial our number, but then I hear their garage door open so I quickly hang up before she answers. I hope I didn't wake her, mostly because she'll call back.

It takes them forever to pay me. I try not to act desperate to get home, but by the time they finally say good night, I practically bolt out the door. Before I'm even halfway up the stairs, I know something is wrong. As I get closer to her room, I hear the shower running. I think many things at once. Now I'll have to talk to her. If she was in the shower when I called, she should be out by now. But if my call woke her, she'd have called back *before* taking a shower. I am tired. Nothing is making sense.

When I see her, I think she's dead. The shower door is completely shattered and her naked body is covered in blood and shards of glass. Holy fucking shit, holy fucking shit, I say. Or maybe I just think it. For a moment, I can't move. I am only able to look at her.

Holy fucking shit. Holy fucking shit. I have to step over her to turn off the water. It's a strange choice, but if my mother is dead, I need quiet.

She moves. Honey, I think she says.

While I wait for the ambulance I sit next to her on the bathroom floor and concentrate on the puddle of blood that is settling in the grout. This will really piss her off. That—and the new bottle of Prell that's now all over the floor. I turn it upright. Even with the thick wet air and fresh floral scent, I can smell the Dewar's. Her broken bottle is mixed in with the shower stall glass. There's no way I can get to it before the ambulance arrives.

I grab a towel from above and drape it over her cut-up body. I don't want them to see her this bare. "You're okay," I whisper. "You're okay," I tell her again, blotting a deep gash on her cheek. And for however long it takes until walkie-talkies and loud footsteps parade up our stairs, I carefully pick glass out of my mother's rich red hair.

33

2007

Morgan and I walked the reservoir as dry leaves and dirt swirled around us like little tornadoes. Wind whipped our faces as I told her about Henny's evaluation. Every few minutes we had to shield our eyes from dusty debris. "This is intense," I said, referring to the cold. "Should we bail?"

"One more loop."

"Anyway...we're going to start with the tutor and take it from there," I explained.

"So, no meds?"

"No meds. At least not for now. Michael wants to try the tutor first," I said, hoping she wouldn't detect that Michael and I weren't in total agreement. "She's supposed to be excellent."

"What does the school think?" asked Morgan.

"Nothing yet. They're reviewing the evaluation."

"But in the meantime, tutor."

"Right."

"And how's mighty Liza taking all this?" Morgan asked.

"We're not really talking about it," I said. "Though she did mention she doesn't see the point in labels."

Morgan nodded.

"Whatever." I shrugged.

"Speaking of bullshit, Eric's lobbying for couples counseling. He thinks we have *unresolved issues*."

"You do have unresolved issues."

"I know."

We walked for a few minutes in silence. I surrendered to the wind. Somehow it seemed fitting; this too, I couldn't ease. "You ever marvel at how important all this stuff is?" I asked.

"This stuff?"

"All these decisions. Life. Suddenly everything feels very grown-up."

"I don't feel grown-up," Morgan said.

"That's what I mean! You'd think I'd be used to it by now. Husband. Three kids. Businesses. Partners. Mortgages. Homes. It's all so...substantial. Very high-stakes, grown-up decisions."

Morgan rubbed her hands together and blew warm air into her cupped palms.

"I mean, people are affected," I continued. Willa flashed in my mind. She'd actually called Michael to ask if he knew anything about the broker Victoria had recommended. He'd said she was reputable. While they were speaking I'd worried that now he'd want to be included in discussions about a potential move; but when they hung up, he'd surprised me by not pursuing it.

"It's true," Morgan said. "These are no-shit decisions."

I dug my hands in my pockets. "It's brutal out here."

"Terrible," Morgan agreed, walking faster.

"Sometimes I fantasize about bailing on everything, and just painting or something," I said.

"Tell me about it," she muttered.

I was reminded of Eden. Years ago we'd had a similar conversation. I surprised myself by having a brief fantasy that Eden and I were still friends who met whenever our feelings or schedules permitted.

"That's one thing about this guy," said Morgan. "He's an excellent distraction."

"Yeah, well, sometimes distractions become decisions," I said. She nodded, but I had the feeling she wasn't really listening.

"Do me a favor; shoot me if Eric and I become one of those couples who always have to process everything. I don't want my marriage to be a lot of...work." I nodded, but the truth was, Michael and I had been lucky. Our problems had somehow always sorted themselves out. Then Oliver's MoMA show came to mind (would he remember to call?) and I felt a thrill in my belly.

Morgan stopped. "I can't take it anymore! I surrender." For a second I thought she was referring to her marriage. "I mean, enough already; it's too fucking cold!"

Of course, the cold.

"Let's get out of here." She looked at her watch. "I think we have time for a drink."

A few days later, I waited in the schoolyard as Miss Nathanson dismissed Henny's class. Adam and Max wanted to get home. It was Halloween and there were pumpkins to carve before trick-or-treating. "Mrs. Lawson," bellowed Henny's teacher.

"Kara," I urged. Whenever she called me Mrs. Lawson I thought she was about to give bad news.

"Kara," she corrected. "Has Henny started to work with the tutor?"

"Next week," I answered.

"Good. I'm available to talk. Tell her what we're doing in class," she said quietly. Henny was digging in my bag for her Halloween costume. They weren't allowed to wear them to school, so now the yard was filling up with princesses and vampires.

"There is something I think we should keep a lookout for." Miss Nathanson leaned in so Henny couldn't hear. "I'm concerned about Henny's social life."

"What's going on?"

"Maybe nothing, but I noticed she's frequently alone at lunch." Alone at lunch. The image was intolerable. Where were her friends? Her best friend from last year moved to Westchester; but there were others, weren't there? I must remember to talk to Liza about this. Maybe there'd been playdates I hadn't known about. Was it possible she hadn't had any this year?

"And a lot of the girls were all talking about a Halloween party. I don't think Henny was invited," she whispered.

"Whose?"

"Charlotte Leeds." I looked around the yard. Charlotte's mother was talking to a group of women. I berated myself for not making more of an effort. Like my daughter, I seemed to have put all my eggs in one basket; lately Morgan had more than satisfied my friend need.

"Let's both keep an eye out," suggested Miss Nathanson.

"Okay." I smiled. "Sounds like a plan."

Henny didn't bring up Charlotte's party. In fact, she seemed happy to go trick-or-treating with her brothers. No to mention, many of the kids from our building tended to stick together. But I was getting irritated by everyone's behavior. None of the children seemed grateful. They just tossed in each acquisition with barely an acknowledgment, their eyes already on the next apartment, and the one after that.

"What do you say?" I prompted my brood.

"Thank you," they answered in harmonic monotone, with all the sincerity of a call girl at quitting time. I kept comparing Henny to the other girls. While she didn't have a BFF, she didn't look like an outcast either. Helping her navigate friendships could be something we'd work on. I didn't need to turn it into a crisis. Being alone at lunch didn't necessarily predict a life of isolation. I vowed to help her. I could—I wasn't my mother.

I started to relax, until I noticed how uncomfortable Liza seemed. I assumed the candy and kids' boorishness were wearing on her. I know they were wearing on me. I missed Michael. This morning he said he'd do his best to get out early. I checked my watch. I guess he wasn't able.

Little Scissors had been busy too; Victoria's daughter, Leah, had invited a bunch of other ten-year-olds to get their hair teased and glittered for their witch costumes... but I'd still been able to make it home.

On the thirty-second floor, Max's pillowcase got caught on a fairy princess's wand. The little girl let out an ear-piercing shriek. Sweaty witches, rock stars, and firemen froze. With a quick jerk of her royal wrist, the wand and Max's stash flew down the corridor as if a piñata had exploded. All at once, the sugar-stoned masses descended on his stockpile.

Adam and Henny sprang into action. With fast fingers and postures resembling the Secret Service, my children came to their brother's rescue. I stood to the side, proud that my kids were watching out for each other. Liza looked miserable. I tried to dismiss her forlorn frown, but I kept wondering if it was directed at me.

I couldn't take the noise any longer, so with several floors left I coaxed the kids out of the building by telling them Trudy deserved a Halloween walk. We headed to East 81st Street. Elegant town houses were decorated with bloody ghosts and intricate cotton spiderwebs. This is more like it, I thought, enjoying the relief of the cool night air. I hated trick-or-treating in a high-rise—Halloween was one of the few things I preferred outside of the city.

Liza and I stood on the sidewalk while the evening turned into night. We chatted with passing parents. At one point I saw my kids admiring an intricately carved jack-o'-lantern while the flickering fire cast shadows on them. I felt a surge of lucky. And then Michael rang. "Where are you guys?" he asked.

"Eighty-first Street. We're almost done." It was a lie; we still had at least half a block, but there was a part of me that wanted him to feel that he'd missed out.

"I'll be right there."

Even Trudy got a second wind when she saw him. She wagged and waited patiently. "Feel how heavy my bag is," yelled Henny.

"That's nothing, feel mine," pushed Adam.

"Mine too! Mine too!" Max jumped up and down, then stopped suddenly. "Here, Daddy. Carry it."

Michael kissed me and took Trudy's leash. A quick hello to Liza and they were off. All was forgiven as I watched my strong and sturdy husband lead them onward. Liza and I followed close behind.

*   *   *

"I'll give you three Bit-O-Honey for one Snickers," Adam said to Henny.

"No way!"

"What about you?" he asked Max. "Do you want three of my candies for just one of yours?"

"Do I?" Max asked Henny.

"Don't ask her. She doesn't know anything. Think for yourself, three of mine for one of yours. Three for one," Adam repeated, while Henny silently shook her head no.

"Adam..." I warned.

"What?"

"Vampires should be nice to Thomas Trains."

"How many can we eat tonight?" asked Max.

"Five," I answered as Liza said, "You've had enough." We looked at each other. They'd had a lot, but I didn't care. What was the point of Halloween if you didn't go to sleep with a cavity?

"They barely touched dinner," Liza explained. I didn't care how much dinner they had or hadn't touched, and the kids sensed it. I stalled, hoping Liza would acquiesce. My perceptive cretins waited for the verdict. Liza was silent.

"Eggs first," I said, blessed with a moment of diplomatic brilliance. When they started to complain, I raised a traffic cop hand. "If you're hungry, have eggs first... then you may have a few pieces for dessert."

"How many is a few again?" Max asked Henny.

"Depends on who you ask," said Liza, taking out a loud pan.

I looked at her, hoping for connection; but she kept to the task at hand—cracking eggs and turning bread into toast. "I'll deal with the eggs," I said. "Why don't you just switch the laundry and call it a night?"

It was an hour before her shift was over. By letting her leave I was agreeing to fold a pile of kids' clothes and do whatever was necessary to get three Halloween heads to bed. I could hear Michael on the phone in his office; evidently his workday was not yet over. As if I'd change my mind, Liza scurried to freedom while I pushed the toaster again. "Let's see if you guys can get in pajamas before the eggs are done," I challenged.

"I don't want to."

"In a minute."

"Help me."

"Let me rephrase that. Get your pajamas on or the candy's mine!" They ran to their rooms.

"That's what I'm talking about," I said to Trudy, feeling exhausted, experienced, and, quite possibly, like a good enough mother.

34

1987

I sit in a vestibule outside of Professor Benton's office and stare at her books. Famous authors I haven't read line the shelves floor to ceiling, transforming this hallway into a makeshift waiting area. A narrow bench positions my face in front of the dusty book spines, a perfect holding cell for my prison of self-doubt. Brontë, Mailer, Hemingway convince me that I'm in deep trouble. I can't imagine what I could possibly say to explain why I haven't handed in my paper on Woolf. The deadline came and went, and though I planned on getting it done, I haven't even really started.

I didn't realize the extent of my angst until now. I wipe my palms on my jeans and hope she won't want to shake my hand. I squint at the mountain of books, making the titles disappear; only the muted shades of color remain. I am considering how I would capture this vision on canvas when Benton's door opens. Thinking it's the professor, I stand, but it's just another student about to leave. As if she cannot get enough, the girl pauses at the door and says something I can't hear. I am busy focusing on what an idiot I must look like standing in the cramped space when I should still be sitting. I can tell from the tone of their voices that theirs is a friendly chat.

I want to get out of here. The girl meets my eye, which is irritating because she is smiling and carefree and probably very smart, and I am trying to figure out if Benton will notice my sweaty palms in the event that the ever-accessible professor offers hers in my direction. I wonder if she resents having to teach students like me. I should have stayed at Cleveland Community College, I think, but quickly reject the notion. Even though I feel unworthy, I already know that while I may not belong *here*, New York is in my marrow. I lean against Lessing or George Eliot or some other legitimate woman, so the girl can pass.

"Kara, come in," Benton says warmly. I am surprised by how petite she is. In class, her voice conveys authority, but standing next to her, she seems soft and sincere. Her brown hair is cut close to her head. Flecks of gray flicker through, reminding me that I'm about to meet with a wise woman. Benton leads me into her inner sanctum and points to a chair. She is ready to relate.

"How are you, Kara?"

"I'm fine," I say, which is a bald-faced lie, because my head is light and my paper is late. I shift in my seat and try to think of something to say, but since nothing comes to me, I sit. And wait. And try not to look at the Georgia O'Keeffe flower on the wall above the professor.

"Really, Kara? Are you sure? Because, frankly, I feel like I'm losing you in class. You started out the semester engaged, and now you feel very far away."

"Really? Far away? No. Really?"

"Really," she says, not looking away.

"Well, I guess I'm not such a fan of Woolf," I attempt.

"Not everyone is," she says with a sigh. "Still, you don't have to love her to have something to contribute." I nod as if I agree, and hope that she doesn't ask me to contribute something right this very moment.

"Because you know, Kara, saying nothing is not the same as having nothing to say." I look at Ms. Benton and wonder how often she tells students this. Every semester? Once a year? I suspect she is usually right, though in my case, both are true.

"So if not Woolf, who are you a fan of?"

"Um, well, maybe I should give *A Room of One's Own* another try," I say. "I've been under the weather," which suddenly seems true because I feel like I'm getting sick.

"You don't have to make excuses, Kara. Let's forget about your paper for a moment, okay?"

"Okay," I say tentatively.

"So humor me. Consider my question. What *are* you a fan of? What do you care about?" she asks again.

How can I tell her Oliver? Only Oliver. I can't. I'm sure the girl who just left cares about all sorts of things, probably has some fascinating passion. In fact, she reeks of it. I have a terrifying thought that Ms. Benton must be beyond bored by me and this whole pathetic conversation. I look at my watch. She looks at me.

And then, maybe because the O'Keeffe print reminds me of art, and art reminds me of Oliver, or maybe because I'm tired of hiding, or maybe it's that O'Keeffe's floral vaginas actually inspire me, whatever the reason—I tell her the truth. My truth. "I don't know what I care about. Not a clue, actually. Except for this guy named Oliver. I know that's not what I'm supposed to say. Not what you want to hear, but it's true. All I care about is Oliver. Pathetic, but true."

I hear a clock ticking and some voices down the hall. A soft silence fills the office, but I'm not afraid. For the first time, maybe ever, I don't feel the need to fill it. It is my turn to wait.

"Truth is always a good place to start, Kara," Benton says softly. I'm not even annoyed by her platitude. "Plus, you do know, feminism isn't anti-love."

"Not this kind. This love furthers no feminist cause." *Oh?* her eyes ask. "Trust me, there is nothing empowering about this kind of love."

"Passion can empower, no?"

"Oh, there's plenty of passion." I giggle. I'm not yet comfortable talking to grown-ups about stuff like this. But I want her to know. "Oh sure, plenty of passion. I'm passionate about him, and he's passionate about his art."

"Ah yes, that imbalance is intolerable. And unrequited love is a concentration killer," Benton says, as if I'm making sense. "But you know, some of the greatest male artists had lovers who were talented in their own right. Does that resonate for you, Kara?"

I think of the tulips. They're nothing like O'Keeffe's flowers, but maybe they aren't as trite as I'd thought, either. "I don't know," I answer quietly. I don't dare speak my dreams aloud.

"Perhaps that's what you love about this Oliver, his sense of enti-tlement."

"Entitlement?"

"The allure of entitlement is very sexy. People who make no apology for their passion can be quite compelling," she says. I don't bother to convey agreement. Nodding or words will not do justice to this bull's-eye feeling coursing through my veins.

"You don't even know me," I say softly. It's like I want to kill her off before I make a fool of myself by believing. Some people just have it. But not me. Not necessarily *me*.

"It's true, I don't really know you," she says. "But that doesn't make me wrong, does it?"

I shrug, looking petulant; I am unable to stop slouching into the wooden chair. I hate O'Keeffe's ridiculous flowers with their soft folds. We sit. Many minutes pass. I start to feel angry, and also exhausted. I wanted to talk about the paper, or be reprimanded. This is so much worse.

"O'Keeffe loved an artist, you know. The photographer Stieglitz," she tells me, gesturing vaguely above her head. I don't tell her what I think of the print. "Perhaps a paper about those two would be time better spent for you?" she suggests. "I think Virginia would agree."

I can tell she's trying to offer me something. Something I didn't ask for. Something I don't even want. How dare she try to give me hope?

35

2007

Liza and I sat at the kitchen table, the large calendar between us. "So the white frosting and gumdrops go to Max's class on Thursday?" she asked.

"Yes." I checked the memo again. "No, wait. They're gummy bears and they go to Henny's class."

"Right. Gummy bears. I knew that."

"To Henny's class," I repeated. Liza erased Max and wrote Henny on her list. "Got it."

I glanced toward the sink. "Oh no. Please tell me you didn't throw out the milk carton?"

"No. It's in the recycling?"

"Crushed?" I asked.

"Yeah."

"No problem. Save the next one. Henny needs it. They're making gingerbread houses, thus the frosting." I was pretty sure I'd mentioned this before.

"Oh. Sorry."

"Which leads to the next problem. She is going to freak when she finds out I can't be there." The shop was crazy busy. There was no way.

"Do you want me to go?" Liza asked.

"Maybe. Michael's supposed to let me know if he can make it." I perused my list, checking off the vanilla frosting. "What else? Oh, Max needs a red sweatshirt for the winter wonderland show. Gap only has the ones with logos, so check Children's Place. If they don't have any, get the one at the Gap and we'll turn it inside out."

Liza added this to her list. "You said something about wrapping presents?" she reminded me.

I exhaled. "Right. That." I envisioned Liza wrapping the loot that we'd been collecting for months. "It's a thankless job," I warned. Liza shrugged. "We went a bit overboard," I added.

"I'm used to it," she said.

Ouch. I looked at my list. "All right. That's great. A big help. The paper's in the hall closet." Liza nodded. "Thank you," I said.

We needed tape. I put it on my list of things to bring home from the shop. "Can you put the presents in a black garbage bag and throw them in my closet?"

"Sure."

"Please," I added. "Let's see, I've already gotten the teachers' gifts..." Translation—*See? I'm not making you do everything.* But then I realized I'd forgotten to bring home the mug Henny had made for Rosie, her tutor. And she'd worked so hard on it, too. But adding more to Liza's load...

"I forgot to bring home the mug for Rosie."

"I can stop by the store on my way to pick up," Liza suggested.

"Do you mind?" Thank God.

"I can do it."

"Thank you! Remind me to give you some tape." She nodded. I hated needing her. I tried to figure out another way to get the mug to Rosie, but every scenario involved me leaving Little Scissors. I moved to the next item. "Where are the envelopes?" I asked myself.

"The envelopes?"

"Money to go toward the teachers' gifts."

"I thought that's what the mugs were for."

"Those are the *personal* gifts. This is for the *class* gift. It's all very complicated," I teased, hoping to minimize the absurdity. I'll bet Morgan didn't put up with this shit. Then again, one kid was not three.

I rummaged through my papers and found the envelopes I'd

prepared. "Can you put these in the backpacks?" I handed them to Liza. "Wait. Did I write the class parent's name on them?"

"Only on Adam's." She handed Henny's back.

"Freudian slip. Charlotte Leeds's mother is the class parent. What the hell is her name?"

"The thin one with the hair?" Liza asked.

"No. The thin one with the teeth."

"Candace?" she asked.

"Kelly!" I wrote it in angry script and handed it to Liza. "Pants. Damn. Adam needs nice khakis," I said, consulting my notes.

"For Kent?"

"No. We're not doing anything fancy over the break. For the winter dance assembly."

"What about the ones from Florida?" Liza suggested.

"Grass stains." And my father-in-law had thought I'd overreacted. "When you get Max's sweatshirt, pick up khakis in a ten and twelve. But keep the receipt." I looked at her. This was the sort of thing that she often screwed up, but saying *keep the receipt* again seemed patronizing.

"They have a great return policy," I said nonchalantly. "It's so convenient. I mean, as long as you have the receipt." Liza nodded.

"He has to try them on this afternoon because they're going to need to be shortened." Again, she nodded. "Like before he goes on the computer." I knew I was being controlling, but I couldn't stop myself.

"By any chance, do you know how to pin them?" I asked.

"Pin them?"

"Forget it." I reviewed other options. Tonight was Michael's holiday party, so tomorrow night was the first chance I'd be able to do it. The tailor might not have enough time to get them done. "I know, leave the ones with the grass stains on the counter. He can use them as a guide."

Liza wrote this down while I scanned my pages. Michael and I still had to figure out the bonuses for his employees and the doormen. Thankfully, Willa and I'd already done Little Scissors. I flipped through the envelopes for the guys at the garage. I'd have time to deliver them on my way to the shop.

I still had to get a gift for Liza. With all the extra work she'd been doing, two weeks' pay and two weeks' vacation didn't feel like enough. I smiled at her and added L. to my list.

"What am I forgetting?" I said aloud; she waited. "The violin teacher!"

"Henny brought her a mug last week," Liza said.

"Did she? I have no memory of this." I flipped through my pages. Liza nodded. "You remember..." I didn't. *Canvases to CT* jumped out from my list. I underlined it.

"It rained that day..." Liza seemed like she couldn't believe I could be so dense.

"Oh yeah! Right," I lied. "I feel like I'm losing my mind." I couldn't wait for these next two weeks to be over so we could unwind in Kent. I was thinking it might be nice to try painting a landscape and I'd always loved the tree in our front yard. I pictured Michael reading by the fire while I painted. Maybe I'd get the kids some new DVDs.

"Oh my God. The chimney guy. I've got to call the chimney guy."

"Text me if there's anything else." Liza gathered her things.

What the hell was his name? I wasn't sure if I had the number. I scanned my phone contacts. "Thanks, Liza!" I hollered, but she was already gone. I hope she's okay, I thought, while waiting for Chuck's Chimney to pick up.

I locked the door behind the last customer. Willa and the others had already left and in a few hours we'd be in Kent. I watched soft snow come down and savored the solitude. The Upper East Side was already deserted. All the cabs had their vacant lights illuminated; it was time to get out of town. I looked around the shop. The next time I'd be here it would be 2008. Willa had said that after the holidays she wanted me to meet the broker. Our lease was coming up in the spring, but I was pretty sure we could negotiate similar terms. But I didn't want to think about any of that now.

Suddenly, there was a tap on the window. It was Morgan. "Come in. Come in." She was the only person I didn't mind spending these last moments with.

She let in a gust of winter. "I can't believe you're still here."

"I'm heading out. We'll walk together."

"I wanted to wish you a happy and a merry," she said, looking neither. We hugged.

"You okay?" I asked.

"Absolutely. Yee-haw. Aspen, here we come." I studied her. "Why aren't I happy?" she asked. "Shouldn't I be happy?"

"Zoe just got over strep. You've been a shut-in."

She nodded. "Finished my book, finally. That's good."

"Congratulations!" I said. She shrugged. "Come on. I'll walk with you." I went to grab my bag.

"He hasn't called," Morgan said.

Of course not, I thought. "Maybe he's away."

"Maybe," she said.

"Go to Aspen. Seduce your husband. Try," I told her, realizing this was my plan. Michael had been so busy lately. Distant even.

"To fucking our husbands," she said. "And to making art. You're going to carve out the time?" I told her I would.

See you in 2008, I silently promised Little Scissors as I set the alarm.

Morgan and I linked arms and headed up the block with the sweet snow falling in our hair. We hugged goodbye at the next avenue. She went her way; I went mine. And in no time at all, our footprints were white again.

36

1981

I can tell she knows as soon as I walk in the house. My mother's scarred cheek and silent scorn are illuminated with each inhale. My heart pounds.

"And where have you been?"

Not answering seems like the best solution. I can smell her amber poison. I carefully place my bag against a bench in the hall. I don't want her to look inside.

"Don't you ignore me, you selfish little bitch!" A clog flies past my head and hits the wall. Tomorrow there will be a dent. She won't remember why.

"Mom, it's late. Let's just talk in the morning." I know this is a mistake, but I can't take it back.

"Are you too busy for me, Miss Hotshot? Too busy for your mother?" I slide to the floor, unable to leave, not wanting to stay.

"How could you?" she demands. "How could you?" This time, it sounds more like a sob than anything else.

"It's nothing, Mom," I try to tell her. "Just a stupid school play."

"Liar! That whore Naomi Wilson told me everyone's talking about how talented you are. Do you know how that made me look?" she asked. I can picture Mrs. Wilson gloating. "You can't act," my mother spews. I want to tell her that I wasn't an actress. And about the curtain call. And the stupid cast party where I actually had fun. But I don't.

"Birds fly, fish breathe underwater, and you, Miss Hotshot, are

not worthy of the stage." She turns away. Her shoulders shake and
I think she looks like a crazy drunk woman laughing at something
not at all funny. But then I see she's crying.

"That idiot woman asked what I'd thought of the dress rehearsal.
She kept going on and on about how talented all you kids were.
Please."

I stare at my mother.

"So that's where you've been? At a school rehearsal?" she sneered.
I don't answer.

"She looked at me with pity, Kara. Do you know how that feels?"

"How it feels to be pitiful?" I ask under my breath. I am young. I
think there will always be time to be angry at my mother.

She lunges. And though she's moving faster than she has in years,
so fast, in fact, that I'm unable to protect myself, she still appears
to be soaring in slow motion. There's a loud smack across my face.
My hand finds the stinging, as if it's necessary to touch my cheek in
order to comprehend what's just happened. "You think I'm pitiful,
Kara? Do you?" Her nostrils flare.

Hot tears burn my eyes. "No, Mama, of course not." I sound so
convincing that for a moment I think maybe I *should've* given acting
a try.

"I'll tell you what's pitiful. And it's high time you knew. Believing a little hick performance means anything! High school actresses
are a dime a dozen. Every whore in New York comes from some shit
town like this. When I played Lincoln Center, now that was a something..."

"I'm not an actress."

"I'll say." She stumbles to her chair. Soon, it'll be safe to leave. I
listen to her go on about her Lincoln Center days. When she leans
her head back, I quietly get up.

"Good night, Mom," I say carefully. I'm about to go upstairs, but
grabbing my bag reminds me there's a world outside of this room. A
world where I am allowed to speak. "If you were so brilliant, why'd
you stop?"

"Don't be smart with me, Kara."

"No, really, I want to know."

"I'm not going to take this shit," she says, but it's clear, this time, I am the one who will not be put off.

"You act like it was always because of me. Always my fault. But it wasn't. It was you. *You* gave up."

"You don't know what you're talking about. You think you do, but you don't."

"Then tell me!" I hate how desperate I sound.

"You don't know what it's like." Her hand sweeps the air, as if she could erase me from her view. "You don't have a clue."

"Then tell me," I plead again. "Tell me why you quit. Why'd you stop performing?" I sit back on the floor, waiting.

"I couldn't bear it," she finally says.

"Bear what?" I plead. This is not her usual rant. She is confessing. I am still.

"Bear being...pathetic. Not in front of you."

"Me? Are you kidding? I've heard you. You're not pathetic. You're...beautiful." I start to cry, which surprises me. I didn't know I was sad.

"To the untrained ear, maybe," she says dismissively.

"But you could've tried..."

"Tried! For what? So I could end up singing torch songs at the Ground fucking Round?"

"Maybe," I answer, knowing this isn't what I mean.

"Believe me, that wouldn't have been trying. That would've been failing." She lights a cigarette.

"Then what about trying and not failing?" I hear how naïve I sound.

"Maybe I wasn't good enough, Kara."

"Maybe you could have tried to get better."

"But that's just it. I didn't want to get *better*; I wanted to be the best."

I do not yet know this conversation will haunt me for years. How I'll imagine all the things I could have said. Like, *It's not too late.* Or, *Try for me.* Or, *I needed you to be happy.* But that night, I said nothing. And in the years that followed, no matter what comebacks I'd imagine, there would always be this: Her giving up was not only her biggest failure, but the one that hurt me more than any other. And the second truth was *my* undoing, and it scared me even then. I couldn't shake it, even though I tried. And it was this: I understood exactly why she had.

"Good night, Mom," I tell her again. This time I head upstairs, leaving her to her certainty.

I shut the door and my light. Warily, I open my backpack and pull out the play program. There it is. *Set design by Kara Caine.* My accomplishment is in black and white, and for that I am grateful. And though I'm sleepy and heartbroken, and don't dare smile, I read it again.

37

2008

In January, Henny's school requested a meeting. Miss Nathanson informed us that this time, the principal and other educators would be in attendance. That morning, I stood in Henny's room and scrutinized the ridiculous tree painting I'd done over the break. I was trying to decide if I should attempt to fix it or put it back in the closet. Henny loved it, but I was beginning to conclude that landscapes were not my calling. It lacked passion and, worse, I wasn't even sure what I could've done differently.

I felt drained and the day hadn't even begun. After the school meeting, I'd agreed to meet with Willa and our accountant. We were going to go over last year's numbers and discuss the possibility of moving. I figured it would be easier to object to relocating Little Scissors if I at least appeared open-minded. I put the painting back in the closet. This wasn't the time to contemplate solutions. People were counting on me. I didn't want to be late.

On one side of Miss Nathanson was the principal, Mrs. Davis; on the other, a school psychologist who'd never met Henny. I wondered if the seating arrangement had been planned ahead of time. Perhaps they had a policy for where parents should sit when they're informed that their child might be held back, or rather that *promotion was in doubt*, their exact words. "We think there may be some benefit to repeating the curriculum," said the psychologist.

"Really? Because her tutor thinks she's making progress," I countered.

"Of course, it's only January," added Mrs. Davis.

"Rosie also said that when a child has a learning disability, she needs to be taught in a specific way. It's not just a matter of repetition or waiting for her to mature." I sat back in my chair, letting the veiled criticism hang in the air.

"Miss Nathanson has training in a multisensory approach," said the principal. "But let's not put the cart before the horse. We just want to inform you that this is a possibility."

Put the cart before the horse? What the hell was she talking about? Suddenly I felt like the school was not on our side, which was upsetting because I thought we all wanted what was best for Henny.

"Are there other possibilities?" Michael asked the principal.

"There are."

Michael's irritation was obvious. *Well*, said his expression.

"We could give her an IEP..."

"What's an IEP?" Michael interrupted.

"It stands for individualized education plan," answered Miss Nathanson.

"Which basically makes her eligible for services in the school setting," said the principal.

"Like what services?" I asked.

"She'd be eligible for remedial services in the school setting," answered the psychologist.

Michael and I looked at each other. It was as if they were all speaking in code.

"I don't know what that means," I said.

"She'd be pulled out of class to get extra reading help," said Miss Nathanson.

"How often?" Michael asked.

"And what would she be missing?" I added. I was also wondering if the other kids would notice.

"Is there any benefit to the school if she gets this...whatever it's called...IEP?" Michael asked.

"I'm not sure what you mean by that?" Mrs. Davis bristled.

"Never mind."

"What would Henny be missing if she was pulled out?" I repeated my question.

"It depends on her assessment," said the psychologist. "And what we deem appropriate."

"Of course, you don't have to agree with our recommendations," said Mrs. Davis. "But again, let's not put the cart before the horse."

Again with the goddamned horse. I looked down. I was getting punchy.

"And other options?" asked Michael.

"She could be placed in a collaborative classroom where special ed and gen ed students learn together," said Mrs. Davis.

My head was spinning.

"A special ed classification would also change her criteria for advancement," said the psychologist. She looked so pleased with how well she was doing her job.

"Changes the criteria how? Like she'd be held to lower standards?" I asked.

The woman nodded.

"But her evaluation said she's beyond her years in what she's able to understand. Can't she be taught with that in mind? Just yesterday, you should have heard her talk about penguins. She went on and on about how they're endangered. Remember?" I looked at Michael. He nodded.

"And apparently the males guard the eggs for months. They don't eat, even. Although, now I'm not even sure if that's what she said. It doesn't really sound right, does it?" They all smiled.

"She's not meeting grade standards," said the psychologist. My plan was to hold her gaze, make her look away first. But I got teary and my throat burned. I looked at Miss Nathanson. Her eyes were on the principal.

I was baffled. There were too many options. I had no idea what would be best for Henny. I wasn't an educator. "Are you asking our opinion? Because if there's a decision that needs to be made, I have no idea." I could tell Michael felt the same. Rosie would be a good person to talk to—she'd been a tutor for twenty years. Maybe I'd call Dr. Stockland, see what he thought. And Morgan had mentioned her sister-in-law had some experience with this stuff. There was work to be done.

"No. No decision has to be made at this time," said the principal.

"Well then." Michael and I stood.

"Mr. and Mrs. Lawson, one more thing. We need your signature to document that this meeting occurred."

We escaped to the street. "Why is this so painful?" I asked Michael. "I mean, we know she has learning issues."

"I don't know, but it is."

Just then Morgan's husband, Eric, turned the corner. He and Zoe were walking in our direction. Her arm was in a cast. "Honey! What happened?"

"Buckle fracture," said Eric. "She fell off the slide."

"When?!"

"Today, at school."

"Oh my God," I said.

"Max is going to be so jealous," said Michael.

"Definitely," I agreed, though Zoe didn't look like a girl who'd inspire jealousy. Her eyes were swollen.

"Have you heard from Morgan?" Eric asked me. "She isn't answering her phone." Both men looked at me. Zoe stared at her feet.

"No. Not today." Oh, Morgan.

"I thought you guys walked this morning."

"This morning? Oh. We were supposed to." This isn't happening.

He shook his head. "I can't keep up with her."

"She's probably writing." I berated myself: Stop speaking, this is beyond unacceptable.

"That's what Mrs. Shurl said." Eric bent down to Zoe. "Mommy's going to be so sad that she wasn't with us."

"Call her again," the girl whined.

I could feel Michael's eyes on me. I wondered if he sensed something was off. Maybe she *was* writing. Here I go, jumping to conclusions. Perhaps I should stop putting that goddamned cart before that goddamned horse.

"I better get her home," Eric said.

"Max'll sign your cast tomorrow," I called after them.

Zoe didn't respond to me. She just grabbed her father's hand and they were on their way.

I called Morgan as soon as I was alone. Voicemail. I tried again. Dammit, Morgan. How could you? With quick fingers I typed a text: *Call home. Zoe needs you.* Then I said a soft prayer and pushed send.

The next day, I tried to reach our landlord. Even though the appointment with the accountant had gone well—it's always nice to hear that business is up ten percent—I still dreaded the idea of relocating our shop. Perhaps if I could negotiate a two-year lease, instead of the customary ten, Willa would be amenable to tabling her plans.

Seconds after I left a message with his secretary, the phone rang. I assumed it was the landlord and steadied myself, but it was Liza—and she sounded terrified. "The principal called. They can't find Henny!"

"What?!"

"They can't find her. She didn't come back from recess."

I was vaguely aware of a ringing phone, which Willa must've answered, because she waved her hands in front of me. "It's Michael. He says it's an emergency."

"Exactly what did the principal say?" I asked Liza.

"That Henny didn't come back after all the other kids came in. She wanted to know if we've seen her."

"If *we've* seen her? Oh my God. Did they check the bathrooms? The library?"

"I, I, don't know. I didn't ask."

"I'll call you back." I switched to the other line.

"The school just called," said Michael.

"I know…"

"Henny didn't come in from recess. What's going on in that place?"

"Did they check the bathrooms?" I asked.

"Davis said they did. And the library. Where the fuck is she?" Michael rarely swore.

"I'm going," I said, grabbing my bag. "If she left, she couldn't have gotten far." Any semblance of calm I'd had disappeared as I headed for the door. Trudy hopped up, but I couldn't stop for her leash. Visions of Henny alone on the street raced through my mind. Did she know her way home? She'd have to cross two avenues. Someone should call the doorman, tell him to be on the lookout.

Then I remembered there'd been a psychotic man on Lexington this morning. He'd been carrying on about bin Laden and Cheney. She'd be terrified. My cell rang. "Tell them to speak to Adam," said Michael. "Maybe he knows something."

"Good idea. And call the doorman."

I flung open the shop door. And I saw her. She was sitting on the bench outside, batting balloons when they blew in her direction. She'd been crying. "She's here. She's right here!" I cried.

"Are you sure?" asked Michael.

"Yes, yes. I'm looking at her. She's here. Outside the store."

"Unbelievable," he said. "Is she okay?"

"Yes. Yes."

"I'm calling the school." And he was gone. I dropped my bag to the ground and sat next to her. I wanted a million things at once. To hold her, tell her how scared we were. And to slap her across the face. Twice. Hard. I wanted to grab her. Make the whole world go away. And lecture. I wanted to lecture. Tell her she'd have to apologize to the school, her dad, Liza.

But more than any of those, I wanted to stay still and seated. There'd be time for lecturing and listening. My girl had run away. And when she did, it was me she came to; her home base. So we sat silently and watched people pass by. It was tranquil, actually.

In time, she leaned in close, her head against my arm, and spoke. "Charlotte Leeds called me a retard." And she began to cry.

38

1987

I sit in the library flipping through a Stieglitz monograph. I'm fascinated by his portraits of O'Keeffe, her soft yet powerful beauty. The images are so intimate I feel I should look away. One, titled *Torso*, is cropped to show only her nude body, without her face. I'm trying to decide if she's being objectified when Eden startles me.

"Does Oliver know you study naked women?" she asks. I pull the Stieglitz book closer while Eden deposits her slinky self across from me. She drops her bag to the floor, causing an unexpected echo. Some students look up, but when they see her, they don't seem irritated. She's that beautiful.

"I do not," I tell her, rolling my eyes.

"Hey, I'm not judging." She grabs my book and opens it from the beginning. She stops at the image of O'Keeffe wearing a black dress with a white collar. It was taken in 1946, at her first solo exhibition. "Exquisite," she says, shutting the book. "But hurry up. We have places to go."

I grab it from her and look for the page she was just on. "I'm working on a paper," I mumble. O'Keeffe stares up at me, proud in her black dress. Pronounced shadows on her face and neck contrast with her pale skin. I will paint this image, I decide. I wonder what Eden would think, if I told her.

"A paper on O'Keeffe?" she asks.

"Actually, on O'Keeffe and Stieglitz."

"The photographer?" she asks.

"Yeah, but at the time, he was known as the most influential art dealer in New York." I sound like I know what I'm talking about.

"Ahhh." She nods. "Excellent plan—fuck the art dealer."

I recoiled. "Actually, he fell in love with her work before he even met her."

Eden puts up her hands. "Okay..."

"She was an artist in her own right. They influenced each other." I'm so glad I didn't tell her that I've been painting.

"Bring it with you." She motions to the book. "We've got things to do."

"We do?" Eden grabs her bag and sweater. I sigh, but I'm only pretending to be exasperated. "Where are we going?" I ask, already gathering my things.

"Brooklyn."

"Brooklyn!?"

"It's Oliver's birthday," she says. "We're going to make a cake."

I've never been to Brooklyn—it always sounded kind of scary to me, beyond my reach. But even though I have no idea what making a cake has to do with Brooklyn, and I've already gotten Oliver a gift (an early edition of Kahlil Gibran's *The Prophet*), I figure if I'm ever going to Brooklyn, Eden's probably a good person to do it with, so I surrender.

Eden's grandmother opens the door to her Williamsburg apartment, setting free the scent of boiled cabbage. "You're too thin," she tells Eden.

"Thanks, Bubby."

"Don't be smart, it's not a compliment." The old woman holds Eden's shoulders while checking her from head to toe. Eden is released with a squeeze and we are ushered in.

The apartment opens directly into a cramped kitchen. A small round table is nestled in the corner. Eden's grandmother motions for her to clear away some old newspapers so I'll have a place to sit. The walls are colored Granny Smith green, and look as if each decade a layer of thick paint is applied in an attempt to cover up the old and welcome the new. I'm guessing a lot of living has been done in this kitchen.

Eden's grandmother lowers the volume on her miniature TV and refolds today's newspaper, as if bidding her unfinished crossword goodbye. Sandpaper panty hose and old-lady bras hang on a clothes rack in front of the open window, which she manages to pull shut, diminishing the sound of competing salsa songs from the courtyard.

"Are you staying for dinner?" She points to the colander. I oblige.

"We can't," Eden answers. "We have to make a cake."

"Ah," her grandmother says, pointing to the bookcase in the corner. Eden removes the black three-ring binder, cradling it like it's the signed first edition from some famous dead author.

"You can make it here if you want," the grandmother says.

Eden shakes her head. "Too risky," she says. "The subway and all..." I'm waiting for her grandmother to ask who we're baking for. I really want to hear how Eden would describe Oliver, but apparently no further explanation is required because she just nods and moves about the kitchen, shifting apples from the counter to the sink and placing carrots and parsley in the colander. Using a paring knife, she peels an apple in one single spiral, and then starts another. Neither woman is fascinated by this maneuver. There, in the grandmother's kitchen, I forgive Eden for always wanting to cook at Oliver's. I understand it's not easy to hide who we are.

"May I use the bathroom?" I ask quietly. Eden points to a door covered with hanging coats, belts, and purses. I step into the closet-sized room, making the grandmother's things bang behind me as I awkwardly close the door. This room, like the last, has a unique scent: soap and hairspray mingled with urine. I sit on the toilet and feel like I'm about to vomit. I hear shuffling in the kitchen and wonder if they'd notice if I threw up. I take deep breaths, and the nausea passes.

After I pee, I realize there's no sink to wash my hands, only the toilet and tub. I consider running my hands under the bath faucet, but when I tentatively slide the shower curtain to one side, the vision of the old woman's tub brings my nausea tumbling back. I sit again. I'm not usually so squeamish.

"You can use the kitchen sink, dear," the grandmother calls from behind the door.

Eden is reading her grandmother's handwritten recipes when I come out. "This is the one," she tells me, pointing. She copies her grandmother's scrawl.

It starts to snow as the old woman stirs cored apples, turning them into a thick, boiling mush. Every now and then, she tells us how much sugar she's adding, or the value of freshly squeezed lemon. A dishrag rests on her shoulder, and as she talks, she blots her hands before moving to the next task. I take turns between watching these two generations of women and looking out the window at clean flakes falling from the Brooklyn sky.

Later, after several rounds of rummy, the grandmother sets our places with foggy glass bowls of hot applesauce. Before the heaping spoonful dissolves in my mouth, I scoop my next bite. And my next again. For many years to come, long after this afternoon, years following the artists' and hipsters' invasion of this neighborhood, I will unsuccessfully try to recapture this taste. I scrape my bowl clean, and thankfully, Eden's grandmother hands me another. I stir the hot sauce a few times to get the temperature just right. Again, I devour the spicy sweetness. When I'm offered a third bowl, I pretend I'm full, but the grandmother holds my final serving steady, settling the conflict.

A sleepy cat shifts from Eden's lap to the table. No one pushes her away. She finds her spot and relaxes into it, knocking a dry African violet from the sill. The soil dusts the floor. Eden picks up the pot while her grandmother retrieves the violet and drops it back into the planter. Using a hand broom, the old woman stoops to brush the remnants into a dented dustpan. Then she pours a glass of water into the thirsty plant and watches me finish her special sauce.

"You know, I used to devour it just the same," she announces.

"When was that, Bub?" Eden looks over the cake recipe once more before tucking it into her bag.

"When I was pregnant, of course." She chuckles, adding, "All three times."

The wise woman's words tumble out of her mouth into her sweet-smelling kitchen, and for a moment or two they seem to hover, unnoticed. But then, as if we all understand at the same moment, our startled eyes bounce off each other. Astonishment and fear settle on me—these not so easily swept away.

39

2008

Morgan came out of the drugstore carrying the most magnificent long-stemmed French tulips I'd ever seen. She was listening to music, and if I hadn't stopped her, she never would've seen me. "Hi." I tapped her shoulder.

"Hey!" she yelled, removing her earphones. "Where've you been?!"

"I know. I'm sorry. I got your messages. We've been swamped. There was a school meeting..." I sounded so phony.

"You look fancy," she said. "Where you headed?"

"I'm meeting Michael." She nodded. "How's Zoe?" I asked.

"A trouper. Only two more weeks in the cast."

I wasn't referring to her arm. "That was fast."

"Yeah, kids heal quickly," Morgan said.

"That's great." We stood awkwardly. "Henny ran away from school."

"Are you serious?! What happened? Is she okay?"

"Yeah, yeah. It all worked out." I regretted telling her. I wasn't ready to confide.

"Oh my God. You must have been so freaked out. How long was she missing?"

"Not too long."

Her eyes met mine. "Listen, Kara, I'm so sorry you had to deal with Eric. I really am. It won't happen again."

I wouldn't have called it *dealing* with Eric, but I didn't want to disagree.

"It was a major wake-up call. Way too close for comfort," she said. "I was panicked. I had all these missed calls. From the school, about twenty from Eric. Your text. I thought she was dead."

It all seemed to be about Morgan's feelings. I kept thinking about how weary Zoe had seemed. "What did you tell them?" I asked.

"That I was working."

I looked away.

"I could've been, Kara. It's not unheard of to be out of contact for a few hours."

"That's true," I conceded.

"So... let me have it. Yell at me or something. You're just standing there. You don't return my calls."

"It's only been a week."

"Almost two." She studied me. "So I'm mistaken? You're not withdrawing? This is all in my mind?"

"No."

"What can I do?" she asked.

"I lied to your husband. I told him we were supposed to go to the Reservoir."

"I know. I'm sorry. I really am." Morgan's attentiveness made me feel foolish. She was taking me so seriously. "I should never have put you in that position. You knew too much. A secret's a burden. I see that now."

She looked sincere. My anger seemed more about principle than genuine feeling. Or maybe it was just this: I missed her.

"I ended it," she said softly.

"You did?"

She nodded. "The whole thing was out of hand. Not to mention, I really didn't want to get caught."

"Was it hard?" I asked.

"It wasn't easy. But I feel good. Like I'm doing the right thing. Maybe now I'll really focus on the couples therapy. The therapist's pretty good."

"That's... great."

"So, call me. Okay? Enough of this bullshit."

"Bullshit!?"

"Not bullshit. Forget I said that. But still, call me. I miss you."

"I miss you too."

I walked into Lupiere's, grateful I still had a few minutes before Michael arrived. I needed to recover from bumping into Morgan. Plus, there'd been the usual chaos of homework, dinner, and baths that I'd just accomplished—with Liza's help, of course. Even with the effort it took to get out on a weeknight, now that I was here, I was glad Michael had suggested it.

I scanned the restaurant. It was busy enough to feel exciting but mellow enough to hear myself think. I enjoyed the striking crowd and felt lucky to be there. And of course their fried olives were perfection. "Good to see you again," the owner, Alessandra, said, joining me at the bar.

"Good to be here," I told her.

"How are the kids?"

"Exhausting."

"Oh, don't say that! They grow so fast."

"I know. You're right, they're amazing." But also exhausting. I switched gears and asked her how things were.

"We're renovating this summer. Just a little facelift, nothing too extreme."

"Wonderful." I smiled. "But make sure you keep the neighborhood vibe." I guess twenty years of frequenting Manhattan cafés and shops had taught me a thing or two.

"Are you in design?"

"Me? No. I own a children's hair salon. But my husband's an architect. And I do murals." The words just popped out.

"Really! I was thinking of doing something, but I wasn't sure what." She pointed to the large wall in the dining room. Call it divine inspiration or a sudden burst of believing in myself, but as I listened to her, I came up with an idea. A warm smile spread across my face. "Well," I said, leaning in, "I know exactly what you should do."

We agreed I'd come by next week with a sketch and color samples. "My pleasure," I said, as if I did this all the time.

"I guess my firm's not the only one whose numbers are up," Michael said, motioning to the full room. I was about to tell him Little Scissors was up, too—but I didn't feel like going into it.

"Speaking of success, Alessandra wants a mural." I discreetly pointed to the wall behind him.

"Really? That's fantastic." Michael dipped peasant bread in olive oil.

"Not just that, but she liked my idea."

"Excellent." The waiter appeared with our drinks.

"I'm thinking of doing a massive olive."

He nodded. "When?"

"But off center, you know? Nothing symmetrical."

"Cool. When do they want it?"

"Summer. You know, when the city clears out." I appreciated Michael not reminding me that I typically cleared out as well, spending July and August in Kent with the kids. I didn't want to think about that. I wanted to paint the mural.

"I have news, too," Michael said tentatively. "Garrett and I were reviewing things, and we're ready to reimburse the personal loans." He looked like Adam after scoring a goal.

"That's a year earlier than you thought!"

"It is." He took a long, slow sip of scotch.

"That's unbelievable." I smiled. "So we won't lose the apartment after all."

"Jesus, did you think we would?"

"No, I just...I'm just glad we can...pay back the mortgage." This was never an easy topic for us. I'd been worried, but not because I didn't believe in him. It was more that I was painfully aware that if it didn't work out, I'd never be able to pick up the slack. Little Scissors was fluid, but not gushing. There was no way I could've carried that debt.

Right before my eyes, Michael deflated.

"I guess I hadn't known how scared I'd been...until your good news." I paused, but he stayed silent. "I mean, if it hadn't worked out...We're just so extended."

"But it did work out."

I meant to ask, *Why now?* But the food came, and we were relieved and hungry, and before I knew it, we were on to something else.

After he ordered dessert, I broached the medicine topic. "I think she should try it."

"I was afraid you were leaning in that direction."

"Well, yeah. I mean, it seems like she's getting worse," I said.

"Didn't you tell me Rosie thinks she's making improvement? And you know what? At this point, I don't trust anything that school says."

"What are you afraid of?" I asked gently.

"She's seven years old. Still a baby."

"Okay. But what's your concern?" I asked.

"I don't want her to grow up thinking drugs will solve her problems. I mean, she *is* genetically predisposed to alcoholism."

I recoiled.

"That didn't come out right."

I lifted my glass; cold water washed away my meal. "Try again," I suggested.

"I just can't wrap my mind around drugging our girl."

I was surprised he'd given it so much thought, which really wasn't fair. He was her father. Why did I dismiss his connection to her? His feelings were understandable. I too was having a hard time wrapping my mind around the idea, but withholding something that might help didn't feel right either. "Well, I called the psychiatrist..." I started.

"You called the psychiatrist?!"

"I called the psychiatrist to ask about that very issue," I said slowly. "He said kids who need medicine and *don't* get it are at a greater risk for abusing drugs."

Michael looked doubtful.

"Except during the teen years," I continued. "When you really need to keep track of how much they're taking."

"Teen years! Jesus, aren't you jumping way ahead?!" Michael sat back in his chair. "I mean, maybe the school's just trying to label her so they can protect their reputation. Did you know the city uses test scores to rate all the public schools?"

I didn't know where he was going with this. Michael didn't usually discuss educational standards. "What are you saying?" I asked.

"Maybe part of her problem is their curriculum and all the testing," he said.

"Well, yeah, but what are you suggesting?" I asked.

"Maybe we should consider other options."

"Other options? Like private school?"

"Possibly. Or something else. There must be alternatives."

"Okay..." I pictured myself at the computer researching private schools and treatment options and my heart sank. I wanted to paint, and now Michael was implying I should become an expert on learning disabilities.

"Like...out of the city," he started.

"Out of the city?" I didn't understand—the city had to have better resources than the suburbs. "Westchester? The commute would be torture."

"Like, Los Angeles," he said.

"Ha. Ha."

The waiter appeared with our cappuccinos. I watched as Michael dropped two brown sugar cubes to their frothy death.

"Are you out of your mind?" But as I articulated the question, I realized that, in fact, he was quite serious. "You got the project in Seoul," I said after a moment.

"Bigger. The West Coast firm we were competing with wants to merge. Seoul's just the beginning. The whole Asian market is going to open to us."

"And here I thought we were talking about Henny." For a moment my anger was replaced by sorrow. Who was he becoming?

"We are talking about Henny. This kind of opportunity will benefit all of us."

"All of us?" My anger was back.

He shook his head. "I don't understand why you can't see that this is just too good not to pursue."

"Too good for whom?" My eyes bulged, as if not blinking would somehow clarify things.

"Too good for us," he said softly.

"Really? Because I'm fairly certain moving to Los Angeles has nothing to do with what's good for Henny," I said, remembering we weren't alone.

"Okay. I guess too good for the firm."

"I see. Thus the mortgage repayment." I laughed one of those laughs people do when what they really mean is, *How could I have trusted you?*

"If you'd calm down for a moment, you'd hear how lucrative—"

"Don't do that! Don't speak to me as if I just need to hear the details."

"Well, that's just it; you don't have the full picture." He seemed to be waiting for permission to enlighten me.

"But we talked about this. We decided you wouldn't pursue it." I tried to remember the exact conversation.

"Kara, I told you this was a possibility."

"You never said that!"

"I did. Last fall. At the Thatchers' party."

"The Thatchers' party! You knew how distracted I was." This was the first time I'd acknowledged that seeing Oliver had been even the slightest bit unsettling.

"It's not only up to me," said Michael. He was making a bargain with me: He would shelve the Oliver issue if I ignored his deception.

"Right. Your partner," I said.

"We felt it was an incredible opportunity," said Michael.

"Did we?" I sat unmoving.

He shook his head. "You used to be supportive. When did it change?"

"I can't believe you're putting this on me. You're acting like moving to L.A. is no big deal. This is our home. You changed, not me!" But as I said it, I knew this was not the whole truth. Something in me was changing. I wasn't the same woman. It wasn't that I had suddenly become unhappy. It was more like I was suddenly aware that I didn't want to be.

"Well, I'm not sure you understand how big this is."

"Oh, I understand. I am well aware of the magnitude of what you're suggesting. That's the point."

"Kara—"

"You'll be completely consumed while my whole life will be about getting the kids adjusted. Set up. Handled. And did you even *think* about Little Scissors?" I asked.

"I assumed Willa..."

"Maybe I want to do it. Maybe I *want* Little Scissors to be the next Dylan's." I feigned sincerity.

"Do you?"

"I don't know. I never have any time to figure anything out!" We sat for a moment. I scanned the room to see if anyone was watching us. Thankfully, no.

"I thought you'd be..." Michael began.

"Happy? You thought I'd be happy?" I pounced. I knew I sounded like a shrew, but I couldn't stop.

"Proud. I thought you'd be proud."

"*You* have something to be proud of, Michael, not me!" Angry tears came to my eyes.

"We're a unit, Kara. My success is our success."

"Your success is our success?" I spewed.

"That's what I'm saying."

"Wow, Michael. That's so generous. We get to share *your* success." My voice was cracking. I tossed my napkin to the table and stood to leave.

"Kara," I heard him say, but I didn't care. It was late. Time for me to get back.

"Be in touch," Alessandra said when I was already at the door.

"Absolutely." I hoped she didn't detect my painted-on smile.

From the street, I glanced into the lovely dining room. There was my husband, and behind him, the bare wall. Michael threw money on the table. I beat him home.

40

1984

I pull my gray Nissan into a parking spot in back of the church. I'm late. The meeting started a few minutes ago and I hate walking in when everyone is already seated. My mother will be worried. I throw my book bag in the backseat. I have a sociology exam tomorrow, but it doesn't really matter. The semester is almost over and as long as I show up I'll do fine.

Cleveland Community College is far easier than my high school was. Tonight I'll tell my mother my plan. I'm going to move to New York. Get a waitressing job. Take some time off before applying to a city school.

"And now, with two years sober, Juliet." Everyone claps, especially Leo, my mother's new boyfriend. She looks across the smoky church basement and smiles when she sees me. I'm clapping, too. I'd considered tonight an obligation, but now that I'm here, I am truly happy. Aurora, my mother's sponsor, is sitting behind me. She squeezes my shoulder as my mother walks to the podium. Next to me sits a sad-looking long-haired woman. I want to tell her, if my mom can quit drinking, so can she, but it's time to settle in. "My name is Juliet, and I'm an alcoholic."

"Hi, Juliet," we answer.

After the meeting, people mill around. Some talk, others stack chairs or toss away coffee cups. I'm off to the side, preferring to be a fly on the wall. Over the past two years, I've come to know these people. Our house is a hangout spot and I suppose they've become the extended family I never had.

I'm waiting for my mother to decide if she'll join everyone at Denny's.

"We should just call it a night," she says, looking at me. My mother feels guilty going out. It's like she's trying to make up for lost time. When she first got sober, she was impossible, always asking me if I thought she'd been a terrible mother. I'd never known how to answer.

Lately, she's been all attentive again. A few nights ago she tried to make this healthy dinner, with the requisite starch and veggie. As if dinner could undo the past. I just sat there picking at the dry, burnt chicken, silently hoping for this guy I kind of like to call.

"Jeez, Kara, put some gratitude in your attitude, at least I'm trying." I'd stared at her like I had no idea what she was talking about. Then she pushed her plate away and rummaged in her purse for a cigarette.

"Guess that quitting smoking thing isn't going so well," I'd said.

"Guess not." She hadn't even sounded angry, which surprised me. "This is normal, you know. Aurora says kids always act crazy around their parents' AA anniversaries."

"That Aurora is a genius. What else does she say?"

"Not to get into a pissing match with a skunk, for starters." She blew a perfect smoke ring in my direction. "You know, Kara. Life isn't all good or all bad. Sometimes things can be fantastic and terrible at the same time."

"Whatever." I rolled my eyes. At nineteen, I didn't always recognize wisdom when I heard it.

There's an old piano in the corner. Sam, a newcomer to the meeting, is playing "Take Five." After this night, he will be known by the group as Piano Sam. I am content listening to him channel Brubeck on the out-of-tune piano. "If you're not going for coffee," Aurora tells my mother, "then at least sing for us…"

"I'm getting over a cold," my mother says, adding a cough for good measure.

"I'm getting over a marriage," Aurora counters.

"I'm getting over the DTs," Sam says. Everyone laughs, but then the room is quiet, waiting.

My mother exhales. "Well then. I guess it's time I get over being terrified." She whispers something to Sam and then says, "This one's for Kara."

Sam plays the opening chords and I immediately know it's my favorite song from *Fame*, a movie about a bunch of New York City kids who are trying to find their talent and follow their dreams. Night after night, I play the song in my room. My mother never mentioned she liked it, much less that she'd learned it. As she sings, she looks at me. I feel my face flush.

Sometimes I wonder where I've been,
Who I am, do I fit in?

Her voice is raspier than usual, but she is lovely. Full of sorrow. When she's done, no one knows quite what to say. "You're not alone anymore," Aurora offers, wiping her eyes.

"Not if I can help it," Leo adds.

We do not yet know that my mother's cold will get worse and turn into pneumonia. And that the pneumonia is not actually pneumonia, but lung cancer. I will not be leaving to start my life in New York. Instead, I will be busy over the next two years, watching my mother fight to live and then wait to die.

The people in this basement church will cook for us (though my mother will eat little) and rotate by her bedside. They'll carpool to chemo and take turns holding the basin to catch her vomit when I can't bear to hear her retch one more time.

When my mother's long, lush red locks fall on her pillow like dead leaves, Aurora will surprise everyone by cutting her own hair. "This isn't some sponsorly support of your chemo-ass self," she'll tell my mother. "I'm off men, thus the dyke look." My mother will laugh until she coughs up blood.

These people will answer my frantic call the night my mother's shit resembles orange juice and again the morning before the night she finally dies.

At the funeral, Piano Sam will say with pride that she died sober; Leo will cry. Aurora will hold my hand. I'll say little, but they won't care. They'll just help me sell the house and get into a Columbia dorm even though I'm a continuing ed student (a friend of a friend owes someone a favor). But most of all, they'll help me not die too.

But that night, we know none of this. My mother sings, and when she does, she stops being my mother and becomes a torch singer belting out regret and resilience. And hope.

I don't move while she sings, which is evidence of a sadness I can't admit or avoid. Like the words to my mother's song, I have always felt on my own. Still, very few things are as perfect as this night. The night of my mother's final performance.

And after she dies, even with all their help, that ever-present loneliness becomes more than a feeling.

For the first time, I really am alone.

41

2008

Michael and I didn't speak for three days. It wasn't obvious to Liza or the kids, but we both knew our yes-and-no responses about tae kwon do pickup or where Henny's toothbrush was (in Max's lunchbox—long story) didn't count.

And then Simone called. Michael's father had had a heart attack.

"He should be out of surgery by two o'clock," Michael told me when I met him in his office lobby.

I handed him his overnight bag. "Keep me posted." While we waited for a cab, Michael described the angioplasty procedure, including the latest statistics from hospitals in Palm Beach, Manhattan, and Syracuse. Just before he stepped into the car, our eyes met.

"I'm not ready for this," he said. We kissed a sad-scared-I-believe-in-you-kiss, and he was gone.

Morgan had a reading in Chicago, so while Max and Zoe played in the other room, I watched her pack.

"He's lucky," she said when I told her about Dennis's angioplasty. "A few stents and he's good to go." When Morgan was twelve, her father died of a massive coronary, which was something we had in common. Sort of. We were quiet for a moment. "But, L.A.? Yikes," she said.

"Tell me about it. At least we made a deal. I'm going with him in a few weeks to check it out, and Michael finally signed off on Henny trying meds."

"Finally," she said. I considered defending him, but let it go. "What does checking it out entail?" she asked.

"Investigate schools. Neighborhoods. See if I could actually live there..."

"And Little Scissors? Does Willa know?"

"No. In fact, in the middle of everything, she called to tell me she found a great space." I threw myself at the foot of their bed. "It doesn't end," I groaned.

Morgan moved between her bathroom and cluttered closet. Clothes were draped on open drawers, but she seemed able to find whatever she was looking for.

"I think it's the medicine's that's making me the most crazy," I said. "Now that she's actually going to try it, everywhere I turn there are damning articles about children and medication. What if twenty years from now she gets cancer? And there are side effects—decreased appetite, sleeplessness." I exhaled, but it didn't help. "I don't know how she's even going to swallow it. She's never taken a pill."

"Is it big?" asked Morgan.

"No, but still."

"You act like you're doing this *to* her. I mean, the doctor recommended this...you're not torturing her."

"I know. But did you read that story in the *Times*? Jesus. Not to mention Michael's really just placating me because he feels guilty about L.A."

"As well he should," said Morgan. "But still, if medicine's going to help her learn better, who gives a shit what anyone thinks?"

"Maybe," I mumbled. I heard Zoe screaming in the other room. It was the second time today.

Morgan rolled her eyes. "She's totally freaked I'm going away."

"What about Eric?" I asked. "Is he supportive?"

She shrugged. "He's fine. Watch, they'll end up having such a great time she won't even miss me." I wasn't so sure, remembering the day Zoe broke her arm.

"Yogurt," Morgan said suddenly. I had no idea what she was talk-

ing about. "When my niece was little, my sister-in-law put her medicine in yogurt."

"Good to know."

"So what are you going to do?" she asked.

"I'll try the yogurt," I said impatiently.

"About California."

"Oh. I don't know." She held up two boots, I pointed to the taupe
ones. "I told Michael I'd go with an open mind, but beyond that I
have no idea."

"Well, you know what they say about L.A.?" she said.

"No, what?"

"Hell if I know, I'm a New Yorker." Then she tossed a black garter
in the suitcase. It's nothing, I reasoned, and looked the other way.

Willa's Realtor flipped on the lights and ushered us in. "Not to
insult your intelligence, but I hope you noticed the street-level window. Obviously, there's excellent visibility."

I nodded.

"And just to let you know, the plumbing was updated for the last
tenant. State of the art. Feel free to try the faucets." Willa stood off
to the side as if to convey that she had no investment in my reaction.
It didn't matter, though; I already knew she loved the space.

"It was a pottery studio?" I asked, even though Willa had already
mentioned this.

"And retail shop. They did birthday parties, paint-your-own, that
sort of thing."

"Why'd they go out of business?"

The broker paused. "The owners split up. Husband and wife. She
moved to Jersey. But their loss is your gain, as you'll see when you
check out the basement. They left fabulous shelving units."

"Which means we'll have plenty of storage," added Willa. "We can
finally order inventory in bulk." This would tighten our purchasing
margin, potentially saving us a lot of money, but I didn't react.

"I'm worried about the block," I said. "Side streets are tough. There's much more traffic on the avenue."

"With the right signage, you'll be fine." The broker waved her hand dismissively. "And in the meantime, you get three times the space."

"Are there any limitations regarding signage?" I remembered several of Michael's commercial clients had been misled about these kinds of restrictions.

"I'm not aware of any," the broker said.

I noticed this wasn't exactly an answer. "Well, could you find out for sure? Please." But the signage aside, Willa was right—it was great. I couldn't help but imagine how we'd break up the space. There was room for at least two, maybe three more cutting stations and we could still double the retail section.

"I'm thinking we could even have a separate tweens' area," said Willa. "I've wanted to target that age group, but we can't put them anywhere near the little kids." My mind went to the henna tattoos Henny had admired. There was no question that Willa would approve. And I'm sure they'd be another hook for Victoria to pitch to the press.

On the way back to the shop, I felt the enormity of what moving Little Scissors would entail. We'd have to put a lot more money into the business, something Willa and I'd avoided for years. And I didn't want to involve investors again. I liked not having people to answer to.

"You look upset," she said.

"I am. The numbers—"

"You liked it." She smiled. "Just admit it."

"I don't see how we can do this without putting a lot of money in, and frankly..."

"You liked it!" Her eyes sparkled. "You did."

"...and frankly, Michael's and my money is tied up." Well, not anymore, but still...

"There are all sorts of scenarios we could consider," Willa offered.

"There aren't all sorts of scenarios," I snapped. I found her nonchalance annoying. Yes, the space was great. But I had real concerns. "I'm going to talk to the landlord," I said, leaving out that I'd already left him a bunch of messages that he hadn't returned.

"That's a good idea. Get your signage questions answered."

"Not *that* landlord. *Our* landlord." I pointed to Little Scissors a few doors away.

"Oh."

"I want to find out what he's willing to do. I mean, we're on the avenue. That counts for something. I get the feeling he might be open to negotiating." Willa raised an eyebrow. "It's worth a try," I said, thinking, Especially if I'm about to move to L.A.

"Fine, Kara. Call him." Our eyes locked briefly. "See what he says."

I wanted to ask her how she'd feel about a two-year lease, but she turned to go inside. I stood for a moment looking at our cramped, familiar shop. If we moved to California, there was no way Willa would be able to buy me out. I'd have to become a silent partner. Although without Little Scissors, it occurred to me, there'd be time to paint, even in California.

I wasn't sure how I felt about anything anymore. I sighed and followed her in.

Henny stood next to me while I placed a tiny white pill in a spoonful of strawberry-banana yogurt. "Just swallow it?" she asked.

"Pretend it's a piece of granola," I suggested. Adam, Max, and Liza were watching her.

"What's it going to do to me, again?" Even though I'd already explained it several times, I took the spoon from her and put it to the side.

"Okay. This medicine helps kids concentrate better on their schoolwork."

"But it doesn't always work, right?"

"Right."

"I want some," whined Max.

"I don't!" said Adam.

"We're not going to make Henny feel bad about this." I flashed Adam a look.

"Wait. Is this drugs?" Henny asked. "Like Liza's mother?" she whispered. Of course Liza heard; she was standing right there.

"No. This is different. This is medicine." Liza began to load breakfast bowls into the dishwasher. "The doctor thinks it might make it easier for you to focus, so you'll try it," I said. "If it helps, we'll know quickly, because it's in and out of your body in four hours."

Henny nodded.

"Do you guys have any questions?" I looked at Liza and the boys, but they were silent. Then Liza left the room. "Do you want some privacy?" I asked Henny. She seemed to weigh the alternatives: enjoy the power of banishing the boys, or allow them to stay and remain the center of attention.

"No, they can stay." The boys watched as she slowly moved the spoon to her mouth. I nodded. She swallowed it. For a moment, we all kept looking at her; but then I cleared my throat and we went about our business. Truth be told, I forgot about it. Then, an hour or so later, we were snuggled next to each other in her room when I remembered. I grabbed her library book. As usual, she bristled.

"Here, I'll read the first page." When it was her turn, a miraculous thing happened. She read. Okay, that's an exaggeration. She was still exceedingly deliberate. But there was no mistaking it. There was a difference.

The psychiatrist had warned that the medicine wouldn't eliminate learning difficulties. He said she'd still have problems processing written information. Pills aren't magic, he'd told me. The whole time, I'd nodded. Yes, of course, I understand. But now, here we sat. And while I could tell she had a long way to go, this time when I helped her with a word, she was able to recognize it a sentence later.

I considered hollering for Liza. She, more than anyone, would notice the improvement. But I didn't want Henny to feel like she was under a microscope, so I stayed seated (practically holding my breath) while my little girl slowly continued to read.

But then a few hours later, Henny had a tantrum to beat all tantrums. It started when Max wanted to play with a toy Rosie had given her after a particularly hard tutoring session. "It's my worry ball!" yelled Henny. "I earned it! It's mine!"

I agreed and made Max give it back, but she couldn't stop yelling. I tried the technique of validating her feelings, said things like, *I see you're angry. It's doesn't feel fair. You worked so hard. Look, he gave it back*, but there was no reasoning with her. I'd never seen her like this. Her face was clenched in fury and she threw things around her room. I got scared when she started to pull her hair.

"Stop that," I yelled. "Stop!"

She continued to scream. "He's a baby, it's mine! It's mine!" She flailed, so I grabbed her arms. It seemed like the only thing to do was hold her. I could feel her torment surging below the surface. Much later, I'd learn on a website for mothers of children with special needs that this was a strategy known as containing. At the time, it was a visceral reaction: She must *feel* me.

I called the psychiatrist. "She's going nuts," I said when he answered. For a moment I was trapped. The situation required me to describe what was happening, but if I spoke, I'd unleash a flood. But the doctor was waiting for me to explain. "She's pulling her hair and screaming." I felt tears behind my eyes.

"She's like a crazy person." It was my greatest fear. "I can't stop her."

"She's crashing," he said.

"She's pulling her hair!... What did you say?"

"She's crashing."

"That's it exactly! She's crashing." Liza came into the living room. I could tell she was listening.

"It's a side effect—inconsolable irritability. It happens." The doctor sounded a bit cavalier, but still, I was relieved he knew what I was talking about. "Usually adjusting the dose does the trick."

"Okay. That's good, because I thought it was working. Until this, I mean."

"Do you want to pick up a new prescription?"

"Can you just call it in?"

"No, it's a controlled substance. Requires a paper prescription."
I hadn't realized this. "Can I send my sitter for it?" I sensed this annoyed Liza, who looked tired. Too bad, I thought dismissively. I had bigger fish to fry. I scribbled the address and gave her cab fare. I needed to get back to Henny.

She was resting on the rug in the corner of her room. Then I realized that she was asleep. I lay next to her and waited. It reminded me of when I was a child; now that the fit had subsided, it was my turn to recover. Suddenly, I was exhausted. I looked out the window, grateful that this wasn't the lonely view from my childhood. I lay there next to Henny and cherished the flickering yellow lights in my slice of city sky.

42

1987

When Eden and I get back from Brooklyn, I don't bake a cake for Oliver. I tell her I'm fine, and watch as she leaves graceful prints on her snow-dusted street. Halfway to their building she turns and yells, "You can still change your mind," but I wave her on. I know she's talking about baking, but on many levels, my mind is already made up.

"Eden," I call suddenly, running to catch up. "Don't tell him, okay?"

She opens her mouth to speak, but hesitates. "It's not my place," she says. This is exactly what I need to hear. "But you're going to, right?"

"I...I don't know. Probably." She looks horrified by my reluctance. "But, in my time," I add.

"It's just, I mean, he's my friend too." She looks at me with what is probably concern, but I only see disappointment.

"Stay out of it!" I snap. "This isn't about you!"

"Kara," she starts.

"I mean it, Eden. Stay out of it!" I need to get away from her sad, serious face.

"I'm just, worried..."

"Well, do me a favor." She looks at me as if she'd do anything. "Don't be," I say, turning to leave.

That night, instead of wishing Oliver a happy birthday, I start the O'Keeffe portrait. Over the next five days, I paint, only pausing when hunger and fatigue are too intense to ignore. I hold the Stieglitz book in one hand, and though I'm careful, I smudge paint on the photo. I quickly dismiss the destruction. I'll pay for the book. It's the first time I experience for myself that when it comes to making art, there's an occasional casualty.

I know the painting is powerful because when I come back from a bathroom break, I'm startled. The image is so lifelike that I no longer feel alone in my dorm-room-turned-studio. She is exactly who I wanted her to be—beautiful, powerful, and proud. I don't need anyone to tell me the painting works, because I spend many hours enjoying its subtleties. This is how I know I have made art; and by extension, how I learn I'm an artist.

And then I call the clinic. A bored girl tells me that my first appointment must be a pregnancy test, which briefly makes me hope that I've imagined the whole thing even though every day for the past week, anytime my arms brushed my breasts, I ached. I start to fantasize that maybe they've always been so sensitive and perhaps I never noticed.

So with the pregnancy test looming, I pray I've overreacted and busy myself writing the Stieglitz/O'Keeffe paper. As soon as I hand it in, I begin another painting of an image I find in *Vogue*. Under my brush, she too emerges as contemplative. I am bursting with the need to create, an irony that is not lost on me.

When my period fails to come and my wooziness fails to go, I see Eden on campus. "How are you?" she whispers. I shrug and tell her I have to get to class. "Do you need anything?" she asks.

"I'm fine." She steps away from me, looking wounded; I tell myself she's glad to not be involved.

Oliver leaves a few messages on my machine, casual invitations to meet at Ralph's, but I don't consider going. After a while, I turn the volume down and the ringer off. The flashing light reminds me that at some point in my future, I have messages to erase.

I get an A on the paper. Then I go for my pregnancy test.

I pretend I'm not sitting in a women's clinic waiting to give some girl ten minutes older than me a Dixie cup filled with my warm urine. I have wrapped a paper towel around the cup, because after all, I'm not a barbarian, I'm just a girl who didn't insist on rubbers and never got around to going on the pill.

I am led into a room where a serious counselor asks how I'll feel if the test comes back positive. I shrug. She would like to know if I've considered my options. This is when it occurs to me that when my mother was in a similar situation, there *were* no legal options—but I don't want to think about this, so I tell her that I have not considered my options, because for me, there are no options. She looks startled and clears her throat. "Okay," she says, stretching out the word.

I have no option, I tell her again. There's a part of me that feels like this isn't really happening. As if instead, I'm some character on an after-school special, and this is the part where the desperate girl acts belligerent. But I guess you're not supposed to say you have no options, because I get referred down the hall to a supervisor's office. Apparently, the test has come back positive, and it's important I understand that, in fact, I *do* have options. Like a little zealot, I tell the supervisor that I have seen the light and I am now aware of the plethora of choices available to me, because I sense telling her to fuck off is likely to land me in another office where I'll be encouraged to explore my emotions or reiterate my options, when all I really want is to not be pregnant by Oliver or be anything like my mother.

The procedure—that's what the supervisor calls it—will take a few minutes. There will be cramping. They accept cash, bank checks, and credit cards. I'll need a friend to escort me home. This is when I ask the first sincere question of the day. My voice cracks before it is halfway out of my mouth. "What if I don't have a friend?"

The woman looks up, and I correct myself. "I mean, what if I don't want any of my friends to know?" And in the time it takes for the woman to purse her lips in such a way that I realize I cannot be released unless I have someone to take me home, I start to wonder what it would be like to live in this office, because one thing is for shit sure, I'm getting that procedure.

"I'll figure it out," I tell the supervisor (and myself) as I sign forms and fold papers. I pay for the urine test and look no one in the eye. Finally finally finally, I open the door and escape into my city; I move through the grimy streets, down one block and around another, where like a mirage I see the subway entrance and head down the sour-smelling stairwell, catching the uptown train just before the doors close, and, being the lucky girl that I am, I miraculously find a seat, sit, and for the first time in what could possibly be three hours, though I know this is not humanly possible: I breathe.

Funny thing about breathing, though; sometimes it makes you cry.

A day later, I go to Oliver's without calling first. He buzzes me up, and before I enter the door he's left open, I'm scared. Eden's there.

"Hi, Eden," I say.

"Hi, Kara," she replies without looking at me.

"What's with you two?" Oliver asks. His reaction reassures me—she didn't tell him.

"Nothing," I say, handing him his belated birthday gift. He moves to kiss me. I suspect this isn't because he loves Kahlil Gibran or that he missed me, or even that he wants to taste me; more like he knows that a guy should kiss the girl he intends to fuck.

It will be a fairy-tale kiss, because like Sleeping Beauty, or one of her fairy-tale sisters, this kiss will change me. I will go in a girl (despite the fetus developing in my womb) and come out a woman. Before our lips even touch, I know things. I know he will not squeeze my hand or offer me crackers or tell me how this is just our first mistake, but there will be a lifetime of success ahead. I know that I would rather die than have Oliver pity me while he tries to come up with the right thing to say, all while not loving me back. I know I will ask Eden to be my escort, and I know I will never quite be the same.

All this I know, and yet, I kiss him back.

43

2008

While Michael and I waited to board the plane, he called his parents. Yesterday was the first time since the angioplasty that his father had golfed, and Michael wanted to hear about it.

"No kidding?" he said, smiling.

"Tell him I said hi," I whispered.

"Yeah well, she's right—you're not Fuzzy Zoeller—eighteen holes might be pushing it."

I dug in my bag for a magazine and found the notes the kids had given me a few hours earlier. I read them and ached. But then Adam called to ask if he had to go to Philip's house because he'd much rather play with Teddy, and I realized I didn't actually miss them as much as I thought. When we hung up, I put the notes back in my bag and prayed to a god I didn't totally believe in to protect this flight, because the thought of my beautiful babies sitting at our funeral was too much to bear. Then I found my *Vanity Fair* and relaxed.

Los Angeles was as beautiful as Michael advertised. We rented a convertible and drove through the twisting canyon roads. Our hotel was on the beach in Santa Monica. Everyone kept telling us how unfortunate it was to be visiting when the weather was so bad, which seemed odd, since the sky was a clear blue. Evidently it had rained the day before, and they were still getting over it.

"Can you imagine driving in a convertible every day?" Michael asked, as if cars mattered to me. Like a tour guide, he kept pointing things out: the breathtaking Pacific, stunning neighborhoods, chic shops.

"Too much propaganda," I said over Greek food in Malibu.

"Fair enough." Ever so slightly, he pulled his chair away.

"Sorry." I hated how argumentative I sounded. "Can we just be here? Like you said—no pressure."

"Absolutely. Zero pressure. None. Nada. Finis with the pressure."

I rolled my eyes. "Thank you."

But the Pacific *was* spectacular, and the shops every bit as fabulous as in New York, only here there was a playground steps away. I watched parents sipping lattes and chatting with each other, and truth be told, everyone seemed lovely. And from where we were sitting, even the sandboxes looked pristine.

The second day, we visited an elementary school and a junior high. Ever efficient, Michael scheduled an appointment with the guidance counselor, who spoke about their cutting-edge approach to teaching kids with learning disabilities. I was impressed: The schools were equipped with the latest technology. Hallways were spotless. People smiled. Libraries were well stocked and the teachers seemed scholarly. In fact, the whole California vibe was terrific. We ate avocadoes with every meal and made love twice a day. Hell, I even felt *athletic*, once waking in the middle of the night craving a tennis lesson.

On Saturday, Michael had a meeting with the West Coast firm. "Is this typical? Do they always work on the weekend?" I asked.

"Obviously, I'll set my own hours."

Obviously, I thought.

But the offices were stunning. Seamless glass windows overlooked breathtaking views of the hills. There were gorgeous exposed mahogany beams throughout the space, and instead of normal partitions, they used sculptural metal screens to break up the common areas. Every detail was attended to, conveying a sense of professional discernment.

"Beautiful textures," I admitted, having a deeper understanding of the scope of this opportunity.

Michael introduced me to the partners. Warm hellos were offered. A woman named Talia approached me. I'd assumed she was with the firm, but quickly learned she was the wife of the senior partner. "Won't you join me? We have a fabulous contemporary art museum."

"That sounds lovely," I said, recognizing that this wasn't a spontaneous gesture. With my eyes I told Michael it would cost him. Striking up conversations with strangers was not my idea of a nice afternoon. Morgan was great at this. I longed for her poise.

"Don't worry, I'll drop you at the hotel in a few hours," Talia told me. I smiled awkwardly.

"Have fun," Michael offered.

"You know I will." As we pecked goodbye, I secretly bit his lip.

At first I wondered if Talia expected me to meander through the exhibit making pithy comments about each of the works. I felt pressured to do what I always did: get her to like me. But the paintings were vibrant and accessible and any apprehension I'd had was replaced by admiration for the art.

I stood in front of a Marlene Dumas painting. It was of a child lifting her shirt above her head, revealing white panties. The shirt was bold and saturated, and the girl appeared both innocent and seductive. I felt like a voyeur enjoying this beautiful yet disturbing image. Talia waved her hand dismissively. "I don't like this."

A photograph of the artist caught my eye. Like her paintings, Dumas's untamed hair and voluptuous curves seemed unapologetic. It occurred to me how brave she was. Certainly Dumas knew she'd be criticized for this work—let alone the ones of corpses displayed on the opposite wall—but she persevered.

"Come. We'll find Monet," instructed Talia. I had a magnificent realization. I didn't like the senior partner's wife, so why on God's green earth should I care if she liked me? I wouldn't mistreat her or be rude, but I didn't need to be all smiles either. I was polite, but reserved. I was, dare I say—honest.

"My husband tells me you're ambivalent about leaving New York," she said on the drive to the hotel.

"Hmmm," I answered.

"May I ask why?" Time stood still. *No, you may not.* Or, *Why do you want to know?* Instead, I went with, "Actually, like most important decisions, it's layered. And to tell you the truth, I'm private when it comes to this sort of thing."

"Oh, well... I didn't mean to intrude," she said, clearly offended.

"No, you didn't intrude. I mean, it's a valid question. Just not my way." It was a beautiful moment. Not as beautiful as the Dumas and Picassos, but damn close. Damn close, indeed.

On our last day, we drove a winding road along the coast. With my hair blowing and the stereo blasting, I felt free. Michael, on the other hand, looked pensive. I knew he wanted a sign that I was as taken with this whole experience as he was. I tried to imagine living in a neighborhood nestled in the distant hills. I could practically see our kids playing in yards that overlooked the Pacific, tan and learning to surf. The problem was, I couldn't conjure an image of me with them.

We stopped for a late lunch at a café. (More avocadoes—I was going to miss them.) There were two women at the table next to us. Their children played hangman and drew rainbows on butcher paper placemats. My heart ached for my kids, but also for Morgan. "What's wrong?" asked Michael.

"Nothing." I didn't want him to think I was irritated by the women at the table. "Just missing the kids." I checked my watch. "And I should call Willa. She thinks we're visiting your parents." I didn't tell him about missing Morgan. He'd worry it was a bad sign. Even the *idea* of disappointing him made my heart pound.

I returned my attention to the women. They wore the same two-hundred-dollar jeans as the mothers back home. They were discussing their marriages (one husband worked too much, the other preferred his Xbox to making love), their babysitters (should laundry be part of their job description?), and their mothers (one was intrusive, the other recovering from a facelift). They set limits with their kids (no soda, finish the chicken fingers, don't irritate your brother), and were funny (What's that on my leg? Oh yeah, my ass). In short, they seemed fine. I could imagine getting to know them, or others like them.

Another woman came in to buy bread at the counter. She spotted my two women and came over to rave about how big the kids had all gotten. It occurred to me that if we moved here, there'd be no one who would have known my babies since they were babies.

During the flight home, Michael was distant. Even as he slept, his jaw was clenched and forehead furrowed. When he woke, we barely spoke. I wasn't prepared to tell him what he wanted to hear, so I watched the movie in silence. When we landed, my usually warm, extroverted husband didn't thank the stewardesses or say please to the taxi driver. I tried to touch his hand in the cab, but it was cold and unmoving, so after a moment I pulled away.

When we finally got home, we scooped up the kids with hugs and kisses. They all spoke at once and I took in each excited story. Liza darted around the apartment efficiently. I kept peeking at her to see if she was trying to give us space or if something was wrong. Perhaps she felt awkward—having been the woman of the house for four days. We ordered in dinner. I invited her to stay, but she declined. There were baths and dishes and laundry... but all in all, it was good to reclaim my kids and home.

Even though I was exhausted, I decided to sort through the mail. And there it was—a postcard from Oliver. I listened for Michael. He was in the den. I read it, and read it again.

Kara—

A long winter. MoMA opens soon. Lunch—two weeks from Tuesday, the Modern @1:00?

Call assistant (Janet) to confirm.

—O

I tucked the card into the rest of the mail and left it on the counter. I'd deal with it tomorrow. I longed for my familiar bed, in need of an escape.

Sometime later, I was awakened by Michael's voice. "I just can't believe you'd consider splitting up our family," he said into the East Coast night. He found the postcard, I thought. *It's just lunch*, I was going to say, but then I realized he was of course referring to L.A.

Defensive responses swirled in my mind. *Me? What about you?* But I was tired and didn't want to fight. "I just can't believe it, Kara," he said again. "Tell me you'll go," he whispered. "Tell me you'll go."

Another wife would have told him. Or said *something*, even if it was indecisive or not what he wanted to hear. But not me. I said nothing and fell safely back to sleep.

I returned to the postcard. His handwriting was still familiar. Even though Michael had been at work for hours, I felt he could materialize at any moment. I should tell him. Gauge his reaction. But I knew I wouldn't. I rationalized that if we were in a better place I'd have checked in, but who was I kidding? *Gauging* his reaction and *checking in* were code words for asking permission, and I was tired of seeking Michael's permission. Besides, I sensed he planned on being withdrawn until I was willing to talk about Los Angeles. I didn't blame him. And yet, of course, I did.

I looked around the kitchen. We were out of fruit. I contemplated the pros and cons of going to the grocery store. Maybe a run would help me reclaim that healthy L.A. feeling I'd lost several thousand feet above the Mississippi. I took a sip of coffee and read it again.

Finally, I called Morgan.

"It's just lunch," I told her.

"Right."

"I mean, Michael and I are going to go to the show together, that makes Oliver a family friend, practically."

"Practically," Morgan agreed.

"Besides, it's friggin' MoMA! I want the inside scoop on that."

"Who wouldn't?"

"I went to this extraordinary exhibit in L.A. I'm dying to hear what he thinks of Marlene Dumas. Do you know her work?"

"Can't say that I do," replied Morgan.

"I bet they're friends. I find her so compelling. I'd love to hear his thoughts." Morgan was silent. "Are you there?" I asked.

"Oh, I'm here."

"Well, what do you think?"

"Are you serious? You're asking me?"

"I don't know who else to talk to," I confessed.

"I think you're playing with fire. You have this huge fucking crisis confronting your marriage, and instead of dealing with it, you're distracting yourself with Oliver Bellows."

"Actually, I've been obsessed for months, since I first saw his paintings. I just never said anything. Michael's merger is irrelevant."

"Kara," she started. Oh sure, she could sleep with someone else for six months, but I can't have lunch (lunch!) with an old friend. "Do you want my honest opinion, or do you just need me to listen?"

"Your honest opinion." As long as you sign off on lunch.

"Are you sure?" she asked.

"Yes." Not at all.

"Your crisis in your marriage isn't about L.A. Your crisis is about you always looking to Michael and the kids to make you feel whole, when what you really need is to figure out how to do that for yourself."

Silence.

"Jesus," I said. "Is it too late to have you just listen?"

She laughed. "Sorry."

"Is this your shrink talking?" I asked.

"Something like that."

"Have *you* figured it all out?" I asked.

"More like, I'm learning the cost of being true to myself." She paused, like she had more to say. "But we're talking about you. And in all seriousness, once you cheat, you can never undo it."

"You did hear me say *lunch*, right?"

"Right. Lunch. Once you lie about lunch, you can't undo it."

Michael's and my first night together flashed in my mind. How he'd paid the Chinese delivery guy and left our bag of dinner on the foyer floor. To this day, it was the best lo mein I'd ever had—room temperature and on sheets smelling of us.

"Look, it isn't easy," she said. "Believe me, I know."

"I'm so angry," I said into the phone. I hadn't owned it until that moment. Why were his dreams more important than mine? But there was also a wise part of me that knew what I wanted was unfair. How could Michael all of a sudden take my desire to make art seriously, when I never had myself?

"I don't blame you. L.A. sucks."

We stayed on the phone for a while. Out of nowhere, I missed my mother. And I almost told Morgan, *I really miss my mother*—but then she talked about her mother, which made me not want to talk about my mother, so pretty soon after that, we hung up.

And then I called Janet to confirm.

I was getting ready to head out for pickup when the doorman buzzed. "Willa is here to see you."

That's strange, I thought. "Okay. Send her up."

"She said she prefers if you can come down."

Willa looked composed waiting on the lobby couch. She stood when she saw me. "Are you okay?" I asked. "What's going on?"

"Sorry, I should've called, but I didn't want to get into it over the phone..."

"Okay... I'm just about to get the kids. Do you want to walk?"

She shook her head no. "This won't take long." I motioned for us to sit. At first it looked like she didn't want to, but then she returned to the couch.

"I think we should take that space," she said. "It's great. I like it. It works, and I don't want to keep putting it off." She folded her hands on her lap.

"Keep putting it off? We just saw it last week."

"It's been three weeks, Kara."

"I've been playing phone tag with the landlord," I started.

She shook her head dismissively. "I'm unwilling to risk losing it."

"Well, I think we have time. It's been vacant for a while. And it's on a side street," I reminded her.

She exhaled. "What's going on? It's perfect."

I looked at her. "How can you act like there are no risks involved!? Jesus."

"Is that it, the risk? Because every time I try to discuss ways to increase our business, you clam up."

I could tell the doorman was listening. "I don't like being forced into making a decision," I whispered.

"Exactly! Neither do I."

"I'm just asking for some time to investigate..."

"I'm taking the space, Kara. With or without you."

I couldn't believe what I was hearing. "You can't! We have a legal partnership."

She stood. "I've secured a lawyer," she said softly. "And I'm told I can."

Henny came out to the yard and I knew something was wrong. Her face was twisted and it looked like it was taking all her might not to cry. *What is it?* I mouthed. She grabbed my hand and pulled me toward the gate. I bent down to her. "What happened?"

"Nothing," she barked. "Let's go."

Not today, I thought. I can't handle anything more. "We have to wait for Adam." She ignored me and headed toward the exit.

"Henny," I called.

Miss Nathanson tapped my shoulder. "Do you have a minute?"

"Well..." I hesitated, keeping an eye on my girl. Adam was across the yard talking to Philip. I tried to get his attention.

"Is something going on with Henny?" she asked. "She had a difficult morning, which wasn't such a big deal, but she's very hard on herself."

"Uh-huh." I motioned for Adam to wait with his sister.

"We were having a class discussion about the election. When I called on her, she couldn't remember Hillary's name." I agreed. That didn't sound so bad. "And then she called Obama 'Oh Mama.'"

"Ahhh."

"The children were hysterical." The teacher smiled. "It was kind of funny, but then I saw Henny's face. She was devastated."

I sighed. Adam and Henny were waiting. "I'll talk to her," I said.

"And there was a problem during writing workshop as well. She was supposed to read Jake's story to the group, but she had a lot of trouble. Even with words she knows..."

"Oh..." Why was Henny being asked to read another kid's work aloud? That didn't seem like the best idea. I was trying to figure out how to respond, but all I could think about was how embarrassed she must have been.

"I'm afraid Jake wasn't very nice about the situation." Which one was Jake? I looked around. "Don't worry," Miss Nathanson said. "I spoke to him and he apologized."

Oh, I'm sure that changed everything. "Okay..." I paused. The yard was chaotic. Adam was getting impatient. I had trouble differentiating what I should say from what I was thinking.

"I'm not supposed to inquire"—she leaned in—"but I'm curious, why'd you stop the medicine? Did she have a bad reaction?"

"Wait, what?" I asked.

"Why did you stop giving Henny the medicine? Did something happen?" Miss Nathanson repeated.

"What? No." What was she talking about?

"Well, the nurse mentioned that you never sent in more, and you didn't return her calls."

"What calls?"

"I think she left messages with your sitter." We looked at each other.

"So, Henny hasn't been getting *any* medicine at school?"

"I'm sorry, I thought you knew..." I couldn't believe it. I had to get out of there. The nurse had spoken with Liza!? What the hell?

As I rushed off, I heard Miss Nathanson in the distance. "We should set up a time to meet."

44

1987

I sit in Oliver's window and watch the buildings across his court-yard. If I squint, they look like the work of the Parisian impressionists. The city hum keeps me company while Oliver paints. The department chair has arranged for a major collector to visit Oliver's studio. For the past week he's been frantically touching up several years' worth of work.

"I can't fucking believe it," he says, coming into his room. "I'm out of turpentine." He looks utterly lost. I have never seen him so undone.

"Completely out?" I ask.

"That's what I'm saying, Kara." He scans the full ashtray on his dresser for a promising butt, but seems to rethink it, and throws himself on the bed.

"I'm fucking exhausted." Reminding him he hasn't slept much will piss him off, so I come down from the window and go to the kitchen. I make some tea and stare across the loft at his work. His figures are arresting. Spectacular, really. But from this distance, it's the murky backgrounds and luxurious fabrics that draw me in.

He comes into the kitchen. Oliver doesn't usually follow me. I enjoy the power, but at the same time feel unsettled by his neediness.

"Naptime over?" I tease.

"I gotta get this done. This is a huge opportunity, a make-or-break moment."

"What do you still need to do?" I ask.

"Everything." He sighs. "And I need fucking turpentine to do it."

"The store will open in the morning. Maybe it's a sign you should get some sleep." Not to mention, I'm tired too.

"Maybe it's a sign I should buy it in bulk," he says. We both look across the loft at his work. It is an impressive sight.

"Which one's the strongest?" he asks. His tone is less abrasive.

I walk to the canvases, taking in each one for several minutes. Most are of Eden, but some are city scenes, close-ups of buildings devoid of people. All are compelling. There is no denying the passion. I praise each one, Eden's hands, his choice of color. But there is something I'm not saying. Now just doesn't seem the time; he's too anxious.

"What?" he asks. "What are you thinking?"

I pause. "Okay, do you see this?" I ask, pointing to the background in one of Eden. "And this?" I point to the concrete in a cityscape.

"Yeah..."

I have his complete attention. "Are you aware of how fucking vibrant those parts are?" I am excited. Excited by his work. And to be speaking my truth.

"I guess. I mean, I have always loved the blue here." He motions toward the buildings in another city scene. It's not one of the ones I'd been referring to, but like the others, it has the same brushstroke.

"Exactly. It thrives." I stand back and take in the work. Then I go to Oliver and pull him toward the kitchen. "Look. Look at that movement. Look at that brushstroke." He is quiet. Thinking. "I can't help but wonder what your work would be like if..."

"If I tried abstraction," he says, finishing my thought.

"If you tried abstraction."

He walks across the loft and pulls out three canvases from behind the TV. "I did these months ago. Just fucking around."

They are stunning, but incomplete. A good beginning. "These are electric. You have to keep going."

He folds his arms and stares. I hoist myself on the island and watch him. I tell myself if I can't have his love, I'll take this consolation prize: proximity. While he seems to be considering my critique, I wonder if I have enough love for both of us. But I know I don't.

"What are you thinking?" I ask, suddenly nervous I've said too much. The studio visit is a week away. Maybe this has been a mistake.

"I'm thinking I want to give these some attention." He points to the neglected abstractions. "And to do that, I need some fucking turpentine."

"Well then," I smile, "This must be your lucky day."

When we enter my dorm room, my paintings appear as if they've been waiting for our arrival. "What the hell?" Oliver asks when he sees my work. He glances around my space while I stand in the doorway. I'm trying to see my room from his perspective. He's never been here, and although I'm nervous about what he'll think, I'm also proud. Five canvases are propped against the wall. They are familiar. Like friends. I want to introduce him.

"Hey!" he says, walking to them. I am perfectly still. "That's great." He nods. *What's great?* I want to ask. *How? Do you really think so?* "Good job."

"Thanks," I say, but of course, I don't feel complimented.

He stands for a moment, looking. "How long have you been painting?"

"Not long." I busy myself around my room. I want to show him my mother's quilt and the view from my window. The O'Keeffe book sits near my bed and the clinic card is still on my dresser. All go unnoticed by him. I tell myself he's tired. Preoccupied.

"I can't believe you didn't tell me."

I realize suddenly that this is what I've been waiting for. The moment when Oliver learns I'm an artist, like him. *We have this to share,* I want to say. *This is what's been missing. We'll grow together. Inspire each other. I have so much to offer. Do you see that now?*

I go to my closet and retrieve the large can of turpentine. I am waiting. Waiting for him to acknowledge my work. And in doing so—me.

"Fuck yeah," he says, taking the can. It will be many years before I purchase another. "Can guys use the bathroom on this hall?"

"No. Upstairs or down."

"I'll just wait until I get back." He is a man on a mission. "Well, thanks." He holds up my mostly full can.

No problem, I am supposed to say. I am deeply ashamed. Who did I think I was?

"Oh, and Kara." He smiles. "You're the best." He kisses me quickly and away he goes, taking my turpentine and confidence right on out the door.

45

2007

I took a deep breath and knocked on Henny's door. "Can I come in?" I asked, not waiting for her to answer. She was lying on her bed, staring at the mural. "Miss Nathanson told me you had a bad day. You must've been so embarrassed."

She scooted closer to me, but didn't say a word. "You know, forgetting names and getting words all jumbled in your mind, that's part of dyslexia."

"I called him Oh Mama." She rested her head on my lap.

"I know." I smiled. We both did.

"What's his name again?"

"Obama."

"Obama," she repeated.

"You know, I could come to your class. Teach them about dyslexia. Sometimes kids make fun of things they don't understand."

She sat up. "No!"

"If you had diabetes, we wouldn't keep it a secret."

"What's diabetes?"

I sighed. "It's a disease that has to do with your blood and sugar."

"I don't get it."

"It's a complicated disease," I said. "I don't even understand it. But dyslexia—now, that I could explain. I bet I'd be good at that."

"In kindergarten, Mrs. Horiuchi taught us how to make sushi."

"I remember."

"You could teach us how to make chocolate chip cookies..."

I tried to be patient. "It's important you understand that there's nothing wrong with the truth." I played with her hair.

"There's something else." I paused. I could hear Liza and Max in the kitchen. They must've just gotten back from his playdate. "Miss Nathanson told me the nurse isn't giving you medicine anymore."

"I thought you knew."

"Knew?! What do you mean?"

"Liza told me you didn't want me to take it at school anymore." She spoke carefully, as if realizing something was wrong.

"What?"

She nodded.

"But you've been taking it in the morning, haven't you?"

"Only when you give it." I'd turned that task over to Liza.

I stormed out of her room and into the kitchen. Liza and Max were about to start a game of Go Fish. I pulled open the cupboard where we kept the medicine. The container was almost empty. If Henny wasn't getting it regularly, why wasn't it full? I met Liza's eyes. "Go watch TV," I told Max.

"We're playing."

"Now, Max. Ask Adam to turn on a show."

"Go on," said Liza, gathering the cards. Max got down from his chair and moved slowly toward the playroom. "Go on, honey," she urged, which nearly sent me through the roof.

"Where's the medicine, Liza?" I asked once he was gone.

"Kara, I don't know what to say."

"Why don't you start by telling me where the fucking medicine is?" My words startled even my ears. But I remembered what the psychiatrist had said about teenagers abusing this stuff; it was the only explanation—Liza must have been using Henny's medicine to get high.

"I haven't been giving it to her," she said softly.

"So I'm told." Liza sat still. "Why don't you just admit it? *You've* been taking it," I said.

"Is that what you think?" she cried.

"Oh please, don't get all indignant."

"I didn't take the pills," she said.

"No? They just vaporized." The conversation was ridiculous. I should just fire her on the spot. Not only was my babysitter an addict, but she had purposely deceived me. First Willa, now this. Maybe the universe was punishing me, I thought, feeling guilty about Oliver's postcard.

"I've been throwing them away," said Liza. "I couldn't watch you drug her."

"*Drug her?*" I held the counter.

"I just couldn't. I couldn't watch you teach her that drugs were the answer to every little problem."

"Oh my God," I said, mostly to myself.

"I'm sorry, Kara, but you never asked me what I thought about this whole thing. I mean, you never even asked my opinion. I spend a lot of time with her, you know?"

"Of course you do, but I'm her *mother*."

"So! Mothers don't make mistakes?" she challenged. My face flushed. We both knew mothers certainly did make mistakes. I couldn't believe what I was hearing. "Did you even consider treating her holistically? Changing her diet? Saint-John's-wort? Fish oil?"

"I have to do what I think is right." My words were calm.

"So no one else's opinion matters?"

"Of course it does, but in the end, I have to do what I think is best."

"Drugging a seven-year-old?"

"Look, when I was a kid, I had all sorts of problems in school and no one noticed." I wanted her to understand. My mind flashed to Liza on the floor of Henny's room, looking at the mural. She'd taken my art seriously. I didn't want to lose her. "In many ways, I've been trying to get over that my whole adult life."

Liza shook her head. "You shouldn't let your baggage cloud what you do with your kids."

"Oh please. Show me a parent who doesn't..."

"What I mean is—I refuse to be part of it. I love your kids, I do. That's the problem. I just can't stand by doing nothing."

"You sound like you think I'm *abusing* her."

Liza raised her eyebrows, as if I was finally catching on. We were both quiet. I couldn't believe she viewed me this way. I wondered if she felt this critical of Michael. Probably not, I decided. This seemed very much between us women.

She stared at me. "You're drugging your little girl. There's no other way to see it."

I wanted to slap her sanctimonious face. She was totally out of line. I was the mother. I needed to do what I thought was best. But another part of me worried: What if she was right?

Just then, Michael called. "I'm in the middle of something here," I said, hoping he'd intuit that I wasn't just trying to get him off the phone.

"Kara," he started. "We have to talk." Hearing his voice reminded me again of my plans with Oliver. I should tell him, I thought. Walk into the hall right this very moment and tell him about lunch next Tuesday. Forget Liza, forget Willa. Forget Los Angeles. Just tell him.

"Okay..." I said.

"Because I can't take the silence," he whispered into the phone.

"Me neither."

"But I guess it's going to have to wait," he added. For a second, I assumed this was because I'd just told him I was busy. "Because I have to go back to L.A."

"What? We just got back!"

"They're meeting with my contacts from Seoul. I can't let that happen without me."

"Can't Garrett go?"

"I don't want Garrett to go." There you have it, I thought.

I looked at Liza and wondered if she was upset I'd taken Michael's call. Now that I knew what she thought of me, I could barely concentrate. This was an old, familiar feeling. "When do you leave?" I asked him.

"In a few hours. So we'll talk when I get back?"

"Fine." As we hung up I thought about how much was going on that he knew nothing about. Morgan's warning came to me: Once you lie about lunch, there's no turning back. That's ridiculous, I decided. There would be plenty of time to catch him up. He was busy. We both were. But the truth was—part of me worried he might not take my side.

Liza stood waiting. She was young and beautiful and angry. I hated that she didn't see things my way. Hated that she judged me. But I also felt sorry for her. There was something sad about her self-righteousness. "You know, life is layered," I started. "Things aren't always all good or all bad." But I could tell she wasn't listening.

"You're the one who needs Henny to be perfect."

"That's not true, Liza. It's just not." I wasn't sure there was anything left to say. I heard the TV in the distance and hoped the kids didn't know what was going on. They loved Liza. Would they blame me? Henny?

"Go home for now," I suggested. "Let's give ourselves a few days to think." I was still hanging on, even when it was clearly time to let go.

She shook her head. "I can't. I just can't. I'll be out within a day or two." A day or two! Where would she go? I'm sure that Nate's wasn't an option. "Just tell the kids whatever you want," she said.

My face burned. Henny's medicine was Liza's deal-breaker. In my whole life, though I'd often threatened, I'd never left anyone. I marveled at her independence. But then I thought of her mother's words: *Think about it... I hope you'll change your mind... If you'll let me explain...*

It was clear. We'd each been damaged by our mothers' addictions. Constantly fleeing or hanging on no matter the cost were symptoms of the same affliction. I didn't want it anymore. Having a reaction was not the same as making a decision. I wanted something different.

I watched in silence as Liza grabbed her bag from the closet and headed for the door. Like most people who are skilled at disappearing, she didn't say goodbye.

The Sunday before I was to meet Oliver, there was an above-the-fold article about Michael in the business section of the *New York Times*.

The photo was perfect. He looked creative and elegant; the quintessential New York architect. Though we knew there'd be an article, its prominence was shocking.

Michael was still in L.A., so I snuck down to the deli late Saturday night and bought the paper. Despite this merger being the source of my dilemma, I couldn't help but be excited for him.

I phoned Michael. "Impressive," I said.

"How's it look in person? I read it online."

"Fabulous."

"Well, the writer did right by the firm, that's for sure. We sound great."

"Seriously, congratulations."

"Thanks," he said into my ear. I listened to his silence and was pretty sure he was doing the same.

"I'll show the kids. They'll be so proud," I said safely.

"Kara, we still have some decisions to make," he started.

"I know. I'm almost ready. When you get back, we'll talk then."

Our phone rang off the hook. People I barely knew called to offer congratulations. They seemed genuinely pleased for us, and not in an opportunistic way.

Even Victoria called. "The *New York Times*!" she crowed. "It doesn't get much better than that! Is he beside himself?"

"He is. Yes, thanks." I felt a wave of relief at the sound of her voice. Like it or not, Victoria was now my connection to Willa. And since Willa and I weren't exactly speaking, I clung to her.

A century later, I collapsed on the couch. I wanted to watch the debate. Handsome Obama was fielding questions about his pastor, and even though I thought it was Hillary's time, I was getting angry that the media was fueling white America's fear. I muted the TV and let the day wash over me. How nice it had been to get those calls. Even Victoria—what a shock. And that's when it hit me. Morgan hadn't called.

46

1987

I am more than a block away and can already hear the Ramones blaring from Oliver's apartment. A crowd of fabulous, untouchable artist types have spilled into the street, and as if laws wouldn't dare encroach upon them, they nonchalantly pass a joint. I step around gangly girls and boys wearing leather pants and pouty expressions and make my way into Oliver's celebration.

I haven't seen him in a couple of weeks. His studio visit went well; the man bought several important pieces, which led to the gallerist Schuyler Terre offering to represent him. At least that's what the article in *Art in America* said. Turns out, when Terre bankrolls a twenty-two-year-old so he can paint in Italy for a year—it's newsworthy. Oliver's New York solo debut is already scheduled for the season he returns.

Thus, this party.

I get off the elevator and find Eden kissing a beautiful woman. "Can you believe this?" she asks, referring to Oliver's success.

"Seems anything's possible," I say, glancing between Eden and the woman, who has a flower tattoo. They are holding hands.

"This is Willa," says Eden. "Willa, this is Kara."

The woman stands tall and smiles. "Hi." Then she hugs me, which I find surprising from someone so hip. Eden looks at us and smiles. They try to include me in their conversation, but it's too loud. I can't hear.

"Nice to meet you!" I yell.

"And you!" screams Willa. When I glance back, they've returned to their cocoon of kissing. She's nice, I decide, feeling sorry for her. I'm pretty sure that being with women is just a phase for Eden.

I scan the room for Oliver. He's standing by the window talking to two men in expensive suits. Behind them are several abstractions I've never seen. They are every bit as brilliant as I knew his work could be. I try to meet his eye. I want to convey what I think of the work, but he's focused on the men. One says something and Oliver releases a hearty full-throated laugh. His apartment is packed with people wanting to be in his proximity, yet he's dressed in his usual ragged T-shirt (a navy Columbia one, worn inside out) and paint-spattered Levi's. I have seen him in these clothes many times, but tonight it seems like a costume, Oliver playing the role of young artist. I watch his movements, and even though I am nowhere near him, I swear I can smell him.

A stunning woman joins Oliver and the suits. This is no college girl; she drips sophistication and wealth. When she speaks, she leans in and touches his elbow. My body tells me it is time to flee, but like a paralyzed deer, I stay.

Someone has changed the music. The Talking Heads fill the room with excitement. Some dance. New bottles of wine are opened. Lines of coke are snorted off his filthy bathroom counter—the very definition of a happening party.

A chiseled young man hands me a glass of wine. "To Oliver's success," he says, but before I am able to drink to that, he's gone. I can't bear to stand alone, so I pretend to see someone in the distance and head toward Oliver's bedroom. This too is crowded, but at least I'm able to perch on my window. The courtyard is dark, as if tonight nothing dares to exist beyond Oliver.

A hippie-looking woman rumored to have a trust fund sits on his bed and attempts to bead a white boy's dreadlocks. "I heard he presold paintings he hasn't even started," says the knowing hippie.

"Is he staying for graduation?" an eager young woman with dark eyes asks. No one knows the answer.

"I thought he painted people," says the guy with dreads.

"Schuyler told me that Oliver's work reached a new level when he switched to abstractions," says a man, older than the rest. I am fairly certain he is an installation artist Oliver once mentioned.

"No shit?" says the girl with the dark eyes, looking the artist up and down.

"Yeah," he continues, moving closer. "She says his passion is best expressed in his abstractions... the way he moves color across the canvas." The girl seems to hang on his every word, while he slowly takes a cigarette from a silver case and lights it. For a brief moment, I look out the window and contemplate jumping to my death, an attractive alternative compared to this night.

"Do you like his work?" the chiseled man from earlier asks me.

"Uh..." I hesitate.

"Whoa, is that a no?" he asks in exaggerated horror.

"That is not a no," I say.

"Well, what do you think of the about-to-be-famous Oliver Bellows?"

"What is this, an interview?" I joke.

"Actually, yes. I'm from the *Village Voice*."

This is bad news. I assumed he was just a guy. In fact, earlier it had briefly occurred to me that fucking him might be an adequate beginning to the rest of my life. But I want nothing to do with Oliver's press. I practically recoil. "Well then, put me down as, no comment." I don't know this is the first time in a line of many when I will be silent on the topic of Oliver and his art.

I hand the reporter my empty glass and hop down from my sill. I am about to give a reason for why I'm leaving, but when I turn to the group, they've already moved on. So I make my way through the swarm. Eden and the chic lesbian are within reach; but I don't go to them. It's time to leave.

About to make my escape, I take a last look at Oliver. He's across the loft, where he's been stationed all night. Only the important, enamored faces surrounding him have changed.

47

2008

I untied Trudy from the preschool gate and looked around for Morgan. School had already started and Zoe still wasn't here. I called her cell. Out of service. She probably left it in a cab again. No one answered the landline. Maybe Zoe had strep again. Last time, Eric had turned off the ringer and it took three days before they figured it out. I wondered if Zoe would have to get her tonsils out.

I checked my watch. I had some time before I needed to get to work. I wasn't looking forward to another day where Willa and I coexisted while my lawyer reviewed our partnership agreement. I'd get Morgan to make coffee, I decided as Trudy and I made our way.

Eric was coming out of the building. "I don't want to talk about it," he said when he saw me.

"Zoe has strep again. I knew it."

"Oh please. Like you don't know." He moved past me.

"What?!" Why was he being so nasty?

He stopped. "You really don't know, do you?"

"Did something happen? Is Morgan okay?"

"Morgan's always okay. You should know that by now." Uh-oh. This time, he'd found out. We studied each other. He spoke first. "She left me."

"Oh, Eric." I had no idea what to say. I was dying for the details, of course. But hearing them from him was—disloyal. Why hadn't she called?

"When?" I asked.

"Friday. In therapy. You knew we were in therapy, right?"

I nodded. "A lot of good that did," he said.

"Was it...like, a fight? You know, she can be impulsive?"

"Not this time. She had a whole plan," he said.

"A plan?"

"She'd already rented a place, gotten a lawyer...A plan."

"I can't believe it," I said under my breath. Just like Willa, I thought. What if I had inadvertently given her the idea?

He shrugged.

"Where's Zoe?" I asked.

"Isn't she at school?"

"No."

"Here we go. The beginning of Morgan's bullshit inconsistency. She probably didn't feel like bringing her," seethed Eric.

I looked at him. It was obvious that I agreed.

"Anyway," he started.

"Listen, we can still get the kids together...like playdates on the weekends or something. I mean...don't hesitate to call," I said.

"Yeah, thanks," he replied; clearly he had no interest. Somehow, none of our friends had divorced, so this was new to me. I wasn't accustomed to the inevitability of *sides*. Though in this case, it would prove irrelevant.

"Not to intrude, but where is she? Where'd they go?" Is she with the guy? I wondered.

"The West Side." His shoulders slumped, which made him look pathetic. Then I felt shallow and guilty for thinking so. But this was also when I knew she'd never go back to him. Morgan was not a woman who returned to a slouching man.

"And get this," said Eric. "She sold her book." I nodded a *that's inevitable* nod. "Two-hundred-grand advance."

Holy shit. Good for her. "Hmmmm," I said instead.

Soon after, I touched his arm and said something warm and meaningless. I don't recall how he responded. But whatever it was, what we both meant was goodbye.

*   *   *

I got to MoMA early. My plan was to peruse the permanent col-
lection, hoping it would steady me before the time came to meet
Oliver. I made my way to the Stieglitz photos. The room was empty,
except for a guard who kindly spent most of his time roaming where
I wasn't. I stood mesmerized in front of an O'Keeffe nude. The
image reminded me of Eden, of course. And oddly, my mother. I felt
old and sad. Michael seemed so far away. Farther away than California. I suppose I was missing my younger self—when I was free but
didn't know it. When loving Oliver was hurtful only to me.

I wondered if O'Keeffe's full breasts and round belly had always
seemed so forlorn or rather were a Rorschach of sorts, indicative of
my mood. Snap out of it, I thought, emerging from my stupor. Life
was good. An exciting day awaited. I was about to see Oliver, something I'd been wanting for longer than I cared to admit.

And then I saw a reflection in the glass. Someone was standing
behind me. I spun around. "Jesus, you scared me!" I said to Morgan.

"Sorry." She stifled a nervous laugh with her hand. "I knew today
was the day. I figured I'd wander around aimlessly, and if it was
meant to be, I'd find you."

"Or you could have called," I said.

"But this is so much more theatrical."

"That is true. This is more theatrical."

"Are you ready?" she asked.

I'd been having imaginary fights with her since running into
Eric, but it didn't matter. She asked; I answered. "As I'll ever be."

"You have nothing to worry about," she said knowingly. For a
moment, I believed her. "What's meant to be—will be."

"You're very Zen today," I said.

"Right?"

"Well, stop it. It's annoying."

"You look great," Morgan told me, ignoring my funk. "Stoic, but
soft. Not easy to pull off." It was exactly the look I'd been going for.
I pretended I didn't appreciate her saying so.

"I take it you know," she said as we wandered.

"I ran into Eric."

"How is he?"

"He looked good, actually." I'm not sure why I lied. I guess I'd have wanted someone to do the same for me. "So, how's Zoe?" I asked.

"She's good. She's young. She'll be fine."

I didn't say anything to this; I might have even nodded. But I think I knew even then, this is where we died.

"Max misses her." Yet another lie; Max had found Reggie, a fast runner and train lover.

"Yeah. The year's almost over. I don't think I'm going to bother to schlep her to the East Side."

She'd already relinquished the East Side. "And you? You okay?" I asked, needing to change the subject again.

"I am. I really am."

"Good. That's good."

"It was hard not telling you, you know?" She touched my arm as she spoke. If I had been honest or courageous, I would've let the tears come. "But I felt like the whole topic was off-limits..." she explained. "I promised I wouldn't involve you. I wanted to keep my word."

I resisted pithy comments about irony.

"Especially once I went from imagining to planning. I didn't want to burden you," she said.

We passed a stunning Alice Neel portrait. Alice was a mother; by many people's standards, a poor one. I wondered how she would've been viewed if instead, she'd been a father.

"My book sold." Morgan brought me back.

"I heard! Congratulations."

"At auction," she said.

"Wonderful. Just what you wanted."

She nodded. "So anyway, I'm going to go. Leave you to your rendezvous."

We hugged. "Good luck," she said. "You're beautiful. I'll text you my new number. You'll come to the West Side."

"Definitely," I agreed. Then we both turned away.

*   *   *

Oliver kissed my cheek. It was official; I still shivered when his skin grazed mine. I raised my shoulder ever so slightly to quell the sensation.

"Quite the article," he said.

"Yeah, thanks. Michael's thrilled." There. We both mentioned my husband. I hoped my doing so didn't make me sound domestic.

"But you must be used to the limelight," I said nervously. He scanned the restaurant; I scanned the appetizers. It was no use; apparently I'd lost the ability to decipher English. When I looked up, his eyes were zeroed in on me.

"It's good to see you, Kara." I couldn't help but wonder, did he think I'd aged well?

"So. How've you been?" I asked.

"Are you nervous?" He had a slight smile.

It was a simple question, but I wasn't some enamored girl. I was a married woman. A grown-up. A business owner. A mother. A friend. It was too personal. The privilege of my vulnerability was no longer his. Or said another way, it was none of his goddamned business.

But for some reason, I answered the best I could.

"Yes." And like magic, the intensity diminished.

"Why?" he pressed.

"You're an old lover, Oliver. I guess that's how I'm wired." Back then I'd never have had the nerve to label our relationship. A rule I'm certain hadn't come from me.

The waitress appeared. Oliver leaned back in his chair and quizzed her on the day's specials. I noticed by the time they deconstructed the risotto, she was blushing. I strategically made my eyes warm and said all sorts of please and thank-yous, hoping to center her.

"Tell me about your art," I said. This was what I'd really wanted to hear. All of it, starting with his studio experience in Italy through to this very moment. How many hours did he paint each day? Did he ever take time off? Was his wife supportive of his process? Did he feel his work had changed? When he spoke of these things, I was reminded of the night he ran out of turpentine. How vulnerable he'd been. Time and experience—not to mention success—had aged him. But even with his expertise firmly established, he seemed desperate to impress me.

"Come...while they prepare our lunch, I'll show you." We walked his floor, where much of the work was still in the process of being hung. Compared to his Madison show, the scale of these paintings was massive. His work was as charged as being with him had been. Bold. Unpredictable—and yet, still balanced. I wanted to possess the whole experience. I wanted him. I wanted to be a part of his power.

He stood off to the side and I could feel him watching me. I vacillated between taking in the work and feeling self-conscious. When I could stand it no longer, I glanced at him, repulsed by his proud-as-a-peacock gaze. But I wasn't ready to take him off that pedestal, so I looked away.

When we returned to the restaurant, our waitress hurled herself across the room to inquire if we were ready for our meal. Oliver nodded and checked to see if the other patrons were observing us. It was an interesting sensation: disgust and attraction at the same exact time.

"What about you, Kara?" he asked much later.

"Well, you met my kids," I started.

"They're beautiful."

"Aren't they?" I tucked the memory of my first pregnancy away, though something must have registered on my face.

"What's wrong?" he asked.

"No, nothing, I just realized I have to pick them up soon." Which was true, I did. "And there's my shop..."

He nodded. "Do you still paint?" This startled me.

"I didn't for a long time," I said. "But more, lately." Since seeing your Madison show.

"Well, I'm sure the kids keep you busy." He didn't mean to patronize, but I felt defensive. Perhaps because that sort of busy involved a lot of wiping: noses, butts, counters, tears.

"Yes...but that's not really why." I paused, waiting for him to ask me to elaborate. There was an awkward silence, filled by eating and discussions of nouvelle cuisine.

"I was heartbroken, you know," I said, out of nowhere.

He put down his fork and swallowed. "I was young; you deserved better."

"But you were an artist. Didn't you know how much your opinion mattered to me?" My voice sounded small, but I didn't care. I wanted him to answer, but he looked puzzled.

"Wait, what are you referring to?"

"You barely said anything about my art. Nothing. I'd been secretly painting for months. The whole time dreaming of what you'd say once you knew, but then . . . nothing."

"Nothing?" he asked.

"Not really."

"That's not how I remember it."

"Trust me, you were hardly encouraging." I took a sip of water.

"Really? Huh. That's not how I remember it. I'm sorry."

I nodded thanks.

"Flowers," he said, as if congratulating himself. "And some figurative pieces too."

I nodded again.

"They were good," he said definitively. "But Kara, I was young. Anxious. School was ending. I was worried about my future."

I had two thoughts at once. He'd just referred to my work as good (I pretended not to be elated), and that we'd both been so young. Even younger than Liza was now. It didn't seem possible. Back then, he'd seemed so powerful.

"Besides, you were so . . ."

I waited. As if I'd waited a lifetime.

". . . desperate," he said carefully. "Your art was fine. Good even. But you seemed so fragile. Too fragile. I couldn't take it on."

"My mother had just died." Tears came to my eyes. I hated the memory of my younger, needier self. For a moment, I was right back there. Shame as thick as pudding for loving him, when he didn't love me back.

"You asked about my process," he said. "Here's an important part. Maybe even more than anything else. For me, I can't take on anyone's..."

Anyone's what? Bullshit? Needs? Love? What!?

"...anguish," he said. "Maybe it's not fair. But having that much power, as flattering as it was in the beginning, I ended up feeling smothered."

My mind flashed to Michael. And not some pretty, romanticized, Hollywood version of what a woman would think about when she was supposed to be realizing how wonderful her husband was; my mind swirled with some of our most spectacular fights, landing on the one about Bill Clinton. In hindsight, perhaps I'd overreacted, but in my defense, I was pregnant with Adam. Only three months, but still.

There we were, one minute happily cuddled next to each other watching the president address the nation, and the next thing I knew, I was throwing on my fat jeans (which I couldn't button) and looking for my purse.

"Where are you going?" he asked, looking amused. Of course, this had calmed me immediately.

"Fuck you, Michael."

"I *agree* with you. He's lying. All I'm saying is—what's he supposed to do? It's absurd we even know about this."

"*That* woman?" I spat. "I did not have sexual relations with *that* woman."

Michael tapped my spot on the bed. "Kara."

"Don't *Kara* me. It's disgusting—I did not have sexual relations with *that* woman! Please. Like she's some stranger to him!" I yelled.

"It's a private matter." He shook his head.

"*Was* a private matter. Not anymore."

"So he cheated on his wife. Some men do. Not that I'm condoning it," he added quickly. "It's just none of our business."

"This isn't about fidelity," I said. "Not to me. I couldn't care less that he cheated on his wife."

"Well, some people do. Very much so. He needs to distance himself."

"Why? Because she's so hideous? So beneath him?" I yelled, looking around for my boots. "What about *her* feelings? Where do they fit in? *That* woman. What? He can fuck her but he can't say her name? She's so repulsive, so hideous." I quickly put on one boot, then the other, zipping them both with rage. "Who cares, she's just some *understudy*?"

"Understudy?" He raised an eyebrow. "You mean intern?"

"Intern..." I quickly corrected myself.

"Kara," he started. I could see that my pain pained him, but our charming leader of the free world was just like every man I'd ever known. Prince Charming didn't exist. No man could be trusted. No man. Not even Michael.

Suddenly, I wanted to take this baby growing inside of me and leave. Leave my husband. Leave New York. Leave. Raise my baby on my own. It was my genetic destiny.

Like a cyclone, I spun into the living room, down the hall, and landed at the front door. I had nowhere to go. Our friends were all couples; I didn't want them to know. And opening Little Scissors at this hour felt dangerous. So I pretended the living room had been my destination and removed my boots and jeans, wrapped up in a blanket, and collapsed on the couch.

Much later, he touched my shoulder, waking me. "Come to bed, Kara."

"I'm fine," I mumbled, turning my back to him. But he lay down next to me.

"I love you, Kara Caine," he whispered. I let him hold me. "And your mother...she deserved better. She did."

The waitress appeared. I watched her clear away Oliver's dish and wipe the left-behind crumbs. The more intensely she worked, the more awkward she seemed. Oliver waved to a couple seated several tables away. His attention was clearly waning. He wiped his mouth and folded his napkin, the culinary signal for a subject handled.

I considered telling him about the abortion. And not for absolution, either, but to hurt him. Instead, I sat and enjoyed the power of my secret. Perhaps I hadn't been as fragile as either of us had thought. It was decided: This part of the past I would keep my own.

When we said goodbye, I told him how much Michael and I were looking forward to his opening. He smiled. We hugged and again I remembered what it was like to be with him. But then he got a call, and I checked my phone, and within moments I was in a cab heading uptown.

I sighed the sigh of someone who suddenly felt safe. And after a few blocks, I looked past the driver and up the avenue. Perfect, I thought, smiling. If the traffic stayed like this, I'd be on time for the kids.

Michael took the red-eye home. In a haze of early morning sleep, I felt him climb into our bed. Ever so slightly, I moved toward him; he pulled me the rest of the way. I could feel his coarse legs on my warm ones. He pushed my nightgown toward my belly. Finally, his skin on mine. Under the faint smell of airplane air was his scent. Unmistakable. My man was home.

I tried to recall the last time we'd made love, but rejected the contemplation as too difficult. We had much to talk about, to figure out. But I didn't want to think.

Afterwards, we dozed. When my alarm went off some time later (minutes, hours?), he dropped his weighty arm over me. "Let Liza get them."

"Go back to sleep." I was reminded of our distance these past few months. I got out of bed and paused at the window. I loved the city sunrise. White brick buildings were transformed into rosy skyscrapers, which to me were every bit as tranquil as majestic mountains or sweeping plains. My concerns drifted away. I went to wake the kids and scoop the coffee. Though I'd never admit it, there was a spring in my step. Now that Michael and I had connected, my life felt manageable again. Why did I always forget this?

*   *   *

It turned out, Michael was appalled by how Liza had handled Henny's medicine. He used words like *unacceptable* and *betrayal*.

"I still haven't told the kids she left," I said.

"We'll think of something." And I knew he was right.

"We could always tell them we're moving," he offered.

"About that..." I said. Michael seemed to hold his breath. "I'm sorry I haven't been able to talk about this. I shouldn't have shut you out," I said.

"You always shut me out at first. I knew you'd be back."

"Oh my God, am I that predictable?" I pretended to be irritated.

"Only your love, baby." His levity aside, it was important and true.

"Good," I said, his words echoing in my mind. "I'm glad you know. That'll make the rest of what I have to say so much easier."

48

2008

I stood in front of Willa's shop and tried to get an unobstructed view of the new Little Scissors façade. The Realtor had been right; with adequate signage there was excellent visibility. The turnout was shocking. At first, I didn't understand. Of course there were the usual sophisticates and print media types, but the place was packed. Children of all ages, and even a few adults, were lined up around the block, waiting to be tended to by stylists wearing pencil skirts and bouffant updos. There was a barbershop quartet, jugglers, and cotton candy too. And most unexpected, several television station news crews.

With clipboard in hand, one of Victoria's underlings approached me, wanting to know if I'd checked in. On the walk over, I'd tried to prepare myself for any lingering feelings of abandonment by remembering that I'd chosen this—but the chirpy gatekeeper caught me off guard.

"She's with me, she's with me," Victoria called, saving me.

"Unbelievable!" I motioned to the crowd. Victoria beamed and handed me a press packet. "Who *are* all these people?" I asked.

"You didn't hear? These are the 9/11 kids. Free haircuts for all."

I looked around. It was a brilliant maneuver, I thought—opportunistic and manipulative, but moving and sweet, too. As far as marketing strategies go, Victoria had hit a home run.

"They loved the bit about the grieving lesbian using her survivor benefits to follow her dream," Victoria whispered.

"Follow her dream?" I whispered. "She bought me out with..."

"This is a story of resilience," Victoria interrupted. "The other side of tragedy."

I bristled, and then felt bad for doing so. For me, 9/11 would never be anything but tragic. But I knew that wasn't what Victoria meant.

"So, is this a Michael week?" she asked.

I immediately forgave her; I missed Michael and the kids and was grateful for any opportunity to talk about them. Once the school year started it would be easier—the kids and I would stay in New York and Michael would be the one going back and forth.

"They're back on Tuesday," I told Victoria. "And Henny's starting the new school." Thinking about this made me anxious—all change did, but we needed to do something. None of the public school's recommendations seemed adequate.

Victoria nodded. The woman with the clipboard appeared—a reporter had a few more questions. "Make sure you say hi to Willa," she urged. "And if the line's not too long, you should get a tattoo."

Willa was so surrounded by admirers, I almost didn't go in. It was a short but genuine exchange, for me, the perfect kind. I got a chance to say bravo; she got a chance to hug an appreciative reply.

Like having to push a baby into the world, I was a madwoman with a primal need. This was not a tender desire to paint a form or capture a feeling. This was an urgent drive to create. The Lupiere mural was done; it was time. A lifetime of not believing in myself (and searching for permission from everyone) brought me to this point; I finally cared enough not to care anymore.

I looked around our apartment, flitting from one magazine to another. An old *Architectural Digest* had nothing, but then, I didn't expect it would. I wanted to paint a person. I opened a *Vogue* and let

the images wash over me. I was looking for someone strong, someone beautiful. Even though I had no one specific in mind, I couldn't
find her anywhere. I went from one magazine to another. Nothing
held my gaze so I moved on.

And then I saw it, hanging on the wall—a picture I'd taken of
Henny last year. She was sitting on the couch; so still, like a cardi-
nal in February. Bathed in shadows from the morning sun, her face
was shielded by hair. I took the photo down. I hadn't realized she'd
been holding a book. I tried to make sense of her expression. Had
she been pretending to read? My heart ached for not understanding
how lost she'd been. I'd only noticed her beauty.

I placed the photo by my easel and went back to the others; our
wall of love in mismatched frames—my visual aid of time passing. I
studied my mother's headshot. Pre-scarred—how lovely she'd been.
Above her was a close-up of Adam—toothless and proud. And Max,
sweet Max, a year old, standing in his crib, a sliver of Chocobunny
in view—clean and not yet cherished.

Next was Simone and Dennis, from our wedding day; I wondered
if they'd get a chance to dance like that again. I hoped so, anyway.
And then my gaze landed on Michael and me napping on a ham-
mock; for some time I tried to conjure it—that sweet feeling of ease.

And of course the one of Trudy. I didn't look, but knew it was
there. That loss was still too recent; I had to turn away.

Back to my easel. The murals had been easy compared to this
waiting, blank canvas. Murals were for decoration. Much less pressure. But canvas? Canvas required skill. Blank, it was full of possibility. But painted poorly, it was the adversary to be avoided at all costs:
bad art. I knew bad art when I saw it, and I wanted no part of that
failure.

I studied the photo until Henny became a medley of lights and
darks. I just had to be willing—even willing to fail.

I soaked a flat brush in turpentine and burnt sienna and said a
silent prayer. Help me, I thought. Help me do this. Help me not care
about the result.

My hand floated gracefully, the posture of a woman who didn't care. Free, and full of possibility; this was how I began. I always forgot that. How each painting was more than a potential failure. It was also chock-full of hope. And vision. Expectancy and dreams.

Just like beginnings should be.

Acknowledgments

My mother, Leslie Hager—for encouraging my artistic endeavors and demonstrating the value of candid communication and a well-told story. Also, for reading every draft and graciously listening when I needed an audience.

My cherished friends Deanna Meyerhoff, Carolyn Meyer, Betsy Krebs and my steadfast and supportive sisters-in-law—Iris Sandow and Leslie Soodak—for their early reads, smart feedback, and allegiance.

Thank you to my agent, the astute Elizabeth Kaplan, for her swift confidence in this project and all the guidance that followed, and to Melissa Sarver, who gives good phone. Also, to my acquiring editor, the discerning and kind Caryn Karmatz Rudy, and to Emily Griffin—editor extraordinaire—her keen eye and perseverance helped bring forth the story I wanted to tell. To copy editor Roland Ottewell and production editors Leah Tracosas and Tareth Mitch—my awe and appreciation.

My gratitude and heartfelt thank-you to the ever-wise Kaylie Jones and the excellent talent that is Lesley Gore.

To my father Jay Land and stepmother Linda Land for (among many things) modeling lives that revere love and work. And with love to my brother Joshua Hager and the splendid Stefanie Shear. And my sister Elizabeth Land, in honor of our girlhood—still salient despite occurring long ago.

Davetta Thacher, Judy Tallerman, Lisa Winick, Elizabeth Kertes,

Sandy Wissell, Sheryl Emch, Mary Patillo, and Ingrid Tarjan—my valued confidantes. And Alicia Reymann, an artist I knew well for a short time, instrumental to my beginning a creative quest.

To these fine women—for their warmth, patience, and hard work with my children: Jean Brown, Anne Peters, Sarah Lemble, Meredith Rose, Nikki Marquardt, Katarzyna Mikus, Leah Kamin, Katelyn Buckley, Christina Wynn, Devon Thacher, Lyndsey Arminio, Kelly Bottoms, and Victoria Wilson. And to Randy Persad as well as my children's talented teachers—past, present, and future—and the many mothers (and a few fathers) who volunteer in my children's schools.

To these artists: Alice Neel, Marlene Dumas, Elizabeth Peyton, Amy Bloom, Nikki Giovanni, Julia Cameron, and Anne Lamott, for keeping me company on this journey.

To the supportive strangers who made contact following the *Times* coverage of my craigslist ad—your benevolence was appreciated tenfold. Thank you for reading between the lines.

And to children who struggle with learning differences and/or sitting still—try to remember every nuanced emotion—you just might write a novel one day.

And finally:

To my children—Rubin, Ellis, Cassie, and Shay (each unique and extraordinary), they make me the luckiest woman in the world.

And my man Mitchell, whose belief in me (vast and unyielding) has become essential and a given—like the ability to walk or talk or breathe.

Reading Group Guide

1. Discuss Kara's relationship with her mother. What decisions did Kara make in childhood about the kind of life she wanted when she grew up? Was she able to keep true to her intention? When you were growing up which of your parents' character traits did you most want to replicate and/or avoid? Have you been successful?

2. Being a good-enough mother is a recurring theme throughout the novel. By the story's end, which qualities did Kara consider essential to being a good mother? What is your definition of a good mother? Do you have similar standards when measuring a good father?

3. One of Kara's college professors suggests that a sense of entitlement can be alluring. Which of the novel's characters are most comfortable declaring their desires, needs, and ambitions? What did those characters gain or lose in doing so? In which circumstances do you feel most entitled to express your needs?

4. There are many moments in which Kara concealed her true feelings out of a sense of shame or feelings of inadequacy. How did her family history, educational experiences, and gender impact her ability to identify and declare her needs, thoughts, and wishes? Have there been times in your life when revealing your truth has been difficult?

5. When Kara and Michael return from the movies, Kara learns from their babysitter, Beth, that Max has had a nightmare. Kara

thinks, "I was glad she was there. That and the exact opposite of glad, something Michael doesn't understand at all." Where does this ambivalence come from? Have you had any like it in your life?

6. When Kara sets out to find Chocobunny, she rails against archetypes portrayed in the media—specifically the caricatures of the all-nurturing nanny and the wealthy, neglectful mother whose children are merely narcissistic accessories. Do you agree with Kara's assessment of the media? Do these portrayals match your experience?

7. In each of the novel's time periods, Kara encounters characters who struggle with what it takes to make art or to declare oneself an artist. What image does a "real" artist invoke? What is your definition of an artist? Does money or critical acclaim factor into your definition?

8. Many of the artists in the novel seem unable to maintain committed romantic relationships while pursuing their art. Is there something about these endeavors that seems to be mutually exclusive? Does this characterization of the untethered artist have ramifications for people who value attachment?

About the Author

Rebecca Land Soodak, a former psychotherapist, lives with her husband and four children in Manhattan and Litchfield County, CT. *Henny on the Couch* is her first novel.